WILDERNESS TRAIL
OF LOVE

BOOK ONE

AMERICAN WILDERNESS SERIES ROMANCE

DOROTHY WILEY

WILDERNESS TRAIL OF LOVE

Dorothy Wiley

First Edition: 2014

ISBN: 1497393582

ISBN-13: 978-1497393585

Cover design by Erin Dameron-Hill

Author website: www.dorothywiley.com

Updated 2020

Wilderness Trail of Love is a work of fiction and is not presented as a precise account, but rather as a fictional novel inspired by history. Except for historically prominent personages, the characters are fictional and the names, places, and incidents either are the product of the author's imagination or are used fictitiously. Any resemblance to actual persons, living or dead, events or locales is entirely coincidental. Each book in the series can be read independently.

For the sake of understanding, the author used language for her characters for the modern reader rather than strictly reflecting the far more formal speech and writing patterns of the 18th century.

DEDICATION

*To "My Hero" whose courageous ancestors
inspired this novel.*

TITLES BY DOROTHY WILEY

WILDERNESS TRAIL OF LOVE

NEW FRONTIER OF LOVE

WHISPERING HILLS OF LOVE

FRONTIER HIGHLANDER VOW OF LOVE

FRONTIER GIFT OF LOVE

THE BEAUTY OF LOVE

LOVE'S NEW BEGINNING

LOVE'S SUNRISE

LOVE'S GLORY

LOVE'S WHISPER

RED RIVER RIFLES

LAND OF STARS

BUCKSKIN ANGEL

PRAISE FOR DOROTHY WILEY'S BOOKS

"My favorite author. Her writing is pure gold." – P. McGinnity

"Beautifully researched and meticulously crafted." – A. Hughes

"Ms. Wiley is a genius! Best wilderness series, ever!!! – 4hjunkie

"I read every one and started over!" – J. Goss

"They are the best books. Read them all and cannot wait for the new one!" – B.W. Davis

"My favorite author! Anxiously awaiting the next one!" – G.M.P. Lewis

"Wiley is a fabulous author in my opinion. I highly recommend her. Truly a marvelous writer. I am hooked on these!!" – S. Wolfe

"I am a huge fan of Wiley's books! Dorothy is a brilliant historical romance writer! 5 stars all the way!!" – L. Ratterman

"Your books are right up on my all-time favorites like 'Outlander' by Diana Gabaldon." – R.D. Huffine

"They are so good! So well researched and well written with passion and heart." – J.D.H. Green

"I have purchased all the Wyllie books. I am on my second time reading now. I love this entire series. It's just my most favorite EVER!" – D. M. Christensen

"Dorothy is an incredible storyteller!" – C. Nipper

"My most cherished author. Her historical research and great storytelling are unmatched!" – R. Ryder

"There are a lot of writers out there, but few great ones like Ms. Wiley. Never turn down a chance to read a book by Dorothy." – A. Foster

"Every Dorothy M. Wiley book is better than the last! This one needs 6 stars! – G. Lewis

"I read a lot. Rarely have I read an author I liked as much. Please don't ever stop writing!" – D. Harper

"I've been reading many books but none compares to Wiley's—still my favorite author! – K. Smith

"I love your books and read them every day. I want more!!!! You are a favorite author." – J. Bainter

"Historical romance writing that is unmatched." – L.A. Smith

"A wonderfully written historical novel set during the settling of the west by a very favorite author." – J. Weiss

"Dorothy Wiley writes engaging characters and paints vivid word pictures in tales of romance and adventure. Treat yourself to love and excitement by reading one of her books." – Caroline Clemmons, Bestselling Western Romance Author

"An extremely beautiful well-written novel. This is not just romance; it's romance you can sink your teeth into. The details and accurate history made me feel as though I was part of the story. It's an entertaining book that was hard to put down. – Kathleen Ball, bestselling and award-winning author of western romance

CHAPTER 1

New Hampshire, Spring 1797

Yes, it would be dangerous, maybe even deadly.

But at least he could live his life as God intended and build a better future for his family. Wouldn't it be far worse to hide from life—to end it doing nothing significant? To choose only what you will not do.

It isn't death that a man should fear. It's never living.

Nearly dark, Stephen Wyllie watched the boldest of the evening's stars push their way through the regal purple of a cloudless sky. He resisted the urge to race home. He needed to think. Sometimes it was just easier to think clearly on the back of a horse. Could 'two minds are better than one' include a horse? Perhaps with a trusted steed like George it could. The black stallion was by far the best mount he had ever thrown his leg over—tall, strong, and even-tempered.

Passing dense stands of timber, he stared west toward the rugged darkening mountains. "It's time to see the world beyond those peaks, George."

He had just confided in his four brothers telling them what he had not discussed with anyone else, even Jane. Going west. Folly or glory? For months, his mind had spun the question around again and again—like some sort of top inside his head. But now he had his answer.

He wanted to move his family to Kentucky.

It didn't surprise him that his middle brother Edward had mocked the idea. The man didn't have an adventurous bone in his body. Stephen had laid his heart on the line only to be met with extreme negativity. It caused his temper to flare. This was a difficult enough decision without Edward making it more so. His cynical middle brother had snickered at the idea of going to Kentucky and predicted that their heads would be swinging from some savage's hand like Daniel Boone's decapitated brother.

But his other three brothers supported the idea. In fact, Sam's feet were already itching to go. And John and William both wanted to leave New Hampshire for their own reasons.

Going west would be a chance to test himself—to see just what he was capable of facing. He welcomed the idea. The frontier would pit him and his brothers against countless dangers—mile upon mile of wilderness, the worst elements, vicious beasts, and savage men—all trying to steal their lives. They would leave civilization behind. Their lives would be in their own hands. The lives of his beloved wife Jane and four young daughters would be in *his* hands. The thought nearly stopped his heart. Could he keep them safe?

He could and he would. He had to.

He patted George's neck, wanting to share his excitement with someone, even if it could only be his horse. The prospect of land opportunities that would enable him to raise fine horses and cattle made his spirit soar. For the first time, he believed he might be able to go where his dreams had already taken him.

He swallowed the growing lump in his throat, realizing just how much this meant to him.

Pastureland in New Hampshire and the rest of the colonies was hard to come by and expensive. And, damn it, he paid taxes on almost everything, even his horse. And the amount collected rose every year without fail.

Granite mountains and hills, abundant forests of pine, spruce and hardwood, and numerous sparkling streams and silver rivers made the state picturesque but discouraging for men who needed acreage for their livelihood. But the new frontier offered the colonists plentiful and rich grasslands. The only rub was getting there…well maybe not the only obstacle. He pressed his lips together and then wiped his grimaced brow.

What about Jane? Would she be willing to leave their cozy home? Most men did not overly concern themselves with what the women of their homes wanted. He didn't think that way.

He needed Jane to share his dream.

He took a deep breath of the cool earthy evening air. How could he make her understand? Heaven knows she could be beyond obstinate and would not hesitate to challenge him. She'd be apprehensive about the girls and their welfare. He didn't blame her. His stomach knotted with concern for his daughters' safety as well.

But his oldest brother Sam had often said that danger has a way of finding us no matter our place. A former Captain in the Revolutionary War, danger had been, and often still was, a persistent part of Sam's life. He never hesitated to face danger. Just that evening, Sam told their brother Edward that we can't float through life in pampered safety.

He agreed. But would Jane? He didn't want to even bring up the idea of moving until he felt certain it was the right thing to do. That's why he sought out the counsel of his four older brothers first. If he couldn't convince them, he didn't stand a chance of getting Jane to agree. She could be more hardheaded than all four put together.

One of the most beautiful women in New Hampshire, in his opinion, he never tired of telling his wife just that. She would laugh and say he only said that because New Hampshire was such a small state. Her Scots

DOROTHY WILEY

parentage gave her eyes as green as new spring leaves on Hickory trees and an abundance of lustrous red curls that he loved to weave his fingers through as he kissed her. Jane's creamy complexion nearly glowed, unmarred except by the beginnings of well-earned laugh lines on either side of her luscious lips.

George lifted his head, then picked up his trot. Stephen chuckled. His farm lay just over the next hill and the anticipation of feed propelled the always hungry horse forward.

He soon stepped off the stirrup and led George toward the stable, all the while studying the full moon glowing through huge maple trees. Sam once said that Algonquian speaking tribes had a special name for each full moon. What was this one? Full Hunger Moon maybe, because food was so scarce by the end of winter and the beginning of spring. Winter food stores would be long gone, and it was time to plant new crops.

Jane's mare whinnied a welcome to George, returning his thoughts to his wife. An excellent horsewoman, she insisted on having her own mount, not content to be limited to a wagon or buggy like most local women. It was just one of the many things he loved about her. She certainly wasn't a coddled fragile woman, like some he'd known. When they first met, her indomitable spirit had impressed him. Maybe that same temerity would make her want to go west as well. Or, maybe it wouldn't. He frowned. It chafed him to admit that he couldn't predict her reaction and realized that was the reason he hadn't yet told her of his plan. But he would soon. He just had to find the right time.

He unsaddled George and scooped his feed into a wooden bucket. Chomping down on the grain, the horse gave a contented snort and relaxed his ears, a sign of his gratitude. "You're welcome," Stephen said. He stroked his steed's long muscular neck, warm and moist from their ride.

As he proceeded toward his home, well lit with candles and firelight, the familiar mellow smell of smoke wafting from the chimney reminded him how much his family loved their comfortable house. The small two-

4

story red brick dwelling, built with the help of his brothers and neighbors, rose above him like a welcoming sanctuary. Jane would have their daughters upstairs tucked into their beds and covered with colorful quilts, embroidered by both grandmothers, keeping the early spring evening chill away.

Each of the four girls held a distinct place in his heart. With the birth of each one, his heart seemed to grow. He wanted to give them the best in life. He could do that with more land.

But if he asked Jane to leave this fine home, would he regret it? Would she regret it? That would be worse. He could live with his own disappointments, but not hers. Yet, the thought of struggling to squeeze enough income for his family out of his meager farm made his heart clench, and his stomach sour. He couldn't provide for them as he should here. He *had* to make a change.

How was he going to tell her?

Jane came up the path to greet him. Her warm smile and twinkling eyes bridged the distance between them like a thousand words could not. As she met him, she slid her arms under his cloak and hugged his waist. The gesture of affection sent a warm pulse through him.

As he gazed into her emerald eyes, happiness shined back at him. He would do anything to keep her happy. He curled his arm around her shoulders and felt her shivering. He took off his cloak and draped the long heavy woolen cape, still warm from his body around her shoulders.

"There's no need for that, we're only a few steps from the front door," she protested.

"We're not there yet," he said, with a grin.

Jane inclined her head, gazing skyward. The soft rays of the moon bathed her in a brilliant radiance, making the hair around her head glow like the halo of a candle.

A shadow suddenly passed over her upturned face. She seemed

troubled.

He cupped her smooth cheek with his palm and she turned pensive eyes towards him.

"Is something wrong?" he asked.

"I just had a strange feeling when I looked at that full moon. Like something wasn't right. Not with me, something out there somewhere."

He wrapped his arm around her shoulders. "Nothing's wrong. Everything's fine. We're together."

Jane shook her head, as if to remove the feeling, and gazed up at him.

"You just need to be loved, that's all." Taking her hand, he brought it to his lips and then softly kissed each of her knuckles. They tasted delightful and left him wanting to taste more of her.

They entered their home and he helped her out of his cloak, letting it fall to the floor. He pressed his mouth to hers. The chill of the night left his body in an instant as every inch of her responded. Warmth, both his and hers, penetrated his clothes. But that barrier didn't last long.

Jane pulled his frock coat off and began to toy with the cravat at his neck. "I missed you." She gave him a smile that hinted at her desires.

"I was only gone a few hours," he said.

"I still missed you."

"How much?" he teased. "A little or a lot?" He hoped it was a lot.

Then he had his answer. She untied the lacings on his shirt and ran her long slender fingers slowly across his chest. A tingling sensation swept through his torso as she took his jaw in her hand and nuzzled his earlobe before feathering a trail of soft kisses up his neck, across his cheek, and, at last, his mouth. After he'd kissed her thoroughly, she nipped impishly at his lower lip, causing his stomach to flutter and ripples of heat to course through his veins. Then she parted his lips in a soul-reaching kiss that caressed his entire body.

She pulled back to take a breath and gazed up at him with eyes sparkling impishly.

Indeed, she had missed him. He missed her too. He always did, even when he worked in their nearby field. Sometimes he would take a break from his labors just to hear her sensuous voice. The sound of it always renewed his energy and strengthened his heart.

He lowered his lips to the sweetness of her mouth and enwrapped her silky tresses in his hands. His lips recaptured hers and he encased her in his arms, pulling her against his thundering heart. The sizzling kiss caused a tempest of passion to roar through his body, like a sudden storm.

Ready to match his hunger with hers, he peered into her luminous eyes, and her gaze locked on his, conveying the same longing that filled him. He wanted to reach into her and fulfill that need in a way that would leave no doubt how much he loved her. How much he wanted to protect her.

"I miss you every moment that you are not in my arms," he whispered into her curls.

"And I miss you every moment you are not in my bed," she said huskily, her face flushing with the passion rising in her.

A secret, almost magical, part of their marriage, passion bound their hearts tighter with every joining. To his surprise, their hunger for each other only grew more fervent as each year passed. Tonight was no exception. Just her nearness thrilled his senses and made them leap to life. His desire flared with an intense yearning and the very air around them seemed to grow hot.

But the intensity of his need was more than mere physical attraction, although her allure was undeniable and total. Their relationship was rooted in a love so profound and so complete that he now knew what the scriptures meant by the two shall become one. It was more than one flesh—it was one spirit. Jane even joked that they would eventually just become one person if they both lived into old age.

Tonight, though, they were young and filled with desire for each other.

She backed out of his arms and playfully hauled him toward their bedroom, beaming warmly. She didn't have to tug too hard. That beautiful smile made him want to race her to their bed. As he glimpsed the curves of her backside, his fingers ached to shed his remaining clothing…and hers.

Locking their bedroom door behind him, he swept her, weightless, into his arms and carried her to their bed.

Married eight years, she still made him feel like he could conquer the world.

But could he go to Kentucky?

And would Jane agree to go?

CHAPTER 2

White Mountains, New Hampshire, Spring 1797

The stiff breeze whipped filthy blond hair back from her swollen face. It looked to Chief Wanalancet as if even the wind hurt her. As Bomazeen led the mare the young woman rode, she stared straight ahead, focusing on nothing, oblivious to the crowded Pennacook village.

At the sight of Bomazeen, little children scrambled to hide behind their mothers, all hard at work tanning furs or tending crops. The women of the tribe averted their eyes to avoid looking at the white woman, although the Chief knew they could not help but pity her. They understood what the young woman had endured, what she barely survived, as a captive of an inhuman man without mercy, unburdened by even a bead of conscience.

Known for his unchecked brutality, Bomazeen's chilling reputation stretched well beyond Wanalancet's tribe. Whites thought of him as a cruel ghost—appearing from nowhere and making women simply vanish, leaving behind only the haunting cold of fear as word spread of their disappearance.

His tribe whispered Bomazeen's name, calling him Wandering Evil, for he left a trail of violence wherever he roamed. Even the young braves stayed clear of the man because of the condition of both the white and native captives he brought to the tribe for trade. This one looked no different from the rest.

He needed to rein in Bomazeen's cruelty or find another slave trader.

Bomazeen untied the strips of rawhide binding her raw ankles and wrists. "Down bitch," he hissed. When she didn't move, he grabbed a fistful of her hair and jerked her off the horse.

Her legs buckled as soon as she put weight on them and Wanalancet watched her crumple to the ground.

Swearing, Bomazeen half dragged, half carried her to the tribe's traders, and threw her at their moccasin clad feet.

The traders circled the young woman, surveying Bomazeen's damage.

Dark stains covered the front of the woman's bodice. A tear in the fabric exposed a knife gash. Besides her wounds, mud and grime blackened what was left of her blue gown and white bonnet, making it difficult for Wanalancet to know what she had been like only days before.

The woman was in such dismal shape the traders offered Bomazeen half the normal beaver pelts paid for a slave.

Behind the blood and mud, the young woman might be comely, even beautiful. Wanalancet wondered if someone loved her. He shook his head in pity for the young woman. When would Bomazeen learn that he paid a price for his cruelty? Someday, he would pay an even higher price.

Grumbling a curse, Bomazeen sold her to the traders. "Try to escape and I'll come back and cut off your tits. Then your babes will starve." He ended his threat with a swift kick to her buttocks, sending her face-first into the dirt.

"Enough!" Wanalancet barked at Bomazeen. Then he ordered one of his traders to turn her over to the tribe's healers.

10

Tears rolled down her face moistening the dried blood covering numerous scratches and cuts. She hung her head low, her long hair hiding her swollen face. It would take their best medicine and many weeks to mend Bomazeen's vile handiwork. Wanalancet would be sure the women of the tribe healed this woman before one of his braves touched her. He knelt next to her. "What is your name?" he asked and Bomazeen translated.

"Lucy," she said, her voice trembling.

As the traders lugged her to her feet, Wanalancet saw the light leave her eyes as hope left her heart. Her dulled apathetic stare was typical of someone who knows rescue is impossible. She probably wanted to die. It was a common problem with new slaves who thought captivity worse than death.

The traders led her away. Lucy was now a slave.

Among the Pennacook tribes, Wandering Evil intimidated everyone except Wanalancet. The despicable man needed his business. And while he hated to admit it, in addition to the slaves to replace their dead lost to smallpox, Bomazeen supplied items his people had grown accustomed to—tobacco, liquor, blankets, copper kettles, weapons, axes, and wampum—colorful trade beads used to decorate their clothing.

In exchange, Bomazeen traded for skins and pelts of all kinds, receiving far more when the hides sold than the value of the goods traded to his people. Wanalancet recalled many others who had profited at his tribe's expense. Double-dealing French traders, doling out disease along with whiskey and guns, nearly wiped out the Pennacook. Others sacked their small villages and often made off with their food stores on the eve of harsh winters. As their numbers dwindled, Wanalancet struggled to control his changing world.

"Wandering one, you bring woman of few years this time, but she is badly broken," Wanalancet said. He tugged his raccoon cloak tighter against the cool mountain wind, covering the long strings of pearls

DOROTHY WILEY

draped against his bare chest. "I want slaves. I don't want the ailing. Bring no more to me who have suffered as this one has by your hand."

Bomazeen grunted. "I cut her some," he answered in Algonquian, the Chief's native tongue. Evil loitered behind the man's dark eyes.

Wanalancet remained silent, not revealing his disgust.

A sneer crossed Bomazeen's weathered face. "She showed too much spirit. But she won't give you trouble now."

"Why do you tear slave bodies with your hatred? A man should not poison his heart with ill will. Some new people to our land are my enemy, but hate does not steal my mind until it is time to fight."

"My mind is as a stone. There is no soft spot in here," Bomazeen replied, as he slowly drew a long yellowed fingernail across his grimy forehead.

Bomazeen's heart was made of stone too. Wanalancet told him, "Whites walk in white man world. My people walk in Pennacook world. You, a métis, wander between."

"Yes, I am métis—my blood is half-Indian and half-French. But my spirit is not one or the other. To the Indian I am different, but I exist. But to the whites, I am outcast, without being, like a stray dog you throw stones at to get it to run away." Bomazeen's eyes darkened even further. "They treat me like an animal so I attack like one."

The bitter remarks almost made the Chief pity the man. Bomazeen would never know the love of a woman. The heartless man was doomed to a life of cold loneliness.

Wanalancet understood loneliness. He longed to feel the warm flesh of a woman he loved against his body. Last summer, his wife, along with many others, died of smallpox. He honored her at the Feast of the Dead with grave offerings and many gifts. But now it was time to turn his honor towards a living woman—to sing to her the song of the stars.

"On your next wander to white man's world, find me a fine woman. I

12

will give you many furs in exchange, but no cuts, beating, or taking her," he warned. "She must be great among women because she will be the mother to our people."

"I know of such a woman. She lives near Barrington Town. Many people live there now. But, for the woman of a great Chief, I will go there. Her face will make you the envy of other Chiefs. Her hair is the color of the sun as it rises from the edge of the earth. Long ago, I watched her from afar—she is like no other woman. She is tall and strong. She will cost much. Your braves must hunt three times the usual beaver pelts and skins," Bomazeen negotiated. "And your women must clean and tan the furs."

Wanalancet's interest peaked. He could almost envision his new wife. "The exchange will be as you say. Come, let us drink and smoke." He waited as Bomazeen withdrew tobacco and liquor from the back of the pack mule, then they entered Wanalancet's warm smoke-filled lodge. Made of bark and hides, numerous woven baskets filled with special flints, mica, shells, and other valuable items lined the inside. They sat on the fur-covered floor and Wanalancet retrieved his Calumet. Made with a rare red catlinite marble head, the pipe had a long quill made of cane wrapped in buckskin adorned with seed beads, bird feathers of all colors, and locks of women's hair, both dark and blond.

Whenever he went to mediate for peace, Wanalancet carried the ceremonial pipe with pride. He was of the blood of the great Chief Passaconaway and his son Chief Wanalancet, for whom his father named him. As was the custom of his noble ancestors, to show this precious emblem of trade and trust meant he could walk in safety even among his enemies. He also used the pipe, as he would now, to conclude pacts and celebrate life's important decisions with the Great Spirit.

Wanalancet carefully filled the Calumet, then lit the tobacco. As the first gray wisps curled up, he asked the sacred smoke to reach out to this woman's spirit and join her to him. This sanctified act would make her life-force his. Soon, her body too would be his and warm his heart and his flesh.

Through the soft gray haze, Wanalancet again saw in his mind's eye the woman with hair the color he prized most. Hair the same color as his pipe's marble bowl. He began to love her spirit already, but he would have to wait until Bomazeen made good on his promise.

Silently, Wanalancet pledged to dream of her tonight and every night until she shared his lodge.

As he held the polished red bowl of his pipe, carved with grooves honoring the four directions, north, south, east, and…west, he sent the sacred smoke upwards to the full moon.

CHAPTER 3

Jane sat with their daughters, trying her best to be patient, as she taught them to sew. Stephen rested, close by, in his chair reading his favorite book *Adventures* yet again. The fire in the hearth cast just enough light for all of them to see by and his nearness warmed her heart as no fire could.

He's read that book so many times he should have it memorized by now, she chuckled to herself. She decided to buy him a new book for his birthday.

She studied his handsome face, noting the furrowed brow and worried look that crossed his features from time to time. Something was troubling him and it was time to find out what.

Jane placed her needlework on the table. "Girls, time to sleep now. Say goodnight to your father, then go wash your faces and get ready for bed," she ordered, as she picked baby Mary up out of her cradle.

"Yes Mother," Martha replied obediently. Their oldest daughter sprang to her feet. "Come on Polly and Amy, let's go." After all three girls planted numerous kisses on Stephen's cheeks, Martha took Amy's little hand.

Jane smiled at Martha's gesture. The seven-year-old never missed an opportunity to assume her role as big sister.

Without argument, because she permitted none, the children began climbing the stairs. Jane followed the three, carrying the baby, and noted how loud the parade of footsteps sounded on the wooden stairs. Her girls grew bigger by the day, including their feet.

෨

They say it's a paradise, all I have to do is get us there.

Laying down his dog-eared copy of Daniel Boone's *Adventures,* Stephen shook his head. What he just told himself belied the hard truth. Getting there would be the most difficult and dangerous undertaking any of them ever experienced. Like the real paradise, dying might be the cost. But his heart was near bursting from the need for land and an opportunity to make a better living for his family. And his soul craved the excitement and adventure a trip west had to offer.

Despite these strong arguments for leaving, his all too logical mind kept asking the same questions. He adored Jane and their four young daughters. Could he forgo their current happiness and put the lives of those he loved through the dangers of a thousand-mile journey to appease his ambition? Most of the journey would be through raw wilderness. A lot can happen on a journey like that—much of it not good. Some of it terrible.

Confused, he wandered restlessly about the room. The walls seemed confining, trapping, as he tried weighing the pros and cons. But the mental drill didn't help. He was stuck in a quicksand where all decisions and actions seemed impossible.

His chest tightened as indecisiveness gnawed away at his confidence. He leaned one arm against the mantel and lowered his head.

The war between doing what was safe for his family, and what he believed to be his destiny, raged on. But he would find a way to win this war. He straightened and pushed his shoulders back. Somehow, he would follow his heart. He picked the book up again and turned to his favorite part,

"...yet in time the mysterious will of Heaven is unfolded, and we behold our conduct, from whatever motives excited, operating to answer the important designs of Heaven."

Jane plucked the book out of Stephen's work-roughened hands and dropped it on a nearby table. As she did, she noticed his calloused palms. She certainly hadn't married a lazy man. As usual, he had worked sun up to sundown, trying to get a rocky plot ready for planting. Resting was something he did only on the Sabbath, but even then, he did so begrudgingly.

Stephen flexed his back muscles and rolled his broad shoulders.

"Lean forward, let me rub your back. I know it must ache after a full day in the field," she offered.

He grinned with anticipation.

She kneaded his shoulders and he leaned into her touch. Stephen moaned with enjoyment, reminding her of similar sounds of pleasure the evening before. The memory warmed her insides as she recalled trying to muffle her own sounds of marital ecstasy. How he managed to make their coupling better for her every time was inexplicable to her.

She felt his muscles beginning to relax, as her fingers pulled out the fatigue. "You seemed worried while you were reading."

"Oh, I was just concentrating," he replied.

"No you weren't," she accused. "You kept staring at the book and pondering something else. What is it?"

He didn't answer. Instead, he grasped her wrist and tugged her into his lap.

Instantly her heartbeat quickened.

Stephen eyed her for a moment. She detected a flicker in his intense eyes and a hesitation before he said, "I'm just thinking through

17

something, that's all. But it's nothing to fret over."

"What?" she pressed. He was evading her questions.

"I said it was nothing, so let it be." He lifted her hand to his mouth and kissed her palm.

Jane moaned as he nibbled on one of her fingertips, astounding her that even her fingers responded so fervently to his touch.

He ran a hand gently down the side of her neck. "Ah Jane, do you know how much I love you," he said, "and our girls." His gaze was as tender as the caress.

"I thank the good Lord every day for your love." For the moment, she put aside her curiosity to focus on what Stephen was doing to her now— kissing her palm again, then working his way up her arm. Waves of excitement rolled through her body. After working in the field all day, did he have the stamina to love her two nights in a row?

"Go be sure the girls are asleep. I'll light the oil lamp in the bedroom," he said, with a mischievous half-grin, and she no longer had to wonder.

Jane stood and he looked her over seductively. Already feeling a tingle in her breasts and an insistent ache only Stephen could heal, she longed to feel the warmth of his hard body against hers. She reached out and laced her fingers through one of his hands. His fingers felt warm and strong and she gave them a squeeze. Reluctantly releasing his hand, she hurried upstairs to her daughters' room, pleased to find them already dreaming. She tucked the blanket around their shoulders, locked their windows, and took the stairs down so fast she nearly tripped on her skirts.

Jane slowed her pace as she entered their bedroom, and paused long enough to lock the door behind her.

Stephen was already in the bed, pulling a linen sheet over his long muscular legs and sculpted chest. He looked at her longingly as he leaned back against the pillow.

Her clothing suddenly felt heavy and warm. She began to remove her gown and could still feel his eyes upon her. He often told her how much he enjoyed seeing her undress. So she took her time removing her layers of petticoats, stays, and the rest of her underthings and putting it all away before retrieving a soft sleeping chemise.

"No need for that. You'll have it on but a minute," he teased, then brought his hand up to stifle a yawn.

Jane laughed and began untangling her hair. The task bordered on a battle every night as her brush and comb fought to subdue her curls. More than once, she'd been tempted to take the scissors to her plentiful tresses. But Stephen fancied her long hair and, despite the current fashion, she wore it uncovered most of the time. She put as much of it into a long braid as she could and then washed her face in the basin on her dressing table.

After dabbing rosewater on her hands and neck, she inhaled deeply. Stephen loved the sweet soft fragrance and it always helped her unwind from her own long day of chores. But it was the comfort of his embrace and the warmth of his touch that soothed her as nothing else could.

Looking forward to Stephen's strong arms enveloping her once again, she turned towards their bed. Her heart plummeted. Despite his earlier eagerness, he was heavily asleep, his exhaustion winning over desire.

She leaned her forehead against the carved bedpost and released her disappointment on a heavy sigh. She studied his ruggedly handsome tanned face, his black hair shining in the dim light of the oil lamp. Her love for him filled her heart and replaced her frustration.

She blew out the oil lamp and climbed into bed. Soft moonlight painted their room grey.

She would let him sleep, but only for a while, then wake him in the middle of the night.

࿓

From his barn, Stephen watched dawn's light explode over the White Mountains illuminating nature's splendor. The lofty peaks rose out of a color-filled canvas painted with wild strokes by a bold sunrise. Tall pines, destined to become sturdy buildings or the masts of ships, stoically awaited their futures. Hardwoods added to their breadth, each year's slow progress recorded in the rings of their hearts. The early spring grass shimmered with a heavy dew, like a field of living emeralds, each blade reflecting the new day's sun. He heard a Purple Finch greet the morning with his boisterous song, as though the beautiful day was created just for the bird. Days like this also stir a man's soul.

He wanted to spend the day just thinking through his difficult decision. But this morning, he would have to ride to Durham for supplies. They were completely out of several essentials and he needed to buy grass seed before the weeds took over his newly cleared field. Reluctantly, he stopped musing about the future.

After hitching the team to the wagon and putting his musket under the bench, Stephen stuck a pistol and knife in his belt and pulled his powder horn's strap over his neck. As he put his cloak on the seat, he couldn't help but grin, remembering how Jane had looked in it. All day he would wear his beaver felt hat with two sides cocked and don the cloak against the evening chill.

Without realizing, he turned to face the west. He yearned to make his own mark on this young country. That desire seemed to grow stronger every day and caused a restlessness that took more and more effort to restrain. When statesmen signed the Declaration that first hot week of July 1776, he was ten years old. Their spirit and courage became a part of not just that historical document, but also the souls of young men like him. Now at 31, he understood he had reached the age when he could no longer wait to be the man he wanted to be. If he didn't live his dream now he would lose it.

But like his tracks in the morning dew, his resolve quickly disappeared. As his three oldest girls ran toward him, he could almost see his dream evaporating right before his eyes. He could not put his concern for their safety behind him. He knelt to their level and opened his arms wide. As he wrapped his arms around them and pulled them against his chest, he realized he had to do both—find land and keep them safe on the journey to Kentucky. And he had to find a way to convince Jane that he could do both. There was no point talking to her until he had the answers for himself.

"You girls stay close to the house while I'm gone. Don't go beyond the fence and keep your eyes wide open," he warned.

"Yes Father, and I'll watch out for these young ones," Martha said, sounding older than her seven years.

"Don't worry Father, Mama can shoot a hunred 'ards," Polly said.

Stephen laughed, recalling that he had recently bragged that Jane could shoot accurately from a hundred yards. He wasn't certain that, at age five, Polly had any idea what an 'ard' was, but he enjoyed hearing her boast that her mother could shoot a hundred of them.

Amy, the third sister, who just turned three, clung to her mother's apron, frowning.

Stephen picked her up. At once, a happy smile replaced her unhappy expression. She grabbed his face with both her chubby hands and smacked a kiss on his nose. Her demonstrative gesture made him chuckle. God, how he loved his daughters.

"Your mother is indeed a crack shot. Just the same, I'd feel better if you stayed close."

He prayed Jane and the girls would be safe until he returned home with their supplies. He hated leaving, but there was no choice in the matter. As strong as Jane was, it still made him uneasy to leave them alone. He would make this a quick trip.

He gave each of the three girls a hug and a peck on the cheek. He turned to Jane, buried his hands in the thickness of her hair, and gave her a soft lingering kiss. Then he forced himself to climb onto the wagon's seat. Taking one last long look at his wife, he set off.

"Don't forget my fabric, the girls and I need new dresses," she yelled after him, "and pick out something nice looking, not just practical."

Jane would normally pick fabric out herself, but three young girls and a nursing baby made travel difficult. This time, she would just have to trust him.

"I won't forget. That's the main reason I'm going to Durham, not Barrington. I'll get a color that goes well with those green eyes of yours," he called back. *Every color*, he realized. He wished he could buy her fine silks, or better yet, store-bought gowns. She deserved more than he provided now with his meager income. But he had plans. He had dreams. Someday, he would be successful.

He turned to look back once more. Jane waved goodbye and smiled cheerfully. But he knew her heart wasn't smiling. She told him many times that she hated every moment separated from him. She said it made a big hollow place inside her that would not go away until they were together again, as if half of her was suddenly missing.

He understood what she meant. With every turn of the cranky wheels, he left a part of himself behind, replaced with a creeping loneliness. It would clench his heart and not let go until she was in his arms, until he too was complete again.

Maybe that's what love is, he thought. Finding the other half of you.

CHAPTER 4

As Stephen's back grew smaller, the hollow spot in Jane grew bigger. She listened to the squeak of the wagon wheels until she could hear them no more. She turned towards the house, feeling alone even with her daughters. Reluctant to begin her chores, her normal boundless energy was absent today. She wished she could just sit on the porch and sew or even read. With four young girls, reading time was rare, but she loved to read and to write in her journal. It made her feel a connection to a vast world beyond herself. But the garden needed hoeing of the first spring weeds to ready it for planting and the clothes needed washing. Like most women, she always had more to do than she could get done in a day.

"Mama, may we have a picnic today?" Polly pleaded.

"What a splendid idea," Jane responded. "But we have our chores, and…"

"Just a short picnic. We won't be gone long," Martha begged.

Her eyes widened at the idea. It sounded far more appealing than weeding and laundry. But something made her hesitate and she turned back toward the house. "No, when your father gets back, we'll have a big picnic Sunday after church. You heard your Father, we should stay close to home."

The girls grudgingly followed. They strolled past Jane's rose bushes, just beginning to bud. She eagerly awaited their glorious full blooms brightening her front yard.

Inside, she checked on Mary, the youngest, now almost one. Still peacefully asleep in her cradle, the babe looked angelic. Jane gently pulled a little blanket over her, then tiptoed away, being careful not to awaken her.

The day passed slowly as she went about her labors, pausing now and then to pray for Stephen. The trip there would take him all day and it would be early evening before he reached Durham. Of all her chores, she hated washday the most. Nevertheless, as her mother had strongly advised, she made herself keep up with dirty laundry. At Jane's wedding, her mother gave her a "Receipt for Wash Day." She saved it in her Bible, treasuring it for her mother's original spelling and for her words of wisdom. She had memorized the list:

1. *Bold a fire in yard to heet pot of rainwater. Set tubs so smok won't blow in eyes if wind is pert. Shave one hole cake lie sope in bollin water.*

2. *Make three piles, wite, cullord and rags.*

3. *For startch, stur flour in cold water till smooth, then thin with bollin water.*

4. *Rub dirty spots on board, scrub hard. Take white things out of kettle with broom stik, then rench, blew, and startch.*

5. *Spred tea towels on bushes and hang bed linens on fence and cloothes on trees.*

6. *Poor rench water on flower bed and scrub porch with sopey water.*

7. *Put on cleen dress—smooth hair with side combs—brew cup of tee—set and rest and rock a spell and count blessings.*

She especially enjoyed the last piece of advice and faithfully practiced this part of the instructions. She definitely had many blessings to count. Having a husband like Stephen was always at the top of her list. He made her happy and brought joy to her life in so many ways, not the least of which was the immense pleasure she found in their bed. Just thinking about it made her face feel flushed. Halfheartedly, she made herself focus on wringing the water out of one of Stephen's linen shirts, but as she shook it out, even his shirt reminded her of his well-muscled chest and made her long for the comfort of his arms.

When she finished laundering, she brewed tea while she changed from her work clothes into one of her favorite everyday dresses, a blue and yellow striped gown trimmed with white lace at the neck and cuffs. She made a half-hearted attempt to style her curls, made wild by the hot steam from the laundry water, but soon gave up and headed to her teapot. She poured the brew into a delicate china cup and saucer enjoyed by the women in her family for generations. She sensed a connection with her past every time she used the precious set. Each week, after doing laundry, the ritual was her reward to herself for accomplishing such a tedious task.

"Martha, watch your sisters while I rest on the porch," she instructed, as she grabbed her shawl. At last, a few peaceful minutes to herself in her rocker. She would enjoy her tea and the cool evening air. She relished these rare serene moments, an elixir to a mother's harried soul.

Jane opened the front door and froze. Sheer black terror swept through her.

The most hideous and loathsome man she had ever seen stood on her porch, staring menacingly at her. He reached for her arm.

Her treasured teacup slipped from her hands and shattered as she jumped backward and screamed. She turned to run toward her daughters, but the man lunged for her instantly. She felt searing pain on her scalp as his hand grabbed a fistful of her hair and jerked her backwards.

She struggled to free herself but each movement only made him pull her closer, tearing more hair from her head. He stank so badly she began to gag. Nausea rose up in her throat.

All three girls huddled together in the corner screaming, but baby Mary still slept peacefully in her cradle.

"Stop fighting or I'll start killing your litter," he hissed into her ear.

At once, she stopped struggling. She forced her mind to return from the initial shock and terror, otherwise fear would quickly paralyze her.

He shoved her onto the wooden floor planks, then like a huge snake slowly slithered further into her home. She scooted backward, quickly stood, and faced him. She recognized him immediately. She knew who he was, what he was. For years, Jane had heard the vivid descriptions of him and the tales of his butchery.

Most colonists thought him half-human, half-demon. He made his living stealing white and Indian captives and trading them. Although Bomazeen hadn't been seen locally in some time, he had slaughtered many people in the area in the past, always scalping them first before running them through with a bayonet. Sometimes he would slit their throat too. He usually scalped the youngest children and the elderly, taking only those who could withstand the long brutal journey through the wilderness afoot and survive with little food. Rumor was he would crisscross dense forests, avoiding roads and trails, a tactic designed to elude the men who gave chase and attempted to apprehend him.

As he stood before her, he appeared even more terrifying than she had imagined. The part down the middle of his long stringy black hair pointed to inky eyes. A sharp chin supported features that appeared incapable of emotion. Like the viper that wore it, it seemed like a face that never laughed and never cried. Only his voice reflected his spirit—a voice greased with venom. Numerous earrings pierced his left ear, severely stretching the lobe, but his right ear was unadorned except for a gruesome scar. His bloodstained clothes, a mix of Indian and white man's attire, looked like once put on they had never left his body.

Some of the bloodstains appeared fresh, and a scalp, with long white hair, hung from his belt. She shuddered at the ghastly sight, fighting nausea once again.

With her heart hammering in her chest, she took a deep breath, trying to control her quivering nerves and mounting fear.

Bomazeen slowly scanned the house with the chilling eyes of a hungry beast. He spotted a loaf of bread and ham on the table and wasted no time devouring it like a hungry dog.

The girls crouched together in the corner whimpering pitifully.

Bomazeen ignored them, at least for the moment. For that, she was grateful.

Her mind raced nearly as fast as her wildly beating pulse. Could she get this monster to leave?

Show him no fear.

She fought for self-control, determined to keep her voice from trembling. "My husband and his brothers will return soon from hunting," she lied.

Very slowly, and emphasizing each word, he said, "If you lie again, I'll cut your tongue out. I saw him leave this morning, alone, in that old noisy wagon. He took Durham road." His words simmered with barely restrained anger.

Her heart nearly stopped as she realized that Bomazeen knew Stephen was long gone. The devil must have been outside all day, watching her, waiting for the cover of darkness before he kidnapped them. But Bomazeen never took young children. He would kill them, viciously and without mercy.

Oh God, oh God. Stephen, please come back.

Her knees weakened, her throat tightened, and she could barely breathe. But her mind had to stay strong. Stephen was gone.

She had to protect her daughters.

Determined to save them, she willed herself to stand tall and focus on the girls instead of the devil standing before her. She stared directly into Martha's eyes trying to give her oldest daughter strength.

Martha glared back at her with as much anger as fear in her eyes and her little hands shook, but she still clung protectively to her two younger sisters. Jane knew Martha would fight Bomazeen herself to protect them. The courage shown by her seven-year-old awed her. In that moment, she realized what she had to do.

She put herself between the girls and Bomazeen. "Do you need water?"

Bomazeen grunted, continuing to greedily gorge on the bread and ham.

She moved slowly to the water pail. Spotting her cooking knife on the counter, she picked it up, hoping he hadn't noticed. She would try that first. She dipped some water and took it to him. Her hand shook so badly much of the water flung out.

Bomazeen snatched the dipper from her, but then grabbed her other wrist. "You think you can whip me with little old cooking knife? Stupid woman. I've been cut many times, but I'm still hunting you whites. You can't kill me. Indian magic protects me." He threw the knife into the fire before slapping her face hard, nearly knocking her over. The imprint of his hand burned her skin, but disgust from the fiend's touch really made her smolder.

Then he reached for her, squeezing her arm painfully, and prepared to slap her again. Suddenly, he stopped short. He groaned what seemed like disappointment, and twisted his pursed lips.

She recoiled at the daggers of evil his narrowed eyes hurled at her. Then she glanced toward her daughters and her heart strengthened again. Angry that she'd let him see her get the knife, she ignored her stinging cheek. Her Scottish temper rose to the surface, repressing her fear. "Sir, we are protected by the Lord Almighty, who is stronger than your heathen superstitions. He will speedily avenge any blood you spill upon this family."

"I not afraid of your God. I kill whites and Indians many times. He never hurt me."

"He will—in hell."

Bomazeen snorted loudly. "A story for weak children."

Rather than rile him further, she reined in her temper. "What do you want?"

"Your oldest girl will make good slave." He pointed at Martha. "And Chief needs a woman. I spied you once near town when I was passing through to southern tribes. I knew then that I could get good price for you. Chief will like red hair. He already smoked his pipe to make you his wife and he celebrated joining to your spirit."

"I'll die first," Jane swore.

Bomazeen jabbed a dirty finger in her face. "Then you'll die."

At that, Polly's echoing sobs froze her heart like a thousand cold winters.

Stephen, if I never see you again, remember I loved you.

CHAPTER 5

S tephen pulled into Durham as the sun slipped behind the western side of the White Mountains. Spring still hadn't overcome the evening chill, and it felt cool enough tonight that they might even wake up to a light frost. Well-dressed shoppers, slaves, servants, horses, dogs, and assorted peddlers crowded the busy city's streets. He stabled his team at the livery barn and then headed across the cobblestone square to Harry's Tavern and Inn, where he planned to eat a nice meal and spend the night.

As he walked, his thoughts turned from food to Jane. As usual, he missed her already.

The popular inn was, as always, crowded and loud, and its distinctive smell, a blend of aromatic food, musky men, and oak burning in the enormous fireplace, assaulted his nostrils as he went in. In addition to drinking and eating, the mostly male clientele used the tavern to unwind, smoke their pipes, read the latest newspaper, play billiards, share gossip, argue endlessly about politics, and lately to learn news of travelers who had gone west. He noticed one of Harry's most popular drinks sitting on many of the tables. Called a 'Flip' it was a potent concoction of beer and New England rum, sweetened with molasses. The tavern owner plunged a red-hot iron into the brew, giving it the flavor of burnt sugar.

Several men he had known since his youth shouted or waved their welcomes as he entered. Looking for a place to sit, he spotted Bear. His best friend and adopted brother's stature and bright coppery hair made the man hard to miss.

"Stephen, it's a fine surprise to be seein' ye. I just ambled in meself," Bear said in his booming Scottish lilt. He stood to shake hands, towering over Stephen.

He shook Bear's strong hand, nearly twice the size of his own, then sat. "What are you doing in Durham? You hate big cities, and I thought you were hunting. If I'd known you planned to come here, we might have traveled together."

"I had to see the doc about a tooth that suddenly made me want to weep like a wee bairn. He pulled it and told me to go drink a few sassafras ales to dull the pain. A fine doctor that one. He knows what good medicine tastes like." Bear gulped his ale with relish. "I should have gone by to tell ye before I left, but I was hurtin' so, I dinna want to see or talk to anyone, even you."

"Glad you're here. It'll give us a chance to talk." Stephen valued his friend's opinions. Bear's keen intellect had a way of getting to the meat of a matter. And despite his coarse appearance, he possessed the qualities of a scholar, having acquired an excellent education as a child beside a peat fire in a lonely Highland glen.

"Aye, and a chance to swig a few ales, if ye have a mind to."

"After that wagon ride through those windy ass hills, I'm ready for a good meal and some of Harry's ale. It made me appreciate that old story about Grandfather Thomas."

"Your grandfather was a Samuel."

"My father's grandfather. The one that was a Scots Coventeer and had to leave Scotland in 1685 because he refused to swear allegiance to the English king. Tradition has it that even at age eighty, Grandpa Thomas frequently drove his ox team to the nearest market town, and none of the other farmers could get there any quicker than he. Or unload their wagons any faster than he did."

"Aye, that sounds like one of yer braw kinsmen," Bear laughed. "Are Jane and the wee ones well now?"

"Beautiful and stubborn—the whole lot of them." He smiled as he thought about how enchanting Jane looked in the moonlight last night after she woke him. He wanted to think about the rest of what she did to him, but Bear was asking him a question.

"So what brings ye to Durham then?"

Stephen cleared his throat. "Jane needed cloth to make the girls some new clothes. They've about outgrown everything. I needed supplies too and I heard they have new spring grass seed," he explained. "But I'm finding it difficult to think about planting."

Bear chuckled, nodding. "Nay, ye're na inclined to farming much."

"True, God knows, but that's not the reason."

"Well, don't be making me guess, what is it then?"

"I'm thinking about heading west. To Kentucky."

Bear's coppery brows rose and his eyes widened on his ruddy face. "Truly? 'Tis a bold move. I would consider it meself. Heard tell 'tis a hunter's paradise. Temptin'."

"As you well know, it's been my dream to find better land. Personal danger seems but a minor consequence compared to the opportunity to secure rich land. But I worry about Jane and the girls. How can I put their lives in jeopardy?" he asked, already feeling his jaw clench.

"Well, the key to safety will be to travel in a large, well-armed group. If ye decide to go, I'd be pleased to be a part of it," Bear offered.

Bear's offer did not surprise him and his family would be safer with his adopted brother along. "If we decide to go, there is no man I would rather have join us."

"I'm honored. Are yer brothers inclined to be going to Kentucky as well?"

"Sam for sure. Like you, he doesn't have a family to worry about and he's been restless lately. He needs a challenge. Footloose William would go anywhere the rest of us go. After losing Diana, John needs a place to start over. But Edward is unwilling to attempt a trip this difficult. I don't know if he's being cautious or cowardly. Sam thinks him a coward."

"Nay, he isna a coward—he's just na an adventurer like Sam. Edward is uncomfortable without four walls around him. I think he would be a burden to ye, if ye dinna mind me freely speakin'."

"I expect you to speak freely."

"I sense you still have some doubts."

"What if the land is not all it's purported to be? Maybe it's only a hunter's paradise. What if I can't make a decent living there? I won't be a failure."

"Och, ye're na capable of failing. Worse is to na try at all. Those who do na attempt that which is difficult are the real failures, and the real cowards. They'll always wonder what might have been—what they might have done. They'll be the ones with regrets at life's end. Ye're na a man to flee from a challenge or to give in to fear."

"But I must be logical about this decision."

"Aye, Stephen, to be sure. And it's understandable to be torn. But some decisions require more than reasonableness. A courageous man does na do a great deed because it is reasonable. Like tossing the caber in Scotland, this is a test of your strength. A brave man acts out of faith and courage and tosses the caber as far as he possibly can."

He stared at his big friend. Bear's wisdom sometimes seemed as grand as his physical size. As he had done with Sam, he let Bear's words sink in, and again his courage strengthened.

"Are you gents hungry or just thirsty?" Harry put a pint of ale in front of each of them.

"Harry, meet my adopted brother Daniel McKee. We call him Bear," he said.

"I've heard of you. You're that wolf and bear hunter," Harry said, quickly wiping his wet hands on his stain-covered apron before shaking Bear's outstretched hand. Harry turned to Stephen. "How long have you known Bear?"

"Since he was a cub," he answered.

Bear and Harry both laughed.

"That's an...interesting neck adornment you wear Bear." Harry stared wide-eyed at Bear's neck.

The impressive band of assorted huge teeth and claws, some more than four inches long, frightened nearly everyone who saw it.

Stephen remembered one man it had literally scared off. The man had stopped at the Barrington tavern while traveling through New Hampshire. He became curious about Bear's unusual neck adornment and inquired as to its origin. William, who often told tall tales, especially to unsuspecting strangers, jumped in and explained why Bear wore it. William told the man, well on his way to inebriation, that his adopted brother had been orphaned and raised by a she-bear. William said Bear was so much like his namesake and knew so much about them, that it was probable that the giant was half bear himself.

Bear, who had been thoroughly enjoying William's embellishment of his ancestry and childhood, while having an abundance of ale himself, roared exactly like a bear, glaring down fiercely at the diminutive man.

It was just too much for the man. He hurried away, stumbling over chairs in his attempt to escape. Bear and William had laughed for an hour after he'd left.

"I've kept one tooth and one claw from each bear I've killed as a tribute to them," Bear told Harry, who still stood staring, clearly mesmerized by the intimidating collection.

"I know folks around here are grateful that you've thinned them out some," Harry said. "Bears and people don't mix well."

"But they are the unmistakable kings of the forest," Bear said adamantly. "They command respect both for their uncanny stealth and for their courage. I've learned to respect and understand them. I've seen them climb a 100-foot tree in seconds and there's an old Indian sayin': a needle falls in the forest, the eagle sees it, a deer hears it, but the bear smells it. Aye, he smells fear too. To be a good hunter, or a good fighter, you can never let your adversary smell fear."

Wise words, Stephen thought. His stomach growled. It had been a long time since breakfast. "I'll have your pot pie, Harry," he ordered. "What's new in Durham?"

Harry's expression grew serious. "Nothing big except that devil Bomazeen."

The name hung heavy between them, a sudden dark threat. Stephen glanced at Bear, who also appeared dismayed to hear the name.

"He's back?" Stephen asked in disbelief.

"Where? When?" Bear nearly demanded.

"Sorry to say, near your neck of the woods. Just heard of it. He left his usual calling card—scalped a widow named Andrews and slit her throat. As if that weren't enough, he ran her through with a bayonet. Stole her few valuables. Something's brought the devil back. Probably looking to steal slaves to trade. She was too old to be of any use to him, poor soul, so he just did away with her. Now they think he must have been the one that stole young Lucy MacGyver."

"Mrs. Andrews, she lived not more than five miles from my farm," Stephen said. His mind and his heart raced and his nerves tensed. "My God. Forget the pot pie, Harry. I'm leaving." He leapt up from his wooden chair, knocking it over.

"It's dangerous traveling at night," Harry protested, while righting the chair. "Wait till morning."

A sense of foreboding filled Stephen, as he gathered his weapons. Jane. His girls. *Please God, keep them safe.* He needed to go now.

I'm coming, Jane.

"You'll need to eat," Harry said, "Take this loaf of bread with you."

"My thanks," Stephen muttered hastily, as he started off, rushing toward the door.

"I'll go with ye," Bear offered, tossing money on the table, and following Stephen out.

"No, I'll need the loan of your steed. My wagon will be too slow," Stephen shouted over his shoulder as he wove his way through the noisy tavern.

"Aye. My new horse is a good stout geldin'. Keep him at a slow lope and ye can ride all night long," Bear said as they started across the square.

"Bear, I need those supplies. Could you get them for me and then come as soon as you can?"

Stephen started to sprint and Bear managed to keep up.

"Aye. Give me yer list. Tomorrow's morn I'll be at their door and then on me way."

Within moments, he and Bear rushed inside the livery barn, lit with a small hanging oil lamp. He gobbled the bread while Bear quickly saddled the big horse and shortened the stirrups. The food made his stomach feel as if he had swallowed a rock, but he forced himself to wolf it down since he hadn't eaten all day. As Bear handed him the gelding's reins, the anxious look on his friend's face told him he understood Stephen's apprehension.

"God's speed, my friend," Bear said, as Stephen mounted and took off.

He rode all night, through a stiff breeze and damp chill. But worry kept his mind from noticing the cold. He alternated between thinking about what might be in the dark forest ahead and desperately praying for his family. Jane's face kept coming into his mind. Normally the vision brought him pure joy, but tonight every image made his gut knot tighter. He couldn't bear the thought of losing her.

Every mile through the night's black silence made him more uneasy. His jaw tightened so much it ached and his back muscles, already tired from his wagon trip that day, felt hard as rock. He focused so intensely on the dark trail ahead even his eyes began to hurt. He couldn't help but remember the dozens of vanished lives and recall the tragic testimonies of the few survivors of Bomazeen's raids. If he had known Bomazeen was anywhere near his home, he would never have left Jane and the girls alone.

Catching a glimpse of a horse and rider coming up the fork to the right, he reined the big gelding in hard, pulling him to an abrupt stop. "Who goes there?" he yelled, pistol drawn. Although nearly sunrise, it was still dark and difficult to see.

"Stephen, it's me," Sam yelled back.

A few moments later, his brother lined his tall steed up next to Stephen.

"Bomazeen is back. He killed again. I just warned John. I was riding to warn you. I didn't recognize you on that dun mount," Sam explained.

"Borrowed him from Bear so I could get back from Durham faster."

Bear's horse snorted, the hot air from his nostrils sending puffs of vapor into the cool air. Sam's gelding, also ridden hard, did the same, filling the darkness between the two men with a ghostly mist.

"Bear is bringing my team and supplies. I left Durham as soon as I heard about Bomazeen. Rode all night," he explained, trying hard to hold his emotions in check.

"Guns loaded?" Sam asked.

"Yes. Both."

"Good. Don't worry, we'll be there soon."

"God, don't let it be too late." Stephen kicked the big horse and gave him his rein.

Sam rode close beside him.

The hooves of both steeds thundered at the same pace as his racing heart.

CHAPTER 6

Taking his time, Bomazeen slowly skulked closer to Jane.

She saw foul lust building on his face, as he stared at her like a wolf ready to devour its prey. It caused her stomach to churn with disgust.

His lips parted, revealing a narrow pointed tongue. He touched himself and his lascivious eyes clouded with animalistic desire. The thought of him touching her made her skin crawl.

Appalled, she stepped backward until she felt the wall against her back. She frantically searched for something to use to defend herself. She spied the musket by the door and darted towards it.

But it was too far away.

Bomazeen quickly followed. She felt his hand grab the back of her neck. He shoved her to the floor, then rolled her over. One hand still held her throat as he grasped her bodice, tearing the garment to her waist, and exposing her breasts. His eyes widened and his mouth opened, revealing rotting teeth.

She cringed as his long filthy nails traveled slowly across her breasts and felt her skin tear beneath his sordid touch.

She cried out as he grabbed her hair with one hand, using it to pin her against the floor. As she bucked and kicked, fighting with every ounce of strength she could summon, she felt her hair tearing from her scalp, her roots ripping.

"Stop fighting or I'll just scalp this hair off your head and be done with it," he threatened.

It was no idle threat. The evidence hung from his belt. She forced herself to quit resisting, at least for the moment. But her anger continued to escalate.

Then he released her hair, grasped her wrists, and with one hand planted them firmly above her head, before reaching for the ties of his leather breeches.

She wanted to vomit the revulsion exploding inside her. *This cannot be happening*, she screamed inside her head. *It can't. I won't let it.* She twisted and turned against his weight.

Bomazeen reached under her gown. His hand moved quickly. Too quickly.

Jane released her shock and horror in a shrieking scream.

Little Mary woke and began to cry loudly. The baby's crying seemed to reverberate through the terror in the room making the sound nearly deafening.

She struggled against the pressure of his body trying to force her legs apart. She had never felt anger so intensely. Then her fury escalated even further.

Obviously distracted by the baby's intense squealing, Bomazeen growled like an angry animal and stood, keeping a grip on her wrists. He turned toward the cradle, a look of pure loathing contorting his face as he stomped toward the baby, dragging her along beside him.

Extreme dread instantly filled her. Would this beast kill Mary to silence her? God, help us, she begged silently.

She resisted with all her might and weight trying to stop him, but the man was strong and he held her wrist with a deathlike grip. But she *had* to stop him. As Bomazeen neared the baby, she jumped to her feet, snatched Mary into her free arm, and clutched her infant daughter protectively against her exposed breasts. "Leave my baby alone," she shouted fiercely.

"Bitch." Bomazeen released Jane and tore the baby from her arms.

"No!" she screamed, lunging at him with a wild frenzy as she tried to take her daughter back, tears of rage burning her eyes.

Bomazeen put his hand around the baby's throat and held the infant out at arm's length, away from her.

She thrashed about wildly, trying to reach her daughter, but Bomazeen kept the baby just out of her reach. Her throat tightened as desperation filled her. She had to save her baby. "*Please*," she begged.

Mary's little legs dangled like a rag doll's as the devil just sneered at her, and continued to taunt her with the wailing child.

She struck out, but he caught her arm midair, then painfully twisted it behind her back. He hoisted Mary in the air like a trophy. When he raised his arm back preparing to toss the infant, all three girls screamed in alarm and Jane felt her heart stop.

Seeming to take great pleasure in frightening the little girls, Bomazeen's evil sneer broadened. He tightened his grip around Mary's throat and squeezed. He dangled her again, tormenting her sisters.

This time, anger trumped fear and Martha ran towards him, her little arms outstretched, clearly intent on grabbing Mary away from Bomazeen. "No, no, no," Martha screamed.

Bomazeen released a sinister cackle and took a step backward, closer to the cradle, maintaining his hold on Jane, and nearly twisting her arm out of its socket. All she could do was watch, helpless, as Martha struggled to reach her tiny sister.

Bomazeen dangled the baby just above Martha's head, mocking the child's desperate efforts by raising Mary further up every time Martha nearly touched her sister. He smirked at her oldest daughter. "Is this what you want? You're a little wildcat, like your Ma."

The madman's actions made Jane furious, but worse, she feared he would tire of his cruel game and just kill Martha.

"Leave my sister alone!" Martha screamed. Her oldest child repeated the pitiful plea over and over.

Jane saw her chance. Martha's act of bravery provided her with a needed distraction.

As Bomazeen continued with his cruel taunting, she slowly stretched her free arm towards the cradle. Every inch of movement caused her other shoulder extreme agony but she would not stop no matter how badly it hurt. She desperately felt for the pistol she always hid underneath the cradle's mattress when Stephen was gone. She found it! Gritting her jaw, she took a slow steadying breath to calm her fury. She was left-handed and held the pistol in her right. She prayed her aim would be true as she cocked the weapon.

Bomazeen turned towards the sound to face the barrel of her firearm.

In that frozen instant, his malicious expression changed, as if his face turned to stone.

She desperately wanted to fire, but Bomazeen held Mary in front of him and held her at an awkward angle, making the pain in her shoulder excruciating.

Then his expression changed again. The stone came to life with the cold blood of evil. "You bitch. You can't kill me." He turned toward her and prepared to heave Mary at the weapon.

Horrified, the mother in Jane rose above her own fear. As his arm came back, she fired.

The ball's impact threw Bomazeen backward.

42

Mary flew out of Bomazeen's hand. Through the smoke of the gunpowder, she saw her baby falling in what seemed like slow motion.

Martha lunged forward to catch her sister.

The baby landed in Martha's arms, breaking her fall. As Martha and Bomazeen both fell to the floorboards, Jane heard a loud thud as the devil's head hit the wood floor.

She gathered Martha and a screaming Mary up in her arms, sobbing in dismay at the sight of blood splattered on her baby. Her hands flew across Mary's face and head, then her arms and legs, desperately wiping at the blood, searching for injuries. Mary wasn't bleeding. It was Bomazeen's blood.

She quickly put Mary back in Martha's arms and stood. Grabbing Bomazeen by both hands, she lugged him toward the door, but pain flared in her strained shoulder. She could only use one arm to pull him. She struggled for some time, against his dead weight, but finally managed, a few inches at a time, to get him out of her home. She glared down at his bleeding head, as he lay motionless on the porch.

She blinked hard and shook his revolting image from her head. She stumbled around his body, tripping on her skirt and fell next to Bomazeen's reeking collection of scalps. A broken shard of her teacup cut her arm. Clutching the bleeding gash against her thundering heart, she hurried inside.

She bolted the door and locked all the windows and shutters in their home. Her hands trembling, she reloaded her pistol and tucked it inside her apron. Only then did she motion Martha, Amy, and Polly to her side. Whimpering, they ran to her grabbing the folds of her gown with their little hands. "Mama, Mama," they cried in unison.

Martha buried her weeping face in Jane's skirt as she gently lifted Mary from her daughter's arms. "My brave Martha," she said soothingly, as she stroked the girl's head.

Unable to stand another moment, Jane sank to her knees and the girls piled around her as she hugged each of them fiercely. She kissed their tear-streaked faces blending their tears with her own. She needed to cry with them, needed to let the tears wash the terror from their hearts.

Then her blood turned cold at the realization of what might have been their fate—the horror that Stephen would have come home to. She started to shake. Her knees weakened, her hands trembled, and her heart raced. She wanted to speak, to reassure her daughters, but her jaw quivered. She struggled to compose herself for the sake of her girls.

She wiped tears away from her face with the back of her shaking hand. "Thank you, Lord, thank you," she finally managed to mutter.

Gradually, her hands steadied and her breathing returned to normal. She placed Mary in Martha's arms again and stood on wobbly legs.

"We're all right now. We're all right. We're all right now," she repeated over and over.

But had Bomazeen come alone?

CHAPTER 7

The house, bathed in early morning light, soon came into view. All the windows appeared locked and shuttered. Stephen's gut clenched. Something was wrong. Both men kicked their horses to a full run.

Moments later, he flew off the side of the gelding, his musket pointed at his front door.

Sam unsheathed his knife and slid off his mount in a single smooth motion.

"Jane. Jane, are you all right?" Stephen yelled, praying that she would open the door and scold him for shouting and waking the children. He pushed against the door, but it didn't budge, bolted from the inside. "Jane!"

The door flew open. "Stephen!"

Jane leapt into his arms, a pistol in her hand. Never had she felt so good in his arms. Never had he needed to hold her more. He hugged her fiercely, his heart still beating wildly.

"Sam, she's here. She's fine," he called out, relief filling his heart.

Sam rounded the corner from the side of the house. "Thank the Lord. I was just about to break through the bedroom window." The long blade he still held sparkled in the bright morning sun, bouncing reflections like a highly polished mirror.

Stephen guided Jane back inside. He cupped her face in his hands and peered into her eyes. He saw pain there he had never seen before. He noticed the torn bodice pinned to the front of her gown and blood on her skirt. Her lips and chin trembled. His heart tightened in his chest as he took in the sight of her. "Tell me," he managed to say.

"He's dead," she cried. "He's dead. He was about to…"

Jane couldn't continue. She pointed outside with a shaky hand and then put her fingers over her mouth. She seemed to be trying hard to hold in the emotions threatening to empty out of her. She pushed past him and headed for the porch.

Stephen and Sam followed.

"Where is he?" Jane demanded.

"Who?" Both men asked in unison.

For the first time, Stephen noticed the smeared blood on the porch. "What happened here?"

"No…he's got to be here. I killed him!" she shrieked, her eyes frantically darting around them.

Stephen gently grabbed her shoulders and turned her to face him. "Who did you kill?"

"Bomazeen." At the sound of the name, unspoken fear came alive in her eyes.

Sam leapt from the porch and began to study the ground. "If he's here, I'll find the bastard. I'll check around back."

Thankful his brother was there, Stephen could focus on Jane. Sam had the trained eyes of a soldier and if anything was amiss, he'd find it.

"The girls?" Stephen asked, holding his breath until she answered.

Jane pointed upstairs. "They're finally asleep. It was after midnight before the poor darlings stopped crying." She looked up. "Oh dear Heavenly Father, thank you for your mercy upon us."

He closed his eyes for a moment and silently also said a word of whole-hearted thanks.

"Stephen, he nearly....killed Mary," she sobbed. "He was going to take me to Chief Wanalancet. He said the Chief wanted me for his wife and married my spirit with his peace pipe. And he was going to make Martha a slave," she said, her voice breaking, barely able to get out the words.

"Is Mary all right?" he demanded.

"She'll have bruises around her neck, but her crying seemed normal, and she finally slept, so I think she'll be fine."

"Did Bomazeen hurt you?" He held his breath, bracing himself for what was coming.

Jane touched her cheek. A blue bruise showed through her pale skin. "He tried. He came close. So close."

Stephen watched as she squeezed her eyes closed. He kissed her eyelids tenderly, wanting to remove the image from her mind, and then laid her head against his chest. "What happened to your arm?"

"I opened the door and I saw him, standing there, his evil eyes staring at me. I dropped my teacup. Later, when I pulled him outside, I fell and cut my arm on the shards. Mother of God, he almost killed Mary." Her voice and lips trembled.

Sam joined them again. "There's a trail leading into the woods. Jane, how did you manage to shoot him?"

"He got angry because the baby was wailing. I picked her up. He grabbed Mary away from me and dangled her by the throat. Martha got mad and charged him. She was so brave. She kept trying to pull Mary away from him." She paused for a moment to catch her breath. "While she distracted him, I managed to get the pistol I keep under the baby's mattress, and I shot him. I had to shoot from an awkward angle because he had one of my arms pinned behind my back, but the bullet hit the side of his head."

He turned to Sam and said, "It's a trick her father taught her. No one expects a gun to be underneath a baby. The girls know not to touch it, and the baby's not strong enough to lift the mattress."

"Your Papa taught you well. Good thing. It saved the lives of three of your girls and you and Martha from the unspeakable," Sam said. "Someone helped Bomazeen into the woods. He was half walking and half drug. Must have been the one hiding their mounts."

"He's still alive?" Jane gasped and pressed her hand against her mouth.

"Your shot must have grazed his head and knocked him out. Someone helped the bastard into the timbers and onto a horse."

"That man's not human. He's a damned demon," she swore.

Stephen could only hug Jane against his chest, where his heart still pounded. He could not believe that monster had entered the sanctuary of their home. His family was supposed to be safe here. His baby was supposed to be safe. He should have been here. His entire body tensed with the effort to control his anger. But now, he needed to help Jane.

"It's over now. Let's get you back inside," he suggested.

Jane raised her head and nodded. She allowed him to usher her into the house, but then stopped, locked her arms tightly around his waist and sobbed into his chest. She had likely kept her emotions under tight control all night. But now, with him here, she was free to let go of some of the hurt.

Stephen gently stroked the top of her head, giving her time to cry. Best to let the poison out. The ordeal understandably traumatized her. "You're safe. I'm here now."

After several minutes of quivering in his embrace, she sniffled and dried her eyes with her apron. "I was so frightened. Thank the Lord you're finally home."

"Jane, your bravery astonishes me. I'm so proud of you." He kissed her forehead. "Most women would not have had the courage to fight back."

"Here drink this," Sam said, as he offered her water.

Jane eyed the water dipper, then shook her head and buried her face on Stephen's chest again. "Once I made sure Martha and the baby were not badly injured, I somehow dragged him out to the porch and then bolted the doors and windows. I didn't want to risk going outside. All I could do was stay awake and keep my pistol pointed at the front door."

"You did all you need to do. Sit down now and rest. You're exhausted," Stephen told her, guiding her to her favorite chair.

"I'm going after them," Sam said.

"You shouldn't go after them alone. But I can't leave Jane and the girls. Wait for Bear. He should be here soon," he suggested.

Sam headed for the door. "There's no time. The trail is already getting cold."

"I'll have Bear come after you when he gets here," Stephen called out as Sam left.

"How did you get home so soon? Didn't you go to Durham?" Jane asked.

Stephen bent down beside Jane and took her hands. "Yes, I was at Harry's Tavern, where I ran into Bear. Harry told us Bomazeen killed Widow Andrews. As soon as I heard, I borrowed Bear's horse and left at once." He told her about the rest of his night.

"Oh, Mrs. Andrews, the poor soul," she said hoarsely. "He must have killed her on the way here. Dear God."

He didn't want to tell her the grizzly details of the killing. She'd been through enough and her nerves were still too raw. As he stood up, he realized his heart was still hammering in his chest. He took a deep breath to steady his own shaky nerves.

After stoking the fire and making certain Jane was okay, he stepped out and scanned the woods around their home, almost hoping he would spot the bastard. If he ever got his hands on Bomazeen…

Jane vigorously attacked the blood on the porch's wooden planks with a bristle brush and strong lye soap. The morning sun bathed her as she worked, the good light aiding in her cleaning efforts. Wanting to rid her home of the last traces of the ordeal, she scrubbed as she had never scrubbed before. Beads of sweat formed on her forehead.

She wished she could wash Bomazeen away from her mind as easily. She pushed a long strand of hair out of her way, so she could see more clearly. She stopped abruptly. Hair. The white hair on Bomazeen's belt belonged to Widow Andrews. She gasped in horror. Choking back sobs as she remembered how lovely that silver-white hair had been. She could see it clearly in her mind as she remembered Mrs. Andrews. "You son of a …," she hissed aloud and smacked the porch with her wet brush. She wished she had killed Bomazeen. "You deserve to burn in hell. Burn forever. Burn without dying. I hope the first thing to burn is the hair on *your* head."

The unpleasant task completed, she stood and stared down at the scattered pieces of her treasured teacup, finding it hard to focus on them through her tears. She slowly gathered the larger pieces up in her apron, then found a shovel and buried the broken shards beneath her favorite tree.

Returning to her bucket, she threw the dirty water as far as she could, hot angry tears pouring down her cheeks. She wiped them away with the back of her hand.

The girls, exhausted from the trauma, still slept upstairs so she took the time to wash herself, comb her hair, and change into a fresh dress and apron. Still uneasy, and with Stephen at the barn, she put her pistol back under the baby's mattress and stuck a knife in her apron.

Next, she cleaned off the mess Bomazeen had made of her table and washed the water bucket and dipper. She got fresh water from the cistern and started a pot of coffee before going out to the hen house, feeding the chickens, and then gathering their eggs. She appreciated how the chickens ate the bugs around the place and turned them into food for her family.

Her sack of potatoes was still half-full and she peeled a dozen and started them frying on the iron skillet. Doing these ordinary things kept her mind busy and off her ordeal. She'd taken these simple tasks for granted in the past, but today these small chores had more meaning. She realized how close she had come to not being able to do them for her family.

Jane finished kneading biscuits and put them in her Franklin iron furnace. Whenever she used the stove, she silently thanked Benjamin Franklin who had invented the new style of stove. It had a hood-like enclosure and an airbox in the rear, allowing a fire that used a fourth of the wood used by cast-iron stoves. She smiled. Stephen had saved for a year and ordered the stove for her to celebrate their fifth anniversary.

She sat in her wooden rocker to breastfeed Mary. As the milk flowed, profound relief slowly filled her. Her baby was safe, snuggled securely against her. Only Bomazeen's scratch across her breast remained to darken the moment. But the wound would heal soon. She cuddled Mary against her and softly kissed the baby's head as she fed. She wanted to weep again, but this time from overwhelming relief and thankfulness.

The delicious smell of the biscuits baking and potatoes frying with onions filled the house. The girls soon woke, calling for her. She detected fear in Martha's voice and couldn't blame her. But children have a way of bouncing back and she prayed they would soon forget the trials of last night.

"It's safe girls. Come on down now." She pulled a well-satisfied Mary away from her breast and laid her back in the cradle.

The girls slowly descended the stairs. Martha held the hands of both her sisters. They peered wide-eyed, warily looking around the room.

She went to them, hugging, and kissing each one. "Don't worry, your father came back early this morning with Uncle Sam. He's out at the stable now feeding the livestock," Jane said. She deliberately didn't mention Bomazeen or that Sam was tracking him.

"Are you okay Mama?"

Martha asked the question so sweetly it made her want to weep again. She turned away from her daughters so they could not see her eyes brighten with tears. "Yes, dear. I'm just tired. Will you girls help me with baby Mary? Her cloth needs changing and I'm done feeding her now." She hoped taking care of their baby sister would help the girls get back to normal. She needed to talk to them about the ordeal, but she wasn't ready just yet. Soon, but not now.

How long would it take to get over the wound Bomazeen inflicted on her mind? Maybe it would eventually just be an ugly scar. That was the irony of it. Physical injuries often heal with little or no permanent damage. But traumas of the mind are not so easily erased. Some never go away. They are always there, just below the surface, capable of returning unbidden with fresh intensity and pain. She stirred the potatoes and banged the wooden spoon against the side of the pan so hard it cracked.

Stephen unsaddled Bear's horse. After their long journey, the worn-out mount would need a good rest. Scowling as he worked, he tugged at the saddle leathers more aggressively than needed, releasing the girth. The gelding sidestepped and he realized that he was making the poor tired animal nervous. He stroked the horse's neck soothingly and then got him a generous portion of feed and fresh water.

He paced across the barn, as an icy apprehension twisted around his heart. He wasn't worried for Sam. It was unlikely his brother could catch up to Bomazeen, and if he did, it was Bomazeen that needed to worry.

What had his stomach in knots was that Jane had only wounded Bomazeen. The fiend will likely come back for her. The threat wasn't over. It was worse now. Men like Bomazeen don't give up.

Well, he didn't either. He would find a way to keep her safe.

CHAPTER 8

A s the sun contemplated setting, Bear pulled up, the wagon team covered in sweat and breathing hard. "I pushed them as much as I dared. Is everything all right here?" Bear yelled.

Stephen had been waiting alone for Bear on his porch, thinking through their predicament. He did not want to worry Jane. She had endured enough already.

"Jane and the girls are safe, but no," he said, coming down the porch steps. "I'll explain later." Thankfully, Bear didn't press him.

They unloaded the supplies—seed, coffee, flour, cornmeal, honey, salt, cheese, oats, and the cloth for Jane.

"Hope she'll be likin' the fabric. 'Twas the first time I ever bought cloth. And I surely hope it will be the last," Bear said.

Stephen grimaced, remembering Jane's torn dress and what nearly happened to his wife. She would need the new cloth to replace the torn gown. Cackling chickens scattered out of their way as the two men took the wagon and feed to the barn, then stacked the sacks in neat piles. His barn was more orderly than most, and he took pride in its upkeep.

"I'm in your debt Bear for bringing our supplies and for the loan of your horse," he said as they finished unhitching and caring for the wagon team.

"'Tis my pleasure to be of service," Bear said. "Tell me what's happened then. I can tell ye're worried."

"Bomazeen," Stephen snarled. "He was here and tried to steal Jane and Martha." The words made him want to choke. "He nearly had his way with my wife and wanted to trade her to the Pennacook Chief. He would have killed the three youngest. Jane managed to sneak out her pistol and she shot the bloody bastard."

"She killed him?" Bear asked, his eyes widening.

"She thought he was dead, and drug him outside, but the bullet must have just grazed him. Someone helped him and they left on horseback. Sam went after them. He's been gone since early this morning. He wanted you to follow him, but you'll have to wait until morning. It'll be dark in less than an hour, impossible to follow their tracks."

"Och! The men of this state have tried to track that beast through the woods for years and Jane manages to shoot him," Bear marveled.

"I'm afraid she's in danger. Bomazeen will come back for her."

"Aye. Disease decimated many of the Pennacooks. Not many remain in the White Mountains. Smallpox killed most of the women of the tribe last year. I just heard in Durham yesterday that they started raidin' from here to the Canadian border, takin' women captive. They're difficult to stop because they sneak in and out quickly, leavin' nothin' to follow. These natives like strong women. They do most of the work and tend the crops. Aye, the threat is real. The Chief could send Bomazeen and more braves after her again. I'll stay with you until we know 'tis safe," Bear offered.

Stephen had little respect for some of the Algonquian tribes. He had heard many stories from Sam. On more than one occasion, Sam saw them fight alongside the British during the Revolution. During a battle in the Mohawk Valley, decimated Continental troops suffered more than 400 casualties, many at the hands of the natives. Sam had not forgotten, and neither had he. But, he also knew that other natives had helped many colonists. Some built trusted relations with them and even owed their lives to the aid provided by friendly Indians. But the British purposely tore through those bonds of trust and kept tensions high, making peaceful relations with the tribes difficult. And it rankled him that men like Bomazeen kept the pot stirred, sometimes to over boiling.

"I'm not sure it's ever going to be safe," Stephen said. "The British continue to arm these natives and encourage them to resist us. You're right, they are exceedingly difficult to fight—they grab women quickly and then disappear without a trace. Bomazeen targeted Jane for the Chief. The fact that she shot a man like Bomazeen will only make her more desirable to the Chief. Bomazeen's wounded pride will make him come after her as soon as he's able."

"They do admire strength. I agree there's reason to believe they will come again."

"Let them come. Better yet, let's take the battle to them," he growled through gritted teeth. "We can get others to help. We'll leave in the morning."

"Ye're na thinkin' right, man. You're talkin' out of rage," Bear said. "That'd be suicide. They would know we were comin' a mile away. They'd set traps for us. Tryin' to fight them in the timber and mountains is near to impossible. It'd be like elk tryin' to hunt a mountain lion."

"Damn it. Defending my family is my job—not Jane's. The bastard nearly raped her. She's my wife. It's my duty to protect her."

"Then start." Soundlessly, Sam had sidled up behind the two.

"What happened? Did you find them?" Stephen demanded.

"I found where they had stopped to rest their mounts."

Stephen and Bear waited for Sam to continue.

"Looks like Bomazeen is on his way to the Pennacook village. I lost his trail in the rocks. Searched for some sign of them for hours, but to no avail. It was getting late and it would have been ill-advised to continue, so I turned back."

"How can a man be so cruel?" Bear asked.

"Some say it's the French in him, some say it's his Indian blood. I tend to think he's just a mean sick bastard," Sam said.

"I hate to even say this, but I think Bomazeen will come after Jane again. She made him look weak to the Chief," Stephen said.

"I agree, but I am afraid next time he'll not only seek to kidnap her, he'll want to torture her. He'll make her pay and he won't give up until she has," Sam said.

"That's not going to happen," Stephen snapped.

"We'll keep her safe and yer wee bairns too," Bear swore. "The question is how?"

"I've been trying to figure that out all afternoon," Sam said. "We've dealt with Indian uprisings before, and we'll do it again if necessary. But this isn't an uprising. This is Bomazeen. He's unpredictable and vicious."

Stephen raked his fingers through his hair. "The problem is we don't know when the sneaky devil will attack or attempt to get Jane again. I don't want her living in fear every minute of her life and I can't stay here at the house all the time. But now, I can't leave them alone either."

"We could take turns standing watch," Bear suggested.

"But how long—a week, a month, six months?" Sam asked.

"Could she stay with kin?" Bear asked.

"Her folks have both passed, and she has no other relatives near here," Stephen said.

"You could move into Barrington, near Edward," Sam suggested, "but there's no guarantee she would be safe there either. And how would you care for your livestock or keep someone from stealing them."

Stephen's heart beat faster. He realized what they needed to do. "There is a way to keep her safe, or at least to get her away from this threat. We go west. You both wanted to go anyway. Maybe this is God's way of telling us it's time. His way of spurring us on."

"I beg ye na to take offense man, but is it possible that ye are usin' this as an excuse to leave?" Bear asked. "Would ye have decided to go anyway? Ye told me ye were worried about the risks. About being reasonable."

"Damn it Bear, what would you have me do?" Stephen tried to throttle his anger. "You're the one who made me realize a decision like this has to be made from faith and courage not from what is rational and safe."

"Aye, I did say that."

"And you were right as rain," Sam said. "Now it's even more right."

Stephen scrubbed his fingers across his tired eyes and gritty face. Lack of sleep made it difficult to think clearly. Had they considered everything? One thing still bothered him. "What will keep them from following us?"

"If they did, I think they would only follow as far as the Merrimack River. Once we cross at Manchester, we should be safe. Natives are rarely seen past there," Sam said. "After we cross the Merrimack, we'll turn south towards Springfield. Of course, we could go to Pittsburgh and then take a flatboat down the Ohio, but we would be unable to take much with us. I think we would be better off going over land so we'd have more provisions when we get to Kentucky. This way, we can take food, tools, extra horses, and a few of your best cattle."

Stephen knew that for Sam a trip to Kentucky would be a glorious adventure, despite the dangers. Sam often talked about moving on. Most of the area's tribes had relocated to Canada or high into the White Mountains and life did not challenge him as it once had. Since the Revolution, Sam made his living as a hunter, tracker, and sometimes a mapmaker. The work provided a reasonable livelihood, but he could tell it did not light a fire in Sam's soul. The fire within his big brother was cold, smothered by some buried pain Sam refused to acknowledge, even to him.

Stephen gently stroked George's face and scratched under his forelock. Touching his horse made him feel somewhat calmer.

"I agree, and a wagon will provide shelter for the children. After Springfield, where would we head?" Stephen asked Sam, already anxious to plan the trip. Sam had studied maps all his life and would know the route to Kentucky from memory.

"South through Hartford towards New York, then Philadelphia, skirting around larger cities as much as we can."

This was no surprise. Sam hated large cities, especially Philadelphia with more than 30,000 people and New York with some 25,000. He'd often said these bustling places made him feel like he couldn't think clearly. Cities held too many distractions and too much potential for trouble. The few times business or the need for supplies forced Sam into a large city, he got in and out as quickly as possible.

"Then we would turn southwest on The Great Indian Warpath, taking us through southern Pennsylvania, the eastern edge of the frontier. After that, we'd continue south through Virginia all the way to Bristol. At that point, we'll pass through the Cumberland Gap and head north into Kentucky. I don't know much about the route after that, but we can find out more from the locals."

"How soon do we leave?" Bear asked.

"We can't ask you to go," Stephen said. "This is our problem and I don't expect you to leave everything behind."

"Ye did na ask me. I want to make the trip. I did some thinkin' on my way here about our conversation at the tavern. I decided that I wanted to go with you if you went west. Your family is my only family. Your problems are my problems," Bear said.

Stephen had known for a long time that Bear felt that way. As a young man, Bear had traveled from Scotland to the colonies with his father and mother, but both parents died in route on the ship. Buried at sea, they left their orphan son a modest sum of money. With no family in the colonies, Bear had become a hunter and trapper, using the skills his grandfather had taught him as a boy in the Scottish highlands to rid the area of the threat of predators. Stephen's father befriended the young man, often buying fresh meat from him for his large family. Their mother would insist that he stay with them from time to time to attend church and receive schooling with her own boys. They had both been like parents to Bear.

"Besides, there'll be more bear for me to hunt there. These woods are gettin' picked over, are they not?"

"Sam and I would welcome your help. Then it is settled. You'll join us, of course." Stephen closed the barn door. Had he just closed the door on his old life?

They started back towards the house.

"But what about Jane? Is she of a mind to leave?" Bear asked. "If I know her, she'll na let Bomazeen run her from her fine house."

"Indeed. She's so stubborn she would probably stay just to prove he couldn't. Before this happened, I wanted her to feel the same way I do about Kentucky. I didn't want her to go out of loyalty to me."

"Does she?" Sam asked.

"I haven't asked her yet," Stephen begrudgingly admitted, rubbing the stubble on his chin.

Sam and Bear, both looking incredulous, stared at Stephen, making him feel more than a little foolish.

"How could you have gone this far in your thinking without talking with her?" Sam asked.

"You're asking for a storm by keeping this from her," Bear added.

Bear was right. Jane's temper could ignite quicker than dry leaves.

"I wasn't keeping it from her. I planned to talk to her after I had reached a decision. Until I knew for a certainty that I wanted to go, there was no point in worrying her about it. Besides, she'll support what I want to do," he said, trying to sound more confident than he felt. He admitted to himself that he should have raised the possibility with her before now, but the right moment never seemed to present itself.

"We'd best wait out here and have a smoke before dinner," Sam said.

Bear quickly nodded his agreement.

"Cowards," Stephen muttered. He swallowed hard, then turned toward the house.

CHAPTER 9

As Stephen reached his porch, the aroma of the cooking meal greeted him, but did little to stimulate his lack of appetite. He heard the girls playing upstairs, laughing now. Again, he thanked God silently for sparing his daughters.

Jane swung the door open, about to toss out some dishwater, and nearly collided with him. She studied his eyes, but said nothing, then stepped back, letting him take the dirty water before turning back inside.

He pitched the water and stepped back on the porch. "Give me the right words," he whispered aloud.

His boot crushed a tiny broken piece of Jane's teacup and the feel of it against his boot sole, made him bite down hard on his lower lip, trying to keep his anger in check.

He watched Jane bustle about her kitchen making stew and biscuits, enough to feed three hungry men, growing girls, and her own healthy appetite. The recipe, used by her family for generations, was one of his favorites and equally good for all kinds of game. As she peeled wild garlic and potatoes, he slid his arms around her waist and gently pressed his lips to the back of her head. She tilted her head forward and he pushed her long hair aside to softly kiss the back of her neck until he felt her quiver.

"That's what I needed," she said and sank back against his embrace.

Stephen managed a slight smile. Jane's obvious physical reaction to his affection warmed his heart, making him even more determined to protect her.

He turned her around to face him and tenderly traced the line of her jaw. "Jane, I am so grateful that you were able to protect yourself and our girls. I'm proud of your courage. But unfortunately, that was not the end of danger."

"Why?" She stared at him, her eyes wide with concern.

He hesitated and swallowed hard, searching for courage. "Sam tracked Bomazeen. The devil headed toward the Pennacook village in the mountains, but tracking him is next to impossible and he had a long head start. The tribe will probably heal his wound. But you also wounded his pride. That won't heal. He'll come back and try again."

Jane unclenched her fist and put the kitchen knife down. "Stephen, I admit this was a close call, too close. This event shook us all, but you must have faith that God will keep us from harm."

She moved to the table and lit some candles, brightening the room considerably, but not Stephen's mood.

"It's not that simple. Savages have butchered many people of faith," he said.

"Then we'll be ready for them. Men around here have fought the natives before. What's different now? I know you're not afraid of them."

"The difference is that in the past they only stole horses or cattle during a raid. But now they're stealing women, and Bomazeen wants to capture *you*. The natives need wives to replace their women who died from smallpox and they need slaves to tend crops. Bear says they have started raiding again from here to Canada. Bomazeen is helping them. It is nearly impossible to rescue a woman or child once stolen. One of the girls stolen recently, Lucy, was just sixteen." Stephen almost choked on the words. He pitied the poor young woman. His heart twisted in his chest when he thought about how close Jane and Martha had come to the same fate.

"Sam and Bear agree you are in grave danger. Our girls are also in peril. I'm not afraid to fight, but it is my responsibility to keep you safe. I believe the best option is to leave."

There, he'd finally said it.

Jane froze in her tracks. "Leave? But this is our home."

Stephen started to pace. "This farm is remote and isolated. When we built here, no one thought the natives would again be a threat. And they probably wouldn't be now if disease hadn't wiped out their wives. I would die fighting to keep anyone from taking you. But I cannot always be here to stand watch. And if, Lord forbid, I were to die in a fight with Bomazeen, I could no longer protect you and the girls. I *won't* let you become a slave. To be certain that does not happen, I have to keep both of us safe. I had been thinking about heading west, to Kentucky, before this happened. Now, I'm certain it's what we need to do. Sometimes it takes courage to make a wise decision. We need to make a wise decision now."

Jane put her hands on his arms to stop him. She stared at him, her face flushing. "How can you be so ready to give up our home? Leaving won't keep us safe. There are countless dangers on the trail to Kentucky. Probably worse hazards. Have you considered that?"

"That's all I've thought about lately. My brothers and Bear will be joining us so we will have five men—six if Edward comes—not just me to protect you. And we won't be sitting here waiting for danger to come to us. I'll not live here with your life in jeopardy or with us worrying about the girls disappearing every time they go outside to play. Why should we when so much opportunity waits for us there? Daniel and Squire Boone call Kentucky a second paradise. Boone's axe men cleared a trail all the way to the Kentucky River. They say the grass there is lush beyond belief."

"Pastures—so that's what this is all about. I should have known." Jane threw down the towel in her hand.

"No! It's not just about land. It's about opportunity."

"What about Indians in Kentucky?"

"The Shawnee, by terms of the truce, agreed not to harm white settlers. Once we reach Fort Boonesborough it will be safe." He truly believed that was true. He stayed informed on the news of the frontier, reading everything he could get his hands on and Sam's contacts with the military and other hunters and trappers provided reliable information. They also learned a good deal from newspapers. He removed a newspaper clipping from his writing-table drawer. "I was going to show you this even before Bomazeen came here. It's from the *New Hampshire Gazette,* December 15, 1796." Stephen read it aloud to her, "*'The Wilderness Road from Cumberland Gap to the settlements of Kentucky is now completed. Wagons loaded with a ton weight, may pass with ease, with four good horses. Travelers will find no difficulty in procuring such necessaries as they stand in need of on the road; and the abundant crop now growing in Kentucky, will afford the emigrants a certainty of being supplied with every necessary of life on the most convenient terms. Joseph Crockett, James Knox, Commissioners.'"*

He put the clipping away and then continued. "Everywhere I go, Jane, men are talking excitedly about the beautiful grass in Kentucky, so rich in color, settlers call it Bluegrass."

He remembered the plentiful grass his father had cultivated on their home place, but a massive mountain slide of rock, mud, and snow buried his parents' entire three-story brick home and most of their property. Tragically, his father, mother, and sister all perished, buried forever at the base of what people would later name Wyllie Mountain.

Jane turned back to making dinner, shaking her head from side to side. "I'm more concerned about the safety of my daughters than a plenitude of pastures." She smacked the biscuit dough with more force than needed.

"I am too. That's why I want to leave," he persisted, fatigue making him even less patient than normal.

"Well, I don't. I can't believe your brothers agreed to this madness."

"They all see the potential and agree it is time for a move. Well, all but Edward," he said tersely, admitting to himself that he wanted his stubborn brother to come. The five brothers, despite their differences, had always been close and he wanted it to stay that way. He still held out hope that Edward would change his mind. He put a log on the fire and stoked it repeatedly.

"We need to think about this. You've waited this long, it can keep until we're both sure."

"Damn it, I am sure. I'm sure we need to leave *now*."

"Well I'm not!" She stomped her foot and glared up at him. A flush of red crept up her throat as her anger flared.

He was running out of options. He had to make her understand. "If we stay, and that devil's spawn grabs one of our girls, will you be able to live with that? This is just a house. We can replace it. We cannot replace one of them. If he comes back, what do you think he is going to do to you? I promise you rape would be the easiest part."

"Don't threaten me with what Bomazeen might do. I *know* what he's like. I felt his hot stinking breath on my face and my breast still bears his filthy mark. He nearly killed my baby," she screamed. "But I won't turn tail and run like a frightened rabbit. This is our home." She choked back a sob.

"Settle your temper. The girls will hear you. They've been through enough. And so have you. I don't want you to go through that again."

She lowered her voice, but not her obvious anger. "Would you have decided to go if this hadn't happened—if Bomazeen had never come here?" She glared at him, her green eyes nearly burning a hole through him.

It seemed everyone had the same question for him. "Yes. I already made up my mind that I wanted to go. I think this is something my father would have wanted for me. And I hoped you would too."

"When did you plan to talk to *me* about upsetting our whole world? I don't care what your father wanted."

"But I do," he said simply. He swallowed his frustration. "And I care about what you want too."

Stephen decided to try to calm her. "You're correct, of course. With all of our futures at stake, we must decide this with great care. There will be only one chance to make the right decision." He took her hand and squeezed it. He could tell she was a long way from committing to leave. There was little conviction in her grip.

He let go of her hand and started to pace again, but then stopped abruptly and faced her. "I want your happiness Jane—more than my own. You mean everything to me."

"Then think about this. We have been so happy here. It would be a terrible sacrifice to leave our home, everything we have worked so hard to build. It might not be much, but it's ours."

He set his jaw and moved closer to her. "Our forefathers made sacrifices and endured misfortunes to come to the New World. They didn't seek ease and comforts in coming here. They expected hardships and discouragements. I don't think they did it just for themselves. They did it for us. They faced exactly the same choice we face, stay or go. They let God's will guide them."

She threw her hands in the air and looked up. "How does anyone really know what God's will is?"

"I don't know," he admitted. He considered her question for a moment and then said, "I do know that we're not here to just exist—to just get by. We're here to accomplish what He puts in our hearts, even if it's difficult. I think those sparks, those ideas that give us hope, that make us want to open a new door, come from Him. If we don't accomplish anything, why are we even here? We must always try, even though we won't always succeed. I know I would rather die trying than die without ever having tried."

She appeared confused.

"Kentucky offers a chance for a better life. Don't we owe that to our daughters?" Worn out by their argument and lack of sleep, he collapsed in his favorite chair and yanked off his boots. He noted he would need to see the cobbler for a sturdy new pair before they left for Kentucky. "You've been through an ordeal and might not want to think about this now. But at least consider how much opportunity lies out there waiting for us before you make up your mind."

Jane didn't respond. Instead, she fetched a pot of coffee from the stove and poured them both a cup. "Stephen, if it were just us, I wouldn't hesitate. This is not about what's right or wrong—it's about choosing between two rights." She stomped back to the kitchen to resume cooking for the moment.

He hoped the streaming brew would refresh him, while he pondered what she had said about two rights.

Jane's head spun with dozens of questions, a myriad of doubts. *What if we get there and he can't find the kind of land he wants? What if the good land is already taken? How will we even know where to look? What if Stephen gets hurt or worse, dies?*

So many emotions thrashed around inside her head she could not think clearly. Her serene world had disappeared. The future approached like a thundering crashing avalanche, not the soft powdery flurry she'd grown used to. It was too fast and too much. She couldn't keep up.

Her confusion sent her to the verge of panic. Tears welled in her eyes.

She didn't want her world to change. She wanted everything to stay the way it was.

She threw down her biscuit dough and stalked over to stand in front of Stephen. "Damn it, we need to just stay here. You will never convince me that even the best pastureland would be worth putting our girls in jeopardy. And you'll never convince me that we need to leave to stay safe."

"Jane, there's a new home for us out there somewhere. Trust that He will keep us all safe on our journey."

"I trust that He will keep us safe *here*." She stomped her foot. "This is beyond impossible. I won't do it!" she yelled. "We can't leave our home."

"We can and we will." His voice was uncompromising, yet gentle.

The straightforward statement deflated her. She groaned and sat down at the table, nearly unable to stand with the weight of what her husband was asking of her. She knew Stephen's heart—he was just trying to keep them all safe. But at what cost?

Was he right? She wanted to trust her husband. But change was frightening. She brought her fingers to her lips and slowly rubbed her mouth, a habit she had when worried.

Stephen just wasn't thinking clearly. This whole incident with Bomazeen had shaken him to his core. A trip to Kentucky would sound like a convenient way to escape that problem. He probably imagined them riding through the woods, side-by-side, sleeping together under the stars. She wasn't so sure. This was where she wanted to sleep with her husband. She had her babies in that bed. She was happy here, so content.

Until Bomazeen. She closed her eyes and shuddered.

Could she forget the horror that took place here? Would the girls remember the terror he inflicted every time they passed through the room? Would the devil come back for her? Or, heaven forbid, Martha?

She had to admit, the thought terrified her.

Maybe she should leave this house. Make new memories in a new home in another place. A place safely away from Bomazeen.

She glanced at Stephen. His eyes held the same hopeful spark she had seen in them when he came back from the barn. He was looking at the future, while she still clung to the past, desperate to hold on to it. Was it time for her to look toward the future too?

Would he do this anyway, no matter how much she objected? No, he loved her too much. But her husband's ambition, if thwarted, would make him a man who would always wonder what might have been.

A man's life had to have a grander purpose than to just feed himself and his family.

Maybe, she could at least consider his proposal. Maybe it was wrong for her to doubt him.

"*If* I agree to this, and I'm still not sure I can, it will be against my better judgment. I will not do it because we are running from danger. But it will be for our future—yours, mine, and the girls," Jane said guardedly.

Stephen's face brightened at once. "Keeping you safe is my future. I have no future, in the west or anywhere, if you're not a part of it. I know we can make a better future for our family there."

She sucked in a breath. "I can't believe you are truly ready to do this."

He came closer to her, looking down at her intensely, and took her hands in his. "It is overwhelming to think about," he said, his voice conveying excitement. "It will not only change our lives but the lives of our daughters and all those who'll come after us. New Hampshire won't be home to our descendants. I want to create a future they will benefit from. Someday, they'll know we did this, and be grateful that we did it. I hope they will love the land as I do. This is going to be a great country someday; maybe even go beyond Kentucky. By God, we might even go beyond Kentucky."

Her blood froze at his words.

Jane could only stare at him, wondering if she could even go beyond her doubts.

CHAPTER 10

With Sam and Bear there to keep a vigilant watch, Stephen felt he could get away for a short while to talk to his other brothers. He wanted to speak to all three together if he could, so he decided to get John first and then go into Barrington where Edward and William both lived.

While he rode, Stephen thought about his discussion with Jane. He marveled at her keen mind. Having her as his wife and confidant was his greatest blessing, but her stubbornness went beyond bearable sometimes. And she called *him* pigheaded. Sam had promised to talk to her while he was gone. Perhaps he could make her understand how important this was for all of them and how serious a threat Bomazeen really was.

He arrived to find John saddling his sorrel mount and Little John's old grey pony. John's steed stood nearly 16 hands high to accommodate its owner's long legs. The horse's copper-red mane and tail sparkled in the morning sun reminding him of Jane's hair. He would do whatever it took to protect that lovely head of hair.

"Where you headed?" he asked John, without dismounting or greeting them.

"Good morning to you as well," John said, smiling. "We're going to Barrington to check the progress of the new schoolhouse. I want to be sure the carpenters and masons are following my plans correctly." He threw his saddle over a blanket and adjusted its weight on the horse's back.

An excellent builder, John had designed and built several area homes, bridges, and churches. Currently, John was working on Barrington's first schoolhouse, something the town was sorely missing.

But today, Stephen's mind was not on his daughters' education, but their future.

"Figure out who can take over for you. We're leaving for Kentucky," he said.

John stopped, and looked up at him. "Why so soon? I thought we were still making up our minds. And if we decided to go, I didn't think we were leaving until early summer, after the heavy spring rains. I can't just leave the school half done."

"Finish saddling. We'll talk in Barrington with Edward and William," he answered.

"All right. There's some coffee left if you're interested," John offered as he grabbed the girth strap and gave it a tug.

"I just want to get to Barrington. Let's go!"

John glared back at him.

Stephen softened his tone. He didn't mind being abrupt, but he did not want to be rude. "Please hurry."

Within minutes, the horses and pony carried them at a steady trot, down the winding valley trail to Barrington. A crisp morning breeze carrying the scent of spring wafted against his face and he inhaled deeply.

"What's the rush Uncle?" Little John asked.

"You'll see soon enough." His mind raced, filling with the numerous tasks to take care of before they could leave. They would have to sell their properties or turn them over to someone to rent. He would auction most of his livestock. They would need six months' worth of key supplies, plenty of ammunition and guns, extra horses, and a roomy wagon. By the time he reached Barrington, he had many of the details already worked out in his head.

He tugged George to a stop in front of William's house. The simple two-room dwelling was suitable for an unmarried man. William kept it neat, but it lacked the warmth of a woman's touch. What would his life be like if he didn't have Jane?

When no one answered Stephen's rap on the door, they let themselves in and found William still sound asleep, lying face down, wearing only his linen underdrawers.

Little John marched over to the bedside. "Wake up Uncle Will. Uncle Stephen needs to talk to you."

William raised his head, grunted, and managed a weak smile at his nephew.

"What are you doing still asleep when the morning's half over?" Stephen asked. "I swear the only reason you wanted to be sheriff was to keep yourself out of real work."

"And out of jail," John said. "Probably figured if he was sheriff, he couldn't get arrested."

"Excellent point," Stephen said, looking over at John.

"Had a long night," William said, swinging his long legs over the side of the bed and slowly pushing himself up. "First there were two young ladies that needed some company and then these trappers started trying to snare my lovely ladies. I had to set them straight. They're probably sore around the jaw this morning." He pushed his long hair out of his face with both hands.

"You look a little roughed up yourself," John said. "But that's not unusual for you."

"Well, there were three of them," William said.

"Get dressed. We're going to talk to Edward about the move to Kentucky," Stephen ordered.

"I'm not going anywhere without some coffee," William said, pulling on his breeches. Stephen handed him his shirt. "You can have coffee at Edward's. Get dressed."

"I'll saddle your horse," John said as he strode out.

Stephen stepped a few feet away, but not out of earshot.

Little John remained nearby watching his Uncle dress.

"He's wound up tighter than a new watch," William told Little John. "I just need to throw some water on my face. Can you hand me my cravat?"

"Sure and here are your leggings and boots," Little John replied. "I think Uncle Stephen wants to tell you something important."

"Indeed, I do," Stephen said.

"Let's go see what's got him so worked up," William said, grabbing his pistol and powder.

The ride to Edward's handsome house was just across the town, so within minutes, they gathered around the home's highly polished dining table. Edward's wife and children had gone to the butcher's shop so they had the big house to themselves.

As Edward got cups and poured coffee, Stephen watched Little John climb onto his father's lap. At five years of age, the boy liked sitting on his father's knee. Like John, he would be tall, already a head taller than other boys his age. His strawberry blond hair hung as straight as a ruler and framed a cherub sweet face. Perhaps because he was motherless, all four uncles gave Little John an abundance of attention and love.

"Where's Sam?" Edward asked. "If we need to talk, he should be here too."

"I'll explain," Stephen said, then proceeded to fill in his three brothers. Little John also listened quietly and attentively, his eyes growing wide when he learned that Bomazeen had nearly taken his Aunt and cousin.

"I can't believe you're willing to take a journey this dangerous," Edward said.

"Staying here is a greater gamble. We all agree Bomazeen will come back for her. He specifically targeted her. How do we defend her against someone that cunning and evil? He's some kind of supernatural fiend. It's like trying to defend her against a damn ghost."

"On the trail, we're more vulnerable to attack. What makes you think he won't come after us?" William asked.

"We can minimize risks if we travel in a group. We're strong together. Sam, Bear, and you are all highly skilled with arms. John and I are competent shooters. We are virtually a small army. I'm confident we'll be able to deal with potential threats—as long as we stay together." He strode over to the window and peered out, already visualizing the group of them traveling west.

Edward let out a long, audible breath. "A man like Sam might stay alive in Kentucky. But not you Stephen. If you lose your life or the lives of those you love, what have you gained? I understand wanting to pursue a dream, but dreams can quickly become nightmares."

Stephen snorted. He was more like Sam than Edward, that was a certainty. Maybe Edward didn't understand because he couldn't. Edward had always appreciated the creations of men more than the creations of God. The man just didn't understand that land is the foundation of life itself. He turned away from the window and marched over to stand by Edward.

"I've tried to make the best of my place. The winters here try both man and animal. I have seen my cows turn as hard as stone as they froze to death in roaring bitter winds. The rest are so poor by spring, they don't breed back. Our horses have to paw through snow locked in ice trying to feed on dry withered grass. Beef and horses need good pastures to keep life in their bodies. I can't sit here, like some bloody fool, waiting for granite to grow grass," he said. He moved away from Edward and faced his other brothers.

"I have just spent a month of back-breaking labor clearing heavy timber and rocks off just one acre of my farm, toiled until my hands are raw and bleeding. And for what?" Stephen asked. "With every rock I throw in a pile, my life is slipping through my hands. I need to look beyond my own front door for a better life."

Edward examined his own well-manicured nails and the shiny gold ring he had purchased with his last month's profits. His lucrative store was one of the region's largest establishments and his mind for business ensured he didn't have to bust his knuckles like his brothers.

"Kentucky is indeed beyond your front door," Edward scoffed, "more than a thousand miles beyond, half of it through raw wilderness."

Stephen turned away from his brothers to look out the window again and studied the morning sky, cloudless and serene. "Imagine what it would be like—a wide valley, a slow, clear creek sparkling through it. Grass that grows green and thick even when God is tight with the rain. The climate's mild and the land is so fertile the grass tickles the cows' bellies." But even as his soul reveled in this heavenly vision, his mind jerked him back to reality. He needed to get back to Jane. He turned back to face his brothers.

"Edward, you can live in your grand house, and sell goods year after year. Or, you can come with us. You may die, or, you may experience the greatness of your life," Stephen said.

John spoke up. "Maybe Edward will experience the greatness of his life where he is. But we can't let fear keep us here."

A quiet, pensive man, the builder in John loved nothing more than the music of hammers and saws. Stephen understood why John never completely recovered from losing his wife Diana in childbirth. A house full of reminders of her made it difficult to recover. Perhaps it would also make it easier for him to make the move. The most important reminder of Diana stood next to John, his little arm wrapped around his father's elbow.

"I feel God calling me to a new life. In a place as fresh as Kentucky, I know we'll have opportunity and so will our sons," John said. "I just need a few days to take care of my building projects and put my affairs in order."

"Damn it, John, your son's future is precisely what worries me," Edward shouted. "The wilderness is unforgiving. Do you want Little John facing vicious heathens? Or some of the rough depraved white men of those frontier settlements? I've heard most of them acknowledge no superior on earth, and it's a question if they do in heaven."

Stephen had heard the same thing but wasn't about to say so.

Edward continued to rant. "Do you want your children exposed to the elements for months at a time? The frontier is no place for civilized men, much less youngsters. Stephen, think of your beautiful wife. She won't be safer on the trail. And your four young daughters. One of them is still in the cradle for God's sake. It's unthinkable. You have all heard about the brutal murders and torture of women and children on the Wilderness Trail. Even Boone's own son was tortured before he died in agony. How many of you won't make it? Whom will you bury along the way in lonely graves you will never visit again? You two can sacrifice your children— but hell will freeze before I will."

Stephen's face contorted in fury and confusion. He slammed his fist against the table, making the pewter candlesticks and Little John jump. He leaned across the table and glared at Edward, wanting to make him shut the hell up. What angered him the most was the truth in his brother's words. Truth often generates more anger than a lie.

Nearly choking on his anger, he couldn't speak. It galled him to

WILDERNESS TRAIL OF LOVE

admit, but Edward was right. He would be putting the lives of young innocents in peril, but he still thought leaving would be the best way to protect Jane and Martha. His stomach clenched as he collapsed into a chair. He watched John hug his son and then drop his head into his big hands. Edward's words clearly stung John too.

Amid the uncomfortable silence, Stephen forced himself to picture the horrible what if…the loss of one of his daughters. The frightening and abhorrent image made him swallow hard. He shook his head but it didn't clear. Like waking from a bad dream, he realized it wasn't real, but the horrible thought remained to make him uneasy.

"People die here too," Little John said.

Stephen glanced up. One by one, his brothers recognized what the child had. Life was fragile wherever they were. Tragically, they had all lost family here. First, both his parents and younger sister, buried by the landslide. Then Little John's young mother.

"Little John's got the right of it. There's danger here too. A few days back, young Lucy MacGyver disappeared. Probably an Indian slave by now. The militia and Sam and I tried to track her, but we had to abandon the chase when the tracks evaporated in the mountains," William said. "I'm afraid we'll never find her."

"There's no hope for her," John agreed. "She could be anywhere from here to Montreal."

"We all die when it's our time, no sooner and no later," William said. He grabbed John Jr., gave him an affectionate hug, and then lifted the boy high into the air, earning William a delighted squeal from the child. "As for me, I'd leave tomorrow. I say, let's go before the best land gets settled. It's safe enough—I read that the Indians there signed a treaty after the Battle of Fallen Timbers. Besides, it'd be amusing for all of us to be together again."

Unlike Edward, the prospect of change never worried William. His handsome brother welcomed it, not because of the challenge it represented for Sam, but because William had not found his place in life. William viewed everything in his life as temporary. The only thing permanent was his love of the law. But William's cavalier attitude infuriated him as much as Edward had. There was so much at stake—the lives of his family and his brothers.

William was his predictable impulsive 'ready, fire, aim,' self. "I'll go talk to the mayor and let him know the town will need to elect a new Sheriff, then I'll pack what I'll need, go to the bank, and be at your place by early afternoon."

"Needless to say, my family won't be going," Edward said emphatically. "Too many risks. Too many." He shook his head from side to side. "This is beyond foolish. Leaving won't keep Jane and the girls safe."

His contemptuous tone sparked Stephen's anger again. "You're making two mistakes, calling it foolish and staying here."

"You're the one making two mistakes," Edward yelled back. "Putting your wife and your children in jeopardy."

Stephen sprang up from the chair and glared at Edward, feeling his jaws clamp together.

John stepped between them. "This argument is pointless. The decision has been made. We'll need your help managing our properties since we need to leave as soon as we're able."

"Of course. I'll take care of all your properties. I can rent them out or sell them, as you prefer. Just let me know what you need me to do. And you may procure all your supplies at my cost from my store," Edward offered. "I'll send a wagon into Durham for whatever you'll need that I don't have in stock. Just give me your list. Sam should have a good feel for what's needed he's made so many trips with the army."

"Sam and I will work up a list," Stephen said, putting aside his anger to focus on what needed doing. "John, will you take care of securing a wagon and an ox team? Make whatever changes you think would make it more comfortable for Jane and more efficient for the trip. It will need a durable cover to protect the children from storms. We will need as much storage room as possible, a large water barrel on each side, and an extra wheel or two. Have it ready by the time Edward gets the supplies together. Sam will secure what weapons and ammunition we should bring. I'll find us a couple of good spare horses. I heard about some geldings for sale here in Barrington. And William, if you would handle all the legal documents involved in the selling or renting of our properties." Because William aspired to become a lawyer, he had studied the law for years, and Stephen was confident that he would expertly handle the necessary papers.

By afternoon, the brothers' hastily made plans were well in place. After all his agonizing, he realized the decision was behind him. At last, it's happening. He grinned and his heart swelled as his mind's eye pictured expansive rolling pastures, his herds of cattle and horses grazing contentedly on lush Kentucky grass in the warm sun. Jane and the children, safe, in a big new home.

He could make that happen. He would make that happen.

CHAPTER 11

While Stephen was gone, Jane invited Sam into the house to smoke his pipe by the open window. Bear was busy feeding the horses and other animals. The scent of sweet tobacco smoke mixed with the pleasant aroma of her baking biscuits.

She'd already begun the difficult task of selecting what to take to Kentucky and what to leave behind. Her heart not yet completely committed to the idea, she found it difficult to concentrate and wandered from one item to another.

"Jane, you seem fretful. Are you uncertain that this move is what's best for you and Stephen?" Sam asked.

She thought for a moment before replying. "I'm not at all sure. I am beyond worried. I'm terrified that we are making a mistake. Is leaving the best plan Sam? Do you truly think Bomazeen will come back?" She fisted her hands in her apron to keep them from trembling.

"I do. There's no telling when. But he will."

"I admit the thought of facing that beast again terrifies me."

"It should. He's not human."

"Even if Bomazeen doesn't come back, I understand why Stephen wants to do this. You can't cage an eagle in a farmyard. If he doesn't go, he will never be completely happy. And if he's not happy, how can I be? How can he be a good father and make his children happy if he feels trapped in a life that's not his destiny?"

"I've watched him all my life. Even as a child, he longed for more than he saw here. He sees with the same vision our ancestors had. He sees the horizon everywhere he looks."

"No, Stephen sees beyond the horizon. He is determined to do this. His will to go is stronger than my desire to stay."

They both agreed it was the correct decision for Stephen. However, she still worried whether it was for her daughters. She wondered if her husband fully realized what her girls would face. What she would face. She was by no means a delicate woman, but the wilderness tested the mettle of even the strongest of men. Did he really understand how much she was leaving behind?

"But what about you? Do you realize how hard this trip will be?" he asked.

"I know it would be the hardest thing I've ever done. Maybe the hardest thing I will ever do. But my father taught me not to shirk from something just because it was hard—because most everything that's important is difficult. That's the way life is. That's not what is holding me back. I am worried about the girls. How could I live with myself if something happens to them on the trail?"

"They are not out of danger here. Bomazeen is as clever as Lucifer. He'll find a way to pay you back—maybe by stealing more than one of your daughters. Heaven forbid they did die on the Wilderness Trail, it would be better than being a slave."

She looked away hastily, then moved restlessly around the room, finally picking up Stephen's favorite book. She added it to the stack of items they would take. "Perhaps you're right. The thought of him trying to steal Martha again makes my heart shake. Even the toughest life is better than slavery."

❧

"Are they going?" Sam asked the minute Stephen returned later that day.

"William and John are joining us," Stephen answered, dismounting, "but not Edward. He thinks we're making a mistake."

"That's Edward's problem," Sam snarled, "he thinks too damn much."

"If you and Bear are willing, we leave in two days," he said, as he led George to the barn.

"Good. It's time to stop lathering and start shaving," Sam said.

Stephen wondered if Sam was trying to appear confident or if he really had no doubts.

As they walked back toward the house, he heard Jane call out, "Stew's ready and the biscuits are hot. Please dust off your boots before you gentlemen come inside."

"Don't let Bear eat my biscuits," Sam yelled back, used to competing for food with his brothers.

"I made an extra pan full just for you," Jane answered.

That was smart. He had seen Sam eat a dozen biscuits at a sitting.

"Jane, you're an angel here on earth," Sam said, climbing the porch steps two at a time and then throwing the door open.

"If she's an angel, then God must have his hands full," Stephen said, wiping some flour off her face. Even in an apron covered with food stains, she was a vision.

Jane swatted him with her dishtowel, but she still gave him a big smile.

Stephen sat at the head of their old pine table, the tantalizing sight of steaming stew, hot biscuits, fresh butter, and a cobbler, all making his mouth water.

"Bear, sit here beside Stephen and Sam sit across from Bear. We'll put the girls down here by me. Martha, put the butter over there by Uncle Sam. You know how he likes to butter up his biscuits," Jane said.

"I don't know why you have to make a biscuit soggy with butter before you can eat it," Stephen complained. "You ought to just eat the thing the way God made them."

"God didn't make the biscuits, Jane did," Sam said.

"I remember eatin' some of Stephen's wee biscuits on one of our first hunting trips. As hard and as flat as horseshoes," Bear said, then threw back his head and laughed.

"Why do you think I married Jane? It wasn't just because she was the prettiest woman in New Hampshire, it was her biscuits," Stephen said.

All the girls giggled, even baby Mary.

"Mommy, Bear let me ride with him on his new horse today. He looks like the camel in the drawing in the Bible," Amy said.

"Who? The horse or Bear?" Stephen asked in jest.

"The horse, silly," Amy answered.

"Camel. You know that would be a fitting name for that big dun," Sam said.

Stephen had thought the horse had an oddly large head but hadn't said anything to Bear about it. A man can be sensitive when it comes to his horse.

"Les call him Camel. Would that be okay with you Bear?" Amy asked.

"Aye, wee princess. We'll call him Camel, but only because ye named him," Bear said, looking at Sam.

"The Bible says the camels carried wise men," Martha said.

"That makes the name even more ideal," Stephen said.

ॐ

"Stephen, I want Sam and Bear to take the girls into town till we're sure it's safe. Bomazeen's words about Martha making a good slave for the squaws kept haunting me all day. They can stay with Edward's family. I know Anne won't mind. I'll keep Mary with me."

Stephen nodded his agreement. "Good idea, but I want Sam and Bear to get them into town before dark. Get their things packed."

Jane set out a small bag and filled it with a change of clothes for the girls then she got their faces washed, hair braided, and their traveling shoes on.

They stood ready to go in no time. "Uncle Sam and Bear are taking us to Uncle Ed's house," Polly cheerfully informed her father as he came into their room. "Mama says we're overdue a visit to our cousins."

He gave Polly a hug. "Indeed, your mother is correct. Now let's go down and find Uncle Sam and Bear. He scooped Amy up and picked up the girls' bag.

As he reached the bottom of the stairs, he yelled back to Jane to get the girls' coats.

Bear and Sam strode out and began tightening the cinches on their already saddled horses.

"Sam, Bear, why don't you return tomorrow after you've had a chance to see about your own places. I know you both left suddenly," Stephen suggested.

Jane kissed and hugged each of the girls in their birth order, as was her custom. "Be good and mind your aunt and uncle," she said.

"It would be good to take care of a few things before we leave for Kentucky," Bear said. "But keep yer eyes open."

Stephen didn't need the warning, but knew Bear felt better saying it.

❧

After tending to George and the other animals, Stephen came inside, bolted all the doors, and shuttered the windows. He peered out a front window before locking the final shutter. "Bomazeen probably wouldn't have healed enough yet to travel and it isn't the custom of the Pennacooks to attack at night, but I'm not taking any chances."

"I'll feed Mary and put her to bed, then let's sit by the fire and talk awhile," Jane suggested, hoping for one last chance to talk him out of this.

After placing his loaded musket and pistol nearby, Stephen towed a chair up to the hearth and sat next to her. For several minutes neither spoke, as he caressed her hand and they both stared into the flames, the peaceful crackling of the fire the only sound in the room.

Stephen peered over at her, sharing his feelings with just a look. She saw so much love in his eyes, so much that didn't need to be spoken aloud. His eyes spoke the silent but expressive language of love.

But there was so much else that did need saying. Too many questions. So many holes in her confidence. But, she couldn't bring herself to crush his dream. Couldn't voice the words to stop him.

"Your eyes are even more beautiful with firelight in them," he said. "Come sit on my lap so I can see them even better."

His voice warm and tender, she was helpless to resist. She moved to his lap, giving up hope of sharing her real thoughts. Instead, she said, "It's not my eyes you want to see."

"Your eyes and every other part of you," he answered honestly. His strong hands held her waist and hips close to him.

"Every part?"

"Every," he repeated.

Her face heated as she wrapped her arms across his chest and back, feeling solid strength beneath his shirt. It seemed impossible, given the weight on her mind, but the feel of his rock hard muscles made her ache with a deep need for him. Giving in to her body's demands, she kissed his forehead, his cheeks, and his eyes tenderly, before ravaging his mouth not so tenderly. She felt his body respond with a surge of desire but knew he would hold himself back, letting her enjoy his unhurried affection before the fire of love consumed them both.

She should resist temptation, at least for the moment. She needed time alone with him to make him understand why she wanted to stay in her home. But against his tender assault on her body, she could mount no defense. And against his dreams, she had no shield. She could not stop herself, or him.

She tugged off Stephen's shirt, revealing his powerful set of shoulders and tight muscled stomach. Despite his medium stature, her husband was wiry strong and she thought spectacularly built. She caressed his broad chest, a wall of muscles rising beneath her touch. Her fingertips tingled as she slid them slowly across his silky chest hairs. Even that simple touch brought her pleasure. A delicious shiver of passion rippled through her.

Stephen lightly fingered a lock of hair that touched her cheek, then sank his hands into her curls and pressed his lips against hers for a long unhurried moment.

The kiss hummed inside her heart. His lips felt soft and warm— always the best thing she had ever tasted—and made a tingle of pleasure rush through her chest. Kissing was her favorite part of lovemaking and he made a considerable effort to be sure she enjoyed it. He would linger at her mouth, teasing her lips, softly, unhurriedly, until she left all the cares of motherhood behind. Transported on a gentle wispy cloud, until the only thing she wanted was more of him.

Then, he would turn his attention to the rest of her, as he did now. His lips left hers to nibble on her earlobe. Then he seared a path down her neck, her shoulders. His lips recaptured hers, this time more urgent and exploring. His hand slipped under her dress and skimmed across her thigh.

The gentle movement of his hand sent a bolt of need deep within her. She curled into his chest.

A smoldering flame in his eyes, Stephen took her hand to lead her to bed. Shivers of desire made her tremble in anticipation.

He would take them both to their own private world of soul-reaching ecstasy.

Afterwards, she knew he would dream—dream of what waited beyond the horizon.

CHAPTER 12

Stephen withdrew his savings at the bank and settled his financial affairs. Land in Kentucky was selling for a minimum of a dollar an acre and he would need all he had inherited and saved, although they all hoped to be able to get land grants and save their money for livestock, equipment, and building homes. He also found a buyer for his cattle, all but his best young bull, and two good-looking heifers. He would take them with him. He had fed corn to the bull separately from the other cattle to tame him and get him used to coming to Stephen's feed bucket. Not yet old enough for breeding, the young bull would be easy to handle. He'd follow Stephen and the feed anywhere and the heifers would follow the bull. They would be the start of his new herd.

With his financial tasks completed, he joined his brothers, still hard at work loading the wagon parked in front of Edward's store. "Aren't you finished yet?"

"You could help some you know," John grumbled.

"I could, but then who would ensure you loaded everything properly?" Stephen said, only half in jest.

He double-checked the long supplies list with meticulous detail, knowing that adequate provisions could make the difference between success and failure in the wilderness. And he had no intention of failing.

John and Bear loaded the last of the supplies. Kegs of salt pork, half barrels of flour and cornmeal, a barrel of fat, rifles, ammunition, candlewicks, and other supplies Stephen had ordered, filled the wagon. Stephen could see that they had arranged everything with care. Space was precious, so they could take only what was essential.

What little space still left when they finished would be all the room allowed Jane for her trunks. She had struggled for hours over what to take and what to leave behind. In the end, she took only what she could not replace, a few items of strong sentimental value, and absolute necessities like blankets, woolen stockings, scissors, needles, and thread. She and the girls were spending the afternoon with Edward's wife and children. It would be their last chance to be together and it gave Jane a chance to give many of her things to her nieces. What remained would go to the needy families in the area or be sold for their value.

Edward went to the back of his crowded stockroom and then returned to the store's porch. "I want you to have this whiskey and this case of wine. When you're sitting around the campfire some cold night, maybe you'll say a toast to me."

"I'd rather you were there toasting with us," William said, taking the whiskey.

Edward's eyes met Stephen's.

"Edward, let's go inside while they finish," Stephen said.

The air inside of the well-stocked store teemed with exotic smells—cinnamon and pepper, rum and port, tea, and oranges. Other merchandise gleamed at them as they passed by—decanters, wine glasses, silver trays, pewter, knives, snuffboxes, and brass shoe buckles.

As they reached his desk, Edward yanked off his coat and slapped it onto a chair. "Don't even start Stephen. I know you and Sam think me the coward of the family, but it's my life—not yours. I will decide what is best for me and mine. Not you," he nearly shouted, as he crumpled the supplies list and tossed it into the potbellied stove.

"I don't think ill of you because you decided to stay. God leads men to different destinies. Yours will be different from ours. And we appreciate you handling our properties. I would have been reluctant to entrust them to anyone else."

Edward appeared stunned. "Thank you. You have relieved my mind. I know Sam thinks me spineless. Compared to Sam, nearly all men might be called cowards."

"Indeed, his standards are set high."

"But there's a difference between cowardice and caution. Recklessness gets men killed."

"He is a tough man to measure up to. Always has been. Sam is passionate about courage and honor. You are about family and security. In his heart, Sam understands that," Stephen said.

"I guess a man can't help but try to measure up to his big brother, especially a man like Sam," Edward admitted. "It's time I quit trying."

Stephen held the same opinion but did not say so because he agreed for a different reason. Edward could never measure up to Sam. "I've come to realize that my dream doesn't have to be your dream. Maybe you're already living your dream. I just know I'm not," he said instead. "And I have to make a better future for my family. I must."

"I think I finally understand," Edward said.

"I think we both do." He patted his brother on the back. "What do you say we get the others and have a farewell drink?"

"Splendid idea. We'll toast to your new home in the west."

On the way out, Edward grabbed a 100-foot coil of rope and a saw. "You only had 25 feet of rope on your list. I thought you could use this 100-footer. You can't have too much rope and maybe this new saw will come in handy when you build your new home. The one you have is so old it was probably grandfather's. And this is the best wool blanket made."

"If we don't get out of here, you'll be sending your whole store with us," he said with a smile. "Then you'll have to come."

੭

The farewell drink together was the first of many difficult goodbyes, both to those still living and those who had passed on. After they left the tavern, feeling especially sentimental with the aid of the whiskey, they rode to the mountain that held their parents, sister, and their childhood home within its base. The four sat their mounts side by side, staring at the site of the massive mountain slide. It looked to Stephen like a huge grave with an immense tombstone. Together, in silence, they recalled their mother and father—parents who had raised them to be the men they were.

The gentle sound of the breeze grazing against his ears soothed his remembered grief. He noted that brush and young trees now grew where their family home once stood. The mountain buried part of him too that day. Stephen's future had been there with his father, working the farm they both loved. He still struggled with the terrible weight of that loss.

He studied the beautiful mountain, where he had explored and played as a child and hunted as a young man. Warm memories filled his mind. His love of the land came from his father. Stephen missed him.

He reminded them of one of their father's favorite sayings, "Always be willing to fight for your neighbor, and kill for your brother."

"A wise man," Sam said.

Stephen dismounted and handed his rein to William. He pulled a pocket-sized sack from his jacket. He strode a few yards away and knelt to the ground, scooping up a large handful of dirt. He carefully filled the sack with the cold dark earth of his father's mountain grave. Then he tied it tightly before placing it inside his waistcoat, in the pocket next to his heart. It would remain there until they reached their new home.

He remounted and gazed up at the top of the mountain. The time had come for new mountains to climb and new memories to share.

And for Stephen, a chance to give his family a better home.

They would have to live by their father's motto to reach that home. They would soon become part of a new frontier Sam Sr. knew nothing about. But they had been raised to be not only well-educated men of faith and courage, but to also be tough, tenacious, and strong. Growing up during a war equipped them to deal with challenges to their courage. They were ready to face the future—a world of infinite promise and untold perils.

CHAPTER 13

*A**pril 26, 1797   Today we began our journey. Ho for Kentucky—
we are on our way. We have stopped to rest about ten miles from
home. Stephen is leading us to a new home. Despite all his
reasons for going, I found it so difficult to leave. I hope we are doing the
right thing, but part of me keeps screaming 'stop'. Departing was
agonizing. When the wagon's wheels first rolled away, carrying the
precious few belongings I could bring, my hands were shaking and I felt
like someone just kicked me in the stomach. Jane read what she'd just
written. She took a deep breath before continuing. But, I have no regrets.
At least not yet. With God's favor, we will all safely reach paradise and a
new home. She underlined 'all' three times.*

It was late in the day when Sam turned to Stephen and said, "I smell
rain on the wind. Let's make camp here before it starts. I'll hunt meat."

Before taking off on foot, Sam checked his Kentucky rifle's load. A
dead shot with it, Sam could put a bullet through a deer at 300 yards and
drill a hole in an enemy's head at 250 yards.

German and Swiss gunsmiths in Pennsylvania designed the long and
slender weapon but named it after the state that inspired its design. The

hunters who stalked the deep dense forests of Kentucky required the accurate long barrel and the lower weight of the slim stock and ammunition. The lighter rifle suited Kentucky riflemen well because they hunted largely on foot, as did Sam.

Once their family traveled beyond densely populated areas, settlements or trading posts would be few and far between, so they needed to be self-sufficient. Their sustenance would come largely from animals, the only consistent food supply. They would need to conserve bullets and powder, neither readily available. For the hungry traveler, a hunter's first shot had to count, because if he missed, he scared off any other animals nearby.

"What did that gunsmith do to make that Kentucky rifle so accurate?" Bear asked. "My old Bess musket could na hit anything beyond 60 yards."

William and John both moved closer so they could also hear Sam's answer.

"He extended the barrel to four feet, decreased the bore size to half an inch, and increased the size of the sights. Long barrels fire a bullet more accurately. And the smaller caliber bullets allow much lighter barrels, making not only the ammunition lighter weight but the rifle as well," Sam explained. "I've brought one for each of you. We'll open the crate tonight. You'll need to shoot it some to get used to it. No two guns are alike so make your mark on your rifle so you only use it and get familiar with how it shoots. Make it a third arm—never far from your body," Sam advised.

"A Kentucky rifle feels different—much lighter than a ten-pound musket. She's a graceful beauty that makes a man smile," William said. He had shot one belonging to a friend in the past, but until now had not owned one.

"This Bess never makes me smile," Bear said, "but she sometimes causes me to curse like a Barbados sailor."

Stephen could not wait to use the rifle. He'd be able to shoot from further away, a distinct advantage when hunting or fighting Indians. "It's fortunate that gun is so accurate, we need to be crack shots to save ammunition."

"Or to stay alive," Sam said woodenly, as he marched off to hunt.

As he was about to leave the clearing, Sam turned back to Stephen and yelled, "Don't use anything but bone dry wood. Less smoke to draw attention to us."

Stephen and Bear unloaded Jane's cooking utensils and the supplies needed to make camp.

After gathering up several armfuls of the driest wood he could find, Stephen retrieved the long-handled axe secured with straps to the side of the wagon. He began chopping up the larger pieces the way his father taught him, his rhythm was so smooth the strikes sounded almost musical.

"William, stop tuning that violin and get a fire started," he said as he carried an armful of firewood to Jane.

"Just getting it tuned for tonight," William said, grinning. "I plan to keep you all entertained on this trip. Just because we're headed into the wilderness doesn't mean we have to leave culture behind us."

"You're entertaining all right," Stephen said, "but not because you're such an accomplished fiddle player." He marched off to get pails of water.

Jane noticed Martha, Polly, and Amy tagging close behind Bear as he unloaded supplies from the wagon. He had to work to keep from stepping on them. Her daughters had become fond of their big friend.

"Bear, how do we know which way Kentucky is?" Martha asked.

"Kentuk," Amy repeated.

Bear put down Jane's heavy iron pans and knelt next to the three girls. "Well now, wee princesses, long before men from Europe came to the colonies, wild animals and native Indians lived here. The animals made many good paths that lead to water or to other things we need like salt licks. The Indians followed those same game paths and made them wider into trails, and white men followed the Indian trails, and made them wider still into roads." Bear drew imaginary roads into the dirt to show Martha. "The northern and southern tribes of Indians traveled along a trail called the Great Indian Warpath for trade or for war. This trail goes around stony ground or dense growths of brush and trees. White men made many of these Indian trails into wagon roads that they now call the Wilderness Trail. We will follow this trail whenever we can. When we get to Kentucky, Daniel Boone and his men have already forged a good road into the wilderness for us to follow."

"What's wilderness?" Martha asked.

Jane could see Bear thinking, trying to come up with an answer they would understand.

"Wilderness is where only God has touched the earth, where it remains as it was created," he finally said.

"Will we get lost?" Polly asked.

"Nae, wee one. Yer Uncle Sam has traveled all over these colonies at one time or another. He willna let us get lost."

"Bear, why did Father want us to move from our big house?" Martha asked.

Martha's question surprised Jane. Stephen had told the girls they were going to a place where there would be more land. Martha obviously didn't understand why her father thought land was so important.

"Sweet lass, your Da must do what he thinks is best. Na just for him, but for yer Mum and for ye girls too. He is a wise man. He is doin' what he must—what his strong mind and his good heart tell him to do," Bear tried to explain.

She prayed this trip would be what was best for her family. She wanted to have faith in Stephen. It was too late to second-guess his decision now.

"Will there be Indians on these trails?" Martha asked timidly.

Martha still had vivid nightmares about Bomazeen. Jane thought the nightmares would probably continue until they were far away from home. Her heart clenched. If only she could have done something to spare her daughters from the terrifying encounter.

Rather than answer, Bear glanced over at her and waited for her to nod her consent before he continued.

"Aye, lass. But do na worry about that now. Not all natives are hostile, but yer Uncle Sam and I are well used to fighting Indians if we need to. With these braw new long rifles, we'll be able to shoot them when they're still a mile away."

"Good," Martha said.

Jane hoped a mile would be the closest hostile Indians ever got to her sweet girls.

❧

Their first evening on the trail passed quickly. After Stephen got Jane's cook fire going and helped her to start the fresh meat to roasting, Sam opened the crate of Kentucky rifles, giving one to each of the men and one to Jane. The .40 caliber weapons cost him more than two year's salary, but they would be well worth the expense. The slender rifles were not only lightweight and accurate they were quick to load. Sam said he could reload his in 12 seconds while running, and that after some practice they would be able to do so as well.

Stephen stroked the smooth maple stock and admired its graceful lines and skillfully made iron accoutrements, including a distinctive patch box in the stock. He pointed the weapon towards the distant hills, pleased with the good sights. His first new rifle, he would treasure it. A rifle like this could mean the difference between life and death or between a full belly and starving.

For target practice, Sam nailed a white feed sack to a tree 100 yards from camp. By the time Jane had supper nearly ready, the sack hung in shreds.

"Let Jane try," Stephen suggested.

"That would na be fair," Bear said, "there's na but a wee bit of threads left to shoot at."

"Give me that rifle," Jane demanded, clearly challenged by Bear's comment.

With Stephen's help, Jane loaded her new weapon. She tucked it securely into her shoulder, took aim, and fired. What remained of the feed sack fell to the ground.

"Those green eyes aren't just beautiful, they're as sharp as a hawk's," Stephen bragged.

"I made it easy on all of you," Sam said. "Next camp, I'll put it out 150 yards."

By sundown, Sam's weather prediction came true. Thunder rolled in a long parade as if the storm played hundreds of drums and cymbals as it marched across the countryside. Wind gusts picked up and large cold drops of rain started to slap their faces.

Jane quickly got the girls and Little John under cover inside the wagon and then started collecting her cooking utensils.

Stephen gathered up their new rifles and stored them away along with anything else that could blow away. Before he and Jane climbed inside too, he swung her around into the circle of his arms. Putting his hand to the back of her neck, he drew her lips to his and gently covered her mouth. She returned the kiss with abandon, letting the rain patter down on them both. Then he forced himself to step back and help her into the wagon.

As he climbed up behind Jane, William and John crawled under the wagon for their shelter.

Sam and Bear took cover under shelters they had made earlier from tree limbs and hides they had placed on high ground.

A lightning bolt cracked overhead. Polly squealed and Amy pressed her tiny hands to her ears. Little John clung to Stephen's damp wool jacket. Martha just looked annoyed at being stuck in the wagon for the rest of the evening.

"Don't worry, lightning is just the Almighty's way of reminding us how powerful He can be," Jane said, wrapping her arms around both Polly and Amy.

"He must be fierce," Little John said. "I wouldn't want to make him mad."

"Many grown men aren't smart enough to realize that," Stephen said.

CHAPTER 14

The next morning Jane made a brief note in her journal. *The storm last night passed quickly, but left the ground wet, just enough to make everything muddy. Stephen is so full of energy and hope. He inspires us all. I pray that God will give him the strength he will need for this journey, and that He will give us all strength. I fear we will need it.*

"We've made good progress today, nearly ten miles. Tomorrow, we should make the Merrimack River before dark. I'll rest easier once we've crossed it," Sam quietly told Stephen and Bear as they rode.

"I won't rest easy until Bomazeen is dead," Stephen replied.

"Aye," Bear agreed. "The demon is still within strikin' distance. We'd be easy to track. We're leavin' a trail an Indian bairn could follow."

"Let's make camp before it gets dark," Sam said. "We're more vulnerable at night so we'll need to hunt some food and be back before sundown."

"Aye. I'm as hungry as big Camel here," Bear said.

"So am I," John said and he and William joined them.

Stephen hoped they could find some turkey or wild hog. Hunger pangs rumbled in his stomach too.

"Little John and I will fish upstream while you two hunt," John said.

Bear and Sam rode off. They would ride some distance away before dismounting and hunting the rest of the way on foot.

Stephen turned to William. "You're looking a little stiff, brother." While William hadn't complained, he suspected that after two straight days on horseback, William felt like he did—saddle-sore in some very private places.

"I'm fine," William growled.

"There's no shame in admitting it. We're not used to riding all day like Sam and Bear. Why don't you keep a watch out and gather up firewood. I'll get these horses hobbled so they can graze some. Looks like some good grass over there," Stephen said, pointing to a meadow not far off.

"Deal," William said.

Stephen removed George's saddle and began brushing the stallion's broad back, where the horse's black hair was wet and matted from the day's ride. He enjoyed the grooming as much as George did. There was something pure and earthy about the salty aroma of the horse's sweat and the brushing seemed to help them both relax after a long ride. When he was done, he stroked George's long neck and hindquarters. The powerfully built stallion had nearly perfect conformation and he counted himself lucky to own such an exceptional mount.

He loved the horse like a dear friend. Riding George was far more than a means of transportation—it made him feel stronger and more alive—as if the strength of the stallion's big heart and powerful muscles passed through to him every time he rode. Of all God's creatures, he thought the horse most worthy of mans' admiration and devotion. And George received ample amounts of both.

"I'm going to the creek to wash the dust off my face and hair. I'll get some water for coffee and dinner too," Jane said.

Stephen looked up and judged the distance to the creek. It was less than 50 yards away. "All right. But stay alert and take your rifle."

William stacked the firewood, then used steel and flint to ignite the leaves and twigs he'd placed at their base. "You should shortly have enough heat to cook if you have a mind to make some of your famous biscuits in your Dutch oven," he said with a grin.

"Thank you," Jane said, "I just need to check on the children and freshen up first."

William opened his bedroll and stretched out his long legs.

The children were running in circles around the wagon, chasing each other and squealing happily, letting off pent up energy from being confined all day.

Jane loaded her rifle, grabbed her soap and pails, then headed down the slope. Tall Cypress trees lined the bank, their branches and leaves rustling like huge wind chimes in the steady light wind. The creek, swollen from spring rains, flowed noisily. The churning water formed white foam around colorful boulders and rocks. Jane wished it were summer and she could disrobe and sit on the rocks, letting warm water swirl around her naked body.

Winding her way around some large boulders, she made a path down to the river bank. She removed her cloak and laid it and her bucket on the rocks, and then unbuttoned the bodice of her gown, pulling it down. With only her shift left to cover her breasts, the cool gentle breeze made her shiver and raised goosebumps on her bare skin. As she bent down to the water's edge, she breathed in the clean smell of the water.

Jane splashed her face with the clear water before dunking her head. Shivering, the chilly water did not feel pleasant, but it felt far better than the dirt and grime of the trail. After dragging the bar of soap through her wet hair, she started scrubbing and didn't stop until she'd done a thorough job. She closed her eyes, dipped her head in the creek again, and vigorously swirled her hair through the cold water.

Then she felt only the cold of terror. Her entire body shuddered in fear when large strong hands pressed against her mouth and held her head down in the water. Jane struggled to raise her head, eyes wide under the water, but she couldn't. She needed to breathe! What was happening? Someone was trying to drown her! Then the man violently jerked her up by her hair. She stumbled and sucked in a breath, choking on water, as a man pulled her backwards. She tried to wrench away, but couldn't.

"Make one sound and I'll gut you like a fish," a raspy voice growled as he pressed an icy blade of steel against her throat, "then I'll steal your oldest daughter instead."

She went limp with fright and ceased to struggle, afraid he would make good on this threat.

He hauled her backwards, dragging her between the boulders, his hand still clamped tightly across her mouth. Her dripping hair covered her eyes and she could not see. She shook her head slightly to clear the hair and water out of her eyes. Her assailant pushed her toward a horse hidden in a copse of nearby trees.

Panic squeezed her chest, making it difficult to breathe. *Dear Lord, send Stephen to her aid.*

With his long blade pressed against her stomach, he hoisted her into the saddle as if she were a sack of grain and climbed up behind her. The fabric of her gown split open under the knife and she felt cold steel scraping against her bare skin. She didn't dare move or scream.

He nudged the horse and they took off slowly, quietly following two mounted braves waiting nearby. Soon, the horses hurtled forward, then broke into a gallop. It was then that she realized Indians were stealing her.

Oh God, this can't be happening.

Then she knew. She recognized his smell. Bomazeen's sharp stench was something she'd never forget, but she could not bring herself to look at his chilling face. She peered down at the knife instead, still held tightly against her stomach. The sight of the blade and the scalps hanging from his belt made her want to retch.

She couldn't let this venomous snake have her, but she couldn't jump off without the knife slicing her belly or leg open. The risk was too great.

Bomazeen, now flanked by the two braves, crossed a large meadow, loping the horse through the tall grass. Within seconds, they would be in the cover of timber again and she feared she would be forever lost to her husband, to her girls, to their life.

Stephen, help me.

Stephen hobbled the last horse and removed the lead rope, throwing it over his shoulder. He turned to look over in George's direction. The stallion wasn't there. He scanned the surrounding hills and spotted George at the top of the next rise. "Damn. I'm going to have to make that big fellow a stronger hobble," he told himself.

He began to march the 100 yards or so to catch up to George when he heard a shot.

He looked up and then gasped, horrified. Anger, like he'd never known before, welled in his chest. A man on a horse was hauling Jane away. It must be Bomazeen! The sight nearly stopped his heart. Then he spotted another horse and a body lying on the ground in Bomazeen's wake.

Stephen sprinted the remaining distance to George, jerked the broken hobble off, and quickly threw the lead rope around the horse's neck to make a rein. He jumped on the bareback stallion, pulled him around, and kicked hard.

The stallion responded, his powerful hips springing into a full run, as Stephen bent over George's withers. Within seconds, they raced wide open across the meadow toward Jane. He saw Sam and Bear a couple of hundred yards off. Had Sam made that shot from there?

Ahead, one Indian disappeared into the woods, but George easily overtook the other mount carrying two people. He urged George close behind Bomazeen and aimed his pistol, but didn't fire for fear of hitting Jane.

As soon as Jane saw him, she bit down hard on the arm holding her. When Bomazeen jerked the arm away, Jane leapt off the other side, falling like a rag doll.

Stephen fired his pistol, but Bomazeen swung away from the ball's path, clinging to the side of his horse's neck. He shot his second pistol, and this time grazed Bomazeen's arm.

His heart clenched with his need to go back for Jane, but he forced himself to stay focused on Bomazeen. He would not allow the man to escape again. He had not been there the first time Jane was in real trouble, but he was this time, by God. And if he didn't kill the man now, Bomazeen would come after Jane again. He wouldn't let that happen.

This bastard was going to die.

He urged his stallion over and charged into the flank of Bomazeen's mount, knocking the devil and his smaller horse over. He tugged George to a skidding halt and spun the horse around.

Like a cat that had fallen, his dark eyes narrowed and hissing through gritted teeth, Bomazeen quickly bounced back to his feet and faced Stephen. Brandishing a skinning knife, Bomazeen bristled belligerently, his expression murderous, ready to attack. "I'm going to use this knife to gut you. Then I'm going to use it to skin your bitch after I take her," Bomazeen taunted, his voice spiked with venom.

Bomazeen was capable of keeping that promise. Stephen had to kill him.

He leapt off George. How dare the bastard touch his wife. Never again! He quickly yanked the hatchet off his belt, more confident using it than his small hunting knife. He'd had a hatchet in his hand since he was a boy. For the first time, he would use it to kill a man.

The nearness of the monster unleashed something within him. Seething with overpowering rage, he advanced, keeping one eye on the long knife in Bomazeen's hand. Then he noticed the scalps hanging from Bomazeen's belt. The sight sickened him, especially the fresh white-haired one. Undoubtedly Mrs. Andrews'. He would make Bomazeen pay for that ghastly deed. Nothing mattered now but killing the viper that threatened Jane and had nearly murdered his daughters.

But he could not let his rage make him reckless.

Bomazeen came at him like a lightning bolt, fast and angry, targeting Stephen's face.

Stephen jumped to the side and swung the hatchet at Bomazeen's head, but the devil ducked and stabbed at him again, this time aiming for his stomach.

Stephen arched his back and narrowly managed to avoid the sweep of the blade's path. He slung the hatchet at Bomazeen's back but struck an arm instead.

Bomazeen's howl filled the air between them and the forest beyond, while blood poured from the man's gaping wound. But like an injured animal, the wound only seemed to make Bomazeen more ferocious. Bomazeen snarled at him, lifting a corner of his mouth. Stephen had never seen a man look more like a wild animal.

Unfortunately, the injured arm was not the one that held the knife. Bomazeen still gripped the weapon and kept the blade pointed maliciously at Stephen. Suddenly, Bomazeen leaped at him, but instead of using the knife, he thrust his leg out and slung his foot into Stephen's knee. His leg buckled and he went down.

Bomazeen sneered at him with mocking ridicule then stabbed again, but Stephen rolled onto his right side, barely escaping the blade.

Bomazeen put his foot on top of the hatchet, pinning it to the ground.

Stephen had to release his grip on the hatchet as the man's blade again sliced the air, plunging down in the direction of his head. Stephen rolled over just as the knife struck the ground where his head had just been. As Bomazeen pulled the weapon from the ground, Stephen sprung awkwardly to his feet and then scrambled away.

Bomazeen kept a foot on top of the hatchet and chuckled nastily. He raised an eyebrow and stared with amused contempt.

Stephen lifted his chin and hardened his eyes, as anger rippled along his spine. He glanced sharply around him, searching for a weapon. He picked up a stone that more than filled his hand, and then barreled toward Bomazeen, clenching his jaw.

Wild-eyed, his greasy black hair hanging in his sweaty face, Bomazeen stomped forward, growling like a rabid animal.

As the beast came at him, Stephen's heart hammered in his chest and his body tensed in readiness.

Bomazeen lunged, but Stephen blocked the knife with his left arm while his right hand slammed the stone against the side of Bomazeen's head. The fiend's knife sliced through his jacket and into his arm. But he felt no pain, his entire body taut with anger.

Blood flowed down the side of Bomazeen's dirty face, but he did not falter. Instead, the man danced around Stephen, circling him, again and again, forcing him to repeatedly turn to keep Bomazeen in front of him. The silence between them became unbearable. Bomazeen was attempting to let fear build in him.

The strategy was ill-conceived. Instead of fear, courage grew within him. Pursing his lips tighter and girding himself with a resolve to end this battle, he imposed an iron control on his anger and waited silently, his face daring Bomazeen.

Bomazeen stiffened at the challenge. With eyes blazing hot, the man's vicious glare burned through Stephen.

Then, like the snake he was, Bomazeen lurched and thrust repeatedly, struggling to plant the knife in his chest.

Stephen kept his weight centered and balanced on his toes. Over and over again, he moved outside of Bomazeen's reach, turning, spinning, waiting for the right moment.

The impotent attempts to stab Stephen made Bomazeen shake with rage. The man's vexation was evident and the serpent soon sprang at him yet again, teeth bared, his face twisted in anger.

Stephen leapt backward and then whirled as Bomazeen plunged on carelessly, losing his balance. Before Bomazeen could regain his footing, Stephen quickly pivoted to the side as he swung his arm powerfully in a wide circle and smashed the rock into the back of the man's head. He heard bone crack.

"Now you die," Stephen seethed.

Bomazeen stood, unmoving, then the knife dropped from his hand. The fiend sputtered incoherently and his face paled before he collapsed to the ground in a crumpled heap.

Totally lost to his rage, Stephen straddled Bomazeen and struck the murdering slave trader's head repeatedly. He needed to dole out far more punishment than this evil man had life.

At last, he found the will to still the rage flowing into his hand. He rose clumsily, exhausted, and breathless. He stood there, his head spinning, looking down with contempt and bitterness.

Then he heard Bear hastily ride up. Stephen looked up. Bear held George's reins in one hand.

"Bomazeen's dead," Bear said firmly. "He'll na harm Jane again. Ye need to go to her now."

WILDERNESS TRAIL OF LOVE

CHAPTER 15

Jane's name called Stephen back from the depths of rage. "Jane? Where's Jane?" he asked, panting heavily, barely able to speak. He vaguely remembered her falling from the horse.

"She's just down the hill a wee bit. Get on George now and we'll go to her," Bear urged.

"Is she…?"

"She's hurt, but Sam is tending to her."

His heart nearly stopped and bile rose in his throat. "How bad?"

"She was not moving when I saw her, but I do na know."

Stephen glared at Bomazeen lying beneath him, wanting to kill the bastard again for hurting Jane. Nearly faceless, the head was a pulpy, bloody mush. His eyes turned to the now red rock in his right hand. He held something evil. He slung the rock as far as he could throw it.

"Forget that Satan's bastard," Bear urged. "Jane needs our help now."

Bear handed Stephen's panting stallion over to him and then offered to tie a band of cloth around his bleeding arm, but he waved Bear off. Jane needed him. He leapt up on George and took off at a gallop.

"Jane, my God, Jane," Stephen cried, rushing to her side. He lifted her limp body into his arms with so much dread he held his breath. His fury quickly yielded to shock as he took in her appearance. Ugly scratches marred her face and arms, and dirt and little bits of rock covered her matted wet hair. Her gown was filthy and ripped in several places and her shift barely covered her breasts, but he saw no blood.

"She's knocked out by the fall is all. She'll come around," Sam said. "I checked and she appears unbroken. Can't tell if she hit her head or if the wind got knocked out of her."

He gently stroked her head, trying to feel for head wounds, adding his blood to the mess of her hair.

"Let's get her back to camp," Bear suggested.

Stephen handed her to Bear while he mounted George, and then Bear lifted her up to him. He cradled her in his arms and hugged her gingerly. Putting his face next to hers, he gently kissed her temple. Then he looked down at her, horrified to see that he had gotten blood all over her. He tried to wipe her face with his hand, but only made a bigger mess of it.

"We'll get you both cleaned up when we get back to camp," Sam said.

"The other brave? Is he still close?" Stephen asked.

"He got away. He disappeared into the foothills," Bear explained. "I can catch up to him"

"No, let that brave return to his village," Sam said. "Better for Wanalancet to learn we killed Bomazeen. Maybe then he'll give up his designs on Jane."

"Take us back to camp," Stephen ordered.

By the time they got back to camp, Stephen saw John and Little John returning from the river with a string of good-sized trout. The two were happily admiring their catch until they caught sight of him and Jane. John dropped his fish and pole next to Little John and ran towards them yelling, "Stephen! Jane!"

112

William woke up when he heard the commotion. "What the devil happened?" William demanded, clearly horrified by the sight of the two.

"The girls. Where are they?" Stephen demanded. When William didn't answer immediately, Stephen urged his stallion to the other side of the wagon. They were absorbed in a game of checkers. Relieved, he pointed George back to the others.

"How badly is she injured?" John asked Sam.

"She's unconscious, but she'll come around. Bomazeen tried to snatch her again. Grabbed her at the creek. We gave chase and she took a fall from the bastard's horse," Sam explained. "That blood on her is mostly from the knife wound on Stephen's arm. Stephen killed Bomazeen. There were two other braves—I killed one, one got away."

After Stephen dismounted, carrying Jane, he pushed past William as his brother reached out to help carry her. He gently laid her down on the pallet William had just vacated and covered her with the new wool blanket John had quickly retrieved from the wagon. He bent to kiss her lips, then stood and strode over to face William. "Where the hell were you when all this was going on? Didn't you see the three of them ride up to the creek?"

"I laid down for just a minute. I guess I dozed..." William answered.

Stephen's fist hit William's face before his brother finished his sentence.

Taken by surprise, William went sprawling on his back.

He leaned over his brother and grabbed a fistful of shirt. "You damn idiot. She could be dead. Your job was to watch camp, not sleep you lazy fool." He threw William back down in disgust and stood.

"Stephen's right," Sam said, anger in his voice, just below the surface. "We'll never make it to Kentucky if we don't stay alert. We can't afford to be careless."

"I...I never meant..." William started, looking at Stephen. "I can't believe all this happened and I slept through it."

Sam stood in front of William. Sudden anger lit his eyes and hardened Sam's face. "It doesn't matter what you meant. What matters is what happened. Within a few weeks, we will be out of these tame colonies and the life of every one of us depends on each of us being alert. More alert than we have ever been in our lives. You have to notice everything. Hear everything. Nothing is insignificant. If there's a twig broken that shouldn't be, if the birds aren't singing, if insects quiet down. If anything is not as it should be, notice it. It could mean the difference between disaster and life."

"I heard the rifle shot," John said, "but I thought it was just you or Bear shooting game."

"No," Bear explained, "when we saw that devil carryin' our Jane off, Sam leapt off his horse and brought his rifle to his shoulder. I told him he could na make the shot. Must have been 200 yards. But he did, with lethal accuracy. He hit the Indian in the lead, sendin' him tumblin' forward directly into the path of his own mount. The horse stumbled over the body, buckled and fell. Bomazeen and the other brave maneuvered around the dead Indian and his horse, but Stephen soon caught up to Bomazeen and sent the bastard where he belongs—hell."

"Is she dead?" Little John asked, his lower lip quivering.

"She just bumped her head is all," John replied. "Can you hurry down to the creek quick as you can and get a couple pails of water? We'll get Aunt Jane cleaned up and dinner started."

"Yes Sir," Little John said, then ran away to complete his task. The girls still played on the other side of the wagon, oblivious to all the goings-on.

"'Twas a close call," Bear said. "Those demons nearly got our Jane."

"I feel horrible," William said. "What kind of a lawman am I? I'm supposed to protect others, especially my family. I could have prevented this."

114

Stephen didn't respond, his focus returned to Jane, he knelt beside her holding her hand.

Bear placed his hand on William's shoulder and whispered, "We'll never know that will we now? Be grateful she's all right because he would na a stopped at one punch if Bomazeen had taken her. Stephen is upset right now, but he'll get over it when his head clears and Jane is up and about."

"I hope you're right, but I wouldn't blame either Stephen or Jane if they never spoke to me again. I let everyone down. Sam's right, there's no excuse." William hung his head.

Little John returned with the water and Stephen began cleaning the blood off Jane. He gently applied a damp cloth to her forehead and neck. She had scrapes and scratches everywhere. He tried as best he could to clean them but was constantly afraid he was hurting her. Sam helped by applying Jane's ointment to the more severe scratches.

"Just let her sleep," Sam finally said. "Her body will mend itself. Strip off your clothes. We'll wash them in the creek. I also want to take a look at your arm. Don't want that wound to fester."

"Bear and William, load your weapons and watch her well," Stephen ordered.

Sam grabbed some strips of linen and ointment to make a dressing and they hiked together in silence to the creek. Stephen kept looking over his shoulder at Jane and the camp every few yards.

When they reached the creek, Stephen yanked off his bloodied jacket and shirt and slapped them into the water. "Bloody hell," he swore as he started scrubbing the garments with a vengeance. With each rub of the fabric, his wound made him wince, but he kept on, almost welcoming the distraction the pain brought. Sam seemed to understand and left him alone.

When he finished, Sam said, "Let me see to that cut on your arm."

He held out his arm while his brother examined the wound closely.

"It's a surface wound, didn't cut the muscle. Wash it well though and I'll put ointment on it. Take your time, I'll watch the camp." With his rifle in the crook of his arm, Sam positioned himself so that he could keep one eye on him and one on the camp. For that, Stephen was grateful.

He washed vigorously for some time, removing all the sticky dried blood. The chilly water seemed to stop the bleeding as well as cool his heated mind. He listened to the soothing sound of the water rushing over the rocks and boulders—perhaps that's why William hadn't heard Bomazeen grabbing Jane. Finally, he thought he would be able to think rationally. Might even find it in his heart to forgive William. But not yet. His brother needed to learn a valuable lesson.

"That's twice I've come close to losing her. Are you sure she'll be all right?" he asked. Sam had been around many battlefield injuries and possessed a wealth of knowledge about wounds and symptoms.

"Yes, I believe so, but she'll be sore and bruised for some days."

"Do you think there will be any more of them?"

"My guess is Bomazeen promised her to the Chief and he meant to keep that promise. By the time the Chief figures out Bomazeen failed again, we will be long gone. I don't think he'd send braves for her again, no matter how beautiful she is."

"I'm beginning to think her beauty may be more of a curse than a blessing." He turned to walk back, carrying his wet shirt and jacket. Sam followed a few steps behind.

William and Bear stood guard and John had dinner underway. The smell of coffee brewing and fish frying filled the air. Although not as good as Jane, John had come to be a skilled cook since becoming a widower with a growing son to feed. He was marinating the fish in hot water with wild onions, fat, salt, and other seasonings, before putting the filets on the cook fire.

"These fish should be tasty," John said, loading a sizzling pan with a second batch of filets. "Have you ever seen such fat trout? We'll feed the children first with these so they can get to sleep."

Stephen stopped and inhaled a deep breath. "Bear and William, go back to Bomazeen's body," he said, "and get that white scalp hanging from his belt. It belonged to Widow Andrews. We'll bury it."

They both gave Stephen a brief nod and strode briskly away.

After Bear and William left, he retrieved a fresh shirt and then spoke to his daughters. The girls were worried about their mother, but he reassured them that she was going to be okay. After the children had eaten, he got them bedded down quickly. The day's excitement had worn them all out.

As usual, Martha led them all in their bedtime prayer, and he watched her with pride.

"Now I lay me down to sleep, I pray the Lord my soul to keep. If I should die before I wake, I pray the Lord my soul to take." In 1781, the New England Primer printed the prayer and it had quickly become a favorite among the children of the colonies.

"And God, please help Mama," Polly added.

At the word Mama, baby Mary starting crying. Hungry and missing her mother, it took Stephen some time to get her to quit fussing, but she finally fell asleep.

Weary, he climbed down from the wagon, eager to check on Jane once again. He went to her and knelt by her side. She slept fitfully, probably dreaming of that demon snatching her. His hands fisted and he wished he could hit the bastard again.

He stood and joined the others by the cook fire. Bear and William had returned and Bear was telling one of his stories. Like most Scots, he enjoyed storytelling and his supply of tales was inexhaustible. It seemed that every evening he had another one.

"I've eaten about everything at some point in time. Snake, squirrel, I even had horsemeat a few times," Bear said. "Once we got caught in the mountains in a terrible howlin' blizzard. We could na hunt for several days. We had no choice. 'Twas either eat one of the mounts or starve. We decided he was na that good of a mount anyway. We cut him up and cooked up a fair amount. We were so hungry we decided he was a lot better horse dead than alive. The other time was when one of my Pa's steeds, old Smoke, broke a leg and had to be put down. My Pa was a true Scot and did na let anythin' go to waste, na even a favorite horse. Both times, it was tasty, milder tastin' than deer meat, and took more chewin' than beef, but it filled the belly just fine."

Stephen only half heard Bear's story. Oblivious to the others, he knelt by the fire, his eyes focused on the colorful dancing flames. He hoped Bomazeen was seeing flames now too. Stephen had killed the man savagely, more brutally than he thought himself capable of. But he had rescued Jane—that was all that mattered. He prayed she would be all right. She had to be. Life without her would be no life. He couldn't imagine going on without her. For the first time, he understood the worry and heartache John must have experienced before Diana died.

Lord, please bring Jane back to me.

After Stephen's prayer, an abnormal calm filled him. He stood up and looked at Sam. "Sam, you saved Jane today. That was a remarkable shot. I'll be in your debt forever," he said, his voice cracking.

"So will I," Jane said.

In a second, Stephen knelt at Jane's side grabbing her hands in his.

She smiled up at him. "My hero."

"The hero is Sam. If it hadn't been for that shot, we might not have been able to catch up to you."

"I knew you'd get me back," she persisted, admiration in her eyes.

"I'm so sore and so sleepy."

"You need rest. Sleep, darling," he said, his voice near breaking with his emotions. "And have only sweet dreams."

"Before you do," William said, bending down to her other side, "I'm truly sorry Jane. I fell asleep. I should have been watching out for you. It was foolish and stupid of me. I beg your forgiveness."

"We all make mistakes," Jane said, still gazing into Stephen's eyes, "that's why God, and we, must be so merciful." She closed her eyes and gave in to the sleep grabbing her.

Stephen pondered her words. Was she telling him that he'd made a mistake?

CHAPTER 16

Jane woke before first light. Stephen slept soundly beside her, but Sam stood guard a short distance away, his rifle cradled in his arm. They must have taken turns standing guard.

She ached all over. But it wasn't any wonder given what she'd been through. First, the attack at the river's edge, then the fall from the horse. Everything replayed in her mind from the beginning, as if it were happening over and over again. As she remembered the feel of the blade against her stomach, it seemed real enough that she pulled away from it, pressing her back against the ground.

She squeezed her eyes shut. "He didn't get me," she whispered, on a shuddering breath. But her attempt to reassure herself failed. Terror grabbed at her and squeezed her heart. Unable to keep her tears at bay, she wept, the salty droplets burning the scrapes and scratches on her face. Refusing to obey her commands to stop, the tears kept coming, a confusing mixture of fear and relief, pouring out of her. This is intolerable, she decided, mad at herself for the weakness. She pounded her balled fist on the ground. I must be strong for the girls, for Stephen.

The first purple-grey hints of morning's light began to push at the darkness. Gradually Jane's mood lifted as well. A bird began to sing happily and others soon joined him as the sun's brilliant orange painted the horizon.

God, you let me live for this new day, she prayed. Give me the strength for it. Immediately, she sensed a calmness and her inner strength returning. She sat up, throwing the blanket off.

Stephen popped up as well, holding his gun in his hand. "Are you okay?" he asked, his face filled with concern.

She understood how much her safety meant to him. The ordeal must have been nearly as bad for him as it was for her. Maybe worse. "I'm sore, but well otherwise."

He pushed himself up. "You shouldn't be up," he scolded, pulling on his boots. "Rest another day or so. We'll wait. You're covered in scrapes and bruises."

"No need. I'm as tough as one of those oxen. A few scratches and bumps won't keep me down." She tossed her red curls behind her back and flashed her green eyes at him. "Besides, I wouldn't want to taste the breakfast you men would make. But I would like it if you would get me a couple buckets of water. I certainly don't want to go down to that creek again."

"Of course. Let me help you up." He put an arm around her waist and lifted her up. "Are you sure you feel like getting up and about?"

"I do. I'm not sick, just a little bruised and sore. And I certainly want to change out of these tattered clothes."

Stephen helped her climb up into the wagon and then hurried away to fetch the water. Trying not to wake the girls, she brushed her tangled hair, changed out of her torn clothing, and covered the skirt of the fresh gown with a clean apron, ready for the challenges this new day would bring.

She still ached, but as she started moving around, the stiffness gradually lessened. Although she moved slower than normal, she went about her morning routine, making breakfast and taking care of baby Mary. The biscuits and Johnnycakes would be ready soon and the smell of pork frying woke those still asleep.

"You're as obstinate as you are beautiful, and that's saying a lot," Stephen said, pouring the coffee he had just made, for both of them. "Five strong men surround you, and you're probably the toughest of the bunch."

Almost the same height as her husband, it pleased her that she had inherited her father's physical strength and athletic stature. She often amazed Stephen by wielding an axe with nearly as much skill as he could. Her father, J. R. MacMillan, had encouraged his daughter to learn everything she could, both inside and outside the home. Much to the chagrin of some of the very proper and docile local women, her father supplemented her regular academic studies with his own lessons—riding, hunting, growing food, and raising and doctoring animals. Someday in this new world, his daughter might need to fend for herself, he had said. He'd seen far too many women, made widows by war or illness, become dependent on others.

"Thanks my darling," Jane said, accepting the coffee and planting a kiss on Stephen's cheek. She noticed that he winced when he extended his arm with the cup. "Were you injured?"

"A surface wound on my arm."

"Take off your shirt and let me see it," she said, alarmed.

"Sam has already seen to it. It's nothing."

She insisted on checking it herself and applied more ointment. When she finished, she wrapped her arms around him and laid her head against his chest.

His hand gently pressed her closer to him.

His solid strength felt comforting and reassuring.

Lifting her chin with a finger, he regarded her carefully. "You are feeling better," he teased, then kissed her tenderly.

She could tell he was trying not to hurt her. She longed to feel all of him against her, to reassure herself that she was truly here and they were both all right. But the kiss had to be the end of it, and she swallowed her regret.

Stephen took the ointment from her hand and carefully applied some to every one of her scratches and scrapes. With each gentle touch of his fingers, the pain of the ordeal seemed to lessen, as though his touch had the power to heal not just her body, but her heart.

The group was loaded and saddled up by the time the sun turned from reddish-orange to golden yellow.

The next few miles proved to be the most difficult so far. As they approached the river, the terrain turned rocky and the road grew narrow. The wagon, towed by two brawny oxen, filled the road. Jane fisted the guide rope tightly in her gloved hands. The well-trained animals responded to voice commands. "Gee," she yelled to turn the oxen right as the trail curved sharply.

Her girls giggled and laughed with each bump. Every time the wheels bounced over a large rock, Jane heard them squeal with the unrestrained amusement children find in simple joys.

"Go faster," they yelled, one after the other.

The girls' glee entertained Jane for the first several miles, but now she longed for a smoother ride and peace and quiet. Every bump coursed through her bruised muscles. It would be a long day.

"Hush up, my head's hurting from all this bumping," Jane finally told her little ones.

"How much further?" Martha asked.

"We've only been gone three days darling girl, and at this rate, it will probably take us three years. You'll be ready to be married and I'll be an old woman by the time we get there," Jane said, a little grumpier than she intended.

"Oh Mama, you'll never be an old woman, but I will be ready to marry," Martha said.

"And what kind of man are you wanting to marry?" Jane asked.

"One as smart as Uncle John, as brave as Uncle Sam, as handsome and funny as Uncle William, as strong as Bear, and one as…as…like Father!"

"Gracious, he will be some kind of man," Jane said. "I can't wait to meet him."

"Stop the wagon," Sam yelled.

The horses began to prance, sidestep, and act like giant horse flies had attacked each one. Stephen gripped George's reins tightly as the big stallion jerked him sideways. The others dealt with similar problems from their mounts.

"Whoa," Jane yelled, stopping the oxen.

Sam jumped from the saddle and tied his nervous gelding securely to a nearby tree. Bear did the same.

"Stephen and William stay close to Jane and the girls. John, put that boy in the wagon and have your gun ready!" Sam shouted.

John followed his brother's instructions. Little John, who rode behind his father's saddle, quickly jumped off the horse and climbed inside the wagon. When Sam issued orders using his Captain's tone, they all knew he expected an immediate response.

"Is it Indians?" Jane asked, alarmed.

"No, probably a mountain lion or panther close by. If it's real hungry or sick, it will attack humans. Let's go Bear, this is your kind of party," Sam said.

Bear took off on foot followed by Sam.

Nearly a half-hour passed with no sign of the scouting party. While the horses had settled down, the mood of the others remained tense. Jane did her best to stay calm and tried to distract the children with games and stories.

"What'd you find?" Stephen asked when Sam and Bear returned.

Jane released a deep breath when she saw the two were unharmed.

"Good sized mountain lion out there. Found fresh droppings na more than twenty-five feet from the trail. 'Tis what spooked the horses. He ran off though and I do na think he'll cause us any more problems," Bear said.

"Good. I'd like to get through these woods with my mount under me, not the other way around," William said. "Horses sure don't like mountain lions."

"Do you blame them?" John asked. "I'd prefer facing Indians or snakes than be some critter's dinner."

"You'll likely get a fair share of all three by the time we get to Kentucky," Sam warned.

Jane glared at Sam, then nodded towards the children. The last thing they needed to hear were stories about being eaten by animals or killed by Indians.

Sam lowered his voice. "Wild beasts aren't the only ones with an appetite for the taste of a man. Some Indians enjoy eating a man. Didn't you hear what happened to the Miami Chief? He got killed, boiled, and eaten by the Ottawa Indians at the Indian village of Pickawillany."

"And I've heard told that there be snakes in some parts of the world big enough to squeeze a man to death and then eat him whole," Bear added.

John's face paled and eyes widened.

"Quit trying to scare him," Stephen said.

"We're not trying to scare him. I'd say we succeeded," Sam said, laughing with Bear as they remounted.

The pleasure of teasing a brother was not something a man outgrew, Jane thought.

❧

They reached the slow-flowing Merrimack by noon. They would cross the river on a large ferry. The operator, who seemed a pleasant fellow to Stephen, said it would take two trips to get them all across. Only Sam and Bear had crossed a river on a ferry before.

Stephen asked Sam to go first with Jane, the wagon, and the bull and heifers. Sam agreed, tied his horse, and climbed up next to Jane. Sam held the guide ropes for the oxen while Jane held baby Mary as the ferry operator slowly took off. About mid-river, the ferry wobbled and wagon jostled a bit.

Stephen gasped and fear knotted his stomach.

"Do na worry yerself, 'tis normal," Bear said. "The current quickens in the middle."

Despite Bear's reassurance, Stephen's pulse beat erratically and his stomach still churned.

The crossing seemed to take forever.

Stephen released the breath he had been holding and smiled with relief when they safely reached the other side and Sam guided the oxen ashore.

On the second trip, the other children followed with him, Bear, William, and John. As Bear instructed, the men spent the crossing soothing their horses with stroking and whispering. Bear spent the ride soothing John, who was not a good swimmer, and holding little Amy in one of his big arms.

"Ye're worryin' yourself for nothin'. 'Tis just a wee bit a water," Bear said. "I've seen the Captain drink more whiskey than this in one sittin'."

"Nobody ever drowned drinking whiskey," John countered.

"Aye, but many a hard sorrow has drowned in the sweet nectar," Bear answered.

Holding Polly's hand, Stephen stood next to Martha and Little John, who watched a snake slither across the water's smooth surface. The two shivered, like the ripples in the water left by the snake. Both agreed a snake in water was a lot scarier than one on the ground. Unlike the adults and horses, the children clearly loved the ferry and, as they reached the opposite shore, said that they wished they could ride it again.

Stephen hoisted Polly up onto George's saddle and led the horse up the river bank. George too seemed to sigh a breath of relief now that they were on land again.

He checked on Jane and then, straightening his back, turned the stallion toward the next trail.

CHAPTER 17

*W*e *have traveled over a hundred miles now*, Jane wrote. *I have started to feel calmer. I worried that the Chief would send more braves after me, but Sam says we are too far away now and they will not follow us anymore. I pray he is right.*

I wonder what new dangers face us.

"Sure glad to see some sign of civilization again," William yelled over to Stephen and pointed to a cluster of buildings not too far away. "It's been entirely too long since I've had a nice-looking woman pay some attention to me."

Little more than a 100 yards long, the village of Petersborough offered the usual assortment of shops and merchants—a blacksmith, shoemaker, gristmill, general store, livery stable, three taverns, and two churches. Like most towns, the number of taverns outnumbered the number of churches.

"No use you looking for a pretty woman. We won't be here any longer than it would take for you to tip your hat at one," Stephen said.

"Now wait. We don't have to keep up this pace. Why are you in such an all fire hurry anyway?" William asked.

"If you had something other than women in that pretty head of yours you could think more clearly," John scolded. "It's late spring. That gives us six months before it starts to snow. If you don't mind sleeping on snow-covered ground, you can take your time, but I'd prefer to be under a roof and not freeze my backside off."

"We can spare enough time for a quick ale," William insisted.

"I've spent a good part of my adult life trying to keep you out of taverns. I guess I'll never cure you of that weakness," John said.

"You'll have no difficulty talking Bear and me into joining you," Sam said. "John's purity hasn't rubbed off on us either."

"I hope it never does. I wouldn't want to have to drink alone," William said.

Several people waved as they slowly made their way through the village. The townsfolk no doubt had grown used to the steady stream of people passing through on their way north or south. Many of them depended upon travelers for the majority of their business.

"Before you go traipsing off for that drink, William, we need to make camp." Stephen pointed to a clearing on the west side of town near some of the village's homes. As they set up camp, he'd never seen William move so fast.

Once settled, John stayed with Jane and the children, sitting by the campfire, teaching Little John to read. Sam, Bear, and William grabbed their weapons and headed for the tavern, but Stephen lagged behind.

"Go with them if you want," Jane said and slid her arms around his waist from behind.

"I don't want to let you and the girls out of my sight," he replied soberly.

"We'll be fine. We're in a town filled with people and the Indians would not dare attack us here. Go join your brothers. I know you want to."

He turned to face her and stared into her wide green eyes, lit with a sensuous light. His heart gave a tug and longing filled him.

"You'd better leave before you decide to haul me off into the forest in broad daylight."

"You know me so well." He kissed her forehead. "Have I told you today how much I love you?" he asked and pressed his lips lightly against hers.

"Yes, you just told me. But you can tell me again if you insist."

"I love you." He gave her hands a squeeze and glanced around for John. He was sitting by the wagon. "John, you're on guard duty. Keep your rifle handy."

After John nodded his agreement, Jane said, "I have some mending to do, but I'll keep a lookout too. This will be a good time for Martha, Polly, and Little John to study their school books. Now get." She turned him in the direction of the town. "Someone needs to keep an eye on your brothers."

Stephen leapt on George and raced to catch up with the others. The men decided on the establishment named Patriot's Tavern because they liked the name.

"Be on guard men. Ye can na tell what kind of man ye're goin' to find in one of these roadside taverns," Bear said.

"That's true, and try not to aggravate anyone Bear," Sam advised, as they lined their mounts up in front of the hitching post.

"Aye, I'll be on me best behavior Captain, but I will na promise anything. If a man needs disciplinin', it should na be put off."

"I agree," Stephen said. "Punishment should be swift and sure."

"I'm glad to know you both hold such profound philosophies on justice," William said.

"Justice has a way of finding its own course," Sam said, pushing open the tavern door.

The cozy room held half a dozen round tables crowded around a large rock fireplace. The scent of stale ale, tobacco, and the smoky fire filled the room. A collection of whiskey barrels stood behind the counter next to a stack of ale pitchers.

The four found an empty table near the fireplace.

A particularly homely big-bosomed woman served a pitcher of ale to the table without even asking what they wanted.

"How'd you know we wanted ale?" William asked jovially.

"If you're not here to drink, then leave with your stink," she declared, motioning towards the door.

"Yes madam, we are indeed here to drink. We appreciate the prompt service. Thank you for the ale," William said quickly.

"Even your good looks and soothing voice had no effect on that woman's disposition, William. Maybe you're losing your touch," Stephen said and stifled a laugh as they all watched her march off towards the kitchen muttering to herself.

After she left, William said, "That woman has served one too many pitchers of ale. Her face would sour fresh milk. Have you ever seen such an uncomely woman?"

"Only once before," Bear said. "My Aunt Finney. The snuff she dipped, among other things, made her hard on the eyes. I'll tell ye though, she could spit further than any man I ever knew."

"I've never known a woman that dipped snuff and spit," William said. "That had to be something to see."

"Will ye look at that old fellow now. He looks passing strange," Bear said.

Stephen glanced in the direction Bear indicated. A long scar ran across the man's weathered face, well into a graying beard that nearly reached to his waist. He wore greasy leather leggings and tall old boots.

"What's that stuck in his hat?" William said. "Let's invite him over here. He might prove entertaining." William stood and strode over to the man's table.

Stephen shook his head in disapproval while the others found William's typical behavior amusing. "He'll never learn to mind his business," he grumbled.

"Sir, my brothers and I wondered if you would care to join us for a drink. We've traveled a fair distance and thought you might have some news of the frontier," William told him.

"Thank you, sonny. I'd appreciate the company of some educated men," he said, his gray-blue eyes twinkling. He stood, without straightening his back completely, and slowly followed William back to their table.

Despite his age, the man appeared to possess strength and carried himself with an air of self-confidence. Stephen suspected that although the older man may have slowed down, if pushed, he would be able to take care of himself.

Sam pulled up another chair. "Have a seat."

"My name's Possum Clark," he said as he sat down.

"Mine's William Wyllie. This is my older brother, Captain Sam, my younger brother Stephen, and our adopted brother Bear. You can probably guess why he's called Bear."

"That I can. But I bet you can't guess why they call me Possum Clark," he cackled.

"You like to eat possum," Bear offered.

"Nope."

"You only come out at night?" Sam asked.

"Nope."

"Because you hunt a lot of possums?" William suggested.

Possum shook his hairy head.

When Possum turned to him, Stephen just shook his head and took a long sip of his ale.

"It's clear you boys ain't going to figure this one out so I'll just have to tell you. When I was about this young one's age," he said, nodding at Stephen, "I was one of the first white men west of the Appalachian Mountains. Maybe the first Christian man on some of those mountains. The thrill of walking on soil on which the foot of a civilized man has never trodden is beyond comparison, like walking in the Garden of Eden, 'cept I had no Eve. Although, not having a woman like Eve, always serving up temptation, may be a blessing, but I'm digressing." He stopped to take a long swig of his ale. "Well one cloudy foggy morning, I set about putting beaver traps by a river near the base of this mountain. The water was icy cold and a first snow dusted every tree and scrub. All of a sudden behind me, I hear the timber cracking, branches snapping, dead trees falling, like an avalanche breaking everything in its path—only there was no avalanche. The timber and brush were as thick as that hair on Bear's head so I couldn't see a darn thing. The next I know, a son-of-a-buck Grizzly faced me with a look on his face I hope never to see again. This old bear stood at least eight feet tall and weighed as much as five, maybe six, men. He opened his mouth and roared at me like the King of the forest. And I guess he was the King, 'cause I sure felt like a lowly peasant about to die right then.

"Now I had heard many theories about what to do if ever a Grizzly confronts you in the wild. One is to yell back at him and wave your arms around. But I was afraid my yell would sound more like a damn whimper. No use trying to run, they can make tracks faster than a horse. Trying to shoot them up close like that is risky. If you don't shoot them right between the eyes, you're just going to make 'em mad. One fella, he tried to shoot the Grizzly that got him. All they found of him was his rifle broke plum in two, a bloodied hatchet, and bear droppings. Another theory is to lie down and play dead. Although it goes contrary to what a normal man is inclined towards, I decided on that course of action, mainly 'cause my knees weren't working so well at the time. So I lay face down and acted just like a possum playing dead. That damned rascal sniffed me up one side and down the other. I could feel his hot breath on my skin. With each snort through his nostrils, I thought I would feel those razor-sharp long claws ripping my flesh apart, his teeth crushing my bones. Even though it was cold enough to freeze bacon, I was sweating in my buckskins. I guess he decided I wasn't a threat to him, or he didn't like the smell of me, or maybe I was just lucky and he'd already gorged on a big breakfast, but he moved off, toward the hills." Possum pointed in the direction the bear evidently went and everyone seemed to take a breath at the same time.

"And I was lucky it weren't a she bear. A she Grizzly will attack viciously if she has cubs anywhere around. Of course, I had to tell the story of my narrow escape at the Rendezvous with the other trappers that spring." Possum paused to laugh and cough for a bit. "They gave me the name Possum after that."

"What's that in your hat?" Stephen asked.

"It's a possum tail of course," Possum said, laughing again. "Reminds me every day how lucky I am to be alive. Be happy while you're living boys because you're not far from dead."

After the story of the old mountain monarch, Possum Clark gave the men more sage advice, describing the best routes, road conditions, and possible dangers. Having traveled to and from Kentucky six times since he'd been a trapper, he knew the route like an old friend. Captain Sam learned long ago to navigate by the stars, but the more information they had the better since they would travel by day.

Stephen borrowed quill and ink from the tavern owner, who was much more cordial than his wife. He felt sorry for the man yoked to such a sour woman. He pulled paper from his waistcoat pocket and, with Possum's help, wrote down the names of towns and villages and landmarks to look for, making a careful list for future reference.

As they stood to leave, William said, "Thank you, Sir, for a most entertaining discussion."

"You have been a valuable source of information, Mr. Clark," Stephen said, as they bid the trapper farewell. "We thank you kindly, Sir."

"Glad I could help. Return the favor someday yourself to some needy soul," Possum said. "The frontier is full of opportunities to help your fellow man. Don't pass 'em by. You never know when you may be the one in need of help."

As they all stood to leave, Possum said, "One last piece of advice boys. There's a good chance one or more of you may die on this trip. The rest of you will have to go on. That's the way it is out there. Just as this beautiful country goes on and on, so does life. Keep moving west, towards the sunset. Some of us just get there sooner than others."

CHAPTER 18

As daylight surrendered to night, every passing minute changed the sky from shades of blue to a soft array of violets, giving a dreamy quality to the evening. A luminous crescent moon glowed brightly on the horizon while a warm breeze stroked the strings of tall pines and lush hardwoods, playing a soothing melody for the couple as they strolled.

Jane's beauty was the only thing challenging the stunning scenery. To Stephen, she appeared more radiant than ever. He'd never grow tired of looking at her.

A seemingly endless variety of fragrant flowers, vines, and ferns wove their way between dogwoods, pines, and large rocks painting a colorful foreground for the surrounding slopes and mountains beyond. She bent to pick a flower. Its velvety petals reminded him of her lips.

"Have you ever seen a more peaceful place?" she asked. "Could there be any place in the world more breathtaking?"

"It'd be worthless to a cattleman—too many trees, boulders, and rock. I wouldn't pay ten cents an acre for this land."

Jane turned and lifted her chin. "Who said anything about cattle? I was just talking about the beauty of this place."

Mystified as to why his comment about land annoyed her, he took a quick breath and then shrugged. She was volatile by nature, and sometimes he struggled to understand her shifts in mood. "My point is that beauty is in the eye of the beholder, even when it comes to land. I admit, the scenery is pleasant here, but it's not what I need."

"Sometimes, you're too focused on the future and don't just enjoy the now."

"My duty is to think about our future. A man cannot do justice to the present if he doesn't make plans for tomorrow."

"What do you mean 'do justice to the present'?"

"I believe every person has both a present and a time yet to come. If we don't prepare for that time to come, we may lose now."

"Why?" Jane asked.

"Every moment of the future is linked to what we do with our lives *now*."

"Don't miss the present while you're taking care of what's coming. What good is a future without a present? Someday you'll look back and wish you still had the past you missed. Let's just take joy in this day."

She had a point. "All right. All right. Give me your hand. We'll walk awhile."

They strolled in silence further from the camp. The moon, now higher in the sky, shimmered with the softness of candlelight.

"Do you miss home?" Jane asked.

"I miss our comfortable bed and what we did in it." He raised a brow and grinned. He wasn't being very subtle. But the truth was he did miss it. Some of the best times of his life had been in that bed.

"We can't do much about the bed, but maybe we can manage to do something about the other." Her eyes twinkled wickedly.

"You were right about enjoying the now," he said, laughing. "But first, do you miss home?" Worried about what her answer would be, he waited anxiously for it. He wasn't sure how he would feel if she was truly homesick. Could he turn around, go back, if she asked him to? No, he could not.

"Honestly, yes, exceedingly. How could I not? You made this decision and while I will have to live with it, I ache for our home sometimes. I miss little things. Like sitting on the porch and sipping tea out of mother's china. Bomazeen made me break that cup. When it shattered, maybe my future there shattered too. That's all a part of my past now, buried forever." She moved closer and smiled up at him. "Yes, I miss all we left behind, but my future belongs with you. And so does the present." Her voice underlined the word 'present' as she dropped her cloak to the ground.

She kissed him softly and he savored the warmth and softness of her full lips.

Jane pulled his powder horn's strap over his head and leaned their rifles against a tree.

He watched, mesmerized, as she removed her gown and hung it on a nearby Hickory limb. His pulse kicked up and his breathing quickened as she shed her stays and petticoats, revealing her shapely form.

He stared. How gorgeous she appeared at that moment. Her hair shining in a shaft of soft moonlight, her sumptuous lips speaking without words. Her soft ivory shoulders and the fullness of her cleavage beckoning him. She was exquisite, enthralling.

"You're so beautiful," he whispered, as she stepped into his embrace.

His fingertip tenderly traced the outline of her gentle, but proud face, committing every detail to memory. Her pale smooth complexion seemed almost translucent in the moonlight. Red-gold ringlets curled on her forehead and her lashes swept down against her pink cheekbones. Then she glanced up and he gazed deep into the shining emeralds of her eyes, bright with her growing desire. Her enticing lips, full and rosy, parted at his touch. He kissed his fingertip and then ran it across her lower lip.

He caressed her lovely long neck and planted a soft kiss at the hollow beneath her throat. Then he drew his finger slowly across the full curve of one breast and then the other. They felt firm and soft at the same time, and he marveled at their allure.

She trembled in his arms and released a soft sigh.

Using both hands, his intimate exploration continued. He caressed her back, pulling her closer as his fingers inched down until he reached her waist. Then he ran both hands over her hips and down her thighs, feeling a tremor ripple inside her.

And every place her fingers touched heated and produced a pleasurable sensation until it was time to yield to the passion that embraced them both.

Stephen removed his clothing, his eyes never leaving her, while she spread her cloak across a bed of pine needles. The soft breeze, gently caressing his bare skin felt cool, but not enough to dampen his heated body.

As a precaution, he laid his loaded pistols nearby and positioned their rifles on either side of them.

Then he joined her on the cloak and wrapped his arms around her. He enveloped her in love, possessively, protectively, wanting to bring her close to his heart. He savored the feeling of just holding her.

She tilted her head back, opened her lips, and he kissed her—a kiss as deep and powerful as his need for her. He sensed her deep hunger in the fervor of her kiss and it only added fuel to his mounting desire.

He tenderly kissed the sensitive spot below her ears before gently nibbling on her neck and then her shoulder. As he lowered his lips to the curves of her chest, she moaned pleasurably. But he took his time, enjoying every minute.

Her body was luscious and the taste and feel of her stirred him even further. He reached down and found her soft round bottom. Filling his hand with it, he pressed her against him. Another moan, this one deeper, more urgent.

She ran her hands through his hair and down his back, then she gripped his hips, drawing him still closer, hugging him even tighter.

"My love," he whispered the words on a breath against her cheek.

The passion between them was undeniable and grew more fervent with each joining—like a perfect secret only the two of them shared. He was hers and she was his. And that would never change.

"Stephen, I love you so much it hurts."

"I know of only one cure."

"Aye," she whispered.

As he linked his body to hers, he did so slowly, savoring the amazing feel of her.

She whimpered and arched against him.

He closed his eyes, reveling in that extraordinary feeling when they were one—the only time they were completely together—two halves of one whole. Each moment joined with her was perfect pleasure and he wanted every second to last forever. Every kiss to be endless.

He found the irresistible taste of her lips both sensual and soothing to his spirit. Not only did his body keenly crave hers, so did his soul. For the need she satisfied was not just physical, it was an urgent need for his soul to bond to hers—to create a link so strong it could not be undone.

She grabbed his biceps, gripping his muscles, hanging on to his arms as her body climbed an exquisite mountain of pleasure.

As she reached the mountain's pinnacle, his entire body grew taut, every muscle submitting to an odd power capable of taking over his will, until it had complete control of him and he had no choice but to yield to its power. He gave her all he had and surrendered.

Then a nearly violent tremor possessed her followed slowly by a melting softness. Her entire body grew limp as if she had no choice but to rest after the thrilling climb.

He held her tightly, guarding her, until her mind and body returned from the mountain top. They had done justice to the present and it made him look forward to the future all the more.

CHAPTER 19

Stephen woke reluctantly, not wanting to leave his pleasant dream. He glanced around, realizing they had all slept longer than normal, as the sunrise stayed hidden behind a massive wall of darkening clouds. He'd dreamt of Jane. The taste and feel of her the evening before left him wanting more, a lot more. But as the menacing storm approached against a wolf gray dawn, the clouds opened up and it began to rain and with dismal insistence rudely extinguished the heat of his desire. Then the cold drops woke the other sleeping travelers one by one.

Unable to make breakfast without a fire, they settled for cold jerky, cornmeal cakes, and water. It would be a long day with five wet men who had missed their morning coffee. Skipping the brew never seemed to bother Jane because she wasn't fond of coffee anyway. She preferred tea.

"Let's go. We might as well get wet moving as sitting here," Stephen said, even more impatient than usual.

"Are you sure?" Jane asked, eyeing the mountainous dark clouds and lightning in the distance. "Maybe we should wait it out."

"If we stop every time rain blows in, we'll never get there," Stephen said. "This downpour won't let up anytime soon."

"No, it won't," Sam agreed. "It's going to be a real frog strangler, but we have no decent cover here. I'd as soon get wet sitting on a horse as hiding under a wagon."

For several long hours, they endured the thunderstorm, making slow miserable progress. The gloomy morning looked more like late evening. Water flowed in steady streams through every low point on the trail. The oxen trudged through sticky mud, every step they took becoming more difficult. Goosebumps rose on Stephen's arms as the temperature dropped, making them all cold as well as wet.

The trail ahead became increasingly difficult to see as the rain turned into heavy torrents. Then the wind picked up, blowing rainwater horizontally and throwing small branches and wet leaves in every direction, as though the storm could not decide which way to turn.

Stephen rode next to Jane and noticed her hands trembling so hard she had difficulty keeping the team moving. He tied George to the side of the wagon and jumped up beside her. "Get in the back and dry off," he ordered.

For once, she gave him no argument. She nodded, handed him the guide rope, and kissed him before climbing into the back. Her lips felt wonderful against his cold face, and he wished she could linger there longer, deepen the kiss. At least the thought warmed him.

"Get under the blankets," Jane told the children.

"But I'm afraid," he heard Polly whine.

"Remember what I taught you, 'fear sees the storm, faith sees God in the storm'," Jane said.

"This doesn't look much like God to me," he heard Martha say.

Stephen had to agree with her.

"Step up!" he urged the oxen. It worked for a few yards and then they slowed again, unable or unwilling to improve their pace in the downpour.

The heavy rain suddenly slowed to a steady drizzle and he turned to look inside the wagon. Jane was trying to dry off as best she could, but it was hopeless, her gown and cloak were soaked. "Get out of that wet gown," he suggested.

"I guess I'll have to. Little John, cover your head with that blanket, so I can change my clothes."

Stephen glanced back inside to be sure the boy complied as she hauled a dry gown out of her wooden trunk.

"He's peeking Father," Polly accused, pointing her finger at her cousin.

"Am not you tattle tale," he shouted, taking the opportunity to lower the blanket again.

"Little John, if you don't keep your head under that blanket, I'll shave all the hair off your handsome little head," Jane threatened.

All the girls laughed.

"Best you do as she says, boy," Stephen said, then grinned.

Little John moved closer to Stephen and threw the blanket over his head. "There are too many girls in here."

He had to sympathize, four girls, plus Jane. No wonder Little John felt outnumbered. He knew exactly how his nephew felt.

As quickly as the deluge slowed, a heavy downpour started up again.

Sam pulled his horse up alongside. "I'll scout ahead, see if I can find shelter."

"Good, this wagon is starting to float," Stephen yelled back.

Sam urged his mount to a trot. The big gelding responded eagerly, undoubtedly anxious to find shelter too. Sam kept the horse at a brisk pace until the muddy trail began a gradual slope downhill. The treacherous path would hold numerous hidden rocks and cracks under the flowing water. He slowed the gelding to a walk and prayed his mount wouldn't stumble and break a leg.

Iridescent white lightning exploded overhead like burning arrows, shooting across the dark sky.

Sam sensed his horse growing tenser under him at each angry bolt. He had to admit, the terrible thunderstorm made him edgy as well.

The trail turned to follow the side of the hill and Sam hoped it signaled a chance for shelter. But each bend in the road only revealed more trail and each section of the trail only led to more woodlands. Sam began to wonder if he should turn back. Finally, he saw a clearing of grass and gravel underneath a large rock overhang. The stone outcropping slanted sharply from the side of the hill, rain falling off its edge in a steady waterfall. It appeared just big enough to pull the wagon under and maybe keep the horses out of the deluge too. He turned around and urged his mount back up the trail toward the others.

In the next moment, lightning hit so hard and so close, the ground quaked, nearly knocking Sam out of the saddle. The bolt's reverberation exploded painfully in his ears as though someone had fired heavy artillery next to his head. Sam tried to cover his face with his trembling arms as splintered smoldering wood and pine bark flew through the air. Out of the corner of his eye, he caught a glimpse of the huge tree beginning to fall. He urged the gelding forward in an effort to escape. But it was too late. He and the horse joined the large tree's deafening collision with the ground. Landing solidly on the mount's hindquarters, he heard the horrific sound of the pine's trunk shattering his horse's back and hips. Instantaneously, his gelding was dead and he lay trapped beneath thick heavy branches.

Sam remained motionless, unable to hear or to think clearly. But he needed to get moving. He shook his head to try to clear it. Winded in the fall, he struggled to draw shallow breaths while he assessed his predicament. He could smell the tree smoldering. Fire? He couldn't move his foot and knee, pinned under the horse and saddle. His ankle screamed as if someone had just planted a hatchet in it. A large branch immobilized his right arm, but he didn't think the arm was broken, he could still move his fingers without pain.

Sam tried to move his other arm toward the saddle but could only just touch the saddle horn. Every movement brought agonizing discomfort in his leg and ankle. He pushed against the horse with his right leg, but the weight of the tree trunk rested fully on the gelding's hip.

The cold rain pelted him incessantly, yet he could feel himself sweating from the effort to free himself. His head pounded and his ears would not quit vibrating, and he still found it hard to breathe. The air smelt burnt and hurt his lungs.

Sam clenched his jaw at the pain and looked for his Kentucky rifle. If he could manage to fire it, he could signal the others. But the rifle lay on the ground just out of reach. He grabbed his pistol, although he realized they would probably not be able to hear it through the storm. Sam pulled the trigger anyway, but the gun did not fire. The powder was too damp. It reminded him why he preferred his knife to the pistol. But even his knife would be of no help to him now.

The deluge pounded his eyes and sent water running into his nose, making him choke. Sam turned his face to the side, but his ear began to fill with the standing water all around him. He held his head up, but after a minute, he laid his head back down, too weak to continue to struggle. What felt like buckets of water, poured over his face. Rainwater continued to pool all around him, as the tree's trunk and the horse's body acted like a twisted bizarre dam, trapping the rising water. Much longer and he'd drown before anyone found him.

"Damn," he swore, as consciousness began slipping away.

Stephen, help me.

CHAPTER 20

Stephen kept the group on the move through the terrible rainstorm, expecting Sam to come back any minute. But the minutes became interminable, with no sign of his brother. The nearly continuous lightning was the worst he had ever seen. A fiery bolt pierced violently through a black cloud up ahead, traveling perfectly vertical. It hit something close by as the explosive clap of the thunderbolt followed nearly instantly.

Stephen began to worry. "He should be back by now," he yelled at William, who rode alongside him in case he needed help with the wagon and team.

John and Bear pulled their horses up beside William.

"We'll scout ahead, check on Sam," John shouted.

"Good," Stephen said. "Hurry, something's wrong."

He watched the two start a slow trot through the downpour. Hopefully, they would keep a careful eye on the barely visible road, now covered in a brown river of liquefied mud. They would only be able to see a couple of horse lengths ahead of them.

Moments later, Bear returned. "Sam's pinned under a tree in risin'

water," he yelled. "Need rope and saws. Hurry!"

Stephen instantly tied the oxens' reins, leapt off, and opened the supply box attached to the wagon's side between the wheels. He grabbed the axe, saws, and the rope Edward had given them, and then gave them to Bear and William.

"Is he hurt bad?" Stephen asked.

"If he's not, 'twill be a miracle. His horse is dead," Bear said.

"Jane, hold the team here until we get back. Keep your rifle loaded and dry and the children in the wagon," he instructed. "If you need us, fire the rifle."

They reached Sam and John as quickly as they could. "How bad is he?" Stephen yelled as he flew off George.

John held Sam's head, doing his best to keep his eyes and nose out of the water. "He's still breathing. Hurry—the water's rising," John pleaded.

Stephen grabbed his axe and the three ran to Sam's side.

"He's knocked out. It could be bad," John said. "I can't lift him any higher—his arm's pinned. His left leg is under the horse—probably broken. It's a heavy tree, but his horse took the brunt of it. We've got to get the weight off that leg before it cuts off the blood or he'll lose it."

"William, use the saw to cut off this branch pinning his right arm," John ordered. "Bear, get the big rope and put a loop around the top of the trunk over there. Once William has the arm cleared, use Camel to drag the tree. Stephen, use the axe to clear all the small branches from around him so they won't tear him up when we pull the tree off. I'll check on Sam some more to see if anything else is broken."

The builder in John had designed an efficient plan to free Sam. It took only a few more minutes before they were ready to move the tree off.

Standing next to Camel's head, Bear urged the big gelding forward. The horse struggled against the enormous weight. The tree didn't budge.

Slick mud, wet leaves and pine needles, made it hard for the gelding to get any traction. Bear coaxed Camel again. "Come on now, ye're a giant among horses, my friend. Our Sam needs your help."

Camel seemed to respond to his master's plea and the sure-footed gelding's muscles tightened as he took a step forward, then another. "Aye, that's the way."

Stephen let out a sigh of relief when Camel managed to move the tree just enough to lift it off Sam's horse. He and William had tied their ropes to the dead horse's flank and used their mounts to lift up the hips. John quickly freed Sam.

"Got him," John yelled, over a loud clap of thunder.

They rushed to Sam's side. His brother's ankle pointed at nearly a right angle to his leg.

"That ankle's clearly broken. We'd better set it before he wakes," John said.

"I'll get Jane," Stephen said. "She knows more about doctoring than all of us put together." As a youth, her father had her doctor animals and as a young woman, she had done some nursing during the Revolution. "William, come with me so you can guard the children."

William turned without saying a word and jumped on his mount, already heading up the trail. Stephen followed.

Spare Sam, Stephen prayed as he rode. They needed him to make it safely to Kentucky, but, more importantly, he loved his brother. And, aside from their father, he respected and valued him more than any other man he'd ever known. He couldn't imagine his life without his big brother by his side.

They reached Jane just as he finished his prayer.

"Jane, Sam's injured. He broke an ankle, maybe more. Need you to set the ankle while he's still unconscious. William will look after the children and bring the wagon. Grab what you need. Ride William's horse."

"What happened?" she yelled as they rode side by side.

"Huge tree fell on the gelding. Pinned Sam and his leg was caught under the horse."

Jane carefully set the swelling ankle, using pieces of bark, cloth, and braided leather. She had to move quickly and do a good job, or Sam would always have a limp. He might anyway, even if she did set the ankle exactly right. Stephen watched, grateful that Sam never woke while she worked. But his brother slept fitfully and from time to time moaned loudly. He worried that the ankle might not be the worst of Sam's injuries.

While Jane worked on Sam, they unsaddled Sam's dead horse and William caught up to them with the wagon. The wind had let up and a slight drizzle was all that remained of the violent storm. They were all soaked and chilled to the bone, but none as cold as Sam.

"His skin feels like ice," Jane said.

"We need to get him someplace warm before he gets a fever," Stephen said.

"I'd best see if I can find shelter up ahead." Bear said.

It did not take Bear long to locate the same outcrop of rock Sam had spotted. By noon, the group managed a rough shelter under the cliff and used a dead log and dry leaves, tucked under the overhang and out of the rain, to quickly build a fire. They placed Sam on a pallet next to the warm flames. Stephen and John took off Sam's wet clothes so Jane could examine him further.

"There is considerable bruising, but no open wounds," she told them, "and I see no signs of burns from the lightning strike. His internal injuries are unknown. They could be severe. I wish we had a physician to examine him." Jane applied ointment to Sam's cuts and scratches.

Stephen had to help Sam somehow, if only in his own small way. He took a dry cloth and dried as much of the moisture off Sam's skin as he could. They would all need to dry off and get warm, but Sam came first. He covered his brother with the wool blanket Edward had sent and tucked it snugly around his chest and feet.

"Will he wake up?" Polly asked meekly, helping to straighten the blanket across her uncle.

"We must pray that he will," Stephen said, placing his hand on the top of his daughter's little shoulder.

"I don't want Uncle Sam to die," Little John told his father through tears.

Stephen understood how unnerving it was for the children to see their hero in such a state. It worried all of them. Sam could have unseen injuries and he might never wake.

"He won't die Little John. The good Lord knows we need him to help us on our journey," John said. "I bet he wakes up tomorrow morning as fierce as ever."

It would be a long time until morning. Stephen would get little sleep, if any, and his stomach would be knotted with worry by then.

Amy scooted up next to Sam and knelt down. She gently kissed his forehead and then his bandaged ankle. "Mama says kisses make hurt bedder."

Polly also knelt down and kissed him. Then Martha did the same.

Stephen studied Sam, desperately hoping that Jane was right.

CHAPTER 21

The prayers and kisses worked. Sam woke the next morning.

Jane examined Sam's swollen arm and knee. The ankle caused him great pain, but otherwise, he appeared to be all right, except for numerous bruises and scratches nearly everyplace Stephen could see.

"You scared the hell out of me," he told Sam, handing his brother a generous cup of whiskey for pain after they finished breakfast. He suspected Sam would not savor the whiskey. He hurt too much to enjoy it slowly.

"I'll try my best not to put you through that again," Sam said, gulping a big swallow. "Was it hard to get the tree off?"

"Indeed, but thanks to that new saw and the long rope Edward gave us, we made quick work of it. We might still be working on it if we hadn't had those."

"Here's to Edward," Sam said, downing the rest of the whiskey with relish. "Too bad about my horse, he was a good one."

"Do you think you'll be able to ride?" he asked.

"I'm as sore as a butchered hog, but yes, if one of our spare horses will let me mount from the off side with my right foot," Sam said. "I can just leave the left one hanging, and ride with one stirrup, especially if I can stay on this medicine. How about another cup?"

He took the cup but filled it with coffee instead. He needed Sam alert enough to shoot straight if the need arose. "I'll give you a stronger cup in an hour."

The group decided to rest up for a week or so and let Sam recuperate.

"I'll start training one of the spare horses to let you mount from the off side. It bothers some horses, but others not at all," Stephen said.

That afternoon, he chose the bigger of the two extra horses he had brought along and started training it. He spent two full days mounting the tall buckskin from the off side to get it ready for Sam. The beautiful golden gelding, with a silky black mane and tail, became indifferent to which side Stephen mounted him. He also spent the rest of the week fine-tuning the horse's other skills. Sam's new gelding was a quick learner and willing to please.

After several days, Sam could take short steps if he used a sturdy branch for a cane. He hobbled over to where Stephen worked with the horse and watched. Stephen remembered that Sam had admired the gelding when he brought the mount back from Barrington, but hadn't been willing to give up an experienced mount for a green one. After this training, the steed would be more dependable.

"He's level-headed but he's got a lot of go in him," Stephen said. "You'll have to hold him back some." He made the horse turn in a tight circle. "As you can see, he reins well too."

"Looks like you've polished him up well," Sam said. "Thank you for getting him ready. You've had several horses over the years. Which one was your favorite? Old Rebel?"

Hearing the name, Stephen fondly remembered the first horse his father gave him. "I don't know. I always like the one I'm riding. But George is exceptional. He'll be hard to beat."

"This one will be called Alex," Sam declared.

"Why Alex?"

"After Hamilton—the rascal who came up with that excise tax on whiskey last year. He's a horse's ass, so I thought it would be a fitting name."

"You can't name your mount after someone you dislike. The horse is a noble animal and you should name him after someone you respect. That's why I named mine George, after Washington."

"You got it wrong brother. A typical horse is an ornery, untrustworthy, unpredictable animal that's only useful if exceptionally well-trained."

"Good steeds are God's greatest gift to man, next to a woman of course. And I suspect most horses give a man less grief than most women," Stephen retorted.

"What did you just say?" Jane asked, just walking up as he finished his sentence.

"I was explaining to Sam why a man should name his mount after someone he admires," he said quickly.

"What I heard was that most horses can give a man less grief than a woman," she declared, crossing her arms.

"That's exactly what he said," Sam said. "I heard those very words myself."

Stephen could tell that Sam was feeling the effects of the whiskey he still drank for pain and had seized an opportunity to cause him problems.

"I said 'most' women, that doesn't mean you, Jane," Stephen said, feeling defensive.

"What women *do* you mean then?"

He swallowed. Jane wasn't going to let him off the hook. "I don't mean any women. I was talking about George. No, I meant horses in general."

"No, you said George was God's greatest gift," Sam injected, clearly enjoying himself.

Alex snorted contentedly and Sam laughed while he brushed the gelding's coat, shining now like new gold coins.

"You're deliberately trying to cause trouble with my wife. I can see you're feeling better. We leave tomorrow," Stephen said and marched off.

After walking only a short distance with the cane, Sam limped back to camp instead of hunting with Bear, unable to put his full weight on the ankle, even after three weeks. "Damn that's aggravating," Sam said, through clenched teeth. Glowering, Sam threw his cane down and took a seat near Jane.

Jane could see that it made Sam mad to admit a physical weakness. It was something a man like him just didn't do. He had always been an exceptionally strong man, able to travel great distances by foot without fatigue. "Don't be so hard on yourself," Jane said. "It has only been a short while since your injury. If you push yourself too hard now your libel to have a bad ankle your whole life and I worked too hard to make that ankle mend correctly."

"You did a splendid job with splinting. It just needs a while longer," Sam said, looking calmer now. "You look pale. Are you feeling well?"

Jane inhaled and let the breath out slowly. Even breathing seemed to make her tired. "I'm just weary. This journey is considerably harder than I expected. It nearly killed both of us. One day we're cold and wet from these horrendous storms and the next we are sweating through our clothes and the air is so heavy you can hardly breathe. And I miss being clean. I'm constantly covered in either mud or dust to say nothing of these annoying insect bites." She paused long enough to scratch her itching ankles. "And we still have so far to go. I don't mean to complain. I'm just bloody tired." She stroked the neck of Sam's new horse, tied nearby. The buckskin's silky hair felt good against her palm. Precious few things on this journey felt soft to her hand.

"Jane, don't fight this trip. You can never win. Draw strength from being tested," Sam said. "That's the difference between those who make it and those who don't."

"How? How do I do that?"

She waited while Sam thought for a moment before answering.

"Like Alex here, he feels soft and looks beautiful on the outside, but when you touch him, you also feel strong hard muscle beneath. When he's pushed, he responds from that power. Think of these challenges as exercises to build your inner strength, not obstacles to sap it."

"I'm not sure I can do that." She didn't feel beautiful on the outside or strong on the inside. She saw only mud and dirt and felt only mounting weariness.

"Nature never fails to challenge us. If we fight it, we exhaust our strength. But if we respect it, both for its power to create and to destroy, it can help us grow stronger."

"You want me to respect the wilderness? Use it to make me stronger?"

"I challenge you to do so. If you don't, you'll grow to hate the wilderness But if you do, you will find the beauty in it, learn to love it as I do."

Sam was right. He was proof of his own words. She lifted her chin and said, "All right, I accept your challenge."

She took a deep breath and marched off to find Stephen. Then they would both bathe in the nearby beautiful pond. The idea suddenly sent her spirits soaring. Picturing the hard muscles of her husband's bare body made her feel stronger already.

಄

The next few weeks passed uneventfully, except that Stephen noticed that the children changed from week to week as children are wont to do. Baby Mary started to walk, Amy grew another tooth, Polly started reading, Martha grew at least an inch, and Little John decided he was old enough to ride his own mount. He begged Stephen to let him have the remaining spare horse. They had sold Little John's pony before leaving Barrington because it was too old to make the trip. The extra horse was especially gentle and reined well and Stephen knew it would be easier on John's mount if it did not have the extra load of the boy every day.

"I think Little John would be a fine horseman," he told John. "It's in his blood. Besides, the horse needs to be ridden if he's going to stay gentle."

"Then you ride him," John retorted, "Little John is just a boy; he doesn't need a man's steed."

"He'll need to become a man quick enough on the frontier. The sooner he gets started the better," Stephen snapped back.

"I'm his father and I'll decide when he needs to become a man," John retorted.

"John, Stephen's right," Sam intervened. "Little John will be much safer if he's a good rider. A fine mount can save a man, or a boy, from disaster. Soon he'll need to learn to handle a weapon too. It's time you let the boy start to grow up."

John glanced at Stephen and then Sam. "All right, so long as Stephen teaches him to become a better rider."

"And I'll teach him to use a knife," Sam promised.

಄

"There's a secret to loping a horse the right way," Stephen told Little John later.

"What secret?" Little John asked.

"It's all in the reins," he explained. "Most people keep the reins in the same spot held over their mount's neck or saddle."

"That's the way I do it," the boy said.

"That's wrong. You see, the horse is moving his head as he runs. It moves forward and back, just as your body does. So the reins need to move with his head. Otherwise, you're jerking him every time he takes a step and it's hard for him to run smooth."

Little John said, "I want to be a good horseman, just like you Uncle Stephen."

"To be a good rider, you need to understand how your gelding moves and, more importantly, how he thinks."

"How do I do that?"

"It's mostly time in the saddle. The more time you spend with him, watching him, learning how he thinks, the more you'll understand him."

Little John, now six, took to the horse instantly and the two became inseparable. With every lesson he gave him, his nephew's skill as a rider and the boy's gratitude towards him grew.

Stephen suspected Little John would have sided with him in the recent debate with Sam on the proper inspiration for naming a horse. Little John named the gelding Dan—after his hero Daniel Boone.

CHAPTER 22

*T*o describe today would be a repetition of yesterday. We have come over 300 miles. We are continually plagued by rain and grey skies. Every storm makes even making a meal a challenge. Yesterday's weather was especially oppressive. I thought I would go mad from the incessant pounding of raindrops on the wagon cover. I have given up trying to keep us all clean, instead focusing on my struggle to keep the children warm. We have stuck a wheel so many times I have lost count. I am trying hard to live up to Sam's challenge, to think of these trials as opportunities to grow stronger. But, nature seems determined to test my resolve.

Despite these hardships, we are also blessed. I have not told Stephen yet, but I am with child. I know our daughters are precious to him beyond measure, but I pray this time we will have the son I know he desires. I know being with child will make this trip more difficult for me, but children come in God's time, not ours.

৵

Jane closed the journal, put aside the ink and quill, then leaned back against a Sycamore tree. A cool breeze wafted over her face, blowing wisps of her hair against her ears and neck. Baby Mary slept next to her knee. A patchwork quilt covered the damp ground beneath them. She enjoyed just watching the little beauty sleep. She thought about Stephen and how handsome he looked when he was asleep—when his cares and ambition did not burden his fine face. Her cheeks and neck heated as an overwhelming urge to kiss him suddenly seized her. And she wanted to feel his strong arms around her. To love him. But their lack of privacy made being amorous rare and beyond difficult. Soon, she promised herself.

She inhaled deeply, taking in the soothing earthy fragrance of this tranquil place, and let her breath out slowly. These few moments to rest and record her thoughts were precious and she savored the serenity.

But the moment's quiet peace did not last long.

Martha ran up. "Mama, Uncle Sam said to fetch you. Amy's face is red and her eyes look strange."

She quickly gathered Mary and the quilt in her arm, grabbed the journal and ink, and hurried with Martha to Sam.

Sam rested against his saddle, holding Amy, her head leaning against his broad shoulder. Amy's tiny fingers played listlessly with the fringe of his buckskin shirt.

"She wandered over here a little bit ago and climbed on my lap. Knew she was sick as soon as she sat down," Sam said, concerned.

"Baby, what's wrong?" Jane asked, feeling Amy's forehead. Her daughter felt blistery hot and red patches covered her cheeks and neck. Jane tried not to show Amy the fear that gripped her heart. The child was quite ill.

She climbed into her wagon to lay Mary down and went back for Amy. She put Amy next to Mary on the pallet the girls used, then stuck her head out the back. "Get your father," she told Martha, who stood with Polly nearby.

"What's wrong?" Stephen asked, peering inside the wagon, the moment he reached it.

160

"Girls, take the bucket and get some water so I can make a broth for Amy," Jane told Martha and Polly, before answering.

As soon as they were alone, her eyes burned with tears wanting to fall. "Dear God, Stephen, Amy's burning up and shaking with chills. I don't know if its exposure to all these rainstorms or yellow fever. I just know she is terribly ill."

"Yellow fever? It killed thousands in Philadelphia a few years ago. It can't be that. She just has a chill is all," Stephen said firmly, dismissing the notion.

"Remember the symptoms of Yellow Fever, fever and chills? Exactly what she has. It killed indiscriminately. Some got it while others in the same family didn't." Biting her lip, she turned her eyes back on her daughter. Her mood veered sharply from worry to anger. "I'll make her some herb and oak bark tea. I don't know what else to do."

Stephen climbed inside and felt Amy's face. "I'll sit with Mary and Amy while you find and mix the herbs."

This time she detected worry in his voice and it alarmed her.

Jane quickly put some of the water on to boil and took the rest to the wagon to wipe Amy down. She removed her girl's dress and mopped her body with the cool cloth, then handed the rag to Stephen.

"Keep wiping her down, especially her forehead," she told Stephen. "I'll go brew the tea."

While Jane made the herb tea, Stephen stayed with Amy. His girls had never been seriously ill before and the shadow of worry hung over him. Before long, a dread—dark and terrifying—crept into him. He tried to ban it, but couldn't. He began to pray.

The sound of trotting horses lifted him back from the retreat of prayer. He wiped Amy's forehead before climbing out of the wagon.

"Hope John's luckier than we were," William said, as he and Bear dismounted.

"Amy's ill," Stephen said at once.

"How bad?" William asked.

"I don't know. She has a bad fever. John's down at the creek. Tell him he'll need to cook the fish he catches for dinner so Jane can tend to Amy."

Bear's bushy eyebrows grew closer and his face looked troubled before he said, "I'll tell him, and I'll water these thirsty horses too."

"Can I do anything?" William asked.

"Pray," he answered.

Jane brought the tea to the girls and then yelled, "Stephen, come here."

He didn't like the desperate sound of her voice. He and William both jumped to the back of the wagon and looked in.

"Mary's getting warm too. Feel her," Jane cried, moving the baby closer so he could reach her. "God, why?"

He ran his palm over Mary's little head, indeed quite warm. "Jane, just do your best. That's all you can do," he said, trying his best to calm her, despite his own rising panic. He glanced back at Martha and Polly who stood nearby. "Help Uncle John get dinner ready," he told them.

"I'll make coffee and bring you both some," William offered.

Stephen climbed back into the wagon. "Here, let me hold Mary while you wipe down Amy. When did Amy go to sleep?"

"A few minutes ago. The fever made her drowsy. The tea didn't help," Jane said, panic entering her voice. "What if she doesn't wake up?"

"Give it time. She just drank it. Can the baby take any?"

"Yes. Here's her baby cup. She just started drinking from it this week."

Stephen was sorry he hadn't noticed that. He gently held the little pewter cup to the toddler's lips. What a beautiful girl. Had he taken the time to notice even that before now? Mary's red curls hung damp and limp as the fever climbed. Her eyes studied his face—eyes that somehow knew he was trying to help her. She took a small sip. Jane had flavored it with honey and Mary seemed to like it. After taking another swallow, she managed a weak smile up at him. Then, cradled in his arms, she too fell asleep. He laid Mary down and covered her with a warm blanket to keep the chills at bay, before returning to the others.

He didn't want to eat but tried to bring Jane some food. She refused it and he returned to the campfire. John fed fresh fish to the rest of the group. After dinner, Little John, Martha, and Polly snuggled by the fire as John read to them. Within minutes, all three children slept soundly and Stephen covered them with blankets and tucked them in.

Sam, William, Bear, and John decided to alternate sentry duty to keep a careful watch over their camp. Now that they were in unfamiliar country, unsure of what they might encounter, at least one of them would be awake at all times.

He rejoined Jane and the night stretched endlessly. The dark sky matched their growing despair as they grimly watched both daughters slowly slipping away. Mary's breathing grew slow and shallow and fever burned red through her face.

Amy began coughing and as the night progressed, the cough worsened. "Mama, Mama," she whimpered repeatedly, each time tearing at his heart.

Jane stared grim-faced at him. "I can't believe they're both so sick at the same time." She started to cry, unable to hold back her tears of worry any longer.

Helplessness made him miserable. With each passing hour, his sense of vulnerability grew, like a black hole growing bigger and darker, pulling their daughters away.

He sensed Jane struggling to remain calm, but as she caressed Mary's sweet face with the gentle hand of a loving mother, her face suddenly contorted with fear. "She's barely breathing," Jane cried out, desperately cradling Mary against her breast.

He looked on, numb with dread, powerless to help. He dropped to his knees, bowed his head. His spirit reached for God. "Lord don't. Please do not take her. Not this little one. She has lived but one short year. If someone must die on this trip, let it be me, not these innocents. Let it be me who pays for my dreams."

Tears slipping down his cheeks, he turned his eyes to Jane. What he saw on her face filled him with terror. He grabbed Jane, wrapping his arms around both her and Mary, desperately hugging them both to his chest.

The tears of both parents fell on their dead daughter.

Grief exploded through his mind and body, nearly blowing him apart. But for Amy's sake, he would not let this nightmare consume him, not yet. He forced himself to throttle his emotions. They had to find a way to save Amy. He helped Jane, who cried continuously, wipe Amy's forehead with a cool cloth more times than he could count. He prayed without ceasing. He held the tiny hand of the three-year-old in his own, as Jane talked to her, trying to keep her alert, trying to soothe all their fears.

"Mama, I see…," Amy said, barely above a whisper.

"See what my darling?" Jane asked, looking into their daughter's dimming eyes.

"Look," Amy said, raising just a finger to point. "It's baby Mary."

Her sister's name would be the last thing Amy would ever say. She died just before dawn.

Overwhelmed with soul-breaking sorrow, Stephen stumbled from the back of the wagon, nearly collapsing to the ground. He could not bring himself to tell the others. He didn't have to. Sam, John, William, and Bear, already awake and waiting nearby, knew as they listened to Jane's terrible wailing cries. They grabbed him to keep him from falling. Bear put an arm around his shoulders and nearly carried him to the cook fire. William poured him a cup of coffee. He shook his head, refusing it.

He stared into the fire and gave his mind up to the shock and horror.

&

His brothers did their best to console him and comfort Jane. But there was no solace, only pain—overwhelming heart-crushing sorrow. And nothing they could do would change that.

Losing two daughters in the same night was beyond brutal. It was misery incarnate. Here, in person, trying its best to conquer him. He sensed its presence, clawing, grabbing for him, wanting to take his soul to dark foul places. He didn't know how to fight back.

And misery found yet another tactic for torture. Watching Jane suffer. Hearing her weep broke his heart. He couldn't stand to see her consumed by sadness. He thought she might cry herself blind. Helpless, this was the one time he could not be her hero. He didn't know how to help her. He couldn't help her.

As the sun rose, so did his anger. He wanted to lash out at somebody, especially himself. "Edward was right. God is punishing me. I wasn't satisfied with what I had. Edward warned us this would happen. Why didn't I listen?" he yelled at his brothers. "Why didn't you make me listen?"

"You are not being punished," John said.

Unable to bear hearing Jane weep any longer, and afraid he would scare the other children with his anger and grief, Stephen took off on foot. But each step away from her only made him feel worse. He should be by her side, but he needed time to figure out how to help her. How to help them both.

He hurried toward the woods. He started to run. He wanted to be alone, completely alone, to flee from misery, before it possessed him completely. He ran as fast as he could, winding through the trees, his feelings taking control of him—his mental strength weakening by the moment. He wasn't used to losing control. But, overcome by the depth and strength of his grief, he did lose control, even of his body. He fell to his knees, unable to take another step.

His head threatened to explode. His stomach rolled inside him. He wanted to vomit but couldn't. He wanted to scream and did—from deep within—the scream of a heart ripping apart from grief. He clawed at the earth and then beat the ground repeatedly with his fists, sobbing uncontrollably for the first time in his adult life.

"I'm so sorry, so sorry, so sorry," he wailed repeatedly, his fists grabbing again at the ground. "This is my fault. What have I done? Amy forgive me. Mary forgive me," he pleaded, looking through tears at first one and then the other handful of dirt he held in each hand. "I gave you up for dirt in some faraway place. Was it that important?"

Never feeling more miserable or alone, he collapsed, lying on his side, giving in to grief and exhaustion. His fists still tightly held dirt in each hand, just enough to bury him in guilt.

"Forgive me, but I believe God wants me to speak to you," John said quietly, walking up behind him.

He stood at once. His fists clenched at his sides, his mouth contorted in a rage of fresh grief. "Leave me," he growled, pointing away. "Leave now!"

"I will not leave you."

"I don't want you here. Go! Go comfort Jane—she needs you more than I."

"Stephen, remember the story of Job. God may allow you to suffer, but he will never forsake you. But, neither can you forsake Him. The one thing you feared the most has happened. Their safety was the only hesitation you had in deciding to come. I know Edward's words haunt you now. But he was wrong. We cannot live in fear, securing ourselves from perils and avoiding the life we are destined to lead. Sam's right— danger is a part of life. The part that makes life real. You were destined to make this trip. That was God's will. We cannot question His wisdom. Your girls were gifts from Him but only for a short while. We will never know why. Only He knows how much time each of us has on this earth."

"Damn it, I shouldn't have brought them. They could have stayed with Edward until it was safe. Now it's too late, too late to keep them safe."

"The girls would have been miserable without you. We all decided this together, you, Jane, and the rest of us. Do not put it all on you. Even your broad shoulders need not carry the responsibility of all our decisions. We are all a part of this—and we will stand together, through whatever tribulations we must endure."

"I don't have the strength."

"You don't have to," John said, "just have the faith."

John wrapped an arm around his shoulders and gently turned him back toward their camp. He let the dirt in his hands slowly slip through his fingers.

"Faith," he whispered, as he began the long walk back to his wife and...two daughters.

CHAPTER 23

That afternoon, Jane slowly climbed into her wagon, dreading what she must do. John had offered, but she refused his help. They were her babies and she would take care of them.

She redressed Amy, and then carefully placed each child in soft cloth. She kissed their foreheads and studied each of their faces one last time before she forced her trembling hands to cover their heads with the shroud.

Her tears fell repeatedly on the fabric as she shakily wrapped them.

"I'm sorry. My kisses weren't enough," she whispered, her lips quivering, and her heart breaking into two halves—one for each of her departed daughters.

Bear dug a single tiny grave to hold both of them under a majestic old pine. He lined the bottom of the grave with pine needles, making a soft bed for them. When Bear finished, Stephen turned to find Jane.

"It's time," Stephen gently whispered to her.

He helped her climb out of the wagon. She seemed on the verge of collapsing, but he saw her force herself to straighten her back and steady her breath. She gripped his hands as though she were desperate for his strength. She would need his strength this day. He would have to have enough for both of them.

Bear carried Amy and William carried baby Mary. Behind them, John escorted Stephen and Jane, his long arms wrapped around each of them. Sam and the children followed slowly.

He stared at the empty grave as they approached. It waited eerily—for his daughters. Waited for them to fill it with two young lives—lives taken away from him forever. It was the worst thing he had ever set his eyes upon. He hated it.

Bear laid Amy in first and then William gently put Mary next to her.

John removed his hat, as did the other men. "Grief such as this has no cure, only a dulling brought on by time," John said. "Do not blame God. He does not cause innocents suffering and affliction. His enemy does. Because he wants to stop us from carrying out God's will. I pray that this experience will only strengthen our faith. For we know that through terrible times, God never leaves us. Though we may lose members of our family, we never lose Him. We believe it is His will for us to go to Kentucky. We will get there, no matter what obstacles fall in our way or what sadness we must overcome. These two angels are His now, no longer ours. He will care for them and protect them far better than we can. Stephen and Jane, you will be together again with your daughters in His Kingdom and in His time. Until that time, Lord bless them. Amen. Let us sing."

"Praise God, from whom all blessings flow;

Praise him, all creatures here below;

Praise him above, ye heavenly host; Praise Father, Son, and Holy Ghost."

Stephen couldn't sing. Neither could Jane. As the sorrowful group sang the old hymn, he watched as his wife slipped away.

&

As Bear and William began gathering nearby rocks, the surrounding forest stood eerily quiet, as though all creatures had indeed heard the old hymn.

Stephen could only watch.

Sam held the hands of his other two girls, who probably had only a vague understanding of what they just witnessed. "Mary and Amy are in heaven," Sam told the children. "All believers will go there. Some have to go sooner than expected."

"But I want to play with Amy," Polly said, her face reflecting the confusion of grief.

"We have to wait till we're together in heaven," Martha gently explained.

Tears slid down Martha's cheeks, despite how brave she was trying to be.

Sam leaned down on his cane and looked directly at her. "Your baby sisters loved you. They knew that you loved them too."

"But Uncle Sam, I didn't get to say it before they died," Martha cried. "And now I can never talk to them again. Never, ever, ever again."

Stephen stood nearby listening to the conversation. It broke his heart even further.

"Talk to them now honey," Sam said.

"But they won't hear me," she wailed.

"Those dear to us can always hear us, even from heaven. Your love for them makes that happen. Believe me, because I *know* it's true."

"Truly?" Martha whimpered. "They can hear us in heaven?"

"Only the ones we love. They'll hear you. Talk to them, we'll wait," Sam said.

Sam took Little John and Polly aside to give Martha time to say goodbye. He picked up Polly, and she rested her head on his shoulder.

"Children need to say their goodbyes too," Sam said.

As Stephen stood there, time seemed to pass in slow motion. His whole world felt like it was coming to a stop.

After a few long minutes, Little John went to Martha's side and put his arm around her shoulder. Slowly they turned, his arm still comforting her until they joined Sam.

"Let's go see if we can help your mother," Sam said. "She's going to need our help a lot for a while. Can you girls and you Little John do that?"

"Yes Sir," all three said in unison.

Stephen watched as Bear stood over the grave and stared down. Bear had cherished the girls like his own. Nearby, stood the stack of rocks they had gathered to cover the earth and a large stone he would use to mark the grave.

Bear had spent hours that day carving the name Wyllie into the stone along with the beautiful Celtic symbol of everlasting love, the Serch Bythol. The design consisted of knots and two trinities. Bear placed the trinities side by side, bonded by a circle showing eternal love, signifying two people joined in everlasting love for eternity. Both Stephen and Jane's ancestors were from Scotland and the embellishment brought him some measure of comfort. Stephen also believed that the two girls would be joined in God's everlasting love and that brought him the most comfort.

Silently, he said goodbye to his daughters for the last time. He swore Sam was right—it felt like they could still hear him.

He nodded for Bear to proceed.

"It would be my honor to do this," Bear said. "Ye do na have to."

"Yes, I most definitely have to," he choked out.

Bear picked up two spades, handing one to Stephen. He began to fill the grave with earth, forcing his hand to turn the first blade full of dirt into the grave. As the earth slipped slowly off the shovel, sharp grief dug a hole in his heart. By the time they had finished, he felt as if he had no heart.

He lovingly patted the soft dirt smooth before reaching for the first rock.

Big tears dampened the earth of the small grave.

CHAPTER 24

For several days, Jane could not speak to anyone of her sadness, as though speaking of it would make it happen all over again. When she did try to talk to someone, even with Stephen, no words would come, only tears. Her feelings were still too raw to voice.

Instead, she floated in daydreams of their farmhouse and the surrounding rolling hills and stunning mountains. They had been so happy there. Motherhood was joyous and warm, not something frozen by grief's bitter sadness. But that wonderful life and two adorable daughters were gone. Gone forever. Nothing would change that. No matter how hard she tried, she could feel nothing but helpless despair.

A week later Jane wrote, *I have never known such sorrow. I feel like my heart is bleeding within me. My two babies are gone—snatched from my arms by a murderous thief I could not defend them against. How can you fight something you cannot see?*

I had to leave them alone, behind me. I hate that thought. Almost as much as losing them.

At least they have each other.

I sat up with them that last night. I knew it would be my last chance to *be with them. The others didn't know I went back to their....*she could hardly make herself write the word...*grave, after we had all gone to bed. Bear must have seen me leave camp. He quietly stood guard over me all night, just a few yards away. He had carved their headstone with a beautiful symbol of everlasting love. I told my girls, there by their tiny resting place, how much I would miss them. I told them not to blame their father—that they were precious to him and they would always be so. I told them that nothing could ever separate them from our hearts and from our love.*

I will be forever grateful to Bear for his vigil, for giving me peace of mind while I spent that one last night with my daughters.

I can't talk to Stephen. I feel like I have lost him too. At first, I wanted him to hold me. He tried, and I pushed him away. Several times. Now, it's too late. He's stopped trying. It's just as well—I don't want to even speak to him, to learn how bitter I have become. I cannot believe what is happening to me. I am beginning to blame him, and that is making me hate myself.

I'm also frightened. I am afraid to have the baby I carry. I fear I will lose him too if we keep on with this difficult journey. We should never have left our happy home. If we hadn't, I'd still have all my babies and a home for our son. Now I have neither.

Stephen stayed away from all of them as much as possible. Normally laconic, the past week he had been even quieter, barely speaking at all. Sam had tried to reach out to him several times, but he wanted none of it. His mind remained tormented by guilt, and nothing Sam could say would change that. But it seemed his big brother would not give up easily.

Leading Alex, with a bright morning sun at his back, Sam strode up to him as he was saddling George.

"From what I recall of what Possum Clark said, we might encounter Cherokee up ahead," Sam said.

Stephen tightened the cinch, tugging it tighter when the stallion let out a breath. "Then I'll keep both eyes open and both pistols loaded," he said, more sharply than he intended. He buckled the strap. "How's the ankle?"

"Doesn't hurt, but I still can't put my full weight on it. It's almost there though. I'll manage."

They mounted their horses and settled into their saddles. "You need to pay more attention to Jane. She's hurting too. I know you are having a hard time, barely able to handle your own grief, let alone hers too, but you need to share your pain, so she can share hers with you. If you don't, there's a real chance she'll become even more melancholy, maybe never get over this."

"She's made it clear she wants to be left alone. She's strong. She'll be fine in time," Stephen said. He pushed his hat on firmly and rode on, staying well ahead of the others, listening to the rhythmic sound of George walking and the creaking of saddle leather. His groaning heart felt like leather too. He had to do something to reach her.

Stephen strolled with Martha beside him, glad he had agreed to the walk with her that evening. There is something important about walking with your child. It's the kind of simple thing you remember years later, when memories of bigger events fade.

They had decided to pick flowers for Jane to try to cheer her up. Martha knew her mother still suffered terribly and she thought the flowers might help.

He held Martha's small hand. It seemed so soft and fragile. He clearly remembered the first time he held the tiny hand of his first daughter—the fatherly pride that filled him and the sudden need to create a substantial future for her. A child has a way of making a man want to do something important with his life.

Their stroll triggered another memory. Sam Senior had made a special effort to take his youngest son out with him as he made his daily survey of their farm and the rugged hills surrounding it. For Stephen, this was always a special time with his father. Something only the two of them did together. His father never asked the older boys to come along. Perhaps because he understood how much more Stephen loved the land than the others did. Maybe his father had seen the passion Stephen felt for their homeplace as he rode bareback through their pasture. Or had the man seen the pure joy in his eyes when his father gave him his first colt? Or the awe on his face as together they watched a calf being born?

Together, they had watched the new calf find the tits of its mother, and his father had told him of the importance of land. He could still remember his words: "As is customary, your oldest brother Sam will inherit our family acreage. But you must find a place on this good earth to call your own. For each man, there is a special woman for him alone. And, I believe, there is also a piece of earth that is yours alone. You must find it. You may not find it here. Land is hard to come by and taxes get worse every year. But find it you must or you will never be the man you're supposed to be."

He never forgot. He could still almost feel his father's big strong farmer's hand and smell the good earth on him. And his father's words would be forever etched in his mind. He touched the pouch of soil inside his coat.

He studied Martha's hand. Would she be able to walk on her own land with her own child someday and hold the small hand of another generation? Could he keep her safe until then? He had to. He would do whatever it took to ensure that future for her. He promised himself he would let no harm come to her. Ever.

And he absolutely would succeed in this quest for land. The need for land was not his alone—it spanned three generations. For his father, for himself, for his children, he had to find their land.

He noticed Martha taking two steps for every one of his, so he slowed his pace. He couldn't believe he had come so close to losing her too to that devil Bomazeen. Ugly emotions rose quickly to the surface of his mind, like an over-filled pot about to boil over. He swallowed hard, struggling to regain control of his already volatile emotions.

"Some pretty ones are over there Father," Martha said, pointing to a cluster of wild yellow daisies.

"Yes, your mother would fancy those. Pick some, but watch for snakes."

She gently picked them, one by one, and carefully formed a large bouquet.

"It was sweet of you to think of doing this for your Mother," he said as they strolled back to camp. As guilt rose up in his chest, he lowered his head and eyes, sorry that he hadn't tried to do more for Jane himself.

He hadn't even been able to talk to her. Even looking at her was hard—the fiery sparkle of her green eyes extinguished. Whenever their eyes met, she looked back at him with the unfocused stare of those helpless against death's terrible power.

"She's still sad," Martha said.

"We all are."

"When will we stop being sad?"

"Some of us will feel better soon. Some will take longer."

"I think you will be longer," she said.

He knelt and hugged her, a tear slipping out of his eyes. Martha was right.

Stephen returned to the campsite irritated with himself because he hadn't tried to help Jane. "Stop sharpening that knife," he snapped at Sam. "It's sharp enough to slice through solid rock."

But just how to help her still eluded him. He remembered hearing the wagon squeaking that day. His fists tightened around the wheel's rim. "Let's get this noisy wheel fixed," he told John. Bear and William had gone off to hunt the evening's meal. "It makes a grinding noise that's probably annoying Jane. Right now I need to do all I can to ease her mind."

"Just needs some grease," John suggested.

As he reached into the supply box to get it, an arrow whizzed past John hitting the supply box lid, missing him by a finger's width. John crouched by the wheel and grabbed his rifle.

Another arrow sang through the air pinning Stephen's arm to the side of the wagon. He howled in pain and clenched his teeth. He tried to yank his arm away from the arrow. His flesh began to tear. His skin and the sturdy wool cloth of his jacket were pinned securely.

"Jane, get the children under cover. Indians!" Stephen yelled. Jane was on the other side of the wagon somewhere and he had to get to her soon, but the arrow had him trapped and exposed.

He turned in the direction the arrows had come from and spotted an Indian pulling back his bow.

"Cherokee," Sam yelled as he aimed his rifle.

The arrow slammed into the wheel, narrowly missing Stephen's leg.

Sam fired and the brave went down. "John, give me cover while I free Stephen." Sam jumped up and used his knife, slicing through the center of the arrow as if it was made of paper. Then Sam grabbed the arrow and yanked it out of the wood.

He gasped as his arm came free and fell to the ground, the arrowhead's shaft still embedded in his skin. The arrow had pierced the underside of his left arm below his bicep. Sweat pooled on his face as he fought against the burning sting splaying around the arm's muscles like the teeth of a trap.

A brave stood up from his cover in the trees.

John fired, but missed.

❧

Jane admired the bouquet Martha had given her just minutes ago. She inhaled the lovely sweet scent, savoring the fragrance. The flowers had softened the pain in her heart, as Martha had hoped. The bright yellow petals made her smile despite herself.

Then she heard Sam's warning and glanced up.

She first noticed the Indian's eyes—gleaming with the eager anticipation of a warrior about to make a kill. She could smell the wild scent of him—a scent raw and savage—more terrifying to her than the tomahawk coming for her head because…he smelled like Bomazeen. The scent paralyzed her.

Time froze.

She thought of seeing Mary and Amy again. She could almost see them both between herself and the Indian. She wanted to reach out, to run her finger along their soft cheeks. She wanted to hug them to her chest. Her breast ached for her baby.

She saw William fire his pistol into the brave's back, then he was rushing toward her, while Bear kept his rifle pointed at the dense timber.

The force of a bullet threw the brave forward. His head landed facedown at her feet. Blood oozed from the bullet's hole.

For some reason, the flowers were falling from her hand, scattering over the dead Indian's back.

She could do nothing more than stare at the petals, some of them now being covered by the brave's blood, turning the cheery yellow petals the color of death.

Jane suddenly realized what was happening. William grabbed her as terror struck.

❧

Stephen sighed a breath of relief as William carried Jane to the back of the wagon and nearly hurled her inside. He and Bear must have raced back to camp when they heard shots fired.

"How many more are there," William yelled. "I just killed one behind you. Bear and I have our backside covered."

"We've shot two on this side," Sam yelled back as he and John finished reloading. Then Sam grabbed the arrow in Stephen's arm, broke off the arrowhead, and yanked the remaining shaft through the other side of the arm.

Stephen clenched his teeth tightly at the pain. Another arrow whizzed by. This was no time to think about his wound. Ignoring the pain, he grabbed his rifle.

"There's at least one more," Sam hissed, turning his rifle towards the woods.

Stephen could not balance his rifle to aim because of his wound. He pulled his pistols instead but knew they would only be effective at close range.

"Stephen, the children are washing up at the creek," Jane yelled, desperation thick in her voice. "My God, I just sent Martha to join them." She jumped out of the wagon, about to dash toward the children.

Stephen lunged and grabbed her, jerking her back.

"No, let me go!" Jane shrieked, struggling to free herself from his tight grip.

"Stay with William," he yelled. "I'm going." Ignoring the intense throbbing in his arm, he ran in the direction of the children, his pistols still drawn. He fired one within seconds as a Cherokee, hidden behind a large cluster of boulders, jumped toward him.

Behind him, Stephen heard more shots, but he still ran toward the creek with all the strength he could find in his legs. He had to reach Martha, and the other children, before the Cherokee did. Only an hour before, while they walked, he had promised himself he would keep her safe. He would keep his promise, or die trying.

As he came over the rise, the children ran, with Martha in the lead, toward him. Crying and desperately clutching her old doll, Polly fell. Martha ran back for her and helped her along.

As soon as he reached the children, Stephen grabbed all three around him and tucked them behind him. He tried to reload his pistol, but blood dripped down his arm, covering the weapon's grip, making it slippery. As he struggled with the weapon, John and Bear ran up, pistols drawn. The two men took a protective stance around the children and Stephen, their weapons pointed toward the trees.

"Sam and William stayed with Jane," John said. "Are there any more of them?"

"I've only seen the one I shot. Tried to come up behind us," he answered, breathing hard. "Any more at the camp?" Stephen scanned the woods and creek for further signs of the attackers.

"Haven't heard any more shots," John said. He put his arm around Little John's shoulder and hauled his son behind his long legs.

"Maybe 'twas a huntin' party that stumbled on us," Bear said.

"Is Mama all right?" Martha whimpered.

"Aye, William saved her," Bear said.

Thank God, Stephen thought. He wanted to get back to her as soon as he could. He grabbed Martha's hand and picked up Polly with his uninjured arm. "Let's get moving, now!"

"If it was a hunting party, we're na far from more of them," Bear warned.

"Let's get out of here," Stephen barked.

❧

It was late into the night before they finally stopped. They picked a

DOROTHY WILEY

location for their camp that gave them some protection from the rear and good visibility from the front. As soon as they were settled, Stephen sat on Jane's trunk, and by the light of a small oil lamp, she cleaned the caked blood from his wound and applied hot whiskey, ointment, and bandages. But neither spoke to the other as she worked. As the silence lengthened between them, he grew more uncomfortable. It felt far worse than his wound.

He had to say something, to ease the mounting tension between them. But what? Clearly, Jane blamed him for their daughters' deaths. He couldn't change that. Nothing he could do or say could change that. But he had to try. "Jane, I love you. What's happened will never change that."

Her mouth opened as she started to speak, and his heart ached to hear what she had to say. Then, without saying a word, a glazed look of despair spread over her face.

His spark of hope quickly evaporated.

Perhaps it would be best to leave her alone and let her sort through her feelings. She would talk to him when she was ready. At least he hoped she would. Could he lose her too? Would she leave him? Return to New Hampshire? He would die inside if that happened.

The first few days after his girls passed, still in shock, he couldn't even talk—now he didn't want to talk, he admitted. He was afraid he would say the wrong thing and make everything worse. Besides, he had no idea what to say. He could not comfort himself, much less her. He remained wretched, despondent, and full of misgivings. He certainly did not want her to know how much he doubted himself. He didn't want anyone to know.

He slammed his pallet onto the ground, remembering his wound too late. At least the pain would distract him from his misery. Damn it, Edward had been right.

CHAPTER 25

The next evening, Stephen decided to try to talk to Jane again.

Her silence, while she had cleaned his wound, unnerved him. This had gone on long enough. She had kept busy all afternoon. He guessed she was trying to do her part because they all depended on her so much, but he could tell her heart wasn't in it. It's hard to care about anything when your heart is breaking. He guessed that it was only Martha, Polly, and Little John's need for her care that kept her going at all.

Now, she sat off by herself, well away from the others, writing by the light of a small oil lamp. But as he approached, she stopped writing. Her hands swiped at her tears with her apron.

His courage sank in his chest, like a rock thrown in a pond, ripples of fear left in its wake. Maybe he should just leave her alone.

What could he say anyway? No words could make this better.

He had never been a man of empty words. He would rather say nothing at all.

But he had to at least attempt to find the words to comfort her, to comfort them both. He stopped in front of Jane and she glanced up with eyes red and swollen.

He leaned his rifle against a tree and slowly squatted down beside her. He almost didn't recognize the woman before him. Tension lined her face and fear, stark and vivid, glittered in her eyes. Her chin quivered. It pained him to look at her. But if he was going to help her, he needed to take some of that hurt.

He braced himself and prayed for courage.

"What are you writing about?" he asked gently.

Jane just glared at him. She swallowed hard, as if she were trying to hold back her emotions. She looked like she would gag on them. Gag on all the words she had held back since their babies had left them. He saw all the dark turbulent feelings she had tried so hard to suppress, a poisonous brew, boiling just under the surface.

He wished she would just let those feelings out. The more she tried to suppress them, the darker they would become.

He had to reach her or he might lose her forever. "Tell me," he pleaded. "Please."

She glared at him. Her eyes filled with so much disdain he wanted to fall to his knees with sorrow.

Then a flood of bitter words pushed their way out between desperate sobs. "I just finished putting their death dates beside their names in our family Bible. Do you know what that took? How my hands shook from the sadness it caused me? Now, I'm writing about how my heart is bleeding from the pain. How I had to leave what was so precious to me back there in the dirt somewhere. I don't even know where it was exactly. Or if I can ever find it again."

The anger in her eyes burnt him like fire. "Jane." He pleaded her name, hoping it would bring back the woman he knew.

She stood and turned away from him and then turned back as more anger came. "You took us to this misery. Why did you put our girls in this danger? Are we going to lose Polly and Martha too before we realize

184

this was a horrible mistake? We almost lost them back there to those hostile Cherokees. God forbid, what if they'd taken them at the creek? Our children cannot even wash the dirt from their faces safely. We'll need to stand guard over them every minute from now on. We came too close to losing all our girls. And Little John. And the girls nearly lost their father. A few more inches and that arrow would have been through your heart. I would have lost you!"

He reached for her, but she pulled away.

"And all you can do is race further into this hell you've brought us to."

Her words sliced through his chest like a blade. He could have handled the agony of losing his girls eventually, but he could not handle this. Not this. "Jane, don't do this," he begged.

"I want out of this endless hell. Take me back," she cried.

"There's no turning back."

"Are you so proud, so stubborn, you won't admit this journey was horribly wrong?" she yelled.

"I don't want to hear this."

"For days you don't talk to me, you don't even look at me, and then you dare to tell me you don't want to hear what I feel? I *want* my babies back," she cried out with such fierceness he took a step away from her.

"Heaven has them now," he said simply.

"Damn you, I know that, but I still want them. I want them so badly I wish I could join them. If it weren't for Polly and Martha I would," she said between desperate sobs.

He couldn't believe what he had just heard. He tried reaching out to her again, but she wrenched away and turned her back to him.

Her palpable scorn filled the air between them like an oppressive fog.

"Stop this. You're not yourself. I accept the blame for their deaths, but that won't bring them back." He was the head of this family. He was ultimately responsible for the decision. He *had* to accept the blame. He exposed his family to peril.

Maybe he had downplayed the risks because he wanted so desperately to leave. Had he used her safety as an excuse to leave? Had he used Bomazeen's threat as a ticket out of there? But he believed this was what God wanted. Had his faith failed him too?

"You're land greedy. What you did was take us on a dangerous trip for the sake of some piece of dirt," she said, her voice growing cold. "You value the prospect of land more than your family. Is your ambition stronger than your love for us?"

He wanted to say something. But, mute with wretchedness, words did not come to his mouth, only a bitter bile.

He turned away from her, his soul breaking apart under the terrible weight of her pain and his guilt.

There was no way to fix this. He stared at the dirt beneath him, nearly swaying with anguish. Was she right? Had he allowed his hunger for land and wealth to become more important to him than his family?

Never! His family meant everything. A sense of strength filled him and his despair lessened. He turned back and faced her.

Without flinching, he boldly met her eyes. There was still a chance he could make her understand. He would not give up.

"No. My ambition is *not* stronger than my love." He shook his head decisively. "There is nothing on earth as strong as my love for you and the girls. Nor is there anything in this world I value more than you." He reached for her arms a third time, but this time she did not pull away. He looked directly into her eyes. "That's why I can't turn back. I'll not fail Martha and Polly, or you, by turning back. A better future is waiting for all of us. I believe that with all my heart, soul, and mind. Someday, you will too."

He studied her face. The tears were gone, but she would say nothing at all.

Stephen wrapped his arms around her and gave her a desperate hug. She tried to yank away, but he halted her escape and placed a kiss on the top of her head. Then he picked up his rifle and strode into the mounting wind.

CHAPTER 26

On this clear bright day, the kind that brings hope to the heart, Stephen could see the solitary wagon for a mile or more as it drew closer and closer to them on the Wilderness Trail. They didn't see any mounted riders, just the wagon pulled by a team of horses.

"Wonder who they are and why they're heading east," John asked.

"It's none of our business," Stephen said. He had little need or tolerance for strangers, unlike his brothers who were always anxious for news or companionship with their fellow man. "Be sure your weapons are loaded in case there's trouble." John often forgot to load his weapon.

"I'll ride ahead and talk to them," Sam said.

"Why?" Stephen asked.

"Because I can throw a knife quicker than you can shoot," Sam said with only half a smile. "Besides, if they're friendly folk you might scare them with that scowl on your face."

"There's no scowl on my face. That's just the way my maker made it," Stephen retorted.

"God must have been in a bad mood that day," William quipped.

All the men laughed, except Stephen. He hadn't been able to manage even a smile since the girls had died. And precious few words had passed between him and Jane for more than two weeks. He had tried talking to her and that had been disastrous. He wasn't going to put himself, or her, through that again. He hoped she would soon heal enough to at least talk to him. He missed her, desperately. He wanted his wife—the other half of himself—back.

"I'm going with you," Stephen told Sam.

A few minutes later, the two trotted their horses toward the wagon, pulling up short of it when they spotted the rifle pointed at them.

"Stop your horses right there or I'll shoot you out of your saddle," a woman yelled, her tone a menacing warning.

They stepped their mounts back some, not wanting to scare her. "Good day to you, Madam. No need to fear us. We're from New Hampshire traveling to Kentucky—the Wyllie family and Bear McKee. I am Sam Wyllie. Most just call me Captain Sam."

Stephen saw Sam taking in the astonishing sight of her as he spoke. Even at a distance, the woman was stunning. It didn't surprise him that Sam would take notice. Her high cheekbones and strong jaw made her look almost noble and reflected the inner strength he heard in her voice. She wore a stunning blue floral gown that seemed incongruous on a woman driving a wagon in the remote countryside. Her pale skin made her dark blue eyes all the more intense. The only concession she seemed to have made to practicality in her appearance was her hair. Woven into a long thick braid, her black hair hung down her back.

She lowered the rifle as Stephen and Sam approached cautiously. "Pleased to meet you, Sir," she told Sam when they reached her. She nodded politely towards Stephen.

"You're alone?" Sam asked.

"Yes. Highwaymen killed my husband yesterday morning. There were three of them. They ambushed us." She swallowed hard and took a steadying breath, obviously fighting tears. "We always knew it was possible that hostile Indians might attack us, although my husband was quite skilled with weapons and we brought trade goods to bargain for our safety. But I never even imagined white men might murder us. After they killed him, one of them tried to attack me. Then they stole my husband's horse and saddle and most of my valuables."

"How did you manage to stay alive through this appalling ordeal?" Stephen asked.

She extracted an impressive dagger from a sheath at her waist. "The one that touched me got a belly full of this. I presume the other two were cowardly, so they took off. Or maybe they couldn't stomach killing a woman."

Stephen got angry just listening to her story. Murdering, assaulting women, stealing, and horse thieving were not to be tolerated. "Don't worry Madam, you're among Christian men now," he said as he dismounted.

She climbed down reached out to shake Stephen's outstretched hand. She yanked off a sturdy glove and extended her hand to Sam after he too dismounted. "Captain," she said. "I'm Catherine Adams."

"How were you able to make it this far alone Mrs. Adams?" Stephen asked.

"I had no choice. We do what we must. Before we left Boston, I would never have dreamed I could survive a day in the wilderness alone, much less kill a man. But I've learned a good deal since then, everything from hitching up a wagon team to building a cook fire."

"Where are you headed?" Sam asked.

"I didn't want to go deeper into unknown country alone, so I turned the team around and headed east, hoping I'd encounter some respectable people like you before nightfall."

"You're not alone now. When you've rested and eaten, you can tell us all more about what happened. I'll help you unhitch this team," Sam offered.

"Pull your team closer to that creek down there," Stephen suggested. "We'll make camp here."

As she met the rest of their group, Catherine seemed especially delighted to meet Jane. And Jane took to her as if they were long-time friends.

"To be able to talk to another woman is a blessing," she said, as she worked the dough for dinner biscuits. "I haven't talked to another woman for weeks. I've been so lonely…especially after… my two youngest girls died last month." She fought back tears.

"I'm so sorry," Catherine said. "How horrific that must have been for you."

Silence hung uncomfortably between them. Finally, she was able to speak without crying. "God will help me through this valley. He'll lead me out of it."

"You seem to be a woman of exceptionally strong faith. I wish I could say the same for myself," Catherine said.

"Someone once said that without faith we are much like stained glass windows in the dark. Only with the light of the Son can our inner beauty shine through."

"That's so inspirational."

"Catherine, my sincere sympathies on the loss of your husband."

"I'll miss him. I still can't believe he's actually gone."

Catherine's voice seemed unnaturally calm and it didn't seem to Jane as though she were grieving as a wife normally would after losing her husband. Maybe that was because Catherine hadn't loved her husband.

"Death is so hard to accept," Jane said. "I keep thinking there must be something I can do to bring my daughters back. I just can't figure out what it is. It makes me feel guilty, even though I know there is nothing I can do, of course. It doesn't make any sense, I know, but it's how I feel nevertheless."

Martha ran up and gave her mother a hug. "She is so beautiful Mama," Martha said staring at Catherine. "May she braid my hair like that?"

"Of course she can, but tonight she's much too tired. The poor darling needs some rest and some peace and quiet. Now go tell the others our meal is nearly ready and they need to wash up."

Along with hot biscuits, the group enjoyed a dinner of roasted rabbits and the last of the sweet potatoes Jane had brought. As they finished, she smiled, pleased that every member of their group tried to make Catherine feel welcome. Even Stephen made her feel at ease, although he didn't say much.

"You could make a decent cowman if you knew how to throw a rope," Sam said, as he observed William practicing his throw after they'd eaten. The loop missed his practice target and fell limply to the ground.

"I can throw a rope just fine. Getting it around the neck is my problem," William said. He gathered the rope up in loops.

"That's because all you've ever practiced catching is women, and most of them weren't running too hard," Sam chided.

"I'm about to get some practice catching the male species. At first light, I'm going after those two bastards that murdered Mrs. Adams' husband. Where do you suppose the closest jail and judge would be? Cat Springs?" William asked.

The only one that seemed surprised by William's announcement was Catherine. "You can't just go after those murderers. They might kill you too. I don't want you to risk that. Please don't go," she pleaded.

"My honor requires it, Mrs. Adams. I may not hold an official title now, but I'm still a lawman and it's my duty to uphold the law. I'm morally obligated to go after them. My brothers will agree."

Catherine looked around. "Will none of you stop him from risking his life?"

"He's right," Stephen said. "They need to be found or they might attack us further down the trail. They killed your husband in cold blood and they will do it again. Better for us to go after them, than risk their ambush later." He turned to William. I'm going with you."

Jane's heart sank, but Stephen was right. The killers needed to be found.

"They have almost two days lead on you. You don't know where they've gone," Catherine argued.

"William is an excellent tracker. So is Stephen," Sam said. "Stephen grew up tracking in the mountains and hills. Once they find the campsite where you were attacked, they'll know where the killers are headed."

"I'll go too," Bear volunteered.

"No," Stephen said. "I want you here to help protect my family."

"I wish you and William would reconsider," Catherine said.

"Wyllies don't let murderers and thieves get away with their crimes," Jane said.

"You'll be well protected. Sam, Bear, and John will stay with you and the children," Stephen told Jane. "It won't take us long to find the killers."

She did not say a single word to him. Nor did she that night.

But she thought about him. About what had happened to her family. She missed her girls. She yearned for a baby to hold and care for. She missed the way Amy would tug at her apron, wanting to be held. She wanted their happy home back.

And, she missed loving her husband. She missed the feel of his strong arms around her. She missed their conversations. She longed to be back in his arms again.

She missed their life.

Could she forgive him?

❧

The next morning, they all agreed to meet at Cat Springs, about one week west of their current location. The night before, Catherine had written down a detailed description of the two men and their horses. She also gave them the approximate location of the attack, and a list of their stolen belongings, including a description of her husband's horse. William read the list over and put it in his waistcoat pocket.

The two left as the sun came up behind them, the strong new rays falling across their backs.

Jane said a silent prayer to the sound of the horses' hooves as they galloped away. She didn't want either one of them hurt. Stephen sat his stallion straight and rigid, his shoulders broad, ready to take on the burden of hunting down the killers. She realized she had put a terrible weight on those shoulders.

"How can you just calmly watch them ride off after murderers?" Catherine asked.

"I'm not calm." In fact, her stomach was tightening with apprehension. But, Stephen and William were in God's hands, on the side of righteousness, and they're Wyllies. She told herself not to fret. As much to convince herself as Catherine, she said, "But I will not worry. Those murdering thieves better start worrying though."

❧

"Why haven't you told him?" Catherine asked after she learned Jane was with child, the reason for her fussy stomach.

"Our two girls died less than a month ago. We're both still grieving. We're having a difficult time coping with their loss. I wanted the pain to ease before I said anything about this son."

"How do you know it's a son?"

Jane caressed her tummy. "I just do. For some reason, I know this child more than the others I've carried. I'm not sure why yet, but I know he'll do something important with his life."

Catherine blinked away tears. "I lost our first baby last year in Boston. That's one reason I wanted to leave on this trip, to get away from that memory. I don't know if I'll ever be able to have another. The doctor wasn't sure."

"I'm so sorry Catherine. You will be blessed with another child if you are intended to have more."

"First, He will have to bless me with another husband when I return to Boston. But this time I'll marry for love, not for my father. Since I was fifteen, Mr. Adams was the man my father thought I should marry. When the time came, I wasn't given a choice. Everyone, including me, took it for granted that I would marry him. He was a nice enough man, with a lot of ambition—that's why we were on our way to Kentucky. He wanted lots of land for a timber business. But something was always missing from our marriage. I guess it was love. I'll not marry again until I'm sure I'm loved."

"Why do you want to return to Boston?"

"What choice do I have? That's where my family is. I hope to meet up with a respectable family like yours traveling north that will let me travel with them to a city on the east coast. I can take a coach home from there to Boston."

"You have another choice. You can come with us. You're welcome to join our family."

"That's generous of you. But I won't be a burden to anyone and I have no one in Kentucky," Catherine protested.

"You won't be a burden and you'll have us. I could use the help and company of another woman. Keeping up with all these men and children by myself is beyond a challenge. Please stay with us, Catherine. I'd be deeply disappointed if you left."

"How do you know we can be friends? How can you trust a woman you barely know with your children?" Catherine asked with a glance at the playing children.

"Just as I know my unborn son. I do," Jane said.

"I would be honored to be your friend."

"Maybe I need you. I never conceived of the extreme difficulties and dangers we would face. It's beyond anything I could have imagined. You've found that out too. We've both lost loved ones. Had I known what it would be like, I would have stayed in my home. It was small but comfortable." Remembering their cozy home, she barely kept her anger in check.

"I know you're still angry. That bitter anger spawned by the death of a child was part of the problem between me and my late husband."

"Stephen should never have taken us on this journey," Jane continued. "Maybe I should have refused to go. But I didn't have the heart to void his dream. And he seemed unstoppable, as he is now. I begged him to turn around. But he won't turn back. For Martha and Polly's sake, I'll make the best of it. Please stay, Catherine. I admit I need you."

Catherine refilled her coffee cup, waiting a moment before responding. "I'll stay temporarily, until William and Stephen come back. I feel responsible that they've left you and I have to be certain they'll return safely. But before I make a final decision, I want to talk to the others first."

"Agreed. And they will return safely." She prayed she was right and remembered Stephens's words. *Nothing on earth is as strong as my love.*

CHAPTER 27

It was the first time Stephen had joined William in a pursuit of lawbreakers. He'd heard stories of his brother's uncanny instincts for tracking down criminals. Funny, William couldn't seem to track a deer or any other animal without his or Sam's help, but his brother had a sixth sense for the criminal mind.

It took until noon to get to the site of Adams' murder, a lonely stretch on the road leading to Lancaster, between the villages of Coatesville and Gap. They studied the area for some time. Fortunately, it hadn't rained since the murder and they found several valuable clues. Catherine had buried her husband, but not the man she killed.

"It must have been hard on her to dig a grave and bury a husband alone," William said.

They gazed at the lonely plot of rock-covered earth. There must have been a couple hundred rocks on the grave.

"You're right, but she strikes me as the kind of woman who could manage," Stephen said. "She certainly tried her best to give him a decent burial. This must have taken her hours."

Wolves had left little of the other man but his boots, bits of clothing, and his gun. "His initials are carved on the butt," William said. "D R T. If he's related to the other two, and that's a definite possibility, their surname name would start with a T."

"Unless he stole the gun from somebody else," Stephen suggested.

"That's a possibility, but I don't think so. The same initials are carved on this knife." William put both in his saddlebag and mounted his horse. "We're done here."

"They won't be hard to track," Stephen said.

"No, the hoof prints of four horses lead away from here—the horses of the two we're after, Adams' steed, and the dead robber's mount. And these guys are lazy. They make their living robbing decent folks—too lazy for anything difficult, like climbing these hills through the timber to make them hard to follow. My bet is they'll just follow the road to their next victim or town."

"Hope it's not more victims," Stephen said.

They rode on through desolate country. Concentrating on following the killers' clear trail, William barely spoke a word. That suited Stephen who was lost in thoughts of Jane. The landscape also fitted his mood perfectly. Empty and lonely.

He missed her love. Could he ever get it back?

They followed the tracks until dusk when they made camp near a natural spring. After a cold dinner of jerky and day-old biscuits, they stretched out to sleep.

"Thanks for coming along," William said into the darkness.

"No thanks necessary."

"Just the same, I'm glad you're here."

Stephen waited a moment before replying. "I'm not sure I'm glad we're here."

"What do you mean?" William asked.

"I don't mean chasing these murderers. That had to be done. I'm talking about this journey."

"West is where your dreams are, where our futures are, all of ours— even Jane's, although she may have forgotten that in her grief."

"Do you think she'll ever forgive me?"

The question hung in the darkness between them for several moments before William answered. "There's nothing to forgive, so no. Dreams always require sacrifices. The important thing is to not let those sacrifices be for nothing."

"By God, I won't let them be." He rolled over on his pallet and tugged his blanket over his back, signaling the end of their conversation.

Out of his grief came a new resolve to find what he had come for— his land and their future.

At dawn, both men climbed into the saddle, eager to follow the path of their prey once again.

"This is like tracking a herd of cows," William said after they had gotten underway. "They're not hard to follow."

Stephen resented the analogy. "These bastards are more like skunks than cows. Mr. Adams was following a dream of going west, just as we are. These whoresons turned it into a nightmare. Left his wife a widow, robbed her of her possessions."

By late afternoon, the road forked at the western end of the valley they had just crossed. William dismounted and dropped the reins. Trained to stand still when the reins were on the ground, the gelding took the opportunity to munch a few blades of grass, snorting loudly between bites. William hiked a short distance up the road and back again, studying the ground, while he did the same in the opposite direction.

"They went north," William finally said.

"Then we head north."

The little-used north trail rapidly became a steep uphill climb. The horses tired as they climbed rock covered inclines.

"Let's give our mounts a rest at the next stream," William said.

"Give them a rest or you?"

"Got to keep up with my beauty rest. It's a habit you should cultivate, judging from that face of yours."

"It was good enough for Father, and it's good enough for me."

"You do resemble him remarkably. I guess that's why we all let you lead us around. We think you're going to give us a whomping like he did with that damn razor strap. All he'd have to do is look at that strap to make me straighten up."

George stepped over a large rock. "If he was speaking to you now, he'd tell you it's high time for you to give up your bachelor ways, settle down, get married, and get to work on your own farm. And he probably would give you a good whomping."

"I'll settle down when the time is right and not before. I have no desire to farm. I want to study the law and use it to help people. Without the rule of law, our hard-won freedoms cannot be assured. Those who infringe on a man's freedom and rights should pay a price. That's what I believe and that's what I intend to do with my life. A place like Kentucky will need sheriffs and lawyers."

"What about a wife? You seem fond enough of women. You should have found a suitable one by now."

"That's just it. I haven't found one I'm not fond of." William chuckled. "They're all appealing in various ways. Narrowing it down to just one is impossible."

"You better start soon. You won't be that handsome forever. A few white hairs are sticking out by those big ears of yours."

William rubbed the hair by his ear. "White?"

200

"Indeed."

Seeing the amusement in Stephen's eyes, William chuckled, but his eyes still looked worried.

They stopped by a stream flowing down from the foothills. Crystal clear water flowed and gurgled over colorful rocks and boulders, formed and polished over centuries with the infinite patience of nature. After taking a drink, he studied the desolate hills around them, studded heavily with thick spruce and cedars. "Keep a watch for bears and mountain cats. They hunt in the higher hills like these," Stephen said.

"Thanks for the tip," William said.

"Look," Stephen said, pointing to a whisper of smoke escaping through the treetops. "Must be a homestead up there."

Both men mounted their horses and headed toward the cabin.

"Don't assume they're friendly," William said.

"The only thing I'm assuming is that they're not."

They rode a short way up the path and then tied their horses to a tree. Both grabbed their rifles and checked the powder in their pistols. Slowly and quietly, they made their way on foot up the rest of the hill. Hiding behind a large pine, they studied the little rustic dugout for several minutes.

The backside of the cabin rested snugly against the side of a rock covered hill, providing natural insulation against winter winds and snows from the north. A dilapidated porch covered a large front door. Rough logs, cut into five-foot sections, formed the three walls. The only sounds they heard were a squirrel jumping from tree limb to tree limb behind them and chickens foraging a short distance from the house.

"That pen is holding four horses and a mule. That's a lot of horse flesh for a place like this," Stephen said.

William nodded in agreement. "That big sorrel with the white stocking on the right rear foot matches the description of Mr. Adams' steed. And the other three are the colors of the three killers' horses she described. We've found them."

"That sorrel's a fine-looking animal. Probably what they killed Adams for."

"I've heard that in the wilderness, horses are more valuable than humans. My guess would be they plan to take it to a fort or settlement for trade," William said. "It's too quiet in there. What do you suppose they're up to?"

A scream of terror and agony pierced the silence.

He glanced at William for a split second before they both took off running towards the small cabin.

"Stay quiet. We'll have the advantage of surprise," William told him.

William stepped quietly onto the porch, both pistols drawn and motioned for Stephen to stand on the other side of the door.

The woman screamed again, sounding terror-stricken.

William burst through the crude front door, pistols drawn.

Stephen stepped into the room and caught sight of a young woman, bound to the bed, and her two attackers, one of them struggling to penetrate her, the other fondling her breasts. She appeared to be little more than a girl.

In that split second, the repressed anger of his girls' deaths flooded through his mind. The raw and bleeding skin on the girl's ankles and wrists enraged him. The sight of those two animals ravaging her slight body made rage explode from his every pore.

William locked his pistol's sights on the man on top of the woman, but didn't shoot. If his brother fired, he might hit her.

With eyes looking through a father's rage, he understood what he had to do. He couldn't help his daughters now, but he could help this young woman. He cocked his weapon. As the one fondling her small breasts stood up in surprise, Stephen shot him squarely in the chest.

The other man jumped up, his eyes narrowed, his face contorted in fury, and lunged through the powder's smoke toward him.

Stephen turned his pistol around and used the butt to club the man's jaw. Then he kicked the rapist in the stomach with his boot. The vicious blow threw the man to the floor face down.

"Help me. Help me. Help me," the woman sobbed.

The woman's pathetic plea momentarily distracted him, but he spun around when William fired his pistol. The attacker dropped to the floor, shot through the heart.

"He went for his knife," William said, as he nudged the man with his boot. He won't do it again."

Stephen heard wretched sobbing behind him. The woman's pitiful cries triggered the need to protect and tugged at his heart. If William hadn't just killed the bastard, he would have beaten the man to death himself.

CHAPTER 28

I t all happened in a blur of seconds. It took more time for them to find a blanket, cover the young woman, and cut the bindings at her wrists and ankles than it did to kill her assailants.

When the last of her bonds fell away, she grabbed her knees and curled up in a ball of anguish, sobbing desperately. Blood from the bullet wound of one of the attacker's splattered her bruised and tear-stained face.

Stephen and William looked at each other not sure what to do first.

Stephen motioned toward the dead men. "Let's get them out of here and then I'll fetch some water so she can wash up."

They each grabbed one and drug the two men out the cabin door, their bodies leaving a path of blood, crooked and smeared, just like the lives they'd led.

William shoved the man Stephen shot off the dusty porch and went back to help the young woman.

Stephen threw the other body face down in the dirt Then he marched on to retrieve their horses. He mounted George and lugged William's horse behind him as he rode quickly back up to the cabin. He tied the men's feet with his rope and used George to drag the bodies into the woods. The last thing that poor girl needed was to see these two again. He decided he'd better search their pockets in case they had any of Mrs. Adams' valuables on them. The first man had nothing, but he found Mr. Adams' watch in the other's pocket. He searched further and found a pouch of money. He secured both in his waistcoat pocket.

After untying the rope and remounting, he peered down at the bodies and noticed unbuttoned pants hung around the legs of one of them. His eyes hardened. "Go to hell," he swore.

Stephen got water from the cistern and brought the bucket to the cabin door. He gave the bucket to William who gave a dipperful to the young woman. She drank greedily, clutching the blanket against her breast. Her crying slowed somewhat and she laid back down on the cot.

"How is she?" Stephen asked softly.

"Still in shock, I think," William whispered. "I found what looked like a rag and wiped the blood from the floor as best I could and then threw the rag in the hearth, along with the scraps of rope that the bastards used to tie her."

She still sobbed softly and it tore at Stephen's heart. He'd kill them again if he could.

Very slowly, William stooped down on the floor several feet from the bed, his hat in his hand. He said gently, "My name's William Wyllie and this other ugly fellow is my youngest brother Stephen. I guess you could say I'm a lawman of sorts because I was the sheriff in the town where we lived before. We were hunting those two snakes for murdering a man named Adams not too far from here. They also robbed Mrs. Adams. But, thankfully, she killed one of them with her dagger before they could harm her. There were three of them. After she killed one, the other two fled with Mr. Adams' horse and we tracked them here. Now they're dead. I know you're frightened and you don't know us, but I swear to you on that Bible there on the table that you are safe now."

"We won't let any more harm come to you. Just lie down and rest now. It's over. They can't hurt you anymore," Stephen said.

"I gathered up your clothes. Some were torn but some seemed to be still in one piece and I laid them all there at the end of your cot," William explained.

Stephen scanned the sparsely furnished cabin for some clean clothes for her. Several pelts were stretched on racks. Not finding much he decided they'd better just leave her alone. She needed privacy anyway. He motioned for William to go outside with him.

As they neared the front door, William glanced over his shoulder at the young woman. "Rest awhile now. Stephen and I will make you something to eat. Are you hungry?"

She fisted the blanket below her chin, but she didn't respond.

Stephen wished he could comfort and reassure her but, as with Jane, he found himself at a loss for words. What can you say to a woman whose innocence had just been stolen forever? How could a man comfort a woman who just experienced the greed of an evil man's lust, void of any love or warmth.

After William shut the front door quietly behind them, he said, "I forgot to ask her name. She probably wouldn't say anything just yet anyway, but I bet it's a pretty name."

"She's scared out of her mind. It'll take her some time."

"What kind of men would do such a thing?" William asked.

"The kind that go to hell. They're being welcomed there right now."

"How old do you suppose she is?"

"Somewhere between fifteen and seventeen. Pretty thing. Wonder where her folks are? She can't be living out here in the middle of nowhere alone. At least I hope she isn't." Stephen began working on a cook fire for coffee.

"Look at those saddle packs on the porch. I bet they contain Catherine's stolen goods." William marched up to the porch and opened them. "The silver teapot is in here. I'm sure the rest of it belongs to Catherine too."

"I found her husband's gold watch on one of them. Also found a pouch of money. Haven't counted it yet. I'm not burying those two skunks. I dumped them off in the woods over that hill. They can be the local coyotes' dinner for all I care."

"Probably give the coyotes a bellyache," William said.

❦

As soon as they had hot coffee made, Stephen warmed the corn cakes that Jane had sent.

William knocked softly and then slowly opened the creaky cabin door. His brother stuck his head in and said, "Miss, the food's ready if you're up to eating some. We set up a stool for you by the cook fire if you'd care to join us. I promise you'll be safe." He moved off the porch, leaving the door open, and rejoined Stephen at the cook fire.

Slowly, like a wide-eyed scared animal, she peeked around the door, then gradually emerged, still hugging her blanket tightly around her.

Timidly, she regarded Stephen. "Thank you," she finally said, barely above a whisper.

He didn't know if she was thanking him for killing her rapists or thanking him for the food. He studied her eyes and they told him it was the former.

"I'm glad you're up and about. We were worried about you. You'll feel even better after you get some food and coffee," William assured her, using a soothing tone. "Here's a stool we found on the porch. Hope it will be comfortable enough." William had covered it with a blanket to soften it.

Stephen had never seen this gentle side of William. Normally his brother was insensitive and boisterous, more interested in making people laugh than attending to their needs. He seemed intent on talking to the young lady to help her mind return from her near paralyzing shock.

"Stephen's the youngest of my four brothers," William said. "But he's probably the smartest. Definitely the most adventurous—that's why our family is headed to Kentucky. He looks mean, but he's not actually. He's got a beautiful wife named Jane and...," William caught himself before he said four, "...two daughters."

It was the first time Stephen had heard them called two daughters. He swallowed the aching lump in his throat. When reality finally hits, it often comes, as it did now, with a cold vicious slap. The blow stung. What he wanted to do was take off for the woods and scream, not make polite conversation with this young woman. He decided, however, to try to focus on this young lady's problems, instead of his own.

She moved slowly toward the stool. She eyeballed both of them, seeming to study them.

"What's your name?" William asked, breaking the awkward silence.

Doubt filled her face as she decided whether to trust them with even her name. She hesitated, blinking, then stared up at William with violet-blue eyes. "Kelly. Kelly McGuffin."

Kelly had long golden hair, the color of fresh butter that reached an inch or two past her waist. Her big eyes looked like they'd be striking if they weren't so swollen and red from crying. Stephen thought she'd have a lovely smile too but knew it would be a while before they would have a chance to see it.

"Miss McGuffin, I'm sure you'd like a bite to eat and a cup of hot coffee. My wife Jane made these corn cakes. They're tasty. Sit down and we'll bring you some," he said, motioning again to the stool.

She sat down and winced, then stared at the ground.

Stephen felt his temper rise in response. He looked over at William, whose lips thinned with his effort to suppress his anger.

"After you've had something to eat, we'll give you some ointment for those wrists and ankles. They must sting," William said. "In addition to baking, Jane has a way with making healing ointments. She made us carry some along. And you'll probably need some warm water to wash with. We'll heat some water on this fire after we've eaten."

With that, her eyes seemed to light up a bit and it warmed his heart. He was pleased with the kindness his brother was showing Kelly.

"Stephen, have you taken a look at that sorrel of Mr. Adams yet?" William asked.

"Only from here. He sure is a handsome animal. After a while, I'll go check over all the horses."

"They told me they'd give me that steed in payment if I let them stay with me awhile. I was afraid to say no. I didn't know they would...would do that to me," she whimpered and began wringing her hands.

Stephen and William exchanged glances, plainly disgusted.

"If they told you that then the animal should be yours. I'm sure Mrs. Adams, the owner, won't mind since we've recovered her other valuables and killed the men that murdered her husband. But if she does, then I'll buy the horse for you myself, if she'll sell it," William offered.

Kelly sniffed, raised her chin, and managed a slight smile. "You would do that for me Mr. Wyllie?"

William nodded and smiled. "Please call me William. Best you eat now."

Kelly wolfed down the corn cake, staring at her feet as she chewed. "They didn't let me eat for the last day or so," she said finally. "They wanted what little food I had for themselves."

Judging from how thin she was, she hadn't eaten much before that either, Stephen noted.

"I'm so ashamed of what they did to me." She lowered her head. Tears slipped down her checks. "I don't know what I'll do now. Am I ruined?"

"There's no reason at all for you to feel shame. Those two skunks are the ones who should bear the shame, but they're far past that now," William said.

"The sin was all theirs," Stephen added.

He could see she wanted to believe him. "Miss, where is your family? Are your folks around here?" he asked.

"My Ma died when I was fourteen. She's buried over there," she said, pointing to a nearby gravestone on this side of the adjacent hill. "My Pa is off somewhere selling his pelts. He's a trapper. Traps in the Hopewell Forest north of here in the mountains. I fend for myself."

"When do you expect him to return?" Stephen asked.

"Don't know. Been gone for more than two weeks. He always comes back. But I never know how long he'll be gone—most times it's several weeks. Sometimes he sells his furs in Harrisburg. At times, I wish he'd just stay away. When he does come back, he stays drunk till his whiskey runs out. He broke this finger last winter." She held it up for them to view the crooked knuckle. "He didn't mean to. He was just too drunk to know what he was doing. He wasn't like that before Ma died. I guess he's still grieving. It's been four years though."

Her father sounded like a real scoundrel. He thought about his own girls and could never imagine treating them so cruelly. He would never harm them. He'd rather die.

"I haven't properly thanked you both for saving me. I am grateful. They were evil vile men. My Ma told me about men like them. I think they had done this before. The one called Grover told his brother to do it like they did the last time." She hung her head. "That's when they tied me up. It hurt so much. The first one took me and then told his brother it was his turn. The second one just started when you came in and saved me."

210

She kneaded her hands in her lap, as though she were trying to reassure herself that her hands were still free of the ropes.

He glowered at William, snarled a profanity under his breath, and then threw the rest of his supper and his plate to the ground.

Accustomed to Stephen's methods of communication, William tried to explain. "My brother's got a notable temper and what those men did to you made him, makes both of us, angry and sick to our stomachs. When he saw those men attacking you, I think he thought about his own daughters. He wanted to keep you from suffering, just like he would have if you had been his own daughter."

"They did hurt me. I'm glad they're dead," Kelly said, anger in her voice for the first time.

"You have a right to be angry. They deserved to die, for what they did to Mr. Adams, and to you. I'm just sorry you had to witness them getting killed," William said.

"I'm glad I saw it. I never want to forget it."

"You need to rest now. Why don't I get that water warmed up?" William offered.

"It will be dark soon, where will you sleep?" she asked while nibbling nervously on her bottom lip.

"Don't fret about us. We're used to sleeping under the stars. We'll put our bedrolls beside the fire, if that's all right with you," William replied.

Kelly's eyes softened, almost seemed to brighten as she gazed at William.

Then she glanced at Stephen. "Thank you again for saving my life. Your daughters are lucky to have you for a father."

Those simple words gave him a warm feeling he would remember for a long time.

Outside, William cleaned his weapons beside the small fire. He was religious about it.

Stephen brushed George, paying as much attention to the stallion as William did to weapon cleaning and Sam to knife sharpening. The horse's black coat reflected the light from the cook fire like a full moon glistening on a lake at midnight. Both men worked in silence, brooding over the day's sad events.

Finally, William said, "I don't believe we will ever shoot men who deserve to die more."

"I just wish we had found them before they found her," he said, putting the brush down. He poured the last of the coffee. What those men did to Kelly left a bitter taste in his mouth.

"They were scoundrels of the worst kind. They robbed Kelly of her innocence, and nothing I can do or say will bring that back. At least the whoresons won't hurt anyone else. But it's too bad they couldn't have been tried for all their crimes. Given what Kelly overheard, this wasn't the first time they raped a woman," William said.

"They got what they deserved."

"What are we going to do with her?" William asked.

"What do you mean? Do what with her?"

"We can't just leave her here, waiting for her drunken father to come back. What if that skunk got her with child? Her father might think she asked for it and beat her, or worse, kill her," William said.

"You don't know that. I don't like it either but we have to leave her here just like we found her. We can't take her from her father."

"If her mother died when she was fourteen, and she said that was four years ago, she's eighteen—old enough to leave if she chooses. I'll never leave that poor girl alone out here in the wilderness."

"I know your intentions are honorable, but it wouldn't be proper for her to come with us."

"Neither is getting raped."

He was getting tired of William pushing him. "I'm not her father. I have my own daughters, and damn it, I'm having a hard enough time taking care of them. She has a father. This is her home. She won't want to leave."

"You heard what she said. Next time the brut might break more than a finger. He can't be much of a father if he treats her like that."

Stephen had to agree with that. He thought about his own daughters and softened a bit. "All right, we'll talk to her in the morning and see what she says. I'm betting she'll want to stay with her own kin. But if she wants, we'll take her to the next town."

"Sometimes a person must leave to find their own life. Maybe we were sent here to lead her to it."

CHAPTER 29

With the sunrise, a Spring cold front blew in with bluster and it began to rain steadily. Kelly asked the two to come inside as soon as it started. "The coffee is already made if you'd like some."

Stephen marveled at the difference in her appearance. She appeared much brighter and more alert than the day they found her. She wore a fresh, although quite worn, smock and her long hair hung smoothly across her back.

As she reached across the table to pour coffee for William, Stephen noticed the terrible raw rope burns on her wrists, but he also studied her face. Except for Jane, he couldn't remember ever seeing a lovelier young lady, even though her eyes were still puffy from crying. She wasn't a classic beauty, but her features had a pleasing charm. She was much too thin, her ragged clothing hanging on her like a grain sack. If she had eaten one meal a day, he'd be surprised. There was little on the shelves in the way of supplies, only a small pile of crudely chopped wood for the fire and no other comforts that he could see. How could her father neglect her like this?

"Kelly, my brother and I were wondering what you would like to do now," William said.

"What do you mean?" she asked. She blew on her coffee to cool it.

"We won't leave you in this situation, alone and awaiting the return of your brutish father. Those men we killed are not the only ruffians and ill-bred men out there. I don't know how your father could leave you out here. It's indecent and outlandish. Not to mention, there's always the threat of Indians," William said.

"My father bribes the Indians with tobacco so they leave us alone. As far as other men, I guess he never thought men would attack a young girl," she said, looking down at her feet.

Did she still think of herself as a girl? Stephen wondered. "You're not a girl. You're a comely young lady and you need protection," he said adamantly.

"I can't leave. I have no finances and no place to go. This is my home, even if it's not much," Kelly said.

"You have some money now," Stephen said. He reached into his pocket and laid the sack on her little table. "That was on one of them, and it's not Mrs. Adams'. She didn't have any money stolen, so you're entitled to it as compensation for the harm you've suffered. Haven't counted it yet. Don't know how much is there, but it feels like a considerable amount."

Kelly stared at the pouch in astonishment. He realized she had probably never had a coin of her own in her life.

"And you can earn more money," William said. "I'm guessing you can read, judging from the Bible and the books by your bed. You could work for a newspaper or at a schoolhouse, or as a nanny. You can come with us till Cat Springs, or all the way to Kentucky if you want to."

At that, Stephen gave William a stern sideways look. This was not what they had agreed upon. He had never said that she could go with them all the way to Kentucky. What was William thinking? Kelly was a sweet young lady, but he had no intention of taking on another person to care for.

"Mr. Wyllie, what do you think I should do?" Kelly asked.

The rain grew heavier and began to drip steadily through the roof in several places. Kelly quickly responded, as though she had done the same thing many times before, placing a bucket or bowl beneath each leak.

Stephen cleared his throat and opened his mouth to speak but stopped when thunder growled above them. He glanced at William and then at Kelly and then back at William.

"What William says is true," he finally said to her. "You aren't safe here. Do you think your father will come looking for you if you leave?"

"Depends. He probably won't care while he's drunk. When he sobers, he might get mad if I'm not here to wash his clothes and make his meals. I just don't know."

"Can your father read?" he asked.

"Oh yes. He and my Ma were both well-educated in Virginia. He got in some sort of trouble and moved here."

"What kind of trouble?" William asked.

"I don't know. Ma would never tell me. She just said 'the past is past'."

"I suggest you write a note to leave here for him. You could tell him about the men who attacked you. Tell him we killed your attackers, but could not wait around for his return and we could not leave you here alone. Let him know you have gone with us for your protection and that you will write him more when you have a chance to send a letter," Stephen said.

"Sounds like a good plan," William responded, sounding relieved. "Do you have indigo and quill and some parchment?"

"Not much, but enough to write a short note," she said. "But…." She lowered her head.

Stephen could understand her mixed emotions. He could tell she wasn't sure she should abandon her home or her father. Even though he treated her poorly, he was still her father.

Kelly looked up at William, then said, "I have to admit, I had thought about the idea of my own life and leaving this place…I just didn't how or when…all right, I'll do it. But I'll have to take my chickens and my milk cow. I won't leave them behind. They're all I've got and someone has to take care of them."

Stephen's heart twisted when he realized they were the only family she had.

"And we'll have to take my old mule, Rocky. We can't leave him. Pa says he's too old to use as a pack mule up in the mountains, but he's still of use if he's not loaded too heavily."

William glanced at him and grinned. They both knew Stephen had to accept Kelly with her entire menagerie.

"My wife Jane will be thrilled to have some chickens around again, and the children would benefit from some fresh cow's milk. All we have are two young heifers that are not yet producing milk. I suppose we could build a cage of some sort for the hens and tie it onto that mule. But you'll have to take care of them. I'm not messing with chickens. Be sure to explain to your father that you took the mule. I don't want him thinking we did. I won't take another man's animal."

"I'll explain, but he won't care. And I'll take care of my own animals. And you will have the first eggs the chickens lay," Kelly said.

William started laughing.

Stephen glared at him. Eggs. He hated eggs. He shook his head as he strode towards the door, muttering under his breath, "God help us—*all*."

❧

Stephen couldn't believe what had just happened. He not only had yet another woman joining them on this trip, but an old mule, a milk cow, and chickens too. Well, at least the chickens would make Jane happy. He had to admit, he was glad they were helping Kelly. After her father abandoned her and those scoundrels robbed her of her innocence, the poor girl deserved a chance for a new life. He knew Jane would welcome her. And helping Kelly might help Jane heal too.

He sat down on an old barrel on the porch and watched the rain. He missed Jane. He missed everything about her. Her beautiful smile. The soft lilt of her voice. The sparkle in her green eyes. The smell of roses in her hair. But most of all, he missed the joy of feeling her arms around him and the thrill of loving her. He would do anything to make that happen again.

He would make her happy once more. He had to. Their girls did not die for nothing. They died for their land. Not his land—*their* land. Somehow, he would make Jane understand that. And, believe how much he loved her.

❧

The weather cleared and the three packed to leave. Stephen wanted to get back to Jane and the others as soon as possible.

William built a pack frame and a couple of crude crates out of the weathered boards of the existing coop, causing him to acquire numerous splinters and to swear more than once. Carpentry had never been one of William's strengths.

Kelly loaded the crates, calling each chicken by their names— Genesis, Exodus, Leviticus, Numbers, Deuteronomy. "I have three more books in the Old Testament to go before I get to the book of Samuel, then I'll have to get a rooster. Can't have a hen named Samuel after all," she explained.

Stephen just nodded in agreement. Couldn't talk much over all the squawking anyway.

William approached the mule. "Do you suppose that old boy will object to me putting this cage full of squawking chickens on his rear end?"

"If he does, they'll have to walk. I'm not putting chickens on a horse. It would be disrespectful," Stephen said as he saddled their mounts.

"He's a pack mule. He won't mind all that much," Kelly said.

"Just the same, I'd be obliged, Stephen, if you loaded him," William said.

"Why should I load it? It's your cage," he asked.

"You're much better with animals than I," William said.

"Hell. You just want me to be the one to get kicked," Stephen retorted.

William winked at Kelly. "I thought you'd respect a stubborn old mule for not liking chickens. Kind of takes after you don't you think?"

Stephen chuckled, surprising himself that he could.

Stephen and William watched, ready to help if needed, as Kelly packed her few belongings. She put the note to her father on their table and anchored it with the oil lamp.

"I have just one more thing to do," she said.

Stephen took her things and she strode out the cabin door and headed toward her mother's grave. Kelly reached down and pulled the weeds away from the headstone. Stephen kept his distance, giving her some privacy to say her goodbye, but his heart clenched when she ran her fingers through each of the letters of her mother's name. Before leaving, she gathered nearby wildflowers and laid them against the stone.

Kelly mounted the horse that had been Mr. Adams' and appeared ready to go before Stephen finished securely tying her belongings and the two crates full of squawking chickens to the mule. Feathers flew everywhere.

Looking down at him she said, "Mr. Wyllie I believe Old Rocky likes you. He normally moves all around when my father loads him. He's just standing there like you were brushing his coat or something."

"I just told him if he gave me any trouble I'd put lead between his long ugly mule ears," he said, scowling as he waved a chicken feather away from his face.

William laughed so hard he could barely stay seated on his horse.

To Stephen's surprise, Kelly smiled broadly as she listened to William laugh.

When was the last time she heard someone laugh? he wondered.

"I always thought you talked sweetly to animals and that's how you got them to do what you wanted. Now I know you just threaten their life and ridicule them. That's your secret."

Stephen tied lead ropes on the other horses and gave the gentlest one to Kelly to lead and he took the other two. "Let's go," he said, as he mounted George.

William went first and Kelly followed. She didn't look back.

He cracked his whip, letting just the tip lightly touch the back of the cow to urge her forward. As they left, Stephen pondered how long it would be until they caught up with the others. Dragging this entourage down rock-covered hills was going to test his scant patience.

"Mr. Wyllie, you seem to handle that whip with skill," Kelly remarked.

"I've seen him cut off a snake's head with that thing," William said.

"Why waste powder on a snake," he said. "I prefer to save ammunition for two-legged snakes like the kind we left back there."

"We need to report what happened to the sheriff in the closest town," William said.

"No, please, no," Kelly begged. "I don't want anyone to know what happened back there. It's bad enough you two know."

"Maybe we should just leave it alone. What do you think?" William asked him.

"Suits me. Justice has already been served. No point in delaying our progress any more. A sheriff would probably want us to stay in town until he could verify facts and write up a report. But we will have to tell Jane and the others. They'll need to understand why we brought her along."

Kelly moved her horse next to Stephen's. "Please, no one else, please," she pleaded, her eyes filled with tears.

"You needn't worry about what happened to you Kelly. Put it all behind you now," Stephen said gently.

Kelly just hung her head, her tears falling on the saddle horn. For a long time, every step her mount took shook another tear loose.

CHAPTER 30

Jane made breakfast that morning with her mind elsewhere. She kept thinking about Stephen. She had slept fitfully, dreaming of him all night. In her dreams, she desperately tried to reach him, to tell him something, but somehow each time she got close to him, he would disappear. She awoke, feeling uneasy, and wondering what she had been trying to tell him.

He had left with only her anger to carry with him. She let him ride off on a potentially dangerous undertaking without even saying goodbye. But he hadn't said goodbye to her either. He just rode off. Rode off with the guilt she mercilessly heaped on him. She could not deny that she had cruelly judged him guilty and made him feel like a criminal.

Could she take back her bitter words? Or would they both have to live with them forever?

The memory of their terrible quarrel—the desperation in his voice, the pain in his eyes—hurt her to the core. But at the time, she still suffered from an unbearable heartache.

She barely noticed as Sam walked up. He bent to turn the strips of nearly burnt venison over with his knife.

"You're thinking about Stephen aren't you?" he asked.

"He went off, possibly to grave danger, with only my bitterness in his heart. I was angry. Still am. But—"

As usual, Sam cut to the heart of the matter. "You hold him responsible don't you?"

"Yes, God help me, I do. She struggled not to cry, but her eyes burned with tears wanting to be shed. "I'm also terrified, scared out of my mind that more of us will die."

Sam took the pan off the fire and set it on a rock to cool. "When we decided to leave, part of the reason for going was Bomazeen. He was an unquestionable threat and eventually he would have come after you. And likely your daughters too. But he was only the final reason. Let me tell you about a discussion Stephen had with our brothers before we left."

She sat down on her trunk. "All right."

Sam continued, "Edward argued against taking a dangerous trip. Stephen thought the potential rewards outweighed the possible risks. So did William and so did John. And, I agreed with them. It was four to one in favor of leaving. Stephen was stumped though because he knew what jeopardy the journey might put you and the girls in. It was tearing him apart.

"Believe it or not, it was Little John who helped Stephen to decide. Little John said we could die there too, just as his mother did, and his Grandpa and Grandma did in the mountain slide. What Little John said was true. Life has no guarantees anywhere. Amy and Mary could have died from a fever there in your home. You know the truth of that. We've all seen it happen in other families, often without explanation."

"I have," she admitted, reining in her temper, and letting out a long sigh.

"Ultimately, Edward did not have the courage to leave. Stephen did. Would you rather be married to a complacent coward? To a man who is only content with what's easy and safe? Or to a man like Stephen? A man with the courage to trust God and pursue his dream, even if it means facing the unknown. The man you chose to marry for those very qualities."

She shut her eyes and buried her face in her hands. "Dear Lord, what have I done?"

"It's not what you did, but what you can do that is important now. Forgive him Jane and forgive yourself too. No one was responsible for their deaths. No one could have prevented it. None of us know our future. It just happened for a reason we'll never understand. Stephen loves you more than his dream, more than the land he wants so desperately so that he can provide a better future for his family. He wants only one thing more than land—to keep you safe. But if you separate the man from his dream, he won't be the same man."

Jane let Sam's words sink in. They felt like a warm salve to her wounded and bruised spirit. She wanted to heal, wanted to love again. If she were honest, her anger had already faded even before she talked to Sam.

Finally, she said, "Thank you, Sam."

Jane felt her heart beginning to heal already. There was no doubt that she would still hurt for some time, but the sorrow would come from missing Amy and Mary, not from bitter, misplaced anger and resentment. She could leave that dark abyss behind now and move on. Move on with her husband by her side, looking forward, toward the west, toward a shared dream. She prayed he would come back to her and give her a chance to tell him she was sorry. And, to spend the rest of their new life showing him her love.

She closed her eyes, willing Stephen to feel her love, to know that she realized she was wrong to blame him. Terribly wrong. Forgiveness began to bloom in her heart.

It was then that she felt the first soft twitch of the new life growing inside her.

❧

The sun blazed high in the sky when Stephen and William caught up with the others. Bear, who was bringing up the rear, turned in his saddle as they approached, peered down the trail toward them, and waved.

"There they are," Bear yelled and pointed, then loped his horse back toward them.

Stephen couldn't wait to see the girls, but most of all Jane. Somehow, he had to make amends. He tapped his heels against George's sides, urging the horse on. Kelly and William followed close behind.

"Ye're a sight for sore eyes now," Bear said as he reached them. "I see ye have a young visitor with ye, and a lot more stock than ye did when you left."

"Good to finally see you too. Dragging this ornery mule has made me want to cut off this arm," William said.

"Bear, this is Kelly McGuffin. Kelly this is our adopted brother, Bear McKee." Stephen slid from the saddle and handed over the lead ropes. "Take these horses will you Bear?"

Bear took the two Stephen had led and got the horse Kelly pulled behind her.

"Is everyone all right?" Stephen asked Bear. He was most concerned about Jane, worried that her heart was still breaking. Afraid that she still hated him. *Please God, let that not be so.*

"Aye. They're fine. We heard about some Indian trouble na too far away though. We've doubled our watch at night," Bear said.

"What kind of trouble?" Stephen asked. He heard real worry in Bear's tone.

"I'll explain later," Bear said, glancing at the young lady.

"Let's catch up with the others then," Stephen said, looking for Jane and hurrying toward her wagon. George followed behind him.

Jane quickly climbed down off her seat and rushed towards him. The children ran ahead of her. The girls and Little John were the first to reach him and grabbed him around the legs. He gave each a hug and pat on the head but his gaze never left Jane.

"You got a mule and some chickens," Little John shouted.

"Why don't you and the girls go see them," Stephen said with a smile.

As Jane drew closer, tears welled up in her eyes at the sight of him. His heart raced as she threw her arms around his neck and hugged him fiercely.

Could this be the miracle he had prayed for?

As though she didn't know whether to laugh or cry, she did both. Her tears actually felt good against his face, washing away the pain, healing the anger. He tried kissing them away but there were too many.

He reached down to hold her waist and looked closely at her face. Had she forgiven him? It was there in her eyes. Love replaced the bitterness.

His heart nearly burst with joy. He hugged her so forcefully he worried he might be hurting her. He leaned back and gazed down at her. She was still crying. But these tears appeared to spring from joy, not pain. He studied her face, soaking in every magnificent detail. Her eyes sparkled again with life and her smile made him want to weep his relief was so great.

She was so important to him. So much a part of him. He was nothing without her. "Jane," was all he could say.

She tried to dry her tears with the back of her hand. "Stephen, I love you. I'm so sorry. I was so wrong."

He wrapped his arms around her and kissed her passionately. He didn't care who was watching. They were husband and wife, reconciled, lovers once again. He needed to taste Jane's mouth, to feel her warmth, more than ever before. He wanted to kiss away all her heartaches, to sweep her up in his arms, and carry her off to a secluded spot where he could show her how much he adored her.

He forced himself to pull back. His need to feel her passion, and share his, would have to wait for now.

After he caught his breath and gave Jane one more spirited hug, he directed her attention toward Kelly, who had been speaking to Bear and the girls.

"Who is this pretty young lady?" Jane asked him.

"Her name is Kelly. I'll explain later after we get her settled," he said, making it clear from his tone that she should ask no more questions.

"Greetings, my name is Jane." She offered her hand to Kelly.

"Hello, I'm Kelly McGuffin," Kelly replied timidly.

Stephen suspected that Kelly might be overwhelmed by such a boisterous group of strangers.

"Are those your chickens on the back of that mule? And is that your milk cow?" Jane asked.

Kelly nodded a yes to both questions.

Jane smiled warmly, linking her arm around Kelly's elbow. "Why don't you come with me and I'll introduce you to my friend Catherine and the others."

He watched Kelly stride toward her new life.

A life now linked by misfortune and fortune to the dreams of others.

CHAPTER 31

S tephen strode up as Jane tucked the girls and Little John into their pallets for the evening. She rejoiced that the sight of him made love swell in her heart again.

"Goodnight my bunnies, may the angels kiss your foreheads and bring you the sweetest of dreams," she told them. She was anxious to find her own dreams. And, she was even more anxious to feel Stephen's rock hard chest and strong arms envelop her again.

"Mama, tell us a story," Polly pleaded. "It's been so long since you've told us one. Please, please, just a short one will do."

"Yes, yes," Martha begged.

"Please, Aunt Jane," Little John said.

Jane glanced up at Stephen. He smiled and nodded at her as though he too would enjoy hearing one of her tales. He often said she was an excellent storyteller. She usually made them up as she went. Her favorites were always about castles and princes. Stephen looked like a prince to her tonight. He had washed, shaved, and wore a fresh linen shirt over his broad shoulders. The dancing light of the fire made his long black hair gleam and his sapphire eyes seemed more mischievous than usual. His warm smile made her ache to kiss his lips. And elsewhere. She'd make this a short story.

"All right, but you must promise to be happy with just this short one. I'm tired from today's journey," she said.

The children all wore happy smiles and settled in for the story.

ঔ

"Well now, about 200, no 300 years ago," she began, "there lived a small group of fairies in the old land called Scotland across the big ocean. The fairies lived in an ancient forest named Glen Affric. The forest, silent, solemn, and dark, stood unchanged for many centuries, and nothing lived there but fairies. No birds, no deer, nothing at all lived in this woodland but these wee fairies. Every evening the fairies came out of their shelters in the trees and played lovely tunes on magical pipes. These tunes were enchanted and few mortals lived who were lucky enough to ever hear them.

"One evening, a young noblewoman rode alongside the forest, through a golden grass covered pasture. She had lost her way riding her horse and could not find her way back to her castle. The sun was far in the western sky and she desperately wanted to get back before dark, because her father, who loved her very much, would be worried."

She paused to look up at Stephen—her handsome prince. Ah, now she knew where this story was going. She looked down at the children and continued…

"Yet, the young woman was not afraid. Those of noble birth must always set an example for others to be brave. The afternoon shadows grew longer and longer, making every tree, shrub, and stone, darken the grass. She kept riding, but could not find the path that would lead her back to her castle. The reds and golds of the evening sunset made her stop to admire, and there she heard the sweetest sound she had ever heard. She rode through the flowers and grasses and pressed her mount right to the forest edge. She listened carefully. Was it merely the wind or a river? Had she really heard the delightful sound? Yes, she heard it again and the fairies' pipes lured her in. At the edge of the forest, she got off her horse, tied him, and strolled slowly into the woods. After a bit, she grew accustomed to the darkness, and searched and peered past every tree. Suddenly, she heard, *'A woman fair and true rides her horse, always following her heart's course. Through field and glen she rides him through, and the land she loves, loves her too.'* The noblewoman sat down and leaned up against a tree to listen to the enchanting magical tune. She closed her eyes for just a second and fell fast asleep, hearing in her dreams the sweetest melodies she ever heard.

"As her lovely dreams kept her entranced, a neighboring prince spotted her tied mount as he rode home to his castle. He went into the forest to see who the horse belonged to because he thought they might need help. He found the noblewoman fast asleep. Her long golden hair, spread all over her shoulders, shimmered even in the darkness under the timber. Her fair skin glowed like the moon. She wore a gown made of silver, shinier than his long broad sword. She was so beautiful the prince could barely breathe as he gazed upon her. Right then, his heart fell completely in love with her.

"She was such a vision to gaze upon, that he did not want to wake her. But the sun was nearly down and he should wake her before darkness fell on the forest. He knelt down and kissed her hand.

"She woke up at once, and she saw love shining in the eyes of the handsome prince. As her eyes gazed into his, her heart swelled with love too, but she said nothing to the prince, except to say that she had strayed from her path and to ask if he could help guide her back to the right trail.

"The prince decided to escort her back to her castle and ask her father for her hand in marriage. Of course, her father readily agreed, for the young man had saved his lost daughter and was a strong, handsome, and wealthy prince who would someday be King.

"Much to his surprise, when the prince spoke of marriage to the noblewoman, she said no."

"Why?" Martha called out.

"Why you ask? Why would she say no when she had fallen in love with the prince the moment she saw him? He wondered the same thing as he went away disappointed.

"He decided to ride home by way of the forest where he had found her. Forlorn, he could hardly keep his mind on his riding. Soon though, he was at the exact same spot where he had discovered her. He decided to sit there awhile and see if he could figure out what he should do. He sat down, at the exact same tree, and shut his eyes, remembering how lovely she had looked the first time he beheld her.

"The fairies had seen him coming and prepared a special tune for his ears only. *'You are the most handsome prince in all the glens and isles, but you will win the comely noblewoman only if you give her smiles,'* they sang. The song was delightful and made him stand up at once. He searched and searched for the source of the music and couldn't find a thing. For you see, it is impossible for a mere mortal to view something as old and magical as a fairy. Nevertheless, they were there, and they sang the same tune again."

"Mama, are there fairies in Kentucky?" Polly asked.

"Indeed. Of course, there are. And one day they may sing magical songs for you. You have to open your ears and your heart just right. Now, let's get back to the prince…

"All right, he thought, I can find many ways to make her smile. So, he brought her the loveliest flowers he could find, but that didn't work. Then he took her the prettiest and most yummy tasting cake his cooks could make, but that didn't work. Then he had the best poet in the kingdom write a poem so perfect it would have made the great Scots warrior Robert the Bruce weep from joy, but that didn't work either. Although these things pleased the noblewoman, they did not make her truly smile from her heart.

"He went away feeling sad and discouraged, and she went upstairs to her room in the tower, very sad as well.

"Being a Scot, he did not give up easily. He decided to ask his father, the King, what he should do. What do you think the King said?"

"What!" the children all yelled at once. Even Stephen looked like he couldn't wait for the answer.

"The King said, 'Have ye told the lass that ye love her even more than Scotland?'

"The prince shook his head no and gawked at his father realizing how wise the King was. He got on his steed and rode as fast as the animal would carry him to her castle. He asked her maid to fetch her, but she would not come down from the tower, for she wanted no more presents. So he stood outside her window and peered up hoping to see her. Sure enough, she was gazing out at her dazzling mountains and lush green meadows.

"'My darling,' he yelled, 'I love you more than Scotland, more than its grand peaks, and lochs, and isles, and lakes. As much as I love this land, I love you more.'

"And do you know what happened?"

"What?" the girls and Stephen all asked in unison.

She winked at Stephen. "The beautiful noblewoman leaned out the window, her long hair flowing down, and smiled the biggest smile a Scottish lass has ever worn on her face, for she knew then and only then, that he truly loved her.

"And so they married and had the most magnificent wedding ever celebrated in Scotland, in the golden meadow next to where the fairies had played for them. As they said their wedding vows, although no one else could hear it but them, they both heard the most romantic wedding music ever played for two people. All the fairies sang together, very unusual for them, and only done on special occasions. They sang *Love the glories of the land, for Scotland is a glimpse of heaven for you to see. But love your sweetheart all the more, for they shall return your love back to thee.*'"

"I do," Stephen said.

Jane titled her head back and peered up at her own handsome prince. Her heart warmed with happiness. She could almost hear the sweet melody of the fairies in the forest beyond him.

CHAPTER 32

After Jane told her story, the children fell asleep quickly, no doubt dreaming of princes and fairies. Stephen thoroughly enjoyed listening to her tell the story, but the time had come to return to the real world of men and women.

He reluctantly filled everyone in on all that had transpired since he and William had left. Jane and Catherine, both justifiably horrified, hugged Kelly when they learned what had happened to her. He saw Kelly fight back tears, but their comforting only seemed to make her want to cry more. She soon quit trying to be brave and gave in to the tears. Finally, William whispered a few words to her and Kelly stopped crying right away. Stephen wondered what William had said.

Later, as the campfire glowed softly on this unusually pleasant evening, he sensed the mood changing considerably. Everyone seemed relieved the ordeal was behind them. He was as well. It was time to focus on getting to Kentucky and making his dream a reality. A dream he could share again with his wife.

He tugged Jane close to his side and peered into her eyes, sparkling now in the firelight. Holding her again made him giddy with happiness. She had forgiven him and all of a sudden, he wanted to celebrate. He cackled inelegantly, as he struggled to hold back his bubbling joy. He started to laugh, then snorted when he tried to stop, and that made him laugh even harder. Then he all but cried. All his emotions were surfacing at once. He needed to do something quick or Jane would think he'd lost his mind.

"I think we need some whiskey tonight," he proposed. A chuckle erupted from him. He fought to smother it, but it only made his mirth worse. Then Jane started giggling, and it made his jollity worse still. Every time she laughed, he would too. He had never giggled this much in his life. Hell, he couldn't remember ever giggling. What was wrong with him?

"Bear...would you kindly... fetch some whiskey from the wagon?" he finally managed to ask.

The others, all laughing or smiling now too, stared at him in amazement. He was always the last to suggest strong beverage.

"I'll get the cups," he said, ignoring their questioning looks, and finally regaining control of himself.

Bear opened the jug and poured a modest amount for each of the ladies and, as was customary, a more generous portion for the men.

Stephen raised his cup for a toast, a rare gesture for him that left even Jane's mouth gaping open. "To our brother Edward, who gave us this worthy beverage. We miss him, but hope he and his are well and prospering."

In his grief, Stephen decided Edward had been right. Now, he realized they had both been right. If he could have prevented his daughters' deaths by staying in New Hampshire, he would have. But there was no way to know that. He knew only one thing for sure. He was not giving up.

"To Edward," they all repeated.

Stephen took a hearty gulp and then did something even more unusual for him. He smiled at each of them as he slowly looked around the campfire. "I guess you are all wondering what rock I hit my head on or some such thing. Well, not every night is a man and his family reunited," he said, looking at Jane, "not only safe, but blessed with another member. Kelly has decided to join us and to head towards Kentucky. Kelly, you should feel as a sister to us.

"We also have the good fortune of Catherine's company. Jane tells me that you have been a companion and helpmate to her in my absence. I thank you for that Catherine. You too are welcome. I hope that we can ease the burden of losing your husband. To Kelly and Catherine, may our family be your family."

Everyone drank again except Kelly who still hadn't tasted the liquor.

Stephen noticed that she only stared at the cup, fear in her eyes. He suspected she had never tasted whiskey and had only seen its abuse by her father. He casually ambled over and stood next to her, and said, "Kelly, strong drink should be consumed only in moderation. When consumed in excess, it can cause men, and women for that matter, to behave unsuitably. A small amount won't do much more than warm your insides. But you don't have to drink it if you don't want to. You're an adult now, and it's your choice, no one else's."

She titled her head in a nod, seeming to appreciate his brotherly advice. Kelly cautiously sipped and managed not to choke on it, then wrinkled her nose and shook her head.

He chuckled at her. "It takes some getting used to."

"Thank you Stephen for your kind toast," Catherine said. "I'll be forever indebted to you and William for finding my husband's killers and recovering my property—especially James' steed." She left unsaid that they had killed the murderers too.

"I thank you too, Mr. Wyllie," Kelly echoed, "and you too William."

"Let's have some fun for a change," William suggested. He strode over to the wagon to retrieve his violin.

They spent the warm evening in relaxed conversation and storytelling, while William supplied a medley of popular tunes in the background. Kelly sat spellbound next to William the entire time, tapping her foot and enjoying the music immensely. She told them she had only heard music once before when her Ma had taken her to town when she was very young.

John had taken first watch, while Bear and Sam stood around Catherine, who sat on her trunk. Stephen and Jane watched with amusement as the two men took turns exchanging exaggerated truths and stories, clearly competing for the most heroic or colorful tale. Nearly as skilled a storyteller as Jane, Bear seemed to be winning this round.

"'Twas the darkest and hottest night I've ever spent in the wild. Na moon at all and clouds covered the wee stars. The air hung still and muggy. As ye know, I'm furred much like a bear, and in the hotter months, these heavy buckskin-huntin' shirts are a curse. I decided maybe the best way to cool off was a dip in the river without clothes at all. I hiked about fifty yards down to the river from my camp. I moved slowly into the cool water, easin' into it, when several squaws came out of the woods on the opposite bank. They were blitherin' happily, as women often do when doin' chores together. When they saw me, they screamed, 'wendigo, wendigo,' and pointed at me."

Their group roared with laughter. Most had heard the story several times before, but it seemed more amusing each time Bear told it.

Bear scowled at them but continued the story. "Ye are probably are na aware, Catherine, but the Indian man is hairless on his face and chest. So, to them, I appeared more animal than man. They ran hysterical and screamin' back to their camp. I could hear their screams for a long while."

Bear paused they were all laughing so hard. "I was na goin' to wait around to see if they had any braves willin' to hunt a wendigo at night, so I made my way back to my camp, packed up and scampered out of there."

"What's a wendigo?" Catherine asked.

"'Tis an Indian name for an inhuman, supernatural demon creature capable of changing from a man into a beast—usually a bear. The bear hunts on moonless nights and rips to shreds any man or woman it finds. It kills for the pure pleasure of it. Na human is strong enough to defend against it," Bear explained.

"We do become more like wendigo than men when we fight," Sam said, turning serious.

"Aye, Captain. True enough. In battle, we are more beast than man," Bear said, taking a large swallow of his second cup of whiskey.

"Sometimes a man must become savage to survive," Sam said.

As he did the first night they came together to discuss going to Kentucky, Stephen hoped that when the time came, he and his brothers would be savage enough to survive the violence of the wilderness.

Sam took a sip of his whiskey and returned to storytelling. "The beast that gets under my skin is the panther, and one nearly did. She stalked me for a mile or more. I was on foot hunting with my dogs. I prefer to hunt on foot. A horse makes too much noise," he explained for Kelly and Catherine's benefit. "Well, this panther stayed downwind of the dogs so they wouldn't sense her. A panther makes no sound when it moves, but I knew she was there. Every now and then, I could see her burning yellow eyes glowing in the timber. I tried to get her in my sights but she moved too swiftly. A gun is a poor weapon against such a quick-moving animal. I saw her spring from the ground to a tree limb higher than a two-story house. She watched me from her perch for a bit, then she climbed down and slowly crept up behind me. She stalked me silently for some time. All the while, I knew she edged closer and closer. It was just a matter of time before she attacked. At last, she decided to make herself known. First, she just stared at me with pure disdain. I have never had a man look at me with such complete scorn and total contempt. Then, she let out a scream, high and blood-curdling. All the dogs ran, except one. Old King was clearly not fond of the sound of that panther either, but he stuck right by my side, growling deep and fierce in his chest as she approached even closer."

"What happened?" Catherine asked, spellbound.

"When you can see yourself in the panther's eye, you know you're in trouble. The cat and I both understood we were going to battle. I once saw a panther bring down an elk more than three times its size, so I knew King and I were in for a fight for our lives. She screamed again, like a woman in pain or in terror. This time, it was a warning. A notice that she was about to make a kill. As she sprang toward King, I fired, but she moved so fast, I just nicked her shoulder. He took a wicked claw up his middle and then she went for his neck. She was big, easily more than twice his size. I pulled my knife and jumped her. She took a swipe at my face. That's where this scar came from," Sam said, pointing to his chin. "We went a couple of rounds. I felt her claws begin to penetrate my back, and just as my blade found her throat, her jaws wrapped around my arm. She collapsed on her side, my arm still in her mouth. King lifted his head, smelled her hot blood. He saw that I was all right, laid his head back down, and died."

"Poor King," Catherine lamented.

"I haven't had another dog since. I could never find one that good again. I skinned that cat. The beast made a fine rug in my old cabin. I like to think King appreciated it every time I stepped on it," Sam said, half grinning at the thought.

The stories went on for some time, the whiskey loosening both their memories and their tongues. After the first hour, Stephen grabbed Jane's hand and briskly led her away from the camp, carrying both their weapons and his cloak. It was time they talked.

And, his body ached for her touch.

CHAPTER 33

The night sky shimmered like a velvet canopy studded with God's most perfect diamonds as they strolled away from camp.

"Stephen I know I was brutal with my blame. I just missed Amy and Mary so much it nearly made me lose my mind," Jane said, her voice near breaking. "I can still smell them on their blankets. Every time I do, it makes me think I can find them if I just look hard enough. And then I realize, there's nowhere to look."

He struggled not to let his own pain surface.

"It breaks my heart every time I touch Amy's doll or Mary's little cup. I can't stop those feelings. I've tried. God knows I've tried." Jane stopped and turned to face him. "I didn't want to blame you, but I did. And honestly, a part of me still does. A small part. But I understand now why you had to make this journey. I'm struggling to completely forgive both of us, not just you. Maybe with your help, I can. In the meantime, I promise I want to be by your side. Just be patient with me and for heaven's sake talk to me."

He reached for her hand and held it against his chest. That promise was enough for now. "I'm sorry I didn't talk to you about it. My despair—for you and for me—was too overwhelming. You were right. I was responsible. This trip was my doing. Mine. No one else's. *I* put their lives in danger. It was a much easier thing to do in Barrington than out here." He realized he would have to work at forgiving himself. "And when it happened…I couldn't do a damn thing to stop it. It made me feel like I failed both you and them." The admission wounded him, but he felt better having said it.

"No, you didn't fail them or me. As Sam helped me to understand, the girls could have died anywhere. Illness often strikes children, no matter where they are."

He took a deep steadying breath. "I do love you and the children more than any piece of land. You know how much I want land, but I want you more. Without you, land is just dirt. All that is beautiful and important about it is lost. As I told you before I left with William, nothing in this world is more important than my love for you and our family."

A tear slid down Jane's check. "We lost two of our girls, but God will bless us with more children, sons as well as daughters." A shadow fell over her face. "But, if ever we face something like this again, we have to talk to each other. I needed you. I needed to feel your arms around me. But instead, like a fool, I shut you out. I withdrew and you left me alone. The more you stayed away, the angrier I got. Damn it, Stephen, we can't shut each other out like that ever again."

"I was trying to give you time to heal. I didn't shut you out. But I did shut me in. I was afraid to let myself out. You wouldn't have liked what you saw. You would have stopped loving me."

"Maybe I did stop loving you for a while."

"When I rode off with William, I believed you had." He shuddered at the recollection.

"I'm sorry. I was just so full of rage, I had no room for other feelings. But that's gone now. There's still some heartache, but no more resentment."

"The pain is still there for me too," he said quietly.

She kissed the back of his hand. "I've missed talking to you."

"I know you've been lonely."

"Yes, though not as much since Catherine's been with us," Jane said.

"It's good that you have some female companionship for a change. What are her plans, do you know?"

"She wanted reassurance that you were amenable to the idea of her joining us. She didn't want to be a burden."

"I made my mind up on the way back. For some reason, fate put these two women in our path. I think they were meant to join us. Why, I don't know. But whatever the reason, it's the right thing to do."

"I'm horrified by what happened to Kelly. Do you think she'll ever get over it?" Jane asked.

"Yes. She seems to be a woman of strong faith. And I think it's helped to have William treat her with such kindness."

"She's a lovely young woman, but the poor girl's as thin as a reed and wearing a beggar's clothes. Do you think she'd mind if I gave her a gown? I think I have one that will fit her if she belts it."

"What she's wearing is little more than a rag. I don't believe she's had a new dress since her mother died about four years ago. Speaking of gowns, is this one getting a little snug?" he asked, wrapping her waistline with both hands.

"It's not from eating too much. It's this big son of yours." She smiled broadly and rubbed her still flat tummy.

His heart leapt. He stopped abruptly, tossed down their rifles and his cloak, and gently placed his hands on either side of her face. "You're with child again?"

Jane nodded. Her green eyes twinkled with the radiance of pure joy, her sorrow forgotten for the moment.

Her news made his heart dance. He had longed for a son to carry on his name. "A son! But how can you know? That's impossible."

"I just do. It's your first son and he's going to be a big one. I think he'll be at least the size of Sam. Unlike the girls, he has me craving food and milk so that I can hardly think of anything else. I think I was more excited to see Kelly's chickens and milk cow than I was to see you," she said, her face breaking into a wide smile.

"Have you told the others?"

"Only Catherine. She didn't understand why I hadn't told you before you left. But I couldn't tell you then. I had nothing to share but anger. But now, I want to share this with you."

He gazed deeply into her eyes. They seemed even greener when she was with child. Maybe it was the magic of new life growing inside of her. He saw a spark there that renewed his determination.

He started pacing as his mind raced. "We'll need to hurry to Kentucky now. My son's going to be born on our land—not in some damn wagon." He realized Jane wanted nothing more herself. She'd want to have her son in a bed in their home. "I promise I'll build us a fine home there—and our bedroom will have an enormous bed, with plenty of room to make more sons. And daughters, of course."

"Ah…so you're already thinking about our bed and how we might use it?"

Stephen felt a smile tug at his lips but ignored her quip. Instead, he gently kissed her, tasting the honeyed whiskey she'd had earlier. He swept her into the circle of his arms. He had missed the feel of holding her. It was like wrapping his arms around heaven.

He wanted to love her, but first, he wanted her to know that she was loved. He continued to just hold her, pressing their hearts together until they nearly beat as one.

She rested her head on his shoulder and he softly stroked her head for some time, content with just holding her until she was ready for more.

Life had been ugly lately, but now he could feel some of the beauty returning. "My love," he whispered into her hair.

She gazed at him with eyes shimmering with happiness. "I've missed you."

"And I you, my darling, with all my heart." Just looking at her made his blood burn, his desire surge, his heart soar. But he wanted more.

He immersed his hands in her long thick curls. He let his fingers savor the silky feel of her tresses and then he let them wander to the luscious curves of her back and hips. He wanted to touch every inch of her. And he would soon. He stopped his exploration of her body and leaned his forehead against hers. "I hope you're right about it being a son," he whispered, "but, I just want you to be safe and well after childbirth. That's all that matters to me."

"I haven't had any serious trouble yet. I'm strong. Many generations of my Scots ancestors birthing big stubborn babies made us especially good at giving birth."

"That's not the only thing you're *especially* good at," he said, smiling and moving his hands to explore the curves of her backside. She felt so good to his touch, strong, yet softly feminine. His hands trembled with eagerness.

Maybe he could love her enough to help heal her shattered heart and perhaps soon she could forgive him completely. And, he knew her love would absolutely help to revive his own crushed heart. Together, they could become whole again.

"What else am I especially good at?" she asked, smiling.

"Storytelling." He touched her lips with his finger.

Her smile lit up the night. "What else?"

"Biscuits."

She laughed. "What else?"

"Your stew."

She cackled even harder.

Her boisterous laugh warmed his heart more than he could have imagined.

He lowered his lips to hers, and kissed her fully and deeply, until he felt her body press into his, asking for more. And he would give it to her—much more.

He longed for that big bed they would soon have, so he could kiss all of her exquisite body. He never tired of finding ways to please her and the longer they were together, the more imaginative he had become.

As he stroked his thumbs across the front of her bodice, he felt the evidence of her arousal through her gown. Time to remove that barrier.

He began helping her take off her many layers of clothing—gown, stays, petticoats, and other sundry items he didn't know, or want to know, by name, and finally her shift—a process which never failed to test his patience. But he was always rewarded in the end.

She stood before him her body unveiled, except for her white stockings and boots. Her ivory skin glowed in the moonlight. Her thick hair seemed to go on forever, nearly reaching her waist. He stared in awe at her beauty. Her breasts full and her limbs long and slim, she took his breath away. Stephen stared like a mad man, but he couldn't help it. He couldn't take his eyes off her. It had been so long, so very long, since he had seen and touched her as a husband.

He moved closer and rested his hands on the curves of her hips, then he slowly eased his hands behind her, filling his fingers with her soft bottom. It fit his hands perfectly. Everything about her fit him perfectly. Everything.

He tossed his cloak to the ground and then shed his coat and waistcoat, while her hands unfastened the ties of his breeches. She reached down and gently caressed him. Her persuasive caress invited more. He groaned as his body, so sensitive to her delicate touch, reacted. He could stand there forever surrendering himself to her attentions.

He buried his face in her freshly washed curls. He inhaled deeply, reveling in the scent that reminded him of rainwater and roses. The hair's striking red color mirrored Jane's personality—fiery and full of life.

And, as he took her hands, she was radiant with that fire now. Her eyes glistened as she licked her full lips. She tossed the thick strands of hair covering her alluring breasts to her back.

His eyes grew wide. He found himself staring again. She was driving him mad with longing. The primal heat rose between them, palatable, powerful, and intense enough to set the wilderness on fire.

She tugged off his shirt, and the rest of his clothes quickly followed. He stood naked before her and her green eyes flashed with passion. She stepped forward and ran all her fingers through the hair on his chest and across his taut nipples, making him shiver. He surrendered completely to her seduction as she trailed light kisses across the muscles of his chest. A moan slipped through his lips when he felt her breasts press against him. She snuggled against his neck and one of her legs wrapped around him as he held her waist in his hands.

When she crushed her lips to his, he returned her kiss with a hunger so desperate it startled him. He loved her before, but now, his feelings for her were even stronger. He had learned what the absence of that love meant. And he never wanted her more than he did now.

He quickly found all his weapons and placed them on the ground next to them. Glad he had brought his cloak to protect them from the night air, he extracted the garment from his pile of his clothing and spread it out before her. A temporary sanctuary for their love.

He gestured gallantly toward the cloak. "My lady." He took her hand.

"Tell me again, what else am I especially good at, my prince?" she asked breathlessly, as she settled down on his cloak.

As he dropped down next to her, she moved toward him, her green eyes flaring brightly with desire. The warmth of her flesh against him was intoxicating. His hand skimmed across her hip and thigh as he thought about his answer. He liked this game.

"Massaging my shoulders."

She placed a hand on each of his shoulders, her touch soft and caressing, yet it sparked a searing need.

"What else?"

"Kissing." His lips came coaxingly down on hers.

Her kiss was as challenging as it was thrilling. Passion coursed through his entire length then swirled around him, encircling them both in its blazing flames.

"What..."

He thought it best to show her.

CHAPTER 34

L ittle John, wake up," Stephen said, shaking the boy's shoulder.

"What is it, Uncle? Indians?" Little John sat up, wide-eyed.

"No, no. We're going hunting, you, me, and Uncle Sam."

"No fooling?" He scampered for his boots and jacket.

"Be quiet now. Don't wake the girls," he whispered. "They need their beauty sleep."

"Martha needs to sleep for a month," Little John said, already exhibiting the Wyllie wit.

They joined Sam who was getting dressed.

"Are you sure your ankle has healed up enough for a long hunt?" Stephen asked quietly.

"Yes, it feels nearly new again and I'm more than ready to test it," Sam answered. "I can always turn back if it becomes a problem."

The three hunters were on their way before daylight. Sam led them through the open dew-covered field toward the timberline to the north. The air smelled clean, like someone had scrubbed it with soap overnight.

"We'll get away from these open meadows and head up into those hills. There should be deer or wild pig up there," Sam said over his shoulder.

By dawn, they climbed the lush green hills at a steady pace. The exercise felt good to Stephen's saddle stiff legs. Little John kept up without too much difficulty but started breathing harder when the climb got steeper.

"Need a lift, Little John?" Stephen asked. "Jump up here on my back."

"No Sir, thank you anyway," Little John said without slowing.

Normally, the boy enjoyed riding on his uncles' back. But Stephen suspected that his nephew wanted to carry his own weight today, to be a hunter, not a little boy.

Little John caught his breath while Stephen and Sam stopped to check the load of their Kentucky rifles.

Sam spoke to Little John quietly. "From here on, don't talk. If you spot game, tap me on the back, and point to it. Walk only behind me, but not so close that branches snap back at you," Sam instructed. "And watch where you step—avoid snakes and dry branches—or you'll scare off anything worth shooting at."

"Hunting sure has a lot of rules," Little John said, "but I'll do just what you said, Uncle Sam, especially the part about snakes."

Little John gawked at Stephen's rifle. Nearly five feet long, it was longer than the boy was tall.

"It goes on forever," Little John said, his neck tilted back to see the end of the rifle. "The Captain's knife is even scarier. It's as long as my arm. The biggest knife in the whole world."

"It might be," Sam said with a wink at Little John.

"This is the best day of my life. No question. Hunting with the two bravest men to ever live. I want to be just like you," Little John declared.

Stephen didn't know if he was one of the bravest men to ever live, but Sam surely was. They both had a lot they could teach the boy.

Sam waved them on. His brother moved so quietly for such a big man. He watched how Sam advanced. Somehow, before he took each step, Sam could see what lay on the path. At the same time, he took in everything around him in the woods too, while stepping around any dry twigs or branches.

The timber grew thick and dark here. Hardwoods covered in tangled vines and giant pines kept the light out. Stephen hoped they would pass through this oppressive darkness soon. It felt like being in a cave, a big cave full of shadows, and you knew you weren't alone. He was sure strange and ferocious creatures lived in this dreary place.

Little John glanced behind him, probably wanting to be sure Stephen was close by. He was. If his nephew wanted to run back and jump in his arms, he wouldn't blame the boy. It seemed like a forest without end as Sam wove his way through the gloom.

Finally, they passed into the light where rocky hills rose and fell like waves on a sea. They hiked until Stephen's feet were sore from the rocks before Sam finally halted. When he did, Little John froze in his tracks. Stephen did too. The last thing he wanted to do was scare off whatever game Sam had spotted. He watched as Sam silently knelt down to balance his long rifle on one knee. Sunlight reflected off the long shiny barrel as his brother lined up the sights.

He heard a bird singing nearby and then the hard click of the rifle's hammer. He peered in the direction of Sam's aim. A deer stood just inside the edge of another thick stand of trees. The animal stood frozen for a moment—an instant that would end its life. He saw the animal fall in the distance. He released his breath.

"Big doe, I think," Sam said, looking back at him.

"Can I go and see?" Little John pleaded, his face and eyes bright with excitement.

"Okay. We'll be right behind you. Be careful," Stephen said, "don't get too close till we know for sure it's dead."

Little John took off, running fast, rocks and pine needles crunching beneath him with each stride.

His nephew's first hunt. He remembered his first hunt and being equally excited.

A log lay in Little John's path. The boy jumped it as Stephen turned back to Sam.

"Great shot Sam. We'll chew on fresh meat tonight," Stephen said, walking through the powder's lingering smoke to stand next to his brother who was already reloading.

"And maybe sip on some of that good wine Edward sent," Sam said with relish.

The prospect of a good meal made Stephen's stomach growl. They had left without eating breakfast.

"I'll find a branch to carry her back," Sam said.

Where's Little John?" he asked.

Sam glanced up. "He was just there." He pointed towards the doe.

He quickly scanned the wooded area, finding nothing. "He's not now!" Stephen exclaimed and started to run.

Sam trailed just behind him, finishing reloading as he ran.

"Little John. John," Stephen yelled repeatedly as he ran.

"Be quiet, we'll see if we can hear him," Sam said, stopping.

They both listened carefully for several long moments, but the woods stood silent, holding on to its secret.

"Little John, where are you?" Sam finally called out as loudly as he could and they both resumed running.

DOROTHY WILEY

"Stephen, stop!" Sam yelled as he came to a halt.

He stopped abruptly. "What is it?"

"Little John didn't just disappear. He must have fallen through a crevice. Be careful, I'm told Virginia is riddled with caverns."

"What if Indians were watching us and grabbed him, or a bear, God forbid?" he asked, mortified by either possibility.

"We would have heard a bear and there are no Indians here," Sam replied.

"How do you know?"

"I just do. Call it instinct. Call it a sixth sense. Grab a branch. Poke the ground in front of you before you take a step."

They both found sturdy branches to use and proceeded towards the doe more cautiously, about six feet apart. They called for Little John as they moved slowly forward, pausing every few feet to listen for sounds of the boy. But Stephen heard nothing; the only sound in the dense expanse of timber surrounding them was the beating of his own worried heart. The forest here smelled of both rotting and fresh wood, of both dead plants and blooming wildflowers, mingling together in a bittersweet potpourri of death and life.

"I've seen this kind of terrain before. A strong rain or a flood washes away the ground over a cavern and creates a natural trap. Pray it's not too deep," Sam said as they went forward.

"What if it is?"

Sam didn't answer him.

CHAPTER 35

For several interminable minutes, the men searched without speaking, Stephen's mind filling with dread. He repeatedly berated himself for letting something happen to Little John. Already, the familiar poison of guilt began to make him feel sick. His brother seemed to refuse to give in to his alarm, maintaining a dark calmness. But Stephen's mind began to fill with blinding panic. He fought to calm his nerves.

"Did you hear something?" Sam asked. They froze.

"It's him. He's crying," Stephen answered. He moved cautiously towards the pitiful sound. "Little John," he yelled as loudly as he could. He couldn't tell exactly where the crying came from.

"We're coming. Hang on boy," Sam yelled.

The crying turned into loud sobs and they quickly found the opening in the earth on the other side of a fallen tree. Both men lay down on their stomachs to peer down. The opening was not large, but the sides of the hole seemed to go nearly straight down, pointing to complete blackness.

"I can't see a damn thing. Can you?" Sam asked.

"No, it's too dark down there. Little John, are you hurt?" He yelled into the narrow hole.

The sobbing slowed, but the boy didn't speak.

Sam tried. "Little John, we're both right here, just above you. You're not alone. We'll get you out. I promise."

"Help…I fell," Little John managed to whimper between sobs.

The two men could barely hear the boy.

Stephen asked again, "Are you injured? Yell, Little John, so we can hear you."

"Yes, my arm…hurts…bad…real bad. It's dark here. Get me out! Get me out!" the terrified child pleaded.

"Hang on. We'll get you out. Don't be scared, Little John. Things like this happen to hunters. This makes you a real hunter now," Sam said.

"What'll we do? He sounds like he's down there a good way. If one of us climbs down to get him, how do we get us out without a rope?"

Sam thought for a second. "Let's see if any tree vines around here are strong enough to bear weight. While I look, see if you can figure out how long it needs to be."

"Uncle Sam's gone to find a strong vine to pull you out," Stephen yelled down the hole. "Can you see me? Try to look up."

After a moment, "A little bit."

"Little John, how far away do I look? If you stacked horses on top of each other, how many horses would it take to reach me?"

"I don know. I don know."

"Think hard Little John, how many would it take?" he pressed.

"Three big ones."

He sounded weaker. They needed to get to the boy soon.

"Need at least 20 feet of vine," Stephen yelled toward Sam, who continued to circle the bases of the nearby larger and older trees.

"None of these are stout enough to hold your weight without breaking," Sam shouted. "And I don't see any near long enough."

"Keep looking," he yelled.

Time lapsed slowly as Sam's search broadened to trees further away, and Stephen's dread mounted with each passing minute. The sky was growing darker as thick grey clouds rolled by. A storm was coming. They had to get Little John out soon or he might drown.

"This old elm has a vine we can use," Sam finally yelled back.

Seconds later, he heard Sam's hatchet severing the vine at the tree base. Then his brother yanked it, pulling with all his weight. The old vine had been growing up the huge trunk for years and refused to give up its embrace of the tree and its branches. Sam yanked harder. Still, it didn't budge. He watched as Sam began twisting the vine, tugging against it with every twist. He circled the tree, dragging the vine in both directions before he tried again. Sam ducked as the vine finally surrendered and fell heavily to the ground.

Sam ran towards Stephen, the vine trailing behind him. A good inch across, it would be strong enough, if it were long enough.

"You go down, you're smaller," Sam said. "Let's test the length first. I'll drop it down and see how close it gets to him. You'll need to tie it around him and let me pull him out first."

Sam leaned over the hole. "Little John, I'm going to lower this big vine now to see if it's long enough to reach you." He dropped one end into the cave. "Can you see the end of it?" he yelled down.

When Little John didn't answer, Stephen tried. "How close is it Little John?"

Still no answer. "He's passed out, probably from the pain," Sam said.

"I'm going down now!" he said.

"Shed everything you can, except your pistol. You'll need it if there's a varmint or snakes."

Stephen quickly removed his boots, hat, coat and waistcoat, and his powder horn, and other equipment he had on his person.

Sam sat on the ground behind the log. He pushed his legs up against the fallen tree trunk. He would use it for leverage to allow him to use both his arms and his legs and let his hips bear most of the weight. Sam nodded for him to go ahead.

He grabbed the vine and headed down into the cavern feet first, balancing against the sides with his legs. As the vine scraped against the earth at the top of the hole, dirt rained down into the cave, probably dropping on Little John. The narrow opening was barely wide enough for a grown man to squeeze through but more than enough to swallow a small boy. As he slowly descended, his eyes grew accustomed to the dim light in the dark confined space.

"You had better be right next to him, or this vine's not going to be long enough," Sam yelled.

"I am. I'm here," Stephen called back as he reached the boy's side. He let go of the vine when his toes touched ground to give Sam a break from his weight. "But the vine's not long enough to tie it around Little John. Can you find a longer vine?"

"We don't have time, the storm's getting closer and it took too long to find that one. I think I can pull you both out if you can get a good grip."

As they suspected, Little John lay unconscious, his left arm protruding oddly at his side. He strained to see past his nephew. There was just enough light to see that they were both at the edge of a much deeper cavern. If he took even one step, he would be off the ledge.

Without warning, bats flew by him and he frantically flailed his arms around his head. He started to take a step away from the flapping swarm but managed to stop himself just in time when he heard pieces of rock falling in front of him into the cavern's depths. "Blind little bastards," he swore.

Stephen took a deep breath after the bats flew up through the opening, carefully bent down, and gently picked Little John up. Then he reached up to grip the vine, dangling just above his shoulder. "I've got him, let me get a good grip," he shouted. With his right arm, his strongest, he wrapped the vine securely around his forearm and hand. He wanted to wrap it around Little John too, but there wasn't enough vine to spare. Instead, he balanced Little John on his left hip and arm. "All right, pull us up."

He prayed Sam would be strong enough to pull them both up and, for once, he was glad he was the shortest of the five brothers and that Sam was both the tallest and strongest. Feeling the strain of their weight in his own right bicep, he hoped all his work clearing rocks off his land made his arm strong enough to maintain his grip on the makeshift rope until they made it to the opening.

He peered up. He could see daylight, a welcome sight in the oppressive dank atmosphere of the cave. He kept his gaze on the light as Sam slowly inched them up. Soon they were nearing the top.

Stephen tried to get a foothold where he could to take some of the weight off Sam. He worried about the vine breaking, but with Little John in his left arm and the vine in his right, he had no choice but to trust that it would hold together.

Then he felt the vine bounce and pieces of dirt and rotting wood began to fall. He heard Sam swear.

He shook his head, trying to get the debris out of his eyes. The boy hung precariously off his side as he struggled desperately to maintain his grip on both the vine and Little John.

Large chunks of earth cascaded onto them and the improvised rope slid more than a foot.

He nearly lost his grip on the vine. The skin of his right palm began peeling away. He ignored the throbbing burn in his hand. His shoulder was pulling apart. He clenched his teeth against the growing pain, knowing that Little John's life lay in the balance and maybe his too. If they fell now, they would both likely crack their heads against the rocks even before they hit bottom.

"Are you all right?" Sam shouted.

"Yes, but hurry."

"I'll get you out. I swear."

"What happened?" Stephen yelled up, trying to distract himself from the extreme discomfort in his right arm. How much could his shoulder take before it did pull apart?

"This rotten tree collapsed. I nearly got dragged in."

"Sam, you can do this!"

Sam only grunted.

It seemed like an eternity before Stephen felt the edge of the cave's opening against his shoulder.

Because a large section of the dirt at the opening had fallen into the cave, there was now enough room for both Stephen and Little John to pass through. With his left arm, he pushed Little John up onto solid ground, and then threw a leg over the opening.

Sam kept a tight grip until he was fully out.

Stephen knelt next to Little John as Sam collapsed on his back breathing rapidly.

"Is he… all right?" Sam asked, gasping for air as he wiped sweat off his face.

"I hope so. All I see wrong, besides scratches and bruises, is the arm. The bone didn't break the skin. No lumps on his head."

As he rubbed his sore shoulder, Stephen noticed Sam's hands. His brother's left fingers were nearly raw and large red patches covered both

258

palms where the vine had scraped the skin away. Sam rolled his shoulders but otherwise seemed to be okay.

"Get the arm set before he wakes up," Sam said, regaining most of his breath.

Stephen gently manipulated the arm back into place while Sam cut a sturdy piece of bark out of a tree for a makeshift splint. Then Stephen used his shirt to make a sling. Little John moaned during the procedure but did not wake.

"Do you think we can get both the doe and Little John back?" he asked, wrapping his raw hand with part of his cravat, then gave the rest to Sam for his injured hands.

"If we take turns carrying Little John and we both drag the doe behind us, I think we can manage. We'll do the skinning at camp. I'll fetch her. You stay with the boy."

Stephen looked down at Little John's tear-stained dirty face. *Please God, let him be without further injury. We can't lose another child. It would crush all of us.*

He choked back his emotions, the memory of his daughters still painful and fresh. He didn't want John to ever feel the anguish of losing a child. It was a pain that, even when buried deep, would last forever.

CHAPTER 36

I *never imagined it would be this far. I feel like we must have ridden around the world twice by now. But Sam tells us we are just two-thirds of the way there. I am bone-weary and ache for the feel and quiet of a real bed. It would be so nice to sleep again without the constant sound of crickets or coyotes or other creatures of the night. Never will I take my bed for granted again. Or Stephen's attentions in our bed.*

I dreamt of them last night. A dream so real it woke me with tears falling from my eyes. But these tears were different somehow. I wiped my wet cheeks, but couldn't wipe away the strange feeling in my heart. In the dream, I looked into the wagon and there they were, Amy and baby Mary playing together. I called out to them and they glanced right at me and smiled. Beautiful, joyful smiles on innocent faces. It thrilled me to the center of my heart. But when I climbed inside the wagon, they were gone. I called out to them, but they did not come back. I yelled out to them, but they did not come back. I screamed after them, but they did not come back. But I could still see their smiles. And they seemed so full of life. I can't wait to share what I know was a vision with Stephen.

Jane put the journal away. Remember those big smiles she told herself. They were so happy. They just came to let me know that.

࿔

Jane decided she wanted Martha and Polly to learn every skill they could, especially those that would enable them to protect themselves and acquire food. One of their first lessons, fishing, was that very morning.

"That was the best trout I've ever eaten," Jane declared, still picking the last tidbits of meat off the bones. "You girls are excellent fishermen and John a superb teacher."

"Bear showed me how to clean them," Polly said proudly.

"And I learned how to bait a hook—with a grasshopper!" Martha declared.

"And I'm so proud of both of you," Jane said. She already knew Bear had shown her girls how to ready the fish for cooking based upon the fresh blotches on Polly's dress but said nothing. She figured a stain or two was a small price to pay for the skills they were learning. She ignored the dirty dress, focusing on her daughter's happy face instead. Something in Polly's face brought fresh pain to her insides. It was her daughter's smile. She had seen the same smile in her dream. She closed her eyes to the hurt. Saw her daughters smiling again in her mind. They were happy, she reminded herself again. If she could just remember that, she believed it would help.

"May we fish again this evening Uncle John?" Martha asked.

"No Martha, as good as that fishing spot was, a storm is on its way. Those big clouds over there have been building all morning and they're coming this way. From the looks of them, it could be quite a storm," John said, pointing to the darkening thunderheads mushrooming on the horizon. "Besides, your father and Sam will bring us something tasty to eat."

"I hope they see the storm brewing too and head back before too long," Jane said, as she and Kelly gathered up the breakfast dishes.

Catherine poured everyone another cup of coffee.

"Do na worry about them. The Captain's the best weather predictor I know," Bear said. "He can smell a storm comin' a month in advance."

"Oh Bear, you're just exasperating," Polly said.

"You mean exaggerating," Jane corrected, giving Polly an affectionate hug.

"She was right the first time," John said.

Everyone chuckled, except Polly who didn't understand what she had said. Obviously annoyed they were laughing, she pinched her lips, stuck her jaw out, narrowed her eyes, and put her hands on her hips. When she did, she seemed so much like Stephen when he was aggravated, they all laughed even more. Polly had inherited not only her father's dark coloring but his facial expressions as well.

Martha, however, looked like her, with green twinkling eyes, fair skin, and untamable red curls. And as Martha grew, Jane could see more and more of her own personality reflected in her oldest daughter. She still couldn't believe how bravely Martha had defied Bomazeen. If not for the distraction she provided, God knows how that day would have gone. She reached for her daughter and gave her a big hug.

"What was that for?" Martha asked.

"Because, my honey bunny, I love you so much," Jane said, smiling. "And I'm so proud of you."

"Why do you call me that?"

"Because you're as sweet as honey and cute as a bunny."

She shared a giggle with Martha.

"We'd best get the camp ready before those clouds decide to let loose," William suggested.

Jane was used to getting wet. In the springtime, rain fell as often as the sun shined. But these clouds appeared more ominous than normal. The sky turned an eerie shade of blue-gray and faint flashes of heat lightning, still too far away for their thunder to be heard, lit the sky in a continuous light show. The flickering lightning was an early warning that serious thunderstorms were approaching.

The wind soon picked up out of the south causing ripples to scoot across the river's surface. The branches on every tree swayed, dancing to the uneven rhythm of the wind. She suddenly wished Stephen were here.

William turned to Bear and John and told the two, "I'm glad we're about to get a good downpour. You fellows smell like a couple of wild hogs."

Bear and John exchanged annoyed glances, but she had to agree with William. They both could use a good bath in her opinion, but she was not about to get involved in their banter.

"I do na plan to stand out here in the weather so your sensitive nose will na be offended," Bear said. "But I will challenge ye to a wrestlin' match in this river after the storm." River wrestling had become a favorite way for the men to get rid of road dust and let off steam. A lot more entertaining than simply bathing, they could 'fight' without being bruised or cut. So far, Bear was the acknowledged champion, although Stephen earned a close second.

"I'd as soon wrestle a real bear as you," William laughed. "I'd come closer to beating one. I think it's John's turn to take your challenge."

"Not unless Bear's going to tie one arm behind his back. I saw the dunking you took last time," John said.

"Well, I see ye know when ye're outmatched," Bear said. "If it would na offend your nose much, let's move these wagons to higher ground and tie them down."

The three men, assisted by Jane, Kelly, and Catherine, worked for the better part of an hour, while the storm flashed brilliant veins of lightning through approaching clouds now circling them in every direction.

By the time they finished, the two wagons, relocated a safe distance from the riverbank, stood securely tied and staked. They were afraid to tie onto any trees for fear the tree would draw lightning. They had already seen what lightning could do to a tree.

When they finished, they tied down everything else, hobbled the horses, oxen, and mule; and made heavy rope halters for the bull and milk cow. They figured the heifers wouldn't stray far from the bull so they left them untied. Kelly penned her chickens and William piled the saddles and tack on high ground up against a hefty boulder, and covered them with a thick layer of tree boughs. They wouldn't stay completely dry, but at least they wouldn't be totally out in the open or in standing water.

Bear stacked a good supply of wood under both wagons so they would have dry wood for the evening fire. After a bad storm, a good fire would be as welcome as a clearing sky.

"Time to say a prayer. We've done all we can do," John said, looking up at the darkening sky.

"The way the sky looks, and the wind is picking up, I think we had better all say a prayer," William added.

The first raindrops smacked the earth and the river.

"Dangerous storm," Jane heard John shout to Bear, after the rain poured continually for what seemed like forever. Both men had taken cover under her wagon and had raised their voices to be heard over the heavy downpour. Confirming John's description, hail started pummeling the ground.

"Aye," Bear bellowed back, "we're in for a rough one, but we're na so bad off as our hunters are out there. I'm more than a wee bit worried about them."

Because the men were hollering, Jane could hear them clearly. As a hunter, Bear spent many a storm out in the open and understood far better than John or William what the three might be experiencing.

It worried her too. Storms like this created hazards hard to avoid—mudslides, falling trees, rising waters, and illness from exposure. And this hail would be difficult to endure for any length of time. She hoped it was short-lived.

A few feet away from Bear and John, Kelly huddled with William under Catherine's wagon, parked right next to Jane's. Ever since the wind had kicked up, she hadn't left William's side. Jane suspected that the only time she felt secure was when William was near.

"The horses are getting nervous," William yelled over to them.

"They're not the only ones," John shouted back. "I'm worried about Little John."

"I think we ought to go after them. They should be back by now," Bear roared.

"I agree," Jane shouted down as she reached for her cloak. "Bear, help me saddle my mare."

"Give them a while longer," William hollered. "Sam knows what he's doing."

"But I can't stand by and do nothing," Jane screeched. "Damn it. I won't lose Stephen too."

At once, Jane regretted admitting her concern as Martha and Polly started crying.

Along with the hail, a hefty branch and fragments of trees and bark flew by, propelled by wind gusts that would make it difficult for a stocky man to stand upright. Jane realized it would be near impossible to saddle the horses in these conditions.

"Don't worry, it'll blow over soon," Bear's big voice boomed. "The worse a storm is, the quicker it's over."

But Bear was wrong.

CHAPTER 37

S tephen studied the huge nearly black clouds lining up on the horizon as they hiked. He could see the violence slowly building within them, like an army of nature preparing to battle men. "We need to beat this storm. It looks like wicked weather."

"Hope Little John stays out cold till we can get there," Sam said. "This bouncing is bound to make his arm ache even more."

"Maybe we should build a litter."

"Don't have time. Hear that thunder? That bad weather's moving closer. I hate to give up this doe, we need the fresh meat so badly, but we'll have to if we can't stay ahead of the storm."

"Game has been truly scarce lately. We need this meat. I know Jane needs it. She's starved. I think she could eat more than you or Bear. I've never seen her this ravenous. She's still hungry even after she eats."

"She's never carried a big Wyllie boy before."

That made him smile. He had to admit, he hoped Jane was right about it being a boy. After four girls, he had nearly given up hope of ever having a son. "At the rate she's growing, he's bound to be a stout portly fellow."

The two picked up their pace, alternating carrying Little John, but their return still seemed to be taking forever.

"Always seems longer going back than forward," Sam observed.

"The storm is catching up to us. It'll be coming down in buckets soon," Stephen said.

Little John moaned and opened his eyes slightly. "It hurts," he cried. His small face grimaced in pain and he began to cry again. "I want my Pa."

Relief filled Stephen when Little John woke, but it meant the boy would be in serious pain. "I know Little John. We'll be back at camp soon. Aunt Jane will fix you up good." The broken arm hung over Stephen's shoulder. It was the only way to carry his nephew and not put pressure on the injury.

"Little John, is your arm the only thing that pains you?" Stephen asked.

"No, my stomach hurts too," Little John sobbed.

"Forget this doe. Let's get him back to camp as quickly as we can," he told Sam.

"All right. I'll cut the backstraps and a hindquarter, so we'll at least have that much." Sam pulled his big knife and quickly got to work.

He gently laid Little John down on the ground and checked him over again to see if he could spot any other injuries. He suspected that Little John had broken or cracked a rib, but knew his injuries could be even worse. He tried to think of a way to ease Little John's suffering until they got back to camp. Jane had a bottle of a drug to dull pain, but he needed something now. He retrieved a short narrow rope from his shoulder bag and cut off a piece. He put it next to the boy's mouth. "Little John, bite down on this, it will take away some of the aching. It's what real hunters do to stop the pain when they get hurt."

Little John took the rope into his mouth and bit down hard with his back molars since his front baby teeth were missing.

He wiped tears away from the corners of the boy's eyes.

"Rope is a good idea, Stephen. That always helps me when I'm hurting," Sam said for the boy's benefit. He finished up with the doe, quickly wiped the long knife and his hands clean on leaves and grass, and then grabbed a good size piece of linen from his shoulder bag to wrap and bundle the venison.

Stephen picked up Little John and they started off again, with a cool wind seeming to chase them back to camp.

Rain started falling and, as he predicted, it came down as if poured from large buckets. They headed down the rocky hills they had climbed on the way up, the blowing rain smacking their faces like slaps from a cold hand. The steepness and lack of visibility made it difficult to hurry.

Moments later, it seemed like a frozen hell. The wind whipped pebble-sized hail into their backs. Stephen covered Little John's face with his hat, which left his own face exposed to the stinging frozen rain, and pulled the boy against his body.

Little John sobbed loudly now, into Stephen's chest, but continued to bite down on the rope.

Stephen stepped down on a rock covered with hailstones, his foot slid backward across the slick wet stones. He stumbled, landing on his knees, hitting both kneecaps on stones as he desperately fought to keep Little John's head and arm from hitting the ground.

The impact of the fall made Little John scream out in pain.

Stephen glanced up searching for his brother, but Sam hadn't heard the scream or seen them fall and didn't look back. He used his body to cover Little John and studied the boy's face. The rope still hung from the corners of his mouth. His nephew was clearly in agony, but he looked back at Stephen with the iron that was in his blood. "Trust me. We'll get you back," he promised Little John.

He carefully scooped the boy up and hurried toward Sam, feeling pain in both knees.

More than an hour had passed since they had cut the meat off the doe. Heavy rain had poured ever since, but thankfully, the hail ceased its assault. Rainwater flowed down his back, soaking his jacket and making the skin on his bare chest feel like a sheet of ice.

As they made their way downward, a nearly solid blanket of liquid flowed around them making every step treacherous. He wondered how long they would be able to continue. But they had to keep going. Water already ran swiftly at the bottom of the hill. He couldn't tell how deep the stream was.

They stopped and peered up and down the surging water for a better place to cross, but it appeared the same in both directions, with the stream rising by the minute.

"Give him to me," Sam shouted.

His brother wanted Little John since he was taller, in case the water was deep. He handed Little John over and took the venison.

Stephen glanced upstream. "Hurry," he yelled, pointing to a rising wall of water coming rapidly towards them.

With their free arms, both men held their rifles overhead as they plunged into the icy swiftly moving stream. Stephen felt his leather knee-high boots fill with water. His hat was a sodden weight on his head and his wool jacket felt like a heavy blanket on his back.

With his big long legs, and clothing made of animal skins, Sam seemed to almost sprint across, but Stephen struggled for each step. He looked upstream with alarm. The flash flood waters approached with frightening speed.

He fought to steady himself, but with each step, the current grew deeper and stronger. Halfway across, he nearly lost his grip on the venison as the rapidly moving current pushed against his hand. He used the butt of his rifle to draw it back, pulling it tightly to his chest and tightening his grip on the meat. Then, the racing wall of water smashed into him like a battering ram.

Instantly, his knees buckled and he lost his footing, falling completely into the frigid churning liquid. He thrashed about trying to recover his balance, swallowing muddy water as he fought to breathe. His feet flailed under him as he searched for the steam's bottom. The churning water swallowed him completely, turned him upside down, and then back up again.

He should try to swim, but he would have to give up his precious rifle and the meat to do so. Refusing to give them up, he wrestled against the surging stream as his lungs fought for air. Stephen thrashed about, his legs failing to locate the river bed. He needed air or his lungs would explode. He concentrated on finding a foothold to push against. Finally, his right boot felt the bottom and he pushed himself up above the waterline, gasping for air and coughing out the liquefied mud. Amazingly, he still held the rifle in one hand and gripped the venison bundle in the other.

Stephen managed to regain his balance and straighten up. As soon as he did, lightning cracked and thunder boomed just above his head making his legs unsteady again. Yet, determined to reach the far bank, he slogged on through the rushing water. All of a sudden, he wondered if it was the right bank. Turned around and upside down several times by the wild rushing vortex, reality had shifted. Nothing was as it had been just moments before. Was he even going the right direction? He glanced down, the water was flowing to his left, the same direction it had been when they entered the creek. At least he was headed in the right direction.

He waded out of the muddy impromptu river. He had lost his hat in the surge of water and had difficulty seeing, as rain poured off his head into his eyes. He tried to find some landmark that would show him which direction to go. He couldn't see Sam anywhere. Disoriented, he stood on the edge of the stream, his teeth chattering violently, wondering if the floodwater had carried him downstream when he fell. Everywhere he looked, water either flowed into the river or stood in pools growing deeper by the minute. It seemed like the whole world had dissolved into an ugly grey-brown liquid.

Another lightning bolt struck nearby, exploding a tree, and made him want to race for cover. But the only cover was trees, and they were all standing in water like he was.

He took off, splashing through water several inches deep, knowing he had to find his brother and quickly. After this downpour and flash flooding, he'd have difficulty finding his way back without him. He thought for a moment. The water must have carried him south, away from Sam. But how far? Trudging a few yards ahead, his anxiety grew as he saw no sign of Sam or the boy. As he should, his brother would be concentrating on getting Little John, who was suffering and freezing, back to camp.

With a growing sense of isolation, he realized he was on his own. I can do this, he told himself. He felt the front's biting wind on his face and its icy chill as it penetrated his soaked clothes. He suspected that the storm blew in from the north so he turned into the gusts, hoping to get back to the place where Sam had crossed. He had to find shelter; the temperature was dropping by the minute. He wound through the sodden trees, all looking like they were floating in water. Repeatedly, he slipped on rocks and hidden holes and had to pull himself up again and again. Each time, paying with more scratches and scrapes, especially on his hands and face. Shivering violently from the bone-numbing cold, he had a hard time keeping his grip on the venison and his rifle. He clutched both to his chest, but the meat felt like a block of ice on his heart. He put it under his arm instead.

The storm's clouds made everything look gloomy and oppressive. He tried to find a path leading away from the muddy stream. He trudged forward, his boots sticking in the mud, and for what seemed like hours, searched for some sort of shelter. Just one more step, he kept telling himself. One more step and he'd be closer to Jane, closer to being warm again. When he wanted to just sit down, he imagined the feel her soft body pressed against his. He could almost taste her sweet lips.

He staggered on. Giving up was not an option. Not when he had Jane to live for. He had nearly lost her twice to Bomazeen and once to grief and the anger it had spawned. He swore he'd never let that happen again. And Martha and Polly. He had lost two daughters, but he still had two. He had to make it back to all of them.

Finally, he found a thick stand of timber on higher ground. He spotted a huge evergreen covered with a wild grapevine. The enormous lower branches reached the ground and curled back towards the tree's trunk creating a canopy. The higher branches, covered with the thick leafy vine, would keep out the majority of the downpour. Exhausted, he collapsed to his knees and crawled on the slippery forest floor until he was under the tree. Just a little further, he urged himself as he headed for the tree's massive trunk. The rain still stuttered under the tree's canopy, but it was more like a shower than a pounding drenching.

Despite how tired his eyes were, which burned from peering through the rain, he drew his knife and made himself watch for creatures that might have moved into the cozy shelter first. Luckily, the shelter was empty, but the leaf-covered ground next to the trunk still bore the imprints and wild smell of previous inhabitants. He hoped whatever it was wouldn't return soon.

He pressed his back against the trunk of the tree, away from the howling wind, and with trembling hands yanked off his wet boots. He tugged off his wet wool jacket and tried to use it as a blanket, wishing he had brought his big cloak along. But the jacket was so soaked, water ran from its edges. He threw it over a nearby sturdy branch instead to let the water seep out of it before he put it back on. He put his icy feet in his hands and set to work rubbing his numb toes, but his hands were so raw and scratched he could not continue. He put his hands under his armpits hoping to warm them just a little as he fought to control his constant shivering and his chattering teeth.

Stephen closed his burning eyes for a moment. He needed to rest. Could he risk going to sleep? What if a bear or a mountain cat found him asleep? He forced his eyelids open, but they seemed to have a will of their own, a will stronger than his.

Behind his eyelids, he saw Little John and wondered if he would be all right. Was it a broken rib or had the boy been injured inside? If Little John died, heaven forbid, Jane might blame him again. Would another child be sacrificed for his dream? *Please God, no.*

He tried to banish the repugnant thoughts, but they were quickly replaced with yet another worry. Had he wandered closer to their camp or away from it? It was late in the day. It would be dark soon. With the darkness, even deeper cold would come. He had certainly experienced intense cold in New Hampshire, but not when he was this wet and this exhausted. His body could not withstand these conditions for long.

Bear, William, and Sam would come looking for him when the rain let up. If it ever did. This was no ordinary storm. If it had blown in from the sea, it could rain for hours. Would they know where to look? He hoped he hadn't strayed too far from where he had last seen Sam. He would be impossible to track after this storm. Maybe he should backtrack if he could. Find the spot where they had crossed. But he had to rest first.

He wearily closed his eyes again. He hugged his legs and lay down, a ball of misery. He pushed his body into the wet earth and pine needles, trying to bury himself away from the chilly wind. His bruised and swollen kneecaps and his strained shoulder hurt, but the pain was almost a welcome distraction from the bone-chilling cold.

He'd rest just long enough to regain his strength, just for a moment.

Something woke Stephen. He hadn't meant to sleep for long, yet he could tell that he had. It was almost dark. The rain, slower now, still filtered through the tree's branches around his makeshift shelter.

What had he heard? Maybe he hadn't heard anything. Maybe it was just the wind, but the wind had mercifully died down. He forced himself to steady his breathing and to listen beyond the rain and into the timber. A shiver went through him. It wasn't from the cold. He strained again to hear something. But he could not locate the source of the eerie feeling creeping through him.

He quietly reached for his rifle. Would the powder be dry enough? He emptied the pan and quickly refilled it with fresh powder, trying to keep his half-frozen hands from shaking. The powder might be damp even inside the typically waterproof powder horn. But what he had just been through was not typical. There was a good chance the rifle would not fire. He had his knife and hatchet he reminded himself.

And he had courage. Faith and courage. He would need both. He slowly stood up. He had difficulty straightening his stiff knees and legs. He leaned against the tree to keep from falling down.

The shiver hit him again, but this time it slithered down the full length of his spine, waking up his tired back muscles. His breathing quickened with the faster beat of his heart. He stared into the semi-darkness, thankful that he at least had some light. He saw nothing. No sounds, no movement. Nothing.

He was just tired, his nerves on edge. He'd been through enough today. Nothing else would happen. Would it?

What would Sam do? He'd listen to his instincts. He wouldn't resort to self-deception—trying to convince himself nothing was wrong. He'd find his courage. He took a deep rallying breath, steadied his nerves, and called upon his senses. Something prowled out there, something malevolent. He scanned the woods again—but this time he looked further, into the trees.

There.

Only visible because of its yellow eyes, hot with intensity, focused keenly on him, a huge menacing head. He was enormous—all massive muscles and fur. The biggest wolf he had ever seen.

The wolf took a step forward and snarled, baring his teeth.

Even through the rain, Stephen could see its ink-black coat bristling. He remembered what Bear had said about wolves having 42 bone-crushing teeth. But like a dream wolf, suddenly it was gone again, leaving him with only a feeling of dread.

It had not gone away. He felt watched. More than watched—studied.

For what seemed like an eternity, it stalked him. Just out of sight, veiled by the tree's huge branches and the incessant steady rain. He decided the wolf had revealed himself only long enough to try to weaken his prey with fear. Well, he wouldn't let fear weaken him. To the marrow of his bones, he felt terror, but he would *not* give into it.

In a blink, the wolf could leap upon him and rip him apart. The wolf's teeth would crush his ribs and tear out his heart—destroying everything his heart had dreamed of for so long.

Here's where it happens. Just like Sam always said. Being brave wouldn't be enough. Victory only goes to the bravest *and* the most savage. He could only survive the wilderness and this wolf if he could be as savage as it was. Stephen reached deep down inside and drew out the strength to battle.

Still unseen, the black fiend growled deep in its throat.

The blood-chilling sound made his teeth clench. A sense of imminent attack filled him, but it was more than that. It was a sense of a forthcoming struggle for life. His or the wolf's?

Crouched low, Stephen turned in a tight circle, trying to find the brute in the shadows. But the demon would not reveal himself.

He shuddered and was tempted to run. He took a step forward, testing his knees, then another. He stopped. No, the wolf could easily outrun him. Besides, running in the rain on slippery mud and slick leaves with stiff knees would only lead to falling and being seized from behind. He could almost feel the wolf's fangs sinking into the back of his neck. As though the wolf was actually leaping on his back, he jerked around and glared behind him.

But the wolf wasn't leaping. With wicked poise, the wolf stepped slowly into view.

Through the ever-changing drips of the rain, he watched the beast's eyes grow narrow, sharpen into yellow daggers, then his nostrils flared and his lips curled exposing huge teeth. The wolf circled to his right, his steps soft and unhurried.

He could nearly read the wolf's thoughts. This was his forest and he didn't appreciate the intrusion. And he was hungry.

Stephen tried to think but his wildly drumming heart drowned out every thought he had. He made himself slow his breathing. If he didn't he'd never be able to aim accurately. Kill it, that's all you have to do, he told himself. Just kill it.

He put the wolf in his rifle's sights, but if the weapon didn't fire, which was likely, the wolf would be on top of him before he could pull his hatchet or knife. He considered climbing the tree, but his swollen knees would make quickly scrambling up the tree impossible. It would only be a good way to lose a foot or a leg.

Best to go with a sure thing. He yanked out his knife, good sized, but he wished it were as big as Sam's blade. He wrapped his fingers, numb with cold, and his raw palm, around the knife's handle. He grabbed his hatchet with the other hand, the wet handle slippery.

He tightened his grip on both as another shiny coat emerged from the other side of his shelter.

CHAPTER 38

"Look," Bear yelled, his hunter's eyes the first to spot Sam. "Sam's carryin' Little John."

Bear, John, and William left the shelter of the wagons and ran toward the two. They all had to hold on to their hats to keep the wind from blowing them off. Anxious to see Stephen, Jane followed right behind them, her heavy wet skirt dragging in the mud. She was more than a little tempted to exchange her gown for a pair of Stephen's breeches and a shirt.

"Help him," Sam yelled over the wind and rain.

"What happened?" John shouted as he ran towards them.

"He fell in a hidden cavern, broke his arm," Sam answered.

"Papa," Little John cried, reaching for his father with his good arm. His little fist clutched the small piece of rope.

John carefully lifted his son off Sam's shoulder.

Jane was relieved to see Little John and Sam, but didn't see Stephen anywhere. "Where's Stephen?" she nearly demanded.

"Lost him sometime back. We crossed a creek of rising waters and I don't think he made it across."

Jane wanted to faint. Was she going to lose Stephen so soon after they had found each other again? No, she wouldn't let that happen. She held her breath as Sam continued.

"I went back to look for him but with Little John hurting so, I didn't look for long. Besides, I couldn't see past a few feet. We'll find him after this rain lets up."

"No, we have to go now!" Jane shouted. "He could be injured."

Sam shook his head. "We'd just wind up with more of us lost or hurt. Don't worry, we'll leave the minute we can."

"Don't tell me not to worry," she shrieked. "That's my husband out there!" Her nerves were getting the best of her. She needed to get ahold of herself. "I'm sorry Sam, I'm just so uneasy about Stephen I can't think clearly. Let's see to Little John. William, carry the girls from my wagon to Catherine's. John, put Little John in mine."

Jane turned and marched back, wondering if Stephen's last thoughts would be remembering that she still had not totally forgiven him. She had told him that even though she understood why he had to make the journey, a small part of her still blamed him for the girls' deaths, and that she would try hard to forgive herself too, not just him.

She did now, completely.

God, just let him come back, so I can tell him.

She lifted her rain-sodden skirts, shook off most of the mud, and climbed into her wagon, her heart aching for him, for what he might be going through.

William and John, who carried his son, quickly followed Jane back to the wagons as strong winds threw waterfalls of rain at them. Bear stayed back with Sam who could only proceed at a slower pace.

"Ye look like ye're half dead," Bear told Sam.

"Then I look like I feel," Sam growled. The hail they'd encountered burned his face as if he'd shaved much too close. His matted and soaked beaver cap felt like a dead wet animal on his head. The raw skin of his palms flamed with pain and both his back and newly healed ankle ached from carrying Little John's weight.

"How bad off is the wee boy?" Bear asked, concerned.

"Arm's got a bad break. Maybe a rib was broken too. Hopefully, the rest of him will be well. Fell in a cave. Lowered Stephen into it to get him and hauled them both out. Used a long vine for a rope," Sam explained, raising his voice above the storm. "Everyone here all right?"

"Aye. We got the wagons moved to higher ground and everything tied down when the storm started comin' this way. 'Twas good we did, that river is risin' fast. The wind's been blowin' with a powerful fury," Bear said looking around. "I worry about waitin' to go look for Stephen."

"I do as well," Sam said, "but I don't think we have a choice."

"Ye should stay, ye're worse for the wear. William and I will go."

"But I know where I saw him last," Sam pointed out, spitting rain out of his mouth as he crawled under one of the wagons, followed by Bear.

"Alright then, take us that far, and then ye can come back. I can look north of the spot ye last saw him and William can look south."

"Bear, you'll only be able to see a half dozen feet in front of you. It's getting dark. The wind is still fierce and the rain continues to pour."

"My eyes are their sharpest at night. The rain will surely let up soon, and we'll have a bit of a moon when it clears. I'll tell William to get his horse and George saddled, and I'll be saddlin' Camel and Alex while ye rest. Stephen will be needin' us." On his hands and knees, Bear awkwardly crawled out of the cramped space through a curtain of water flowing off the wagon's side.

Sam had to admire Bear's persistence. He was right—Stephen could be in trouble and might not survive this night. If he'd been thinking with his head instead of his exhausted body, he'd have said the same thing. His brother needed their help now.

He hesitated to leave the camp with only John to guard it, but he needed both Bear and William to help with the search. They would have a lot of ground to cover trying to find Stephen.

Sam rested his head against the wheel as he ate the piece of dried meat and cold biscuits Catherine gave him before she darted back into her wagon.

☙

"John, this is a strong medicine. I'm familiar with the proper dose of Laudanum for an adult, but Little John is the first child I've ever given it to. I'm not even sure you can give opium to a child. I'm just not sure. And with Stephen missing, I'm not thinking clearly. What do you want me to do?" Jane asked, her heart worried and anxious.

She wrung her hands, nearly in a state of panic because of Stephen and mad at herself for never learning what a child's dose should be. Before they left on their journey, Sam ordered the painkiller from Edward as part of their long supply list. Stephen asked her to review the list, but it never occurred to her to ask about the Laudanum.

John gazed at his son, a father's compassion filling his eyes.

Suffering terribly, Little John whimpered pitifully. Exhausted from the excitement of the day and enduring severe pain, it seemed as if he didn't have the strength left to cry.

Jane touched Little John's face and feet. He felt cold as ice. She covered the shivering boy with a wool blanket while John removed his boots and stockings, both soaked through. John rubbed his son's toes vigorously between his hands trying to warm them while she thought about what to do.

"Would you give it to one of your girls if they were suffering?" John asked.

280

She recalled the suffering her two girls had endured before they died. "It's your decision John," she said quietly.

"Give it to him. I can't stand to see him suffer like this."

The rain continued to patter steadily on the wagon cover.

Jane turned so Little John couldn't hear her and whispered, "I'm still not sure. If he overdoses, it might kill him."

John reached for Little John's small hand on his uninjured side and kissed it.

Tears now glistened through the pain in the boy's red eyes.

"How much would you give me?" John asked. "He weighs about a fourth of what I weigh. Divide an adult dose in fourths."

"Are you sure?"

"Just do it, now!"

Still apprehensive, she took a deep breath, carefully measured the dose, and gave the drug to Little John. "God let that be the right amount," she whispered to herself.

"Pa, Uncle Sam said I'm a real hunter now," Little John said, his voice weak. The boy soon closed his eyes.

John and Jane both held their breath until they saw him breathing evenly. Within seconds, he slept soundly, his little hand still clutching the small rope that had tethered his pain.

"Yes son, you're a real hunter now," John said, sounding relieved that his son's suffering had ended at least for the moment. "I'll stay with him and get him out of these wet clothes. You've done all you can. He'll be able to sleep now."

"His spare clothes are in this bag. I'll make him a better splint and sling as soon as the weather clears and I'll put it on him in the morning."

"Thank you, Jane. Little John's mother and I are both grateful for your help."

"I'd better go check on Martha and Polly. I'm sure they're both worried about Little John and their father."

She was too. Something told her Stephen was in serious trouble.

"Jane," John said. "They'll find him."

CHAPTER 39

J ane climbed out of the wagon and searched for Stephen's brothers, relieved to see their horses gone. They had taken Stephen's horse too.

She started pacing in the rain. Her hair felt heavy on her back. Her muddy boots felt leaden. All the trees drooped with heavy branches. And her heart wilted with the weight of her worries.

She stared into the dismal gloom. Where was he?

For a moment, she contemplated saddling her mare and following them, but then remembered that Little John might still need her. He could have other injuries and she wanted to be there when he woke. She also didn't want to leave her daughters.

She would just have to put her trust in Sam and the others.

They would find Stephen and he would be all right. He had to be. That's all there is to it, she decided, as though her strong will would be enough to save him from whatever dangers he faced.

With some difficulty, Sam got them close to the spot where they had crossed the rising waters.

There was no sign of Stephen.

The water flowed harder and higher now. The churning muddy waters rushed past them with amazing force, carrying branches and other debris. It would be difficult, if not impossible, to pass to the other side.

The men stuck together. Conditions were too unsafe to split up. They followed the west bank heading north, hoping that Stephen had made it across to the correct bank and that the rising water hadn't trapped him somewhere downstream.

Sam theorized that the wall of water they saw coming would have carried his brother south. But Stephen would have realized this and headed north to try to get back to where he'd entered the water. Without landmarks though, it would be easy for Stephen to become confused.

Sam and the others urged their horses, unhappy with the conditions, to continue plodding through the standing water. Each of the men repeatedly dug their heels into their mounts' sides.

A straight route was difficult as they continually encountered impassable areas where the creek was out of its banks. He steered them around these boggy areas and led the way through thick trees and tangled undergrowth.

Haste was difficult. Only their concern for Stephen kept them moving forward.

When they were able, they fanned out about thirty feet apart to cover a wider area as they searched. They tried calling Stephen's name, but they could barely hear each other through the rain, and quickly gave up that effort.

Instead, they focused on trying to find some clue that Stephen had passed this way. If he hadn't, his brother could be in serious trouble because they wouldn't find him tonight. If conditions worsened, they could be in trouble too. Trudging through mud and water was causing the horses to tire. Soon their mounts wouldn't have the strength to continue.

But Stephen needed help, so Sam pushed Alex and the group even harder.

After some time, the heavy deluge finally let up, and the swiftly flowing waters began to slow and recede. They still rode through a fine mist that felt like a liquid breeze.

Bear motioned Sam and William over to him. He pointed to a torn branch.

"The storm may have broken it," Sam said.

Suddenly, Camel reared—not an easy task for a horse carrying a man of Bear's size.

Sam glanced down. A large Copperhead, with dark hourglass-shaped crossbands, slithered between Camel's legs, skimming the top of the shallow water. Bear managed to stay in the saddle, but now all four spooked horses snorted and pawed the ground, sidestepping into each other in panic.

William's mount abruptly cut to the right while Stephen's horse, led by William, jerked to the left. William ended up laying on his stomach in about three inches of muddy water, facing the yellow elliptical eyes of the snake, now coiled near William's head on a piece of rotting wood.

"Son of a..." William hissed.

"Don't move," Sam warned. "I know you want to bolt, but don't."

William froze, not even breathing, and kept his wide eyes on the snake.

They'd all seen what a Copperhead bite meant. Although seldom lethal, the bite made a large area of skin and muscle turn black with rot. The putrefaction often had to be cut out causing great pain and disfigurement. In addition, the victim quickly experienced extreme pain, tingling, throbbing, swelling, and severe nausea.

Menacingly, the Copperhead repeatedly stuck out a long red forked tongue, then it coiled tighter preparing to strike William's face. A bite to the head could be lethal.

Sam unsheathed his knife, aimed carefully through the rain, and threw but with his wet raw hands, missed. He swiftly jumped from his horse, distracting the still coiled snake from William.

He would have to be fast. Quicker than the snake and that was saying a lot. And he could not miss again. Sam stepped toward the snake gripping his hatchet. His other hand reached for the end of the piece of wood holding the snake. The snake opened its jaws to strike. With a loud howl and supernatural speed, Sam struck, slicing the snake's head off and hacking the wood in two. Pieces of bark and snake flew in two different directions.

William let out a slow breath at the sight of the viper's severed head and twitching body. With trembling hands, he pulled Sam's knife from the muddy water and handed it back to him. "Thanks, I owe you one."

Sam put the snake's yard-long body in a sack and stuffed it into his saddlebag. It was food and food was something he never wasted.

"Quit playin' with that snake. Let's go," Bear said, returning with three mounts. Alex had quickly joined Stephen and William's horses.

"How far do you think Stephen could have gone?" William asked, mounting his horse and still looking a little shaken. "Could the water have carried him downstream from where you crossed?"

Sam peered over at the now smaller steam of muddy water to his right, barely visible in the fading evening light. Stephen must have sought shelter. He could also have tried to find their camp. Or, if Stephen had gotten turned around and crossed to the wrong bank, he could be anywhere by now. They could be getting further away from him with each step of the horses. Yet his instincts pointed him north and the broken branch gave him a small hope that he was right.

"Sam?" William asked again.

"Stay quiet, start listening, and stop talking," Sam said harshly, fatigue catching up to him.

The three rode in silence until Sam stopped. He dismounted and motioned for the other two to do the same and then he started walking, leading his horse. Immediately, without the creaking of saddle leather beneath their weight, it was quieter.

About a quarter-mile up, Sam tied Alex. He motioned for Bear and William to do the same, then said, "We'll walk from here. It'll be harder going for us, but at least we'll be able to hear. I can't hear a damn thing with four horses splashing through this muck."

They trudged some distance in silence, their feet beginning to freeze in the cold water. Until now, he had successfully fought the cold, but at this point, his teeth began to chatter. He'd been wet and in the storm for hours. Every step was grueling, but he forced himself to put one foot in front of the other. The clearing skies and a sliver of moon allowed him to stare into the gloomy darkness ahead.

Sam heard a wolf howl. The skin on the back of his neck prickled. Then a second wolf howled. "Hurry," he yelled, taking off at a near run.

The three splashed through standing water for several minutes and then William slipped and fell to his knees. Sam and Bear kept going.

"Stephen," Sam screamed at the top of his lungs.

"Stephen," Bear roared even louder.

Sam dashed ahead with only his instincts to guide him as to where the wolf howls had come from.

William caught up to them. "Did you hear him?" he yelled.

"Just keep going," Sam shouted, struggling now to continue rushing. He slowed somewhat but motioned the other two to keep on. He sensed Stephen was ahead and that his brother needed them.

Bear turned on the speed and charged through the timber, reminding

Sam of a real Bear on the run. William trailed closely behind him.

Sam heard a rifle being fired, probably Bear's. Bear usually managed to keep his powder dry. In inclement weather, he and Bear both kept their rifles and powder wrapped tightly in deer hide. But even with that precaution, in weather like this, dry powder required a small miracle.

Within moments, he saw Bear standing over a large dead wolf, its silver-black hair fluttering in the stiff breeze. Blood oozed from a hole in its side where Bear's bullet entered.

"Keep going, there's another one!" Sam yelled.

The men ran another few yards and found it. The wolf looked like it could barely run, dragging one of its back legs. Its defiant yellow eyes glowed bright with viciousness, even in the dim moonlight. The wounded black monster snarled at them through a bloodied mouth and teeth stained red.

"Bloody hell," Sam said at the sight.

CHAPTER 40

Sam heaved his knife, this time hitting his growling target.

They all heard the sound of the blade slamming into the wolf's thick chest followed by the animal's dying whine.

Sam quickly retrieved his knife and they continued searching.

It didn't take long.

Stephen lay nearby under a tree canopy, his knife clutched in one hand, his hatchet in the other. Both were bloodied. His throat torn, blood pooled at the base of his neck.

Sam froze for a moment, his mind denying what his eyes were telling him. Then he sprung towards Stephen as Bear and William also rushed to their brother's side. Stephen's face and hands were nearly blue with cold and loss of blood. Sam took a quick look at the neck wound and motioned for Bear to put his hand against the tear to stop the bleeding. The laceration didn't appear to be deep, but the ragged gash was about three inches long. William pulled off his cravat, folded the necktie into a bandage as best he could, and then tied it around Stephen's neck.

Stephen seemed barely conscious, but Sam suspected it was mostly from fatigue and exposure. He checked his brother's pulse. It beat slow but strong. For that, he gave thanks. He quickly checked for other serious wounds. A scratch ran across his chest, and bite-marks punctured both arms. Jane would need to clean the wounds with whiskey and stitch them. Blood dripped into one of his brother's eyes from a small scalp wound but he was otherwise intact.

Everywhere Sam touched, Stephen felt like ice.

The three put Stephen's boots back on him and then his coat.

"Where's his shirt?" William asked.

"He used it for a sling for Little John's arm," Sam explained. "We've got to get him warm now, or he won't make it back to camp."

"But how?" William asked. "There's no hope for a fire with everything so saturated, including us."

"I'll hurry back for the horses. Then ye can put him on my saddle in front of me. My body will warm," Bear said. He took off, splashing through water, even before he finished the sentence.

Stephen needed help now. Bear was as cold and wet as the rest of them and even his big hairy body would provide little warmth. "Drag that damn wolf over here," Sam told William, urgency in his voice. "Then go get the other one."

William had one wolf back in a minute, and then quickly went after the bigger of the two.

Sam turned his brother on his side and pushed the still warm animal, up against his back, and then as soon as William brought it, pushed the second beast against his front side. Then Sam draped the neck of the front wolf onto Stephen's neck.

He noticed both wolves had severe cuts and slashes on nearly every leg and one leg on the larger black fiend hung nearly severed. The stomach of the other had a deep gash, evidently opened by Stephen's hatchet. He marveled at the courage his brother found to survive the attack.

He cut the tails off both wolves, wrapped, and then tied them around Stephen's hands. The heavy air held the musty scent of the wild animals and the shared apprehension of the two men.

Sam finally stood.

William looked worried. "Is he going to make it?"

"Hard to say," Sam whispered.

"If he comes around soon, he'll recover quickly. If he stays out, he's chilled to his core. His heart may be too cold to get his blood flowing again," Sam said.

William knelt down, pressed the carcass nearest him up closer to Stephen's chest, and held it there with his hands.

After several long interminable minutes, Stephen started to stir and finally opened his eyes. They glistened unnaturally in the dark.

Stephen screamed as his eyes flew open. The wolf was right next to him! Horrorstruck, he thrust the beast away and pushed himself up. Flailing his arms around him in a wild frenzy, he grabbed his hatchet. Never comprehending the wolves were motionless, or that Sam and William stood nearby, he slammed the hatchet into the wolf's neck.

He stood, swaying on his feet and glaring at the wolves. They weren't moving. Were they dead?

"Stephen," Sam shouted. "They're dead. The wolves are dead!"

When he stopped and looked up, Sam grabbed the hatchet and handed it to William.

His brothers were here? They seemed to be trying to tell him something, but he could barely hear him. He couldn't think. But he remembered that he just fought a battle for his life, his entire being consumed with trying to stay alive. He shook his head, trying to understand what had happened and what was happening.

"He's delirious with rage and fatigue," he heard Sam say.

"We're here Stephen. We found you. We'll help you," William said. "Bear's bringing our mounts."

"Savage fury isn't something easily turned off," Sam said. "Give him a few minutes."

Slowly, Stephen started to calm and his breathing began to slow somewhat. He glared directly at Sam, then at William. Recognition finally came into his head.

"Did...I ki..kill them?" he stammered, blood dripping from his shaking hands.

"Fending off an attack by two wolves is a remarkable feat. Both were dying and started running off when they heard us coming. We only finished them off for you," Sam explained.

"If they were running off, why were they next to me?"

"We put those beasts close to you to get you warmed up," Sam explained.

Judging from the warmth coming back into his body, Sam's plan had worked, although he didn't appreciate waking next to the fiends.

"Take it easy, you're leaking blood too fast for you to be moving around," William said.

William applied pressure to Stephen's neck wound, while Sam helped lean him against the tree trunk.

"Sam, they nearly had me." Stephen panted the words. "When that big black monster ripped my neck, I thought I was about to be eaten alive. But I didn't give up. I kept fighting like I knew you would."

"You did fine," Sam said, "mighty fine."

"Jane? Is Jane all right?" he asked, still shaking somewhat.

"Yes, and so are the girls. John's with them," William said. "She's sick with worry though. We need to get you back to her soon or she'll be out searching for you herself."

"Little John?" Stephen nearly pleaded the question.

"Jane's tending to him. In a lot of pain, but he should be fine. Going to make a good hunter one of these days," Sam said.

"And a good man," he said, feeling weak but more like himself. He slid down the tree trunk to sit and after several minutes his breathing calmed and the blood stopped dripping from his neck.

"I'm sorry you got separated," Sam said. "I tried looking for you, but the rain was so heavy I couldn't see a thing, and I needed to get help for Little John."

"I'm just glad you found me when you did."

"Me too," Sam and William both said at once.

Bear arrived with their horses and as soon as he saw his owner, George yanked away and galloped to Stephen, snorting and stomping his feet. The stallion acted as though he knew something was wrong.

"Whoa now," he soothed. "I'm just fine now." He reached up and with still cold fingers, stroked George's wet nose. The stallion calmed and stood still, letting the rein drop in Stephen's lap.

After tying the other three horses, Bear helped Sam skin the wolves. Better than blankets and waterproof, Sam wanted to use the furs to keep Stephen warm until they made it back to camp. Now the two wolves would help save his life, not take it from him.

In the meantime, William took a cloth from his saddlebag, moistened it with water pooled on leaves, and started cleaning as much blood and dirt off Stephen's face and neck as he could. "Your face is bruised and filthy," William said as he began, "but remarkably, it's only nicked in a few places."

"Good, I wouldn't want you to be the only handsome one in the family," Stephen said, feeling more like himself.

With each passing minute, he seemed to gain strength. He had survived. As soon as he could hold Jane in his arms, everything would be right again.

"I still have the meat," he said, pointing to the bundle that hung high up in the tree.

"I knew you would," Sam said.

CHAPTER 41

Thankful to be alive, beyond anything he felt before now, Stephen and the group slowly made their way back to their camp through the dark wet wilderness. He could not wait to see Jane again. He had come so close to making her a widow. Now, he just wanted to be back in her arms again.

The miserably cold wind and rain moved further south and they were all beginning to thaw out. With the help of the wolf hides tied to him, warmth crept back into his body. The damp air smelled like wet earth and leaves. Every sodden tree, branches drooping, dripped with the last drops of the violent storm.

Before long, with each step of his horse, the drops seemed to grow heavier with menace. The forest seemed unnaturally quiet. Instinctively, he knew something was wrong. He also saw Sam growing more apprehensive by the minute. His brother's senses, honed by years in the wild, seemed to be on high alert. Stephen watched as Sam scanned the surrounding woodland again and again. This went beyond his ordinary watchfulness.

Now, his own skin crawled. Yet, he couldn't figure out what was making both of them so uneasy.

He glanced over at Bear and William. They seemed to sense danger too.

The unknown threat made the group slow as they drew closer to their camp.

He steered George alongside Sam and asked, "Is something wrong?"

"Possibly," Sam whispered. "Wait here."

"No, I'm going with you," he said, his tone leaving no room for debate.

"Tell the others to wait here. Tell them to stay silent and load their weapons. Then follow me."

Now Stephen worried in earnest. Sam's instincts were never wrong.

Stephen silently made his way forward, following behind Sam, the only sound coming from a forest of dripping leaves and pine needles. Dark speculation filled him with unease.

Within minutes, hidden in heavy brush, they studied their camp. Using the dry wood they stored under the wagons in a storm, the group had managed to get a large fire blazing. The firelight made the drops of moisture on the branches surrounding his head sparkle and let him see the campsite clearly.

Then his stomach vaulted with the intensity of his horror. He blinked hard, hoping that fatigue made him see an illusion. But it was no illusion—it was Chief Wanalancet himself and four muscular braves. He recognized the Chief, having seen Wanalancet once before when Sam helped to mediate a peace pact between several tribes and the colonists.

"Bloody hell!" Stephen mouthed silently.

In addition to a bow, each Pennacook brave carried a rifle and knives. Their dark wet hair and exposed skin looked polished in the fire's light. Except for mud on the legs of their horses, tied nearby, they seemed unaffected by the storm.

Jane stood by the fire, as Wanalancet circled, studying her. Her long hair appeared damp and even wilder than normal. Her bright eyes shot daggers of anger at Wanalancet and followed the man's movements. He prayed Jane's temper would not get her killed and hoped he could control his own mounting rage.

John lay motionless on the ground nearby, his hands and feet tied. Other than a bloodied face, he appeared to be unharmed. The children were tied together around one tree, the two girls weeping quietly while Little John, in obvious pain, whimpered pitifully. Anger swelled in his chest and he gnashed his teeth.

Two braves held Catherine and two held Kelly. Both women appeared disheveled and highly agitated, as if they had fought hard, but finally gave up struggling. All four braves seemed to be awaiting instructions from Wanalancet, while they gaped at the two women eagerly and longingly. He suspected it wouldn't be long before Wanalancet gave his braves what they wanted.

He glanced over at Sam. He could tell his brother itched to pull his knife, but Sam would think with his head not just his gut. Men who didn't wound up dead.

Sam turned silently, and they quickly headed back toward William and Bear.

His mind raced faster than he walked. The Indian that had escaped when he killed Bomazeen must have told Wanalancet about Jane escaping and confirmed that she was as beautiful as Bomazeen had undoubtedly claimed. The more striking a woman, the more Bomazeen would have gotten for her in trade. As they all suspected, Bomazeen had singled Jane out for the Chief for her beauty and red hair. The Chief would also have learned that her family was following the Great Indian Warpath. Wanalancet would be familiar with the trail, used for centuries by the northern and southern tribes for trade and war. For the Chief, it would just be a matter of staying out of sight of other travelers until he caught up to Jane.

As soon as they were out of earshot of the camp, he quietly asked Sam, "Why did that son-of-a-bitch follow this far into the wilderness? And how do we kill them?"

"The Chief must have made a wedding pact with his Great Spirit," Sam whispered. "In Wanalancet's mind, he was already wed to Jane. I've heard of similar spirit pacts when they chose wives from neighboring tribes. Wanalancet suffered the humiliation of losing Jane twice and must have decided that the Great Spirit demanded that he claim her himself. Whatever his motivation, Wanalancet is obsessed with having Jane. If we don't respond correctly, we could all die."

"Make yourself think like a Captain again. We need a strategy," Stephen urged, refusing to give in to his panic. "I'll do the same."

He started moving back toward the others. By the time they reached William and Bear, a plan gelled in his mind. It was risky, but it stood a chance.

Under normal circumstances, he would have no doubts. However, he had just been through hell and they were all about to go there again. But he felt considerably stronger and warmer, and his wounds had stopped bleeding. He could do this. He would do it. For Jane. For his daughters.

Bear and William stood together loading their weapons, with ball and powder, on the slim chance that the powder would be dry enough to fire.

"Everyone at camp appears to be unharmed. But," he hesitated still unable to believe it himself, "Wanalancet and four braves are holding them all captive."

"Wanalancet!" Bear exclaimed. "The Pennacook Chief?"

"Keep your voices down, and listen carefully," Sam warned. "Wanalancet has come for Jane. In his mind, they are already married."

"She's my wife!" Stephen swore. His hands clenched. He wanted to strangle the bastard.

"That's unimportant to him. His braves will want the other two women as well. Stephen, you're weary, cold, and injured, but I need you to act stronger than you feel."

"I feel fine," Stephen spat.

"Good. The rain's drizzle washed the remaining blood off you. You must appear fearless and strong. The wolves' hides on your shoulders will impress Wanalancet. The Algonquian tribes revere the wolf's spirit and believe the animal's hide can make you strong, savage, and cunning. Believe that yourself."

Stephen did believe it. "I'd gladly turn into one of these damn wolves if it would stop the bastard from taking Jane," he cursed. His blood hot with his wrath, he stood taller and clenched his fists.

"Good. Wanalancet will sense that," Sam said. "What are your ideas, Stephen?"

"We intimidate him, make him realize I killed Bomazeen, and will kill him too. We show him our strength," Stephen said. "Then we appeal to his honor. Make him understand that stealing a man's wife is dishonorable and evil. That I have an ability to kill evil men. If it works, we stand a chance of changing his mind about stealing Jane."

"How?" William asked. "He won't be easily intimidated."

"Bear, you have the strength of bears in your body, and in your necklace. Let Wanalancet see that too. William, do you have one of your old lawman badges in your coat?" Stephen asked.

"Yes, right here," William said, reaching into his waistcoat. "I kept one for luck."

"Good, we could use some luck. Put it on. He may know what it means and believe you are a warrior because of it. With or without the badge, you are a warrior, so look like one. Wanalancet will know of Sam and his knife. Sam is intimidating just standing there. The four of us must stride into that camp as though we have no fear and they do not worry us."

"I agree," Sam said. "Hold your heads high and let your strength show on your face. Hold your weapons at the ready but do not use them until I do. Understand?"

"If he has hurt Jane or if he even steps upon her shadow, I'm using my weapon. And I'm going to kill him," Stephen vowed.

"He hasn't come this far to harm her. Clearly, he's obsessed with her. Besides, she's no good to him dead or injured. He *will* want to kill you. Probably what he's waiting for," Sam told him. "You must make him realize that your spirit is strong and that your spirit also claims Jane."

"Will that work?" William asked.

"It just might," Bear said, "if not, we'll kill them."

"Indeed. But our goal is that nobody dies. Not us and not them. Jane will only be safe if we can finally convince Wanalancet that he cannot have her," Sam said, "and get him to go back to the White Mountains. No matter what Wanalancet says, be careful what you say. Put steel in your eyes and let them speak for you. If you have ever trusted me, trust me on this. If we are forced to use our weapons, I'll kill the Chief. Bear you take the brave closest to you with your hatchet. William and Stephen, spread out a little and stand ready to fire at the brave closest to each of you. Then both of you fire your second pistol at the remaining brave. With all this moisture, your weapons may not fire so be prepared to move fast and use your knives or hatchets. Understand?"

"What about John?" Bear asked.

"He's tied up and bleeding a little. They've tied the children around a tree. All three women have their hands tied. Wanalancet is just waiting for us," Sam explained.

"Let's get this over with," Stephen said, pulling his pistols. "They took Jane once. I'm not about to let that happen again."

Leaving their horses tied, the group made their way to camp. As Stephen suspected, Wanalancet heard them coming.

"Watch out!" Jane screamed.

"We come to talk," Sam yelled calmly, in the Algonquian language.

As they entered the clearing, four bows pointed arrows at each of them, but Wanalancet held his braves back with a motion of his arm. Stephen assumed Wanalancet would want to see his enemy before he ordered them killed and because the Chief held the women, he had the advantage and he knew it. They could not charge the Pennacook without risking the lives of the women.

They approached slowly and cautiously, Sam clutching his long knife in a clenched fist, Bear gripping his big hatchet and a pistol. Stephen and William each held two pistols. All four strode forcefully towards the cook fire. He glanced at Sam and saw the warrior in his brother—his defiant jaw set, lips pursed, and hard eyes intense. Bear looked nearly as threatening as Sam, and William's features were dark and menacing.

Then he turned his gaze forward and his eyes met Jane's. His heart leapt out to her. She needed him. His girls and Little John needed him. His family needed him.

He would be a warrior too, by God.

CHAPTER 42

J ane gasped at the sight of Stephen. She was overjoyed to see him alive but his wild and daunting appearance shocked her. Black stubble covered his face in a dark intimidating shadow. His hair, which had grown to shoulder length on their journey, hung dark and wet, framing his pale and scratched face. He looked exceedingly powerful, his broad chest clearly visible without his shirt. What appeared to be two wolves' hides, hung across and down both shoulders, making him seem like a frightening barbaric warrior and his cobalt eyes held an enigmatic look she had never seen before.

The sight of him renewed her strength. But the danger he was about to face filled her with foreboding and apprehension.

The four stopped, with William and Bear flanking Stephen and Sam. She could now see their faces clearly. The four bristled with anger as if they wanted to tear these Indians apart and break every arrow in their quivers! She could not believe how menacing and fierce they all seemed. Even William's handsome face twisted in a vicious sneer. And Bear, the gentle giant, could not look any more blood curdling if he were a real bear. In Sam, she saw more than a daunting appearance. He exuded valor and a bold courage. That's what she had seen radiating from Stephen's eyes! Bravery. She glanced again at her husband and his courage filled her heart.

For a moment, no one spoke and no one moved.

Then Sam said, "Chief Wanalancet," and nodded his head in acknowledgment.

Wanalancet! So this was the Chief who sent Bomazeen to steal her. Hell fire! The situation was worse than she thought. A terrifying realization washed over her. This man was after *her*.

Jane kept her eyes pinned on Wanalancet. The fire's reflections bounced off the many strings of beautiful pearls on the man's broad chest. His intelligent ebony eyes, sinister and threatening, sparkled in the fire's light. He stood taller than most natives that she had seen and his powerfully built arms spoke of great strength.

She quickly decided that the Chief and the other four ominous braves, who appeared muscular and warlike as well, would be formidable opponents for Stephen, Sam, William, and Bear. She would have to help. That would even the odds. She would do something, anything to help. She could pull a burning log from the fire, throw it in the Chief's face. She would probably die trying, but if it saved Stephen's life it would be worth it.

Her heart beat so rapidly she could barely breathe. She grabbed her skirt with her fists to hide her shaking hands. She forced herself to stand tall. Her rigid back muscles knotted with anxiety as her gaze shifted constantly between Wanalancet and Stephen.

A palatable tension swirled around them all, the air nearly dripping with hostility and friction. She could sense the barely controlled anger that boiled in Stephen's body.

He would find a way out of this. He had to.

Stephen watched as Wanalancet studied each of the four men. The Chief peered into each man's eyes and held them for several long moments.

He felt Wanalancet read his soul and knew the Chief had seen the angry part of him.

The Chief moved to stand in front of Sam. "You are Bloody Hand," Wanalancet said.

"Some call me that," Sam answered.

The Chief moved to Bear. "You are Bear Killer, the giant," Wanalancet said to Bear.

Sam translated. Bear gnashed his teeth and snarled.

Only glancing at William, but clearly noticing the badge, Wanalancet turned his attention to Stephen.

Stephen glared back, boldly, his jaw defiant. Pistols in both hands and the wolves' hides contributed to his feeling of wild strength. He would need that strength. This would likely be a battle.

"You are a wolf man?" Wanalancet asked him.

Sam said, "Yes, he is a wolf man. Wolves and men both fear him. You would be wise to fear him too."

Stephen could hear the bridled anger in Sam's voice.

Wanalancet turned toward Jane. "Which man you belong to?"

Sam continued to translate and Jane pointed to Stephen.

He fixed a cold stare on the Chief.

"Then he is the one I must kill. The spirits of the wolves on his back give him power," Wanalancet said, "but my powers are those of a Chief and come from the Great Spirit in the stars. You men must lay down your weapons. After I kill the wolf man, we will take three women and three horses. If you do not follow us, the rest of you may live and keep your little ones. If you even begin to follow us, I will send two braves back to kill the children when no one is watching. Now lay weapons on the earth. Then, wolf man dies."

Sam translated slowly, keeping his voice low so the children could not hear.

Stephen considered Wanalancet's threat. He weighed the fighting skills of the braves. This could not end well if they fought. But if they didn't fight, all three women might be raped within minutes after he was killed and the other men tied up. Catherine and Kelly would each be raped twice and probably many more times before the night was over. The possibility made him want to be sick. Wanalancet would find the whiskey in their wagon and be emboldened by it. He doubted that the Chief would keep his promise to let the others live.

"If you want those two women to keep their life, step forward now wolf man and put down your useless weapons. They will not fire in this wet world. Out of respect for this woman," he said pointing to Jane, "I will make your death swift."

All of a sudden John sat up. "Please, be reasonable, he is a brother dear to me. He got caught in the storm. He was only hunting for food. He means you no harm. Neither do the rest of us. I beg you, do not hurt him."

A corner of Sam's mouth lifted in a half-smile and he translated what John said as, "You will never be able to kill a man as strong as the wolf man. His Great Spirit gave him great powers over evil. Those who carry evil in their hearts should always fear him. That is why your evil friend Bomazeen is now dead. And why you too will die if you do this evil thing."

"The wolf man killed Bomazeen?" Wanalancet asked, seeming impressed.

"Yes," Sam said, "in the afterworld, even the evil spirits could not recognize Bomazeen. Dark and evil blood covered his head when my brother the wolf man finished with him."

"We called him Wandering Evil. Now Bomazeen will wander forever, unrecognized by anyone," Wanalancet said. "But Wandering

Evil's killer must also die. I do not want this woman wanting to return to him. If he is dead she will not long for him."

Jane turned to Sam and with authority and strength in her voice said, "Tell him I'll go with him willingly and act as his wife, but only if he lets *all* of you live."

"Like hell," he swore.

Ignoring Stephen's outburst, Sam calmly translated Jane's statement.

He struggled to keep his mouth shut. The pistols in his hands shook slightly with anger. He was reaching a boiling point.

Sam eyed him and subtlety put a finger over his mouth. One wrong word and this could end in disaster for all of them.

Stephen clenched his jaw even tighter and lowered the pistols slightly. Only the brave's arrow pointing directly at him kept him from leaping on Wanalancet, but he wouldn't be able to hold himself back much longer.

Wanalancet held Jane's chin in his hand and stared penetratingly into her face. Looking beyond the green of her eyes, the Chief seemed to be studying her heart. "Your love is that deep?" he finally asked, and Sam translated.

"I would die for every one of these men, my brothers, and I would die a thousand times for my husband," Jane answered.

"You would die for them, but I ask you to live for me. To come with me is not death. It is life. I will sing the sacred song of the stars to you. I will honor you with many slaves and gifts. You will rule over our people with me. Your beauty is worthy of a Chief. You are tall for a woman and your spirit is strong. You will be the mother of all our people."

For the moment, Stephen would continue to give Jane a chance to stand up to the Chief. The pluck she showed impressed him and she had chosen her words wisely. He prayed that would continue, because not only did her words need to reach Wanalancet, they could not cause the

Chief's temper to flare.

"I am already a mother," Jane declared, pointing to the three children, "and I have already heard the song of the stars and have it written on my heart. My God permits only one man to sing the precious song of love to a woman. To leave that man would mean spiritual death for me and dishonor. But if you let them all live, and leave the other two women, I will no longer follow my husband and go with you. I will willingly be a wife to you in all ways. As God is my witness, I speak the truth."

"Never!" Stephen growled.

"Tell him," Jane ordered Sam.

After Sam translated, the Chief straightened his broad back. "You are in *no* position to bargain. You will go with me, after I kill the wolf man, or I will kill them all if I need to," Wanalancet said, his voice harsh, his eyes threatening.

"Then I will never stop fighting you," Jane said, her eyes suddenly blazing, "especially when you want to lay with me."

Stephen noticed Sam watching Wanalancet's every breath and studying every muscle on the Chief's proud face. The slightest flicker of hostility in the man's eyes would release the knife clenched in his hand because that fraction of an instant would be the only advantage they would have. If Sam acted at the right moment, he could kill the Chief. Bear's hatchet would sink into the brave closest to him and he hoped the weapons he and William held would fire and hit their targets. And Wanalancet would be a dead man. He would make sure of that.

But Wanalancet had probably brought his best braves with him and they could be equally lethal. Quick as a snake. With his hands and feet tied, John would be dead in a moment. Several of them would definitely die, heaven forbid, even the children. He had to stop that from happening. However, he would not let Jane make this terrible sacrifice even if Wanalancet agreed. He couldn't betray her trust in him.

Stumped, he couldn't decide what to do or say next.

Wanalancet turned from Jane to Sam. "Bloody Hand, I must kill wolf man. Tell him to prepare himself."

CHAPTER 43

Before Sam even translated, Stephen understood what was about to happen. His heart pounded in fury. They were caught in that moment between life and death. What happened next would determine if they were going to live. He would not back down. He was more than ready to die if need be. He would *never* let Wanalancet take Jane.

She carried his heart. She carried his son.

Stephen had to convince the Chief that Jane was his. He turned to Wanalancet and said, "Trying to kill me would be a mistake. I destroy evil. Are you so sure that your heart holds no evil? If it does, I will prevail. My spirit has the courage of good, not evil. Unafraid of the wilderness, I have come far and journey further only to make a new life and a better home for my family. I respect you great Chief and have no desire to take your life and those of your braves. But my honor will not let you steal my wife. Stealing her would be an act of evil."

Wanalancet seemed to consider what Sam translated and then replied, "I too have traveled far to claim my new wife and start a new life with her. I did this because my spirit joined hers through the smoke of my sacred pipe. I love her spirit already." The Chief hauled Jane over to stand beside him. "And I will love her body soon."

Jane didn't resist but her face went bright with anger.

Stephen quickly stomped toward Wanalancet, his teeth bared, his own face burning with wrath. He ignored the brave's drawn arrow closely following his movements. It was time to end this, one way or another.

"Sam, tell him exactly what I say—exactly." Stephen forced himself to speak slowly. "We can fight now for which life and which spirit wins—yours or mine—but some of you will die and some of us will die." He waited for Sam to translate, then continued. "Those of us who live will hunt you until we kill you and we will bring these women back to us. This woman is already a wife, *mine*, and by all that is sacred, she always will be. Taking another man's wife is evil. And I must fight evil where I find it."

"My heart is not evil," Wanalancet said firmly.

"It will be forever evil. If you take my wife." His gaze on Wanalancet remained steady.

Sam translated, then added, "I too have traveled far—to leave behind bloody wars I have fought with both the Indians and white men. We have been enemies for many years. You, your braves, and other tribes fought us with great courage. And the white men fought each other bravely. But the time has come for us to live in the same world and let the same sun enlighten us all. We all need land to grow food and game to hunt. The Algonquian tribes must have their world and their lives. And we must have ours. There is enough land for you and for us."

Then, Stephen continued, "It is not brave or honorable for you to steal women from among us. Even though the numbers are few, the grief you cause is great. If you stop, it will be easier for the white man to respect you and call you wise. A wise soul understands that there are good and bad among any tribe and any nation. But good men will always be greater in number than the bad. You and I must not let bad men determine how we treat each other. My brother does not want his hand to run red with Indian blood, especially the blood of a great Chief. But his knife is savage when it needs to be. We *will* kill you, but only if you harm our family or steal these women. We can be brothers or we can be enemies. You must decide. Now."

"His knife is savage, but it is also a noble blade," Wanalancet said, "unlike the blade of Bomazeen. He was one of the bad men that you speak of. I regret now that he sometimes acted for me because I am not one of these bad men. I see truth in the blade of the big knife because his heart is true. Your spirit, wolf man, is the strongest I have known among white men. But I have come far for this woman. I must consider what to do and what the Great Spirit tells me."

The imposing Indian circled Jane, seeming to study her body and soul. With each circle, his movements nearly graceful and his self-assurance unmistakable, Wanalancet drew closer to her. Each loop the Chief made around Jane lessened Stephen's self-control. Soon he would have none. Forgetting their plan, he decided he would kill the man himself.

Then, Wanalancet bent down and, for what seemed an eternity, studied the fire. Stephen wondered if the flames tied the Chief's soul to the ways of the old spirits. Wanalancet's eyes soon blazed, as though some unknown life force spoke only to the Chief. He hoped they were words of wisdom and peace.

Stephen barely breathed but his hands gripped his weapons tightly. The dripping leaves surrounding them sounded like a thousand ticking clocks. Sam and the others remained quiet. Stephen prepared himself to kill if needed.

Finally, Wanalancet stood tall, his long raven hair billowing in the breeze, and spoke again. "Bomazeen was right. This woman would make good mother to my people. I see great strength in her eyes and her body. But I do not want a woman whose spirit will die. Her beauty would wither like winter leaves. It has been so with others we have taken. Perhaps, as you say, it is false-hearted for us to continue to steal slaves. It is not my desire to do evil. We will leave you now with your lives and women. We will travel on to southern tribes and trade for women there."

Wanalancet motioned for his braves to put away their weapons and they obeyed immediately.

Stephen lowered his weapons somewhat and finally breathed but kept relief from showing on his face.

Bear, who understood the Algonquian language better than he could speak it, put away his hatchet and slowly stepped forward. He removed his necklace and presented it solemnly to the Chief.

Stephen knew what a great sacrifice Bear was making to seal the agreement with the Chief. He also saw in Bear's eyes a new respect for the man Wanalancet was and suspected that he no longer thought of the Chief as merely a wild savage.

Wanalancet's eyes widened in surprise and obvious pleasure as he studied the string of bear claws and teeth.

Stephen removed one of the wolf hides from his shoulder and slowly brought it to the Chief.

Wanalancet's eyes, bright with the fire's reflection, considered Stephen for a few moments before the Chief reached out for the dark skin. "This symbol of the spirit of the wolf is a costly gift. A wolf pelt is worth more than 40 beaver skins and presenting a gift of the fur of a wolf is an act of reconciliation. I accept this gift and your gesture of peace with it."

After Sam translated, Stephen said, "I will keep one skin and you the other. As these wolves were linked in strength and alliance in life, so will we be."

Wanalancet moved to the side of his horse, who sidled uneasily at the smell of the fresh wolf hide, now hanging from the Chief's muscular forearm. He reached into a deer-hide pouch and removed his Calumet, sheathed in the neck of a loon. After filling the pipe's red marble bowl with tobacco, and lighting it with a stick from the fire, he smoked the peace pipe for a few moments before offering it to Stephen.

"My spirit gives this woman's spirit back to you," Wanalancet told him.

Stephen took the pipe respectfully and smoked several puffs before passing it back to the Chief. Wanalancet then solemnly passed it to each of the other men in turn before taking a final drag on the long pipe decorated with bird feathers and locks of human hair.

With the pipe cradled in his arms folded across his chest, Wanalancet said, "I ask only one thing of you."

"What?" Sam asked, warily.

"That you use your noble blade to cut a length of this woman's hair," Wanalancet said, pointing to Jane.

Sam glanced uneasily at Stephen and then translated.

Stephen hesitated a moment but then nodded his assent, and motioned for Sam to give him his knife. If this had to be done, he would do it himself. He took the knife and cut a length of Jane's hair, as she stood motionless, her face revealing nothing. He offered the locks to the Chief.

Wanalancet sat down by the fire and used one of the rawhide strips hanging from the pipe to carefully secure Jane's hair to the quill. Silently, they all focused on the shining copper curls now adorning the Chief's sacred pipe.

Stephen sat down next to the Chief. "Now, I ask only one thing of you great Chief."

Wanalancet studied him as Sam translated.

"Would you clean your heart of Bomazeen's evil by returning the yellow-haired girl back to her people? I believe her Christian name is Lucy," Stephen asked.

Wanalancet gazed again at the fire's flames and smoke, his face impassive.

DOROTHY WILEY

"I ask you to do this good thing," Stephen said. "If you do, and take her back to where Bomazeen stole her, we will all thank our God for your wisdom and ask for his blessings for many seasons upon you and your tribe."

"It will be done," Wanalancet finally said. He stood abruptly, removed one of the many strings of pearls on his chest, and placed the strand around Jane's neck.

Jane's face remained impassive, but her eyes, filled with gratitude, met Wanalancet's. "God's grace onto you," she said with dignity.

Sam translated and Wanalancet nodded and turned away.

Moments later, the Chief and his braves disappeared into the woods.

Stephen turned to his wife. *His wife.*

Jane, crying from joy and relief, jerked the wolf skin off Stephen's shoulders and tossed the rank hide aside before hugging him fiercely. She wanted to never let him go. She wanted him by her side every moment for the rest of her life. To love him forever and ever.

He kissed her as though it were their first kiss—gently at first and then with a passion as wild as the wilderness itself. Then they both ran toward the children. Stephen untied and picked up both girls, hugging them against his chest as she repeatedly kissed their faces. Bear helped Jane quickly untie Little John and he carried the boy over to John, while she ran to retrieve the painkiller the child would need. Sam and Catherine assisted John. William untied Kelly and putting his arm around her still shaking shoulders, guided her to a seat by the fire.

As she came back with the medicine, Jane observed her family, her heart filling with gratitude that they were all unharmed. After getting Little John and the girls settled and comfortable again, she slipped her arms around Stephen's waist. Suddenly overwhelmed by the torment of the last few hours, she smothered a sob against his chest.

He drew in a sharp breath and shuddered. He ran his hand lovingly over the spot where he had just cut her hair. "I'm sorry."

"So am I," Jane said, "but not about the hair. About ever doubting you. About causing you even more heartache. About even a small part of me not forgiving you." Gazing up at her husband's eyes, conveying all the tenderness and compassion she felt, she truly and completely forgave him, and herself.

A cry of relief broke from his lips. "I love you," he whispered.

There would be no more heartache. Only love. She yielded to the sobs that shook her and wept for joy, encircled in his strong arms. She had him back and she would never let go.

Tonight there would be no shadows across her heart. Only the light of love.

With a weak smile and his tired eyes glistening, Stephen presented her with the meat he had fought so hard to keep. "For you," he said, "always for you."

They collapsed to the ground together hugging and crying, the salt of their healing tears seasoning the fresh meat.

As he held her against him, an amazing sense of completeness filled him. He was now sure of himself and his rightful place—beside his wife on the Wilderness Trail. A trail that would lead to a lifetime of passion and love.

Epilogue

1797, The Wilderness Road, Kentucky

L ittle John, who sat in his father John's dusty lap, asked, "What does the word Kentucky mean Uncle Sam?"

Sam glanced up from the wheel he rested his back against. "It's an Indian word—Ken-ta-ke—that has more than one meaning. My favorite meaning is Land of Tomorrow."

"That's poetic and beautiful," Catherine said.

"What's the other meaning?" William and Kelly both asked.

"The Dark and Bloody Ground," Sam answered.

"I much prefer the first meaning," Jane declared, shifting the emerald lights of her eyes to Stephen.

"Aye," Bear agreed.

Stephen gazed at his beloved wife and took her hand in his, caressing the top of it with his thumb. Her warm eyes were full of love. "Indeed," Stephen agreed. "It *will* be our land of tomorrow."

The look Jane gave him was so trusting it sent a shudder through him. He would do everything in his power to keep her trust. As usual, her nearness kindled feelings of fire. He ached to reach over and pull her close, cover her body with kisses, but it was time for them all to get moving again. The animals had rested and watered long enough.

The further into Kentucky they traveled, the more Stephen found it to be a country of extraordinary beauty—lush seemingly endless meadows carpeted abundantly with great patches of clover and tall thick nearly blue grass, incomparable to any they had seen before in color and beauty. Numerous sparkling creeks flowed steadily, often climaxing in picturesque waterfalls. In other areas, clear cool pools of water sweetened by ancient beds of limestone collected around springs shaded by huge sycamores.

Deer or buffalo grazed peacefully nearly everywhere he looked. On their third day into Kentucky, he saw a drove of several hundred buffalo. Martha and Polly delighted in watching the young calves play and skip about like children at play. It was good to see his girls happy.

Despite all the hardships on their journey, Stephen's heart remained strong. He would find what he had come for. He looked back at his young bull and two heifers, which had faithfully plodded alongside them for more than a thousand miles. They had grown quite a lot on this long journey, closer to the maturity needed to be the foundation of his new herd. He had matured too. He was wiser now, and stronger. And he loved Jane even more.

"Do you think we'll find what you're looking for in Boonesborough?" she asked him the next morning, as they all shared breakfast together near a blue-green meadow. "Or will we have to keep going?" She studied his face as she waited for him to answer.

He recognized that Jane was beyond tired of traveling and he wanted to find a home for her soon. He sincerely hoped reaching Boonesborough would be the end of their journey.

"What are you looking for?" Little John asked before Stephen could answer.

DOROTHY WILEY

All eyes focused on him. All ears waited for his answer. They had come so far together, endured and lost so much. He reached inside his waistcoat pocket and pulled out the pouch of soil he had placed there before they left New Hampshire. The soil from the mountainside that held his father's grave had been a long time getting from there to here. But the trip had taken much more than time from them.

He gazed down at the pouch of precious soil, remembering the love of the land he learned from their father, as fathers and sons had for generations whose time had already come. He hoped future generations of their family, whose time was yet to come, would honor that past as they learned to love the land too. When it was their turn to live and to love, he would be gone. Their chance for a better future would remain.

Stephen returned the pouch to its pocket and looked at Jane, who stood at his side. He reached for her hand. As much as he loved the land, he loved her so much more and, at long last, she believed that he did.

Their love, tested in tragedy and forged in forgiveness on this difficult journey, emerged stronger and deeper than ever.

In the future, their marriage would be measured by more than just years—it would be measured by living, by laughter, and a dream they shared.

He swallowed the knot rising in his throat. Ready now to answer the boy's question, he glanced down at Little John. "For God's own pasture, son, I'm looking for God's own pasture."

"Will he share it with us?" Martha asked.

Stephen smiled at his oldest daughter, happier than he had ever been. "Yes. He will. Look at that Kentucky grass," he marveled. "With good rains, we'll raise a fat cow on one acre on grass like that. We'll have a large herd in no time. Right, Jane?" He pulled her into his arms. The nearness of her gave him comfort.

"Right, my husband."

He cupped her face gently in his hand as he looked into her beautiful eyes—the same dazzling color as the meadow that stretched out before them. "I promise you and the girls a better future here in Kentucky," Stephen said and then sealed his vow with a tender kiss, a kiss as light and warm as the summer breeze on his face.

He took in a deep breath. The meadow smelled glorious, like Jane's skin after she'd bathed, intoxicatingly fresh.

And like Jane, the sight of his future made his heart beat stronger.

THE END

A NOTE FROM THE AUTHOR

Thank you for selecting my novel to read and I hope you enjoyed reading Book One of the *American Wilderness Series Romances*,

WILDERNESS TRAIL OF LOVE

The series continues with a

READERS' FAVORITE GOLD MEDAL WINNER!

Book Two

NEW FRONTIER OF LOVE

the story of Sam and Catherine

If you enjoyed reading WILDERNESS TRAIL OF LOVE, I would be honored if you would share your thoughts with your friends. Regardless of whether you are reading print or electronic versions, or listening to the audiobook, I'd be extremely grateful if you posted a short review on the book's Amazon page. This is so helpful to both authors and readers and helps the book to stay visible on Amazon.

Please visit www.dorothywiley.com to sign up for my newsletter or to send me a note under the 'Contact' tab. You can also follow me on Amazon at www.amazon.com/author/dorothywiley to be notified of new releases.

Thanks for your support!

All the best,

Dorothy

TITLES BY DOROTHY WILEY

All of Wiley's novels, in her closely related series, are available in both print and eBook, and many in audiobooks at www.amazon.com/author/dorothywiley

So far, the story of the Wyllies is told in three series—

AMERICAN WILDERNESS SERIES

Book One — the story of Stephen and Jane:
WILDERNESS TRAIL OF LOVE

Book Two — the story of Sam and Catherine:
NEW FRONTIER OF LOVE

Book Three — the story of William and Kelly:
WHISPERING HILLS OF LOVE

Book Four — the story of Bear and Artis:
FRONTIER HIGHLANDER VOW OF LOVE

Book Five — A story of Sam and Catherine and the entire family:
FRONTIER GIFT OF LOVE

Book Six — the story of Edward and Dora:
THE BEAUTY OF LOVE

WILDERNESS HEARTS SERIES

Book One — the story of Daniel and Ann:
LOVE'S NEW BEGINNING

Book Two — the story of Gabe and Martha:
LOVE'S SUNRISE

Book Three —the story of Little John and Allison:
LOVE'S GLORY

Book Four—the story of Liam and Polly:

LOVE'S WHISPER

WILDERNESS DAWNING SERIES

Book One—the story of Samuel and Louisa

RED RIVER RIFLES

Book Two—Part One - the story of Samuel and Louisa continued and

Part Two - the story of Steve and Rebecca

LAND OF STARS

Book Three – the story of Rory and Jessica

BUCKSKIN ANGEL

ABOUT THE AUTHOR

Amazon bestselling novelist Dorothy Wiley is an award-winning, multi-published author of Historical Romance and Western Romance. Her first two series, the *American Wilderness Series* and *Wilderness Hearts Series* are set on the American frontier when Kentucky was the West. And because nothing stays the same on the frontier, not even its location, her third series, *Wilderness Dawning—the Texas Wyllie Brothers*, continues the highly-acclaimed Wyllie family saga but brings some of the family to the new edge of the West—Texas. All of her novels blend thrilling action with the romance of a moving love story to create exceedingly engaging page-turners.

Like Wiley's compelling heroes, who from the onset make it clear they will not fail despite the adversities they face, this author is likewise destined for success. Her novels have won numerous awards, notably a Will Rogers Medallion Award, a RONE Award Finalist, a Laramie Award Finalist, a Chatelaine Finalist for Romantic Fiction, an Amazon Breakthrough Novel Award Quarter-finalist, a Readers' Favorite Gold Medal, a USA Best Book Awards Finalist, and a Historical Novel Society Editor's Choice. And Wiley's books continue to earn five-star ratings from readers and high praise from reviewers, including several Crowned Heart reviews from *InD'Tale Magazine*.

Wiley's extraordinary historical and western romances, inspired by history, teem with action and cliff-edge tension. Her books' timeless messages of family and loyalty are both raw and honest. In all her novels, the author's complex characters come alive and are joined by a memorable ensemble of friends and family. And, as she skillfully unravels a compelling tale, Wiley includes rich historical elements to create a vivid colonial world that celebrates the heritage of the frontier.

Wiley attended college at The University of Texas in Austin. She graduated with honors, receiving a Bachelor of Journalism, and grew to dearly love both Texas and a 7th-generation Texan, her husband Larry. Her husband's courageous ancestors, early pioneers of Kentucky, Louisiana, and Texas, inspired her novels. After a distinguished career in corporate marketing and public relations, Wiley is living her dream—writing novels that touch the hearts of her readers.

YOU'RE INVITED TO CONNECT WITH THE AUTHOR:

Amazon – To be notified of new releases, follow Dorothy on Amazon – http://www.amazon.com/author/dorothywiley

YouTube – Enter Dorothy Wiley in YouTube's search box to see beautiful book trailers

Author's Website and Newsletter Signup – https://www.dorothywiley.com

Facebook – https://www.facebook.com/DorothyWileyAuthor/

and https://www.facebook.com/DorothyMayWiley

Twitter – https://twitter.com/WileyDorothy

Goodreads – https://www.goodreads.com/author/show/8441725.Dorothy_Wiley

BookBub – https://www.bookbub.com/authors/dorothy-wiley

Pinterest – See Dorothy's inspiration boards for each book https://www.pinterest.com/dorothymwiley/?etslf=8021&eq=Dor

Instagram – https://www.instagram.com/dorothymwiley/?hl=en

ACKNOWLEDGMENTS

Foremost, I would like to thank the daring and brave first-wave pioneers of America. Their amazing journeys into the wilderness were not just about a piece of land. They were about God given faith and courage in the face of an uncertain but promising future.

I am especially grateful to my husband's ancestors whose brave stories inspired this novel. Research indicates that the Wyllies actually came from New York, not New Hampshire (where I chose to set the opening for this novel). They traveled through Kentucky, to Louisiana, and then in 1818 to Mexican Texas, making them among the first few dozen families to settle in what would become Texas. As you can well imagine, there are many stories yet to tell about those amazing journeys.

Secondly, I would like to thank my husband, who patiently read my drafts and also served as my amusing muse. I'm very grateful to my dear sister, who (lucky me) is a professional editor and helped with both proofing and layout. My thanks also go to several friends who read the early versions of this manuscript (some when it was just a skeleton of its current form). Thanks for your valuable input, but more importantly, thanks for your encouragement and faith in me.

I also want to thank my critique partners, historical romance authors B.J. Scott and Deborah Gafford, both talented writers, who each provided many great suggestions.

And my thanks to my cover designer Erin Dameron-Hill whose amazing creative talent transformed my vision for the cover into a beautiful reality.

And most importantly, my sincere thanks to my readers. I hope you will enjoy Book Two in the *American Wilderness Series Romances*, NEW FRONTIER OF LOVE, a heart-jolting historical romance that blends high-action, heroism, and humor with the tender love story of Sam and Catherine. Available in print, eBook, and audiobook formats at http://www.amazon.com/author/dorothywiley

.